THE STAFF OF BECKONING

PRANEET MENON

BOOK 1
A SYMPHONY OF SPHERES

Contents

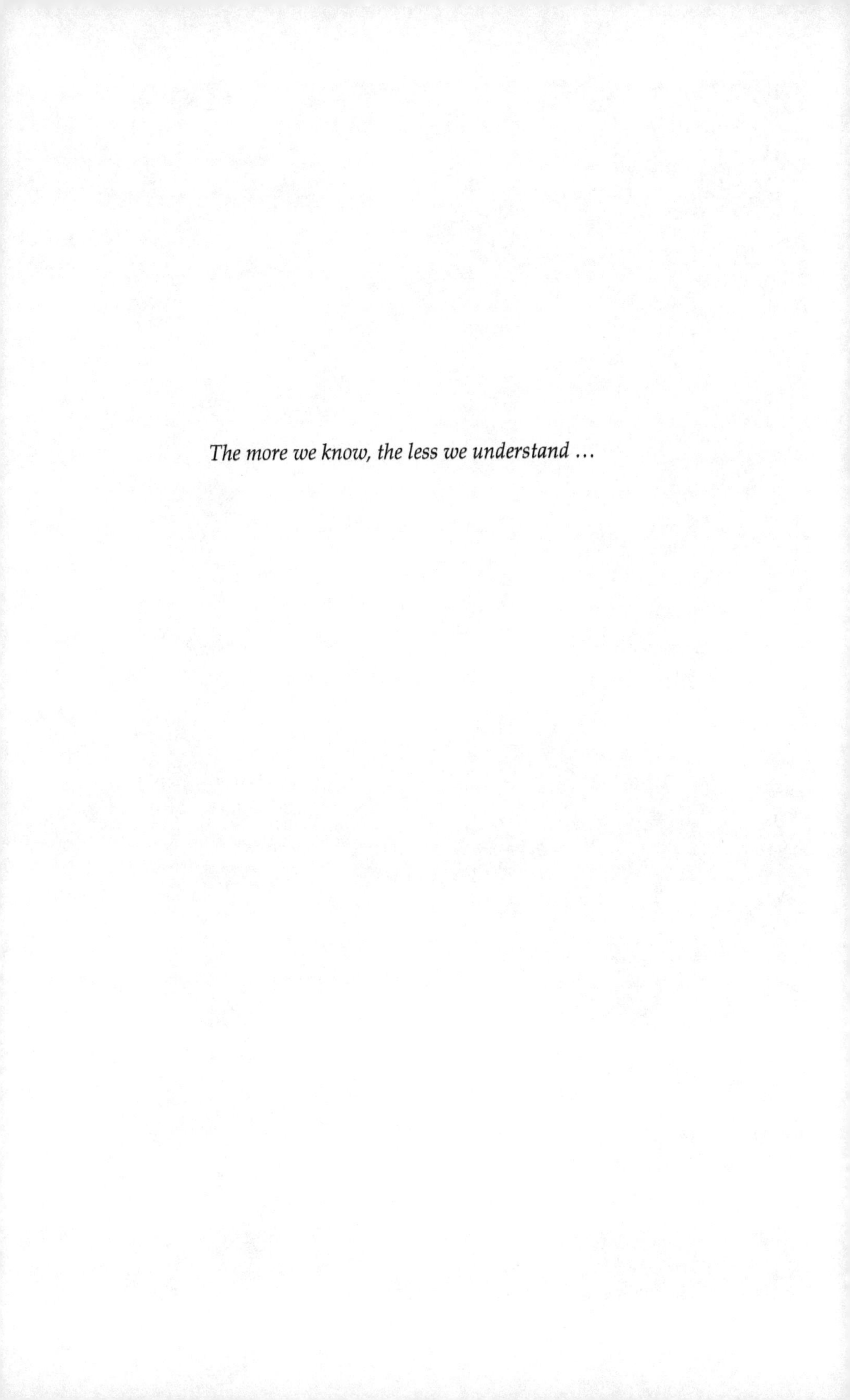

The more we know, the less we understand …

LEAKARHA
The
Leomat Ocean
PELERIA
PORT RATTAWIA
Peleria Bay
Othar Plains
Akkasha
Badallur
Nagra
Marafel
MENERES
Penner River
NAVEN
Vaarallinen Wilderness
OMANNA
CAYAN
Sanctum of the Seven
Cauverri River
LONIDAS
Gronelle Delta
Shi'jazha
Ardun Mtns
PHUCAO
River Korox
QUERRADRUTH
Gronelle River
Boloppa
GHIMA
OSTARIUM
Ghatirodh
River Hena
HERRALAND
Irake Koyou
LANMERIA
PACCA NIRUM

Precipice
THE LAND OF KHERYNE
Salgakh River
Kheryne Steppes
Bahzenelyn Range
Kvor Dunes
Gad River
LYKUSIRA
AEMONNE
Reman
Ocean
Mount Schinay
Aedenin

Prologue

A long breath of abrupt origin filled his lungs with air. He inhaled deeply through his nose and exhaled out his mouth, each breath returning a sliver of sensation to his body, as his mind clawed its way towards painful wakefulness. Fear and confusion churned nauseatingly at the realization that his arms and legs were bound by cuffs and chains.

Vision eluded him. His left eye was sealed shut with something caked over it, while his swollen right eye barely opened a slit. But that was enough to discern a vague light ensconced in a wall, radiating a circular field of light that faded into darkness. Through immense effort, he looked farther down the wall, discovering alternating circles of light and patches of dark.

With a blunt pop, his hearing returned. The sudden barrage of sound emanated echoes of pain from the base of his skull. Waves crashing far away further added to his confusion. The Kheryne Khuun did not often camp near the ocean, preferring to spend their time on the high plains.

Two sets of perfectly synchronized footsteps reverberated from up ahead, sending tremors of panic through him. Fighting it, he willed himself to look in the direction of the noise, revealing two points of light that grew larger with each nearing step. A few moments later, two figures halted in front of him—one tall and one short, motes of light floating above their palms like bright, buoyant dandelions suspended in air.

Gods save me! How!?

The tall figure loomed in a hooded brown robe, the face hidden in the shadow of the cowl.

The other, clad in black, stood a couple of hands shorter. The black clothing seemed to be of one piece, with a black belt around the waist, soft shoes, and a mask that revealed nothing but the eyes. The belt carried two curved black sheaths on each hip, one short and one long. Two black sword hilts protruded over each shoulder.

Shadow operative!

"Where … where am I?" he asked, each syllable stinging his throat.

"Ah, you're awake," said the hooded figure, his voice rumbling like two boulders rubbing against each other. He clenched his fist, extinguishing the mote of light, then stepped forward. "You don't look too damaged," he said, stopping a mere hands-length away. "If you do what we ask, there's no further need for pain. And then we can heal you up and send you home. Are we clear, Altansar?"

"You know my name?" Altansar asked, shock tingeing his painful speech. He had been captured. *How? When?* The last he remembered, he had retired for the night on his straw mat.

"Of course! We know everything about you." The hooded figure paused a moment. "So, are we agreed?"

Altansar was not sure what he was getting himself into, but he nodded.

"Good," came the reply in that deep rumble. "Since you don't know where we are, I'll tell you. We are on Mount Schinay."

Mount Schinay, Altansar thought. He knew of Mount Schinay. Well, everyone knew of Mount Schinay. It was spoken of in myths, in fables of Gods and demons that did fantastical things—towering tall in the middle of Aedenin, the Island of the Gods. But no one had ever been there.

Am I in a fantasy? A dream? He could not be as this dream felt painfully real.

"Now that I've answered your questions, it's your turn to answer mine," the brown-robed figure said. "And be truthful." He stepped back a few paces. "Do you know why you're bound like a dog?"

If this was not a dream, then Altansar knew the answer to the brown-robed man's question. If this was not a dream, then Altansar dared not speak the truth. "No," he answered.

The brown-robed man laughed. "Do you really expect me to believe you? You're Kheryne Khuun. Your people and we are the only ones who do know."

Altansar shook his head despite painful protests from his neck. "I don't know."

But he knew.

"You're making this more difficult than it needs to be, Altansar." The hooded figure pulled out a small glass tablet from his sleeve. It lit up, revealing several strange symbols littered over its surface. "You're forcing me to do unpleasant things to you." With that, he moved a finger across it.

Instantly, Altansar felt a slight chill creep up his arms and legs through the chains that bound him. The next instant was pure agony. It was as if his whole body was aflame while thousands of knives stabbed at him simultaneously. He shook and convulsed in an effort to rid himself of this torture, but that only made it worse.

Then, as suddenly as it had begun, the pain stopped, although remnants of it echoed throughout Altansar's body as he vomited blood and bile. He searched himself for signs of stabbing but found none. *How is that possible?* He kept his sanity, however. He was from the Land of Kheryne and the Kheryne Khuun were hard folk.

"Why do you resist, brother?" asked a smooth, whispered female voice. The roll in her *R*s and pop in her *T*s revealed that the operative, too, was Kheryne Khuun.

Altansar met the Shadow operative's eyes. They looked ... *disturbed*?

"We know you know," she added.

"I"—he spat a crimson amalgam of phlegm, blood, and bile onto the circular stone floor—"truly do not know."

"Don't lie!" shouted the hooded figure, tapping on the glass tablet.

Once again, pain ebbed and flowed through Altansar like the crashing waves far away. It surged in pulses, alternating between intense pain and relief—each moment of relief serving as a sharp contrast to the pain. But he welcomed the pain, for he knew pain. He could deal with what he knew. But he did not know what was to come if he admitted the truth. He would not break!

Through his silent torment, Altansar observed irritation in the hooded figure's posture. He moved his finger over the glass tablet again, tapping on a few symbols. Altansar felt compelled to open his mouth as his tongue was being stretched out from it. Attempts to pull it back in and clamp his mouth shut proved futile. The initial tug progressed rapidly to the point where it felt as though his tongue was about to rip from the back of his throat.

"Khasir, we will need his tongue if he is to talk," the Kheryne operative said, concern—or impatience—dripping in her voice. "Perhaps, if we heal him a little, he might be willing to comply."

"Good, Tallena," the brown-robed Khasir said. "Sometimes sweetening the pot can get you results. You will make a fine Khasir one day." The hooded man flipped the tablet, which dimmed a little at first before brightening again. He tapped on some of the new symbols that appeared on the tablet's surface.

A mild tingle bloomed at the tip of Altansar's nose and spread out across his head and down to his shoulders. Slowly his vision cleared and sharpened, and the stiff pain in his neck faded away. The rest of his body, however, still hurt horribly.

How is this possible? Such injuries usually took weeks to heal. He must be in a dream. *Wake up!*

Lifting his head to survey his surroundings, Altansar found himself to be at one end of a chamber with two rows of stone columns stretching down its length. Looking to either side, he realized that the lights ensconced in the walls were in fact motes of light, much like the motes that floated on the palms of his captors, only larger.

Then Altansar fixed his eyes on Tallena, clad all in black. The hand that held her mote had a glove with what looked like metal bands embedded in them. She looked dangerous, weapons sticking out of every corner. Her eyes, though, showed concern. *For me?*

"Now that you feel better, why not admit that you are a venna." The Khasir spat out the last word laced with revulsion.

There it was. The one truth Altansar had so desperately been trying to hide, trying to forget. Over the last few years, he had exhibited all the warning signs that Kheryne mothers had so judiciously drilled into their children for countless generations. The blackouts, his inexplicable proximity to deaths. He had hoped it would all just go away, but rarely did that happen.

I am a venna and the Khasmia Shadow has found me.

"What are you going to do with me?" he asked with an apprehensive resignation. Venna captured by the Shadow were never heard from again.

"Well, that depends," the Khasir said. "Can you control it?"

"No. It just happens."

"That is the wrong answer."

Altansar's chains went cold as they funneled an ever-expanding surge of pain through his limbs. Every fiber of his being screamed with the intensifying pain, but he did not utter a sound. The relentless pain made him vomit over and over till he was empty, but still he retched.

The pain kept intensifying. Again and again and again. Altansar could no longer bear it. He knew he was going to die. He had to die to put an end to this torture.

This has to be a dream! Wake up!

And then something happened. He felt himself *shift*. Not a physical movement, but rather a displacement within himself. His skin began to radiate a prismatic glow that covered him in a rainbow-hued haze.

What ... what is happening!?

"Quick, get the staff!" commanded the Khasir.

A soft breeze began blowing through the chamber and into Altansar's rainbow-hued haze. The glow brightened as if feeding off the air, like a flame. Suddenly the prismatic glow flared, and the soft breeze whipped into a gale force wind that ripped through the chamber with a deafening howl.

"It's too late!" cried Tallena, shielding her eyes. "It came on too suddenly!"

"We have to stop this!" the Khasir yelled.

The wind picked up more strength, slowly accelerating the Khasir and Tallena toward Altansar. He, however, remained anchored in his spot; his glow was sucking up the wind. As the Khasir and Tallena drew closer, they began gasping for air, as if they had entered a vacuum between the glow and the wind.

The glow grew brighter, the wind blew harder, and Altansar felt himself fade. Not just his body, but also his very self. *Maybe I am waking up.*

The glow flickered and went out, releasing an explosion of force that threw the Khasir and Tallena back about ten paces. The wind died down and the chains that held Altansar slumped to the floor. Altansar's body was nowhere to be found.

But an intangible part of him remained. Somewhere. And it heard someone say in a rumble, "At least the world is rid of him ..."

PART I
ADAGIO

Chapter One

As the deep black of night faded into the dark blue of dawn, Arvan Nathar ran on a quiet trail that zigzagged through Daaman Woods. The woods ran along the northeast border of Marafel, just west of the Pharrahmin Mountains. It was cold for a late spring morning, or maybe his memories of younger days were fading.

It was always this cold. Just never felt it in my bones. But the cold didn't bother Arvan. In fact, he loved it. Distant memories had left an impression of cold air blowing over his naked chest as he ran through wildflowers in the pastures to the south. He distinctly recalled jumping into the frigid snowmelt pool a few miles away from his farmhouse when he was ten or eleven. As he'd jumped into the pond, he'd broken through a thin layer of ice that left gashes on the soles of his feet. It had stung something fierce, but he'd been dared to jump into the pond and Arvan Nathar never backed down from a challenge.

Birds started their morning song as if urging the sun to rise. Feet crunching on the underbrush, Arvan listened to his breathing, with each inhalation and exhalation cooling his lungs as they burned mildly from the strain of his quick pace. It was important to keep a steady breath to pace yourself. He'd learned that during his time in the Navengaard—sound advice, and not just for running.

Like all Nathar men before him, Arvan had joined the Navengaard as part of an unspoken rite of passage in the family, ever since Arvan's grandfather fought in the War of Remaking. Starting as a lowly footman, Arvan had reached the rank of captain by the time he'd retired. His service record spoke for itself and was reward enough for him, but the Navengaard had awarded him a few medals. During his tenure, he'd been involved in a variety of operations, from distributing food in disaster areas to quelling a rebellion in northeast Naven. He'd even spent a summer training with a battalion of the elite Watchmen. That had been a memorable summer for Arvan, as he had been able to train with his late brother. Arvan missed him dearly and hoped that his brother's soul had entered Amarna.

These morning runs always made Arvan nostalgic. But, nostalgia was necessary as it provided an avenue for introspection. He wanted to remember his past, remember the events that had made him the man he was—for better or worse.

As Arvan rounded a bend, the woods abruptly ended at an open field, bringing the Nathar farmhouse into view. Moments later, a chorus of mooing flooded his ears amidst the shouts from farmhands near the cowshed.

I wonder if the cows are still getting sick, Arvan thought. Several of his cows had recently taken ill from an unknown disease, and no cure had yet been found. The Nathars were herdsmen by trade, had been since his grandfather's time, and the animals were their lifeblood. In addition to the herd of milk cows, they also had a flock of sheep kept mainly for its wool. Arvan hoped that, someday, his sons would take over.

Entering the farmhouse through a side door, Arvan climbed up the flight of spiraling wooden stairs to the upper floor. He walked down the hallway and into his room, where Nilane or Misuma had already made his bed and laid out his clothes. Gathering them up, he entered his bathing room and quickly washed himself with soap and hot water from a steaming bucket on the floor. Then he donned his clothes and headed out to the veranda.

The morning sun had barely reared its yellow crown from behind the Pharrahmin Mountains. The perpetually snow-capped peaks made for a long climb for the sun before it could provide its light and warmth to the plains to the west. As Arvan walked out of the house, he pulled his coat around him a little tighter.

The veranda was a large extension on the northeast side of the house. It had a roof but was open on all sides, save for a hip-high wooden railing. A tall shade tree stood in the back courtyard formed by the veranda and the house. Kirsch, the Nathar family steward, was already there with some hot tea, jotting something down on a piece of paper.

Arvan sat in his customary spot on the wooden bench that ran the length of a long table at the center of the veranda. An oil lamp stood atop the table, glowing faintly. Kirsch handed him a fresh cup of tea, which Arvan accepted silently. Sipping it, he picked up some ledgers and began poring over them.

"The cold has got a bite this morning," Arvan commented after a few moments.

"Yea, sir. The flowers are all in bloom, but the air still holds a strong memory of winter."

Arvan nodded taking another sip. "Pretty typical. Say, has the sickness in the cows been contained?"

"I believe so, sir," Kirsch replied. "We lost six and the three that are still sick have been quarantined, of course. I hope they recover soon. Although, given that we have lost every cow that took ill, I don't believe these three will make it. But, Gods' favor, no new cows have taken ill."

"Did the sarawaan determine the illness?"

"No, sir."

"What are we paying her for?" Arvan clicked his tongue with annoyance. What was the use of years of learning if the sarawaan could not figure out a simple bovine disease? *If Malia were still sarawaan, this would—*

Arvan put an end to that thought, realizing the futility of dredging up memories of his wife. It had been eight years and Malia was still missing. Most considered Arvan a widower, assuming Malia was dead. But to Arvan, Malia was neither alive nor dead. She was just missing.

"I believe she has narrowed it down to a few diseases, but is having trouble pinning it down to one," Kirsch answered matter-of-factly. "Apparently, the sick cows are showing symptoms of various diseases and no one disease explains all of them."

"So? Can't the cows have multiple diseases at the same time? Gods save us all, but if a man can have many sicknesses at the same time, so can a cow!"

"Yea, sir. However, the sarawaan says that the diseases that could be ailing the cows cannot occur at the same time. They would essentially kill each other. They are each other's antidotes."

"Diseases are used as antidotes for other diseases?" Arvan furrowed his brow. "Sounds a little strange."

"Yea, sir. But not too strange. We see it happen in nature quite often. Taygars kill deer and men kill taygars. So, it's not too farfetched a notion that diseases can kill each other."

Arvan felt a small amusement at Kirsch's analogy. "So," he began, "if the three diseases are *taygar*, *deer*, and *men*, wouldn't one of the diseases still live? The ones that are the *men*, in your analogy? Or are you trying to say that there are man-hunting deer?"

Kirsch let out a small laugh. "Yea, sir. In my analogy, the deer hunt men."

There was a short pause, then Arvan asked, "So, if the diseases are supposed to kill each other, why are the cows still sick?"

"That's what the sarawaan's trying to figure out."

Arvan regarded his steward as Kirsch returned to his papers. About a decade and a half older than Arvan, the sturdy man, with his balding head and neatly trimmed beard, didn't look anything like a steward—he looked more like a seasoned brawler—but Kirsch was the best steward one could ask for. Kirsch had always been around the farmhouse, as far back as Arvan could remember, as Kirsch's father, Dahn, had been the steward before him. Dahn would task Kirsch with various house-related errands and responsibilities, teaching him the ins and outs of stewardship. And when Dahn passed away, Kirsch took up his torch and quickly proved his resourcefulness. He was a wizard with numbers and had a memory like a steel trap. Kirsch was no sarawaan, but Arvan doubted that even she could explain this cow situation as simply and clearly as Kirsch had.

"We haven't felt the losses yet," Kirsch looked up, "but once the other three die, we will have a hard time fulfilling our orders. The Leinierds have a wedding in a few weeks and have asked us to provide milk for the ceremony and dinner. It'll be about a hundred and fifty people. We'll need about twenty-five cows for the day. That's in addition to our regular orders."

Arvan let out a long sigh. "Basically, we have no reserves."

"That's correct, sir."

"All right." Arvan emptied his teacup. "Could you go to Nagra and look for some cows? I don't want to be left with no options once we lose the other three."

Kirsch nodded and made a note. "It'll be taken care of, sir."

Arvan poured himself some more tea and continued looking over the ledgers. His days as a Navengaard soldier had hammered into him a strong sense of discipline, which permeated all parts of his life. And having served as captain in the final days of his career, he'd been used to a certain level of obedience from those under him. Arvan appreciated that Kirsch needed to be told something only once for it to get done. He wished that he could get his children to respond similarly.

The sun fully crested the towering peaks, prompting Arvan to extinguish the oil lamp on the table. "Have you spoken to Morena lately?" he asked. Kirsch was his only source of news about his daughter.

Kirsch nodded. "A few days ago, sir. She is well, but Laraan seems to have a lingering cough. I'm sure it's nothing the mayor cannot shake off."

"Will she be at Holy Hour tonight?"

"I didn't inquire, but I'm sure the mayor and his wife will be in attendance."

Morena, Arvan's oldest child, was very much like her mother—headstrong and passionate. Once she put her mind on something, she'd poured her heart and soul into it. She'd been his little girl till Malia disappeared and Morena was forced to play mother to an angry Adir and a confused Athvan while Arvan was fulfilling his obligations to the Navengaard.

What must have it been like to take on that much responsibility at that young an age? But Morena had done well; her mother would be proud. It'd been a while since he'd last seen her, and he was looking forward to seeing her tonight. He knew that she would be civil to him in public, but he also knew that beneath that civility lay strong resentment for his absence after Malia's disappearance. Morena would never understand, though. The Navengaard was bigger than the family of a simple herdsman from Marafel. He had a duty to perform.

Arvan returned to his ledger, but his mind kept drifting back to the sickness ailing the cows. A disturbing thought occurred to him. "The sickness hasn't spread to the sheep, has it?" he asked.

"No, sir," Kirsch replied with a casual lack of concern, scratching below his eye with the top of his pen. "That reminds me, the sheep are ready to be sheared. We're short a couple of farmhands this year. We could either hire a couple of new hands or just use the ones we have now and deliver the wool to the loom a few days late."

"I'd like to at least break even this year, Kirsch. And delivering late to the loom is not an option."

"Understood, sir. I'll see what I can do." Kirsch made a note.

Arvan suddenly heard the familiar screech of metal on metal. Looking over at the cowshed gate, he saw Adir—a lean young man with long limbs—tying his horse to a fencepost by the cowshed. A finger-long curtain of hair poked out from under his wool hat, flaring upward around his neck.

Adir glanced at Arvan, then quickly averted his gaze and hurried into the cowshed.

"Is Adir just getting ready to take the cows out now?" Arvan asked. He should have been halfway to the pastures.

"It appears so, sir." Kirsch replied.

Arvan was not sure what to do about Adir. *Will that boy never learn to be a responsible man?*

Though capable, Adir was defiant in a very vocal way. That sweet child, who'd always been so eager to help, had vanished the day Malia disappeared. Arvan knew that, like Morena, Adir blamed him for being absent from their lives. And he could not fault Adir for that. He wished that he could have been there for his son and guide him to manhood, like his father had.

Teenage years were tough on everyone. That was when the fantasy of childhood began to crumble away into the reality of life. Like a newly awakened butterfly seeing the world for the first time through a new understanding. A time when a person began searching for their place in this world. A time when a person was trying to figure out who they are. And Adir had to go through those years without a mother. *Or a father.*

Chapter Two

ods save me, Adir thought, panicked. *Akka saw me!* He wasn't sure why he was panicked, though. When he came of age a couple of years ago, he became a man, and men weren't supposed to panic. He inhaled deeply, the cold air filling his lungs and slowing his racing heart. A sense of serenity washed over him. But as with everything, it was fleeting. Adir huffed in frustration.

As tradition dictated in Naven, when Adir came of age his father began involving him in their dairy business. He was being *groomed* for a job he didn't want. *Who would?* Milking cows, herding them around, and yelling at farmhands was anything but satisfying, especially when having to wake before the roosters. But such was the life he was born into, though he wished it wasn't.

Adir led the cows out of the shed, two at a time, wondering where two of his farmhands were. *It's not like Amaar and Tamaar to not show up, especially not both on the same day.* Their absence had led to a disastrously long delay in milking the cows, which meant everything that came after had also been delayed. He'd tried the best he could to hasten the milking, but a herd of cows took so long to milk and there was nothing he could do about that. *Akka will be furious. He won't accept any excuses for the delay.*

What was wrong with him? Why was he still worried about what his father would think? *He*, not his father, was in charge of the cows. Besides, he'd been handed an unfortunate circumstance and he'd made the best of it. At least the various families that employed his milk delivery service had received their milk with little delay. But that'd meant that the cheesemaker, Master Kaleb, had to wait for his delivery.

Once all the cows were out of the cowshed, Adir untied Veyka from the fencepost and hopped onto her, letting out a sigh for the day to come. His breath formed misty tendrils, curling upward like ghostly fingers reaching for the heavens. The sun had just conquered the Pharrahmin Mountains, bathing the plains with light, but the warmth had yet to catch up.

Pushing the herd south, Adir made his way down the cowpath bordered by green thickets and trees. After a few miles, the path opened up onto the pastures of the Othar Plains. The plains rolled on for leagues to the west and south with short grass where the animals grazed, and farms here and there. Wild flowers dotted the landscape with vibrant hues of red, blue, yellow, and white. The flowers were all turned to the sun, whose radiant heat had finally won its battle against the cold. Adir celebrated the warmth by pulling off his wool hat and coat, stuffing them into his saddlebag.

A little farther south, Adir noticed another herd.

Rein's here!

Leaving his herd to graze, Adir put Veyka into a trot and headed over to where Rein sat atop his horse.

The Nathars and Marandas had been sharing the pastures north of the Penner River for almost four generations, and were close friends. Reinard Maranda and Adir had been the best of friends for as long as he could remember. Being born within weeks of each other, Rein being the older, the two boys had grown up as brothers. Whether it was riding horses, swimming, or even making trouble, the two of them did it together.

With his round face, blue eyes, and pale cheeks that turned sunset crimson when he was cold or blushed, Rein was the one all the village girls fawned over. Adir was a little jealous of that. Each girl tried her hardest to outdo the other, but Rein was as awkward with a woman as a mule on a tightrope. By Rein's own admission, Adir knew that Rein could never work up the courage to respond to their advances. "They behave so strangely," he had once commented.

"Hey, Rein." Adir stopped Veyka next to Rein's horse. "What are you staring at?"

"Those ravens down by the river," replied Rein. Some were perched on branches while others swirled above, occasionally swooping down into the tall grass. "I wonder how many I can shoot down before they fly away," he added while absently raising his bow, arrow nocked. "How far do you think they are? About a hundred paces?"

Before Adir could gauge the distance, he heard the twang of Rein's bowstring followed by the caws of an injured raven. Instantly, a mad cacophony erupted among the rest of the birds. They took off, coalescing into a single, shifting black ball of feathers, beaks, and bones. As one, they made a frenzied flight to the south, looking for safety among the trees along the riverbank.

Rein pulled another arrow from his quiver that looped around the cantle of his saddle. He looked at Adir with a smile and shot the arrow in the direction of the fleeing black ball.

A blind shot? Rein did like to show off. But Rein's arrow hit true and another raven was flapping its wings in a futile attempt to stay aloft.

"That's two!" Rein grinned while nocking another arrow. Pulling the bowstring to his cheek, he appeared to be tracking a lone raven that was desperately trying to catch up to the others. Rein released the bowstring.

The arrow flew toward its target, skewering the raven. The lifeless bird arced downward toward the river.

"And that's three! Let's go grab them before something else does." With that, Rein nudged his horse into a gallop toward the nearest fallen bird, bow still in his left hand.

Adir brought Veyka to a gallop, following close behind. After riding a short distance, he spotted an arrow sticking out of the ground, impaling a dead raven. "There's one!" Adir exclaimed, dismounting and pointing at the bird. "Those shots were incredible, Rein! That last one was easily a hundred and fifty paces!"

"More like a hundred and twenty," Rein said as he dismounted, feigning humility. Freeing the arrow from the bird, he tried to hide an amused smile. He inspected the arrowhead, planted it into the ground, turned it a few times then flaked off the mud with his fingernails. "I'm thinking about competing in the village games, Adir. Gods' favor, I might even make it to Daroongaamen."

Adir smiled. "If you make it to Daroongaamen, I will pay your fare."

"With what money?" Rein laughed as he walked over to another raven lying, wings sprawled, among some grass and feathers. "You should compete too," he added, pointing the bird's beak at Adir's staff.

"Ha! That's a fine joke!" Adir laughed.

True, Adir had crafted the long rod into a staff. After pestering Captain Marwar for details on how to make one, he'd spent weeks scouring Daaman Woods looking for the right hardwood branch. After shaving off its bark, he'd cut the branch to fit the measurements given to him by the good captain, then fire-hardened it.

That said, however, he'd only ever used his *staff* as a cattleprod. Sure, he'd swung and twirled it around and even defeated a shrub or two in the name of practice; he felt like he had to practice after the captain had been kind enough to teach him the basics of staff combat. But dueling with a shrub was nothing like facing another person. Besides, if he competed in the Regional Games, he wouldn't win. Only one could win and that would inevitably be Boar Sayarna. *That man's arms are as big as my thighs!*

"Yea, it's certainly a fine joke," Rein replied with a chuckle. "You can barely swing the thing, but that'll do. Come on, Adir! Let's compete this year!"

Leading their horses farther south toward the river, they eventually arrived at the spot where the ravens had congregated. A foul odor tickled Adir's nostrils at first, gradually growing more and more overpowering.

"What's that?" Rein said, pointing at a heap on the ground, partially hidden by some tall grass. He swatted at a few flies that had come to investigate the newcomers.

As the two closed in—horses grazing behind them—Adir's eyes

widened in horror as his mind gave shape to the heap. *It's a body.* Who this man was, Adir could not tell; his neck ended with a bloodied, jagged stump. His guts lay strewn all over, like shredded sausage. Three long rends gaped across the chest, revealing ribs that seemed to have been sliced off cleanly. Dark red blood saturated the ground around the body. And flies were defiling every inch of it.

Adir looked over to see Rein sick up. Adir himself was fervently trying to hold his own breakfast in. The stench, buzzing flies, and sounds of Rein vomiting overwhelmed him. He turned and walked away. But looking away was no remedy to unsee what he had just seen. Flashes of the mutilated body zipped through his mind. He'd never seen such a sight before. All that blood!

As Adir walked, looking down at the ground, he spotted something odd in the grass ahead of him. It looked like … *a tuft of hair?* He walked over slowly, each step sharpening the image, which formed into a head. Into a face. A face he recognized.

"Tamaar!" he cried out, his voice breaking. One of his missing farmhands. His breath quickened, like a dog panting in the hot afternoon sun. *What if whoever did this is still here?* And before he knew it, a visceral fear gripped him. "We need to get out of here!" Adir said, his voice shaking. "Saddle up now!"

Rein looked confused but did as told. He wiped his mouth with his shirtsleeve, nodded, and ran for his horse.

Adir ran too, heart pounding. He had to get away from the pastures. He leapt onto Veyka's back. The mare must have recognized his urgency, for she instinctively turned and galloped toward the herd.

AFTER WHAT SEEMED like an anxious eternity, Adir was back at the farmhouse, wishing it hadn't taken as long. At least none of the cows had strayed or been too difficult on their way home.

Once the last cow was secured in the cowshed, Adir made his way to the farmhouse with a quick step. He walked around to the left of the house, passing the large well where Nilane was drawing some water.

After crossing the courtyard, he walked up two steps onto the veranda where Arvan sat in his customary spot, working.

Arvan was a man of average height and build. His thickly mustached face, which once might have come close to handsome, now showed signs of age around his eyes and forehead. Though his physique gave him no prominence, his voice was a different matter. To Adir, Arvan's voice always sounded like a cool, calming breeze. Yet he was somehow able to weave in the exact emotion he wanted to convey without changing the calmness of his voice. Even heated discussions never fazed the man. His patience could shame a mountain.

"Akka! In the pastures—" Adir began, holding back a rush of emotions.

"I got word from Master Kaleb a little while ago," Arvan cut in, in that cool voice all too familiar to Adir. But there was a bite of anger in it. "Seems the milk was late." Arvan's brown eyes met Adir's. "Have you no sense of responsibility, lad?"

Adir tensed. With all that had happened, he'd forgotten about the milk delivery. He'd known Arvan would be furious. "Amaar and Tamaar didn't show up this morning," he protested. "And all the houses got their milk on time. I assumed Master Kaleb wouldn't be in a hurry for the milk." But none of that was important. The late delivery was insignificant compared to what he'd seen. He felt a little hot under his clothes. "Akka, in the pastures, I found—"

"Lad, soon you'll take over the farm. You can't afford to be this irresponsible. Farmhands not showing up is a problem that will occur time and again and you need to learn to deal with it ..."

As Arvan rambled on about responsibilities and milk and cows, Adir's grip on himself wavered. *I'm not a boy anymore. I am a grown man!*

"Tamaar is dead!" Adir said, his voice quite a bit sharper than he'd intended. What was wrong with him? *Control yourself, Adir!* He'd tried to match his father's cool voice, but his temper had got the best of him. With effort, he collected himself. "His body was in the pastures. Close to the river," he said, still sounding angry. *Cool, not angry. Gods!*

"Tamaar is dead!?" Arvan exclaimed in shock.

"Yea," Adir replied, a little calmer. But his mind had begun replaying the gory scene from the pastures, which made his calmness as fleeting as a drop of water in the K'vor Dunes.

"And you found his body by the river?"

"Yea." Adir paused, a lump forming in his throat. "He was, uh … decapitated." He tried swallowing that lump to push it far down, but it didn't budge. It just sat there. Uncomfortably.

Arvan's eyes grew large. "Decapitated? Gods save us!" His tone changed to one of concern—empty concern, Adir knew. "Are you all right?"

"Yea."

Arvan nodded, his shock mingling with curiosity. "Did you find Amaar there too?" he asked.

Gods save us! Amaar hadn't shown up that morning either. Had he fallen prey to the murderer as well? But Adir had found no sign of Amaar, though he hadn't searched very hard. "No, we just found Tamaar."

"We?"

"Rein was at the pastures too. He'd shot some ravens. We went to look for the birds and that's when we found—" The pasture scene started up again in Adir's head.

After a ponderous moment, Arvan broke the silence. "Eli will go to the Village Watch as soon as Rein tells him about what you lads saw. I'll go meet him there. We'll take care of it, find out who did this."

Who could have done it? No Marafellen he knew would do such a thing. But on the other side of the river lay the thick and unexplored Vaarallinen Wilderness. "Could the Vaaren have done it?" Adir asked.

Arvan looked at Adir for a long moment, brown eyes piercing, as if reading his mind. "If it were the Vaaren, you wouldn't have even found a body. Those taken by them are never seen again." He paused. "We also don't know if he was by the river at night. No one's ever disappeared from there when the sun's out."

Adir considered that for a moment. "It probably wasn't the Vaaren," he said, uncertainly. "Could it have been a beast that wandered over from the Wilderness before the snowmelt began? It could be trapped on this side since the river is flowing high. There were claw marks across his front."

"Beasts don't decapitate their prey," Arvan said. "They also eat what they kill—" Arvan abruptly stopped speaking. His face tensed, faint creases of age appearing at the corners of his eyes. "These claw marks," he said slowly, "how many?"

"Three," Adir replied. "And large ones at that."

Arvan laced his fingers and rested them on his mouth. He didn't speak for a long moment. Then, finally, he coolly said, "Adir, I think it was a rakhor …"

Rakhor! Here? The Word called them demonspawn, the Watchmen hunted them, and those traveling the perilous mountain paths feared them. All who'd seen them and survived to tell the tale spoke of the creature's three long black claws. "How did they make it this far south? Past the Watchmen." Adir's voice was but a fearful whisper.

"Even the Navengaard Mountain Watch cannot patrol every inch of mountain around the Precipice," replied Arvan. "Those men and women are adept at tracking, spotting, and killing rakhor, but some always leak through."

"Are we safe, akka?" Adir asked. The rakhor had always been a distant threat, but suddenly it felt alarmingly close.

Arvan paused for a moment. "I'll head to the Village Watch, hopefully meet Eli there." He furrowed his brow. "It's best to let them deal with such matters."

Adir noticed how his father hadn't answered his question. *He's quite adept at evading. Typical!*

"And I'll bring this up with Laraan and the Advisory Council tonight," Arvan continued, "after Holy Hour of Worship." Arvan regarded Adir. "You've had a tough morning, lad. Why don't you go and get some rest."

"I'm fine," Adir protested. "I'm going to go see Tia before Worship."

"I'd rather you not leave the farmhouse till we've spoken to Laraan. I don't want this news spreading before the Council has had a chance to decide what to do."

"You think I'm going to blab about this to the first person I see?" How could his father even think that? No matter how old he got, Adir felt Arvan would always meddle in his affairs.

"This isn't about you, Adir," Arvan said.

"It isn't about you either," Adir shot back, then turned and strode away from the veranda, mildly pleased with himself. Did his father really think that he could just pop into his life one day and order him around? Not anymore!

But he *had* had a tough morning. Maybe he should rest.

Chapter Three

The sun was on a downward trajectory, wishing farewell to the world with soft, dimming, golden rays. The dirt roads that led in from the outlying farms and houses of Marafel were lined with trees that bent, swayed, and danced to the music of the evening winds. These roads converged at the Village Square where oil lamps burned brightly.

Arvan, Adir, and his brother Athvan passed by the smithy and the Rainbow Inn. A couple of handcarts squatted here and there, hawkers crying out their wares. Other vendors were setting up their stalls and claiming their usual spots.

At the north end of the square was a fifty-yard-long cobblestone pathway wide enough to fit four people side by side. Lined with oil lamps shaded in the rainbow colors of the Heptagon, the pathway guided the Faithful to the Temple. Tonight, the night of the Holy Hour of Worship, the Faithful milled about in a steady flow down the pathway and into the Temple.

Men were garbed in their neatest trousers, cleanest shirts, traditional Naven coats that flared at the bottom, and formal turbans with long tails. The older women wore their more conservative, high-necked dresses, and each hair on their heads was precisely in place, displaying their maturity. The younger women, especially the unbetrothed, donned colorful tight dresses with low necklines, and let their hair of black and brown dance with the winds. Children ran around yelling and screaming at each other, hiding behind shop wagons and adding mirth to the moments before Worship.

Turning onto the pathway, Adir searched for Rein, but instead spotted Tia staring at him with those soul-searching black eyes. She was helping her mother, Marcy Ellar, arrange crumbcakes. Some of her waist-long black hair was pulled forward, covering her bosom; it lay straight and black, like fine strands of ebony silk, sometimes swishing in to cover her face. And her face—quite pretty. *Pretty? She's beautiful.* And right now that face carried a smile that created pleasant tingles in him.

If it'd been up to Tia, the two would have been married the day Adir had come of age. He, however, was not ready. It wasn't that he didn't want to get married and father children. They were—as everyone married with children harped—some of life's great experiences. But not right now. Giving her a quick smile and pointing his thumb toward the Temple, Adir continued down the pathway with Arvan and Athvan.

A little farther, the trio came upon Logath Kaleb, the cheesemaker, talking to Baely Marrat, who owned a few acres of jute farms. Passing them, Arvan nodded to the two.

Adir took a couple of steps, then turned to his father. "Akka, you and Athvan go on ahead. I'll find you in the Temple. I have some … business to take care of."

Arvan studied Adir, then looked at Master Kaleb, then back at Adir and nodded.

Adir nodded back, turned, and approached the portly man. "I'm sorry about the late delivery this morning, Master Kaleb," he said apologetically.

"I can't blame you for today, lad," replied the balding middle-aged man, looking sympathetic. "Gods! I'm sorry you had to see that. Such violence."

How did Master Kaleb already know? So much for Arvan's plan of keeping the matter quiet by keeping him at home. Frustration at his father mounted but quickly dissipated as images from this morning flickered in his mind. He stared at the cobblestones below to hide a slight quiver on his upper lip.

"Lad. Are you all right?" the cheesemaker asked.

"I'm doing fine," Adir said after a moment, gathering himself. Then, looking up, he switched the conversation back to the delivery. "I promise you there won't be any more late deliveries, Master Kaleb."

"The Word says 'Make not promises that cannot be kept,'" Master Kaleb said with a small smile. "Deliveries will be late from time to time and there's nothing you can do about that. I'm willing to bet a silver scepter that your father gave you quite a lesson on responsibility." His round face took on a look of guilt. "Gods pardon me! I shouldn't be talking about gambling at the doorway to the Gods." He adjusted his turban. "But, bet or no bet, that did happen, didn't it?"

Adir nodded, his uneasiness dying down a little, although the images still flickered through his mind.

"I knew it! That's Arvan all right. Always clamoring on about responsibilities and duties. But as hard and stubborn as he is, the man is usually right. I hate that." Master Kaleb smiled. "A late delivery here and there is fine, but don't go about making a habit of it."

"Yea, sir."

"Now, how's your sister doing? Heard Laraan wasn't keeping too well."

"I didn't know that. I haven't seen her in a while."

The Temple bell drowned the Square with a permeating resonance.

"Well, that's the first bell," Master Kaleb said. "Let's get going. Go find your father, Adir. I have to find my wife and children. Gods watch over you and keep you out of harm's way." With that, Master Kaleb hurriedly waddled down the pathway to the Temple.

The Temple was a tall structure of brick and clay. Large enough to comfortably hold the Faithful of Marafel and then some, the Temple was capped by a tall steeple in the middle and four bell towers, one at each corner. The front facade held three large wooden doors, each crowned by a heptagonal stained-glass window. Each heptagon was split into seven triangles stained red, orange, yellow, green, blue, indigo, and violet—one color to a triangle—symbolizing the Union of the Gods. Or, as the Annadi simply called it, the Union.

Adir walked through the door on the left as the resonance of the third bell faded. A low murmur of conversation rose from those gathered.

A wide band of intricate woodcarvings ran the length of the two side walls, about a hand below the ceiling. One showed Daroon containing the rakhor at the Precipice of the World, while another depicted a hunting scene with Herra riding a taygar, bow in hand and fletching to ear. She was chasing down a giant reptilian beast running on two legs, with teeth as sharp as sword-points and claws as long as a man's arm, its name since forgotten to the ages. Some carvings showed scenes from the history of man, like the Exodus from the lost island of Aedenin and the Battle of Brothers.

At the other end of the Temple stood a plain wooden pulpit with the Union on its front, facing three columns of benches for the Faithful. Behind the pulpit were seven triangles, each shaded with a color of the Union. In front of each triangle stood a white marble statue of a God, a small brass oil lamp set at the foot. The red, blue, and indigo triangles backgrounded Daroon, Hrenwaldt and Berron, while the orange, yellow, green and violet triangles were backdrops for Menera, Pharrahmin, Herra, and Corranine.

Looking around the room, Adir found Arvan and Athvan seated next to the Marandas. Adir walked up to the row, shuffled his way through, and accidentally stepped on Mistress Lora Maranda's toes; she let out a little yelp. Adir apologized profusely and seated himself between Rein and Athvan.

The fifth bell rang.

"Did you talk to your father about"—Adir felt a lump forming in his throat—"about the pasture?"

Rein just stared off toward the pulpit for a few moments. "Yea," he said finally. He looked at Adir. "Akka grabbed his sword and rode off to the Village Watch and told us to stay inside until he got back." Rein rubbed the back of his neck with his right hand. "He came back a little while later saying that the Watch had recovered the body and were taking it to Tamaar's home." He fell silent as the sixth bell rang, then stared at the pulpit again.

The seventh bell signaled the commencement of the Holy Hour services. The murmur in the Temple died down, as Akka Rammel Hallen walked through a door on the far wall. A man in his later years, with white hair and a kindly face, the Akka was dressed in the ceremonial garb of a Sage of the Temple of the Seven Truths: a saffron linen robe adorned by the Union at the center, Union-colored sash across the waist, and a necklace with seven Union-colored triangles centered between the shoulders. The congregation rose as the Akka took the pulpit.

"Our Gods in Amarna," the Akka chanted, "bless us this evening as we shower praise and glory unto you."

"O Gods, hear our prayers!" replied the Faithful in unison.

The Akka gave a hand signal by flaring his fingers, and seven children, three boys and four girls, stood up from the first row in the middle column of benches. They each held a lighted candle perched on a gilded candlestick and fanned around the Akka.

The whole congregation sang.

Praise be to our Gods
Our final salvation.
Praise be to Daroon
For courage to endure.
Praise be to Menera
For love in our hearts.
Praise be to Pharrahmin
For light so we can see.
Praise be to Herra
For food that we eat.
Praise be to Hrenwaldt
For water that we drink.
Praise be to Berron
For wisdom in our minds.
Praise be to Corranine
Whose judgment shall open Amarna.

> *Praise be to the Gods*
> *Our final salvation.*

After the hymn was done, the children lit the lamps in front of the statues of the Gods with their candles then returned to their seats. The flames on each lamp reflected off the colored triangle backdrop, giving each white marble statue an aura of its color. The Akka then bathed each statue with milk from a small brass pot before returning to the pulpit.

"Welcome to all the Faithful in attendance," Akka Hallen said. "Tonight, the seventh night of the seventh month, we are gathered together to worship and celebrate our Gods. And so it is only appropriate to remember our genesis." Akka Hallen paused, looking at the congregation, then smiled.

"Almost seven thousand years ago," he began, "our ancestors lived among our Gods on Aedenin, as carefree as children. We thrived in their glory and protection. But the Gods had bigger plans for us. They wanted us to grow and better our minds, bodies, and souls. And so they decided to leave us to our own devices.

"They said, 'Our children, we know you are strong. We know you are brave. We leave you now to test your resilience and your faith. We shall return one day and celebrate your accomplishments in our service.'"

With a practiced tremor in his voice, the Akka continued. "But our ancestors were afraid and all cried out for the Gods to stay."

Sticking his chest out and raising his arms in imitation of the Gods, he continued. "'Fear not, children, for we shall leave gifts to aid you,' said Daroon. He waved his hands and a red light emanated from them, filling his children's hearts with courage. Next, Menera's hands radiated an orange hue and her children's hearts were filled with love. Pharrahmin stepped forward, hands waving and enveloped in yellow, and said, 'I shall leave you with the sun, the moon, and the stars so you may always have light to see.' Herra's hands were glowing green as she waved them and all of Leakarha was filled with plants and animals for our sustenance. Hrenwaldt's blue hands gave us water, filling the rivers, seas, and oceans. Berron stepped forward with indigo hands, and his children's minds gained wisdom. Finally, Corranine stepped forward and spoke. 'I leave you with many Gifts that will be of use to you. Stay true to your faith in us! Live a Worthy Life! And you shall enter Amarna for eternity.' She then waved her hands and a violet light burst out of them, darkening the world. When the darkness faded away, the Gods were gone."

Akka Hallen paused for a long moment, surveying the congregation. "Our faith in the Gods is strong and our devotion to living a Worthy Life cannot be shaken, even though we are tested every day. But only by staying true to our tenets shall we pave our path to Amarna."

With that, he reached for a handful of incense placed next to a book on the pulpit. Akka Hallen walked over to each marble statue, lit two sticks of incense using the flame from the lamp, and stuck them into holes at its base.

Returning to the pulpit, the Akka opened the thick book placed on it—the Word of the Gods. From it, he began reading the Plea for Forgiveness, which asked the Gods to pardon the unintentional misdeeds of the Faithful and reconsider their entrance into Amarna. But if they were found unworthy, they would gladly be reincarnated and pursue worthiness in their next life. The Plea was followed by readings of scriptures and verses, all of which was either praise to the Gods or a lesson for man. This went on for a while, and the congregation mostly sat in a solemn silence, watching and listening. Sometimes they sang hymns. Sometimes they prayed.

Adir did the same, but deep inside, he wasn't sure that prayers were ever answered. After his mother had disappeared, he had prayed every night to the Gods to bring her back—he felt slightly foolish for continuing that practice to this day—but she never came. He had prayed every night for his father to return from the Navengaard; however, by the time Arvan did return, Adir didn't need his father anymore. He was convinced prayers were nothing but the wishes and hopes of people who had no means of attaining them by themselves and therefore, to Adir, it seemed useless to pray.

No prayer would bring Tamaar back. And if prayers were unanswered, did that mean that there was no one listening? No. Most of the village believed in the Word and the Gods. In fact, most of the world believed in the Gods. All those people couldn't be wrong. Nevertheless, countless unanswered prayers could shake any person's faith.

Akka Hallen closed and picked up the book, then walked in front of the pulpit. "Though the Faithful are numerous," he said in a serious yet kindly tone, "many have lost their way or have chosen not to see it. We are no longer united as one people. We are split into many nations, many beliefs. Man killing man." He shook his head of long silvery strands in disgust. "News from the south talks about war between Aemonne and Guerradrith. The savages east of the Bahzenelyn spend their lives killing and slaughtering each other on a whim. Such senseless violence." He paused. It seemed as if he was regarding each and every member of his congregation individually. "Now, I know many of you are thinking 'What can *we* do about this? *We* are but a small village in Naven. Obscure. Unimportant.' But I assure you, *we* can make a difference!" Raising the thick, saffron-stained, wood-bound book with the Union on its front, he exclaimed, "Spread the Word! For the Word of the Gods shall bring peace and prosperity to all!"

"Heed the Word! Heed the Word! Heed the Word!" chanted the congregation.

The Akka placed the book back on the pulpit and signaled his congregation to stand.

"Let us rejoice in our faith and recite the Seven Truths." The congregation recited in unison.

> *Our Gods created Leakarha.*
> *Our Gods created us in their image.*
> *Our Gods love all their children.*
> *Our Gods shall take the worthy to Amarna.*
> *Life in the service of the Gods is a Worthy Life.*
> *As the Gods provide, the Gods take away.*
> *Our Gods shall return one day.*

After the Seven Truths were recited, the silence in the Temple was broken by the Akka. "A couple of announcements before you leave. First, good luck to all who will be competing in the Regional Games in two days. And second, if you'd like to say a personal prayer to your patron God, you may approach the statues. Please don't rush. The Gods have time enough for us all." He smiled as a mild chuckle traveled through the crowd.

As Adir made his way out with his family and the Marandas, he overheard snippets of conversation.

"... when will Guerradrith learn that war never accomplishes anything?" one man asked.

"They never will!" replied another. "Gods smite them! Why does the godsforsaken Grand Council not step in? They stick their noses into everything like a horse eating from a feedbag ..."

And in another conversation, "... maybe the Aemonnils are getting what they deserve. Himsal did stick the knife in Syanuenan's back ..."

Adir, along with the other Nathars and Marandas, exited the Temple into a cloudless night. The sky was dotted with stars in all directions but the northeast, where it glowed dimly from the Precipice Aurora. After walking the length of the pathway, they approached a group of people in the Village Square. Ellyn Kalathar, Gray Larrion, and Mel Naldatree were deep in discussion—most likely some Village Council business.

Arvan walked up to the trio and asked, "Where's the rest?"

"At the inn," replied Ellyn Kalathar. She was of an age with Adir's father, but the years had been good to her. Her slightly tanned, slim figure was draped in a blue embroidered dress with a modest neckline. She wore her jet-black hair down save for a small bun neatly placed on the back of her head. She was as astute as she was beautiful, if not more so.

Arvan turned to Athvan, handed him a few copper crowns, and said, "Why don't you go and buy some crumbcakes from Mistress Ellar and go play with Martha and Dolaran?"

The scrawny boy's brown eyes brightened as he snatched the crowns and darted off toward Marcy Ellar's wagon, Martha and Dolaran following.

"Lora, could you keep an eye on him for me?" Arvan asked. His question was met with a smile and nod from Mistress Maranda that said he didn't even need to ask.

"We should make our way there." Smoothly slipping her arm through Arvan's, Ellyn led him toward the inn.

BORDERING the southeastern end of the Square, the Rainbow Inn was the biggest structure there, though that wasn't saying much. Its common room and bedchambers were half the size of inns in other villages, and the stable was nothing to brag about either. But no matter its size, the Rainbow Inn was a warm respite for the weary traveler and a cozy, familiar place for the village folk to unwind with a mug of ale or lounge on the breezy veranda with a pipe. Even the squeak of the inn's sign sounded like comfort.

Climbing the three wooden steps to the inn's veranda, Adir walked ahead of the others and opened the heavy wooden door. Passing through the small foyer, the group entered the common room that boasted a few tables, benches, and chairs, but few customers. The night of the Holy Hour of Worship was not a night for revelry in Marafel. However, Adir found Morena sitting at a table, sipping out of a mug.

"Keki!" Adir called, walking toward her. Her brown hair was down, looped by a thin red ribbon.

Morena stood up and straightened her dress. "Adir!" She stepped out from behind the table and hugged him. "It's so good to see you!"

"It's been some time. How is everything?" Adir said.

"Couldn't be better," replied Morena. "We just finished our vegetable garden, hoping for a good harvest."

"How's Laraan? Heard he wasn't keeping well."

A flicker of annoyance crossed Morena's face. "You too? It's like everyone in this godsforsaken village has nothing to talk about but Laraan's cough." She looked away. "It's just a cough, for Gods' sake!"

"He's the mayor and I'm sure the people are concerned."

Morena met Adir's eyes. "No, it's not concern. People just get bored with their lives and look at others' lives for excitement."

That's about to change, Adir thought.

"Hello, Morena," Arvan's voice interrupted. His father walked up to stand beside Adir. Arvan opened his arms and almost took a step to embrace Morena, but stopped when Morena pointedly looked away.

"Hello, akka," Morena said. "How are you doing?" She sounded less like his daughter and more like a distant acquaintance.

"I'm doing well. How's Laraan? Heard he has a—"

"Cough. Yea, I know. I am his wife, after all." Talking to Arvan always put Morena in a foul mood, a reaction Adir shared with his older sister. If Athvan had been old enough to understand his father's purposeful absence, Adir was sure he, too, would have the same reaction.

"I was merely inquiring," Arvan said coolly, a tinge of anger in his voice.

"Thank you," Morena said, facetiously. "If you have any more concerns about the mayor's health, you can ask him when you see him shortly." Morena sat back down and took a sip from her mug.

Uncomfortable silence followed. Arvan opened his mouth to say something a couple of times, but refrained from doing so.

"Ah, welcome," said Sarina Knafelle as she entered the common room through the kitchen doors. She was perhaps half a decade younger than Arvan, with a stout figure and pretty face. She and her husband, Thane, owned the Rainbow Inn.

Adir kissed Morena on the cheek. "I will see you soon, keki," he said and began stepping back, almost bumping into Arvan.

Morena smiled fondly. "You should come by for dinner sometime."

"I will," Adir replied, turning and heading to the rest of the group. His father joined him without another word to Morena.

"May the Gods be good to you," Mistress Knafelle said, approaching the group.

"Thank you, Sarina. It's been a while," Arvan said.

"It sure has. We don't see you around here much, since you decided being mayor wasn't for you. Do you still feel that way?" Sarina smiled.

"Laraan is doing a fine job. The village seems to be running smoothly," Arvan said coolly, as usual. However, Adir sensed a touch of exasperation—possibly at Sarina's implication that Arvan run for mayor again. His father had retired to the farm once his tenure was up, as he had been sick of the petty political squabbles of the Village Council. But folk still came to him for advice.

"Yea, yea. Laraan is doing well and all. With a lot of *help* from your daughter." Glancing at Gray Larrion, she continued, "The girl knows how to straighten out some of the more stubborn councillors. She does take after you, Arvan." Shifting her gaze to Adir and Rein, she spoke to them with a concerned tone, "Are you boys doing all right?"

Adir nodded, as did Rein.

"Good," Mistress Knafelle said, smiling at them. Addressing the group, she continued, "Now, please follow me."

The group trailed after her into the private dining chamber. Arvan had once mentioned to Adir that this chamber had been used for Village Council meetings since the inn was built. A single chandelier hung from the ceiling at the center of the room, right above a large wooden table bordered by ten wooden chairs. Two windows stood on opposite walls, open, filling the room with a cool cross-breeze. A small, unlit fireplace was at one end of the room, above which hung a painting of Eddher Knafelle, donning the fur-lined green-and-white uniform of the Navengaard Mountain Watch. He was Thane's great-grandfather and somewhat of a local legend—hailed as the greatest rakhor slayer to have ever been a Watchmen.

"What are the lads doing here?" barked Niman Mummfar, seated on the far side of the table. He was an old—really old—councillor, who could beat a mule in stubbornness and had the charm of a skunk. His creased and wrinkled face and spotted bald head was a perfect reflection of his personality. Niman poured himself some wine from a jug on the table, took a sip, and continued barking. "This is no place for children."

"I am not a child," Adir said, bristling. Men did not bear such insults. He'd tried sounding cool, like his father, but, as usual, his temper got the best of him. It bubbled at the most inopportune moments, like rice left on the boil for too long.

Niman scowled, but Adir held his gaze. Niman opened his mouth to say something, when Eli jumped in. "The lads were the ones who found the body. We need to know what they saw."

"I agree," seconded Arvan.

"You two don't belong here either!" Niman was shaking with anger.

"Enough! They stay!" exclaimed a voice from the end of the table. Yet diffidence was all too obvious in its tone. Laraan Alameah, the mayor of Marafel and Adir's brother-in-law, was a good, well-regarded man, always willing to lend a helping hand. Unfortunately, being well liked wasn't the only job requirement for a mayor and Laraan seemed to struggle with the other parts of mayorship. However, Adir didn't care about that—Laraan was a good husband to Morena.

"You can't dictate how these meetings—" Niman began, but was harshly interrupted by Mistress Knafelle.

"Niman Mummfar, you be quiet! This is my inn and they're my guests. I'll not stand by and watch you insult them. They can stay if they want, and you can leave if you don't like it!" She was so forceful that Niman quietly sank into the shelter of his chair, like a snail receding into its shell when poked. "Good," said Sarina, sounding like her sweet self again. "If you need anything, just holler." With that, she stepped out of the room, shutting the door behind her.

When everyone was seated, Laraan turned to Adir and Rein. "So, let's hear what happened."

"I met Rein this morning when I took the cows to graze on the pastures," Adir began, breathing out and collecting himself.

"I had shot down some ravens. There was a large flight by the river," Rein added. "And when we went to grab the birds I shot, that's … that's …" Rein trailed off, as if something had barricaded his voice in his throat.

Adir knew what Rein felt. That lump in the throat. The slow, uncomfortable churn in the stomach. He knew what Rein felt because he felt it too. The flies. The blood. The guts! Would he ever be able to get it out of his mind? Or would he forever be haunted by the events of that morning?

"That's when they found the body," Eli said, finishing Rein's thought. A heavy silence engulfed the room.

"Yea," Adir said, breaking the silence. "We found Tamaar's head a few paces away." *He'd looked like he was screaming.*

There was another long silence. The councillors shot shocked glances at each other. This time it was Arvan who spoke. "Can you describe the body?" he asked.

Adir didn't want to. But he gritted his teeth, like a man, and described what he had seen earlier. "The body had no head," he began, breath quickening as he focused on the images looping in his mind. "His front was torn open, his guts were everywhere." He paused and looked around the room. Mel and Gray were perspiring. Ellyn looked calm, but her eyes showed what could have been fear or apprehension. Niman wore his usual grimace.

"And the claw marks?" Arvan asked.

"I didn't realize they were claw marks!" Rein chimed in, surprised. "But now that I think about it, they *were* claw marks! Very large claw marks."

"That's what the Village Watch report said," Laraan added.

"There is no doubt in my mind that Tamaar was killed by a rakhor," Arvan said matter-of-factly. "It's rare that they make it this far south, but it does happen from time to time."

The Village Council stared at Arvan, their faces displaying shock and surprise. After a moment, Ellyn spoke. "Are you sure, Arvan? No one's ever heard of a rakhor coming this far south."

"I wish I were wrong, Ellyn, but I'm sure," Arvan said, his voice simultaneously cool and grave.

"We'll need to keep this quiet," Ellyn said. "No need to start a panic by mentioning rakhor."

"We could do that," Eli agreed, placing his turban on the table. The middle-aged man with grey around the temples pushed his chair back and began pacing the length of the table. "But the news of the murder will spread—"

"Master Kaleb mentioned it to me earlier," Adir interjected, remembering his earlier conversation with the cheesemaker.

"Already?" Eli seemed surprised. "Well, there you go. This news is bound to cause panic. If we keep our mouths shut about the rakhor, people will think that a Marafellen killed Tamaar. Neighbors will mistrust each other. And we certainly don't want that. I think it best we come out with the truth."

"Arvan, what do you suggest we do?" asked Laraan.

Arvan stared out a window, eyes unfocused. "Send word to the Watchmen," he eventually answered, his cool voice pulling everyone's attention. "I'm sure they'd spare a detachment to patrol Marafel." The former mayor paused for a moment. "And I agree with Eli. We should just tell the truth as best we know it. There's no need to hide such things from our friends and neighbors. It would only serve to erode their trust in us. Once the Watchmen get here, people will surely believe that it was a rakhor, and not a Marafellen, that killed Tamaar. Let's hope that's enough to calm everyone."

"Anyone have any objections?" Laraan looked about the room, but seemed to spend a few extra moments regarding Gray and Niman. No one piped up and Adir knew no one would. His father's words carried a lot of weight in this village, even if he didn't run its day-to-day operations. "Then it's settled," Laraan concluded. "We'll send out a rider at first light. And let's try and squash rumors before they start. Let people know that Tamaar is dead and it was a rakhor that did it. And stress the fact that the Watchmen will be here to protect us." Laraan stood up and was abruptly seized by a fit of vigorous coughing. He sat back down, holding his stomach.

"Are you all right?" Ellyn poured a mug of water and handed it to Laraan. "Drink."

Laraan took the mug, nodded his head in appreciation, and took a couple of sips. "I'm all right," he said, then emptied the mug. "If there's nothing else, I'd like to get home and get some rest."

Chapter Four

"How are your studies faring with Preceptor Koray?" Ekren asked as she cut a piece of sausage.

"They are faring well, mara," Dina said, seated to Ekren's right at the large dining table. The young woman spread some ghee on a simiti roll. "We have been talking about current events."

"Oh? And what events are those?"

"The rebellion in Herraland." Dina took a bite of her roll, fixing her eyes on Ekren and flashing a knowing smile. "I am sure you know all about it, mara."

"Yes," Ekren replied. It was true. The Regent of Ostarium had to stay abreast of world events, especially a rebellion in a neighboring nation. She held up her glass and signaled a servant, who topped it off with tamarind sherbet. Taking a sip of the cool drink sent a wave of refreshment through her, washing away the discomfort of the late spring heat. "But I would like to hear what you have to say about the matter, daughter."

Dina's eyes sparkled. The young woman, this morning garbed in a blue cotton tunic with a gold-embroidered neckline, looked so much like her father. Her dark auburn hair, held in place by a floral-patterned bandana, was a stark yet stunning contrast to her light green eyes, placed perfectly on her olive-complexioned face. "Well," she began, sipping tea from a porcelain cup, "the rebellion has put King Dooghlas in a bind. Even before the rebellion, some of his forces were already tied up securing his eastern borders against the Guerrans. And now with the rebellion in northern Herraland, he has had to dispatch more troops to quell it." She paused and grabbed a small bunch of green grapes from the flower-worked porcelain fruit bowl on the table and began popping them into her mouth individually.

"Good," Ekren said. "That is a decent analysis of the Herran forces. The Preceptor is—"

"I am not done yet, mara," Dina said respectfully, a playful smile dancing at the edges of her mouth.

"Then by all means, Heiress Regent"—Ekren made a grand gesture—"please continue."

"Thank you, Lady Regent," Dina replied with a chuckle and a small nod. "So, with his forces already spread thin, Dooghlas won't be able to defend Pacca Nirum well if it is attacked. And I wouldn't put it past the Guerrans to do just that. I think that Dooghlas's best chance at regaining stability is by seeking help. He may come to us, which will pose a significant opportunity for Ostarium …" She trailed off with a quizzical expression. "What are you smiling about?"

"You," Ekren said, filled to the brim with pride, some of which had apparently spilled onto her face. Her daughter had started with something as simple as a rebellion in a foreign nation and cleverly worked through various steps objectively and methodically. "I am not entirely sure if Bilgan is teaching you or you are teaching him."

"I still have a lot to learn from Preceptor Koray," Dina said modestly. Her cheeks turned a pale red.

"We are *always* learning," Ekren said, cleaning the yolk off her plate with a piece of simiti. "But you are doing well, daughter. You will be the greatest Regent our nation has ever seen."

The red on Dina's cheeks deepened. "Thank you, mara!"

The ornate wood-worked clock chimed ten times, reminding Ekren of Dina's appointment. "You better be on your way, Dina," she said. "We do not want to keep Lord Malasi's son waiting."

"Mara!" Dina pouted. "I really do not want to go meet a puffed-up lordlet." She gave Ekren that cute, helpless look she had given her so many times before—the look of a sad, lonely puppy waiting to be rescued. It could soften even the hardest of hearts. However, this puppy had a sly spark in her eyes that made her supposed plight quite suspect. "The greatest mother our nation has ever seen wouldn't let her only daughter go meet a strange man, would she?" Dina said sweetly, with a smile that could will the Gods into submission.

Ekren had fallen for this sympathy-seeking display many times before and was no longer fooled by it. She simply laughed at Dina's attempts to wiggle out of her commitment. "Flattery won't get you anywhere, daughter," she laughed. "Time waits for no one. Now get going."

"Fine!" Dina said, elongating the word. She waved and two servants stepped forward—one cleared off her plate and cutlery, while the other placed a washbowl in front of her.

Ekren watched with an annoyed amusement as Dina washed each of her fingers with painful delicacy, then washed them again twice more. She was obviously stretching out the process to make her displeasure known. Finally, she dried her hands on a napkin. Then she stood and gave Ekren a light kiss on her cheek.

"May the Gods keep you safe till I see you next," Dina said, with half a smile.

"You as well, daughter."

Dina exited the room through the tall, intricately carved wooden doors, held open by a guard. Her baggy salwar fell all the way to the floor, hiding her feet, which made it seem as though she were gliding.

What a graceful woman she has become! Ekren hoped to the Gods that Dina would find Lord Malasi's son to be a suitable consort. And that was all she could really do. Dina had turned away every suitor Ekren had found for the last two years. Ekren had raised Dina to be strong and rely on herself, but the physical and spiritual companionship of the right man would help her realize her full potential. Like Garron had for her.

The doors opened once more and Ferrith strode in. The grey-haired Vice Regent held a portfolio in his long, bony fingers. "May the Gods favor you, Lady Regent," Ferrith said as he bowed deeply. He was the epitome of a frail, aging man, but his bearing held an unmistakable surety of self.

"You as well, Ferrith," Ekren replied, then finished off the last of her sherbet. "Let us head to my study."

"Very well, Lady Regent," Ferrith said, standing erect once again.

Before exiting the dining room, Ekren stopped in front of one of the guards by the door to inspect his uniform. The guard stood as motionless as a marble statue, staring straight through her as if she were made of glass. His domed, steel helmet was well polished, and the spike at its center was sharpened to a point. His boots were polished to a midnight black, and his loose white salwar was tucked into them. His curved sword hung sheathed at his left hip, ready.

The guard's yellow tabard, however, hung a little askew over his full-sleeved mail shirt. Ekren straightened the tabard, examined the guard once more, and nodded. A personal inspection of her soldiers, especially the low-ranked ones, lifted their spirits and made them stand a little taller, something she had learned from Garron when he had commanded her forces. How she missed her husband!

The guard bowed reverently. As Ekren strode out the door, the two guards knocked the butts of their spears on the ground in salute, then followed behind Ferrith.

"So, what news?" Ekren asked as they walked through the brightly painted brownstone hallway that overlooked an atrium through arched portals.

From his portfolio, Ferrith pulled out a rolled piece of paper sealed with green wax and handed it to Ekren. She promptly recognized the seal that showed an image of Herra. "A Herran messenger came in this morning with that," Ferrith said, pointing at the rolled paper. "By her ragged appearance, it is evident she barely rested during her journey."

Ekren thumbed at the seal and cracked it. She unfurled the paper and read as she walked.

Day 33 of Ponth, 6996

Lady Ekren Arinol, Regent of Ostarium, Alamand of the Grand Council,

Herraland is on the brink of collapse. We've been fighting the

Guerrans since the War of Remaking and the Grand Council has done nothing about it! I'm not sure I understand the relevance of the Council anymore—no offense to you of course.

Now, this Sorcha Camran and her rebels are raiding my outposts and burning farms in the name of some misplaced justice. She thinks she can undo decades of rebuilding over a land squabble? No, not while my heart still beats!

That's where you come in. I need troops, weapons, and food. Horses, if you can spare any. We can negotiate terms if you agree.

I am hoping that the Ostarks will ride to the Herrans' defense once more, like in the days of our grandfathers. My messenger will wait for your response. Don't take too long.

-King Kierand Dooghlas
Sovereign Ruler of Herraland.

"That was straight to the point," Ekren said.

"That is why they say 'as blunt as a Herran,'" Ferrith said, picking up on the joke. "What did King Dooghlas want?"

"He is looking for aid—troops and food and such," Ekren said, remembering how her daughter had accurately predicted the Herran king's actions. "Dina brought up this very thing during breakfast today," she added, welling up with pride. "She said the Herrans would court our aid."

"She is a very astute young lady."

Ekren nodded in agreement. Then her mind drifted back to Dooghlas's message. During the War of Remaking, even after Cayan had been liberated from the combined armies of Phucao, Aemonne, and Guerradrith, Herraland was still under Guerran occupation. The Ostark Regent at the time, Ekren's grandfather, had led the campaign into the neighboring nation, helping Herraland overthrow their occupiers and marking the definitive end of the war.

Treaties signed at the war's conclusion restored all borders to prewar status in an effort to *maintain everlasting peace*, her grandfather had said. However, that arrangement, among others, did not sit well with her. Ekren felt that her grandfather should have bargained for more. After all, without Ostark help, the Herrans—or even the Cayani for that matter—would still be under Guerran occupation, their ways of life crumbling into the Guerrans' pit of Faithlessness. As far as Ekren was concerned, the Herrans and the Cayani owed Ostarium a great debt.

But maybe this rebellion in Herraland was a chance to subtly extract payment for that debt. If she maneuvered her pieces correctly, she could end up annexing parts of Herraland. "I need to think on this a bit," she said. She had the vision, but now she needed to work out the details before sending a message back to Dooghlas.

"Very good, Lady Regent," Ferrith said.

As they approached the large wooden doors to the Regent's Study, the guards who'd been following them posted to either side of the door and held it open for their Regent and Vice Regent. As Ekren walked through the doors, the guards knocked their spears on the floor in salute.

Ekren loved her study. It was an escape from the burden of demanding courtiers and citizens. The spacious room ran across one end of the palace, with arched windows on three walls overlooking the city of Lanmeria. The windows were open, letting in a cool, curtain-fluttering breeze. The Regent's Desk sat in the exact center of the room, at the point where the light from the windows converged. The corners of the room on the opposite side of the door—the ones that formed the corners of the palace—had alcoves that made the room seem as if it had ears. The alcoves were part of circular minarets that extended above the roof of the palace. Potted plants, paintings, and other aesthetically pleasing objects decorated the room in typical Ostark fashion.

As per her morning ritual, Ekren walked up to the window behind her desk and peered out at her beautiful capital. Decorations from the previous night's festivities for Holy Hour hung in colors of the Union in various parts of Lanmeria, particularly concentrated around Temples of the Seven.

"Any trouble in the city during last night's celebrations?" Ekren asked.

"The City Watch reported some mild disturbances—nothing serious."

Ekren nodded appreciatively. Only in her nation did people of all faiths and no faith coexist peacefully. "Anything else we need to talk about?" She turned to her vice regent.

Ferrith fished in his portfolio. "I have some papers for you to sign," he said, pulling out a stack. "All routine orders."

"Leave them on my desk. I will get to them shortly."

"Very well, Lady Regent," Ferrith said, placing the stack of papers on her desk. The old man seemed to ponder something for a second, then said, "There is another matter ... although it is not of state import."

Ekren caught a look in Ferrith's eyes that revealed the nature of the topic. "This is neither the time nor the place for that sort of discussion," she said curtly. Ferrith recoiled a bit at her tone, but Ekren felt no remorse. Ferrith should know better than to discuss such delicate matters here. Without taking any bite out of her voice, she added, "If there is nothing else, you may leave."

"Yes, Lady Regent. My apologies." Ferrith bowed sheepishly and stepped backward.

Ekren turned to regard her beautiful city once again as the door opened and closed behind her. She spotted Dina's carriage rolling down the road surrounded by seven Regent Guards on horseback, their white capes billowing behind them. She hoped that Dina would pick a husband soon. She wanted to ensure that her lineage was secure before the end of her days. And ... she liked the thought of becoming a grandmother.

Chapter Five

Dina arrived at Lake Koyou to find that the lordlet had not arrived yet. It was not an auspicious start for him. One should never keep a lady waiting, especially not the Heiress Regent. She was thankful for his absence, however; such blind meetings were often awkward affairs. How she loathed the scripted dance of small talk as her suitors tried to win her affection.

Win my affection, she thought disdainfully. As if it were a prize to be put on a shelf. And based on the so-called suitors she had met so far, she was fairly confident that a shelf would indeed be where her affection would end up. Unlike women, men had no clue how to deal with such things.

Yes, she had rejected each man her mother had arranged for her to meet, much to Ekren's dismay. It was not her fault that Dina had found each of them utterly repulsive, like meat that had rotted after being left out for days.

The sun slowly climbed to the peak of its journey across a blue sky, intermittently ducking behind fluffy white clouds. A kingfisher splashed into the lake some distance away, then resurfaced after a few moments with a flailing sliver of silver in its beak. Dragonflies of various colors buzzed around, hovering in places as if to make sure the world was in order.

At the lake's edge, Dina climbed up a large boulder, slipped out of her shoes, and folded the legs of her salwar to just below her knees. Perched up on the rock, she sat with her feet dangling off its side into the cool waters of the man-made lake.

Lake Koyou was considered a marvel of engineering the world over. Through her studies, Dina had learned that the builders of the lake had picked a perfect spot nestled between hills to dig. They subsequently had lined the bottom with rocks and gravel, then had dug a canal from the Gronelle River to fill the lake. Over centuries of eroding banks, the canal had widened and morphed into a tributary in its own right. This feat had been accomplished some fifteen hundred years before, though records did not indicate why the lake had been built. To her knowledge, the Gronelle Delta had always been a lush land, thereby making a man-made lake unnecessary. But none of that detracted from its natural splendor.

The familiar sounds of hooves and carriage wheels drew her attention uphill. Two horses pulling a white carriage awkwardly picked their way along the uneven hillside, followed by four horses that carried burly men. The men, by the cocky confidence they portrayed, appeared to be bodyguards. It seemed the lordlet had arrived.

The horses pulling the carriage snorted and stamped, unable to get sure footing while trying to balance an inclining hillside and a sliding carriage. After a lot of careful maneuvering, the horses came to a stop, refusing to move another step despite angry lashes from the coachman. That brought the whole entourage to a halt—the carriage tilted with the slope of the hill—a dozen yards from her. Stories always mentioned the gallant prince riding to his beloved on a white horse, but a white carriage? That was new.

The carriage door swung open with a bang and a tall man with a pointy black beard and thinning hair stepped out. He wore a finely woven lavender cotton jubba with flower-work around the neckline, a white salwar, and white shoes with tips as pointy as his beard.

The lordlet looked at his feet with an unflattering grimace. "Gods smite you, Hernel!" he bellowed. "Where did you learn to drive a carriage?" He looked back at his bodyguards, expecting support, but they sat lazily atop their horses in utter disinterest of his plight. Hernel fidgeted with the reins but remained silent. "You stopped right in the middle of this … this"—the lordlet gestured around him with his hands—"FILTH! And now my godsforsaken shoes are dirty. Mara will not be pleased!"

A grown man worried his mother would not be pleased with his stained shoes? Dina was learning many new things today.

The lordlet rubbed his shoe with his hands, his grimace deepening. Shaking his head in disgust, he looked up, his eyes widening as he met her eyes. With a swagger that reminded Dina of a newly born lamb attempting to stand for the first time, the lordlet walked toward her. Though he was as far from a lamb as one could get.

Dina pulled her feet out of the water and hopped off the rock, shoes in hand. She noticed him furrow his eyebrows in disapproval at the sight of her bare calves. Respectable Ostark women did not lay their legs bare! She, however, did not care much for that custom, nor for the lordlet's discomfort. Ostarium was no longer ruled only by men.

"Heiress Regent," the lordlet said, bowing deeply. "I am Lord Mertca Malasi. I believe we are to meet." He smiled suggestively, revealing a few blackened teeth. It seemed the lordlet must have a sweet tooth.

"May the Gods favor you, Lord Malasi," Dina said as graciously as she could, while straining to not stare at his teeth.

"Thank you," he replied. "I apologize for having kept you waiting, but my idiot coachman has no clue of what he is doing."

"He seems to have done well, given the circumstances." Dina was sure the coachman was smarter than the lordlet, who undoubtedly ordered him to go *across* a slippery hillside.

The lordlet snickered uncomfortably.

"Did my coachman not warn you against riding in here? Was he not at the road?" Dina asked.

"He did, Heiress Regent," Mertca said, "but I assured him that my carriage could cross any terrain." He paused and looked toward his carriage as if realizing the folly of his words, but then he added, "Well, the carriage *can* cross any terrain, if the coachman is skilled."

Dina could not help but sigh in exasperation. Even if she had fallen madly in love with this man, his eagerness to push blame onto others would make him a lousy consort. She walked back to the shore with Mertca by her side as an awkward silence expanded. It was as if nature itself was holding its breath waiting for this meeting to end.

"Why don't you tell me about yourself?" Dina said, finally. The lordlet was a poor conversationalist.

"Well, I am the first and only son of Lord and Lady Malasi," the lordlet began. "Akka holds lands to the south. A couple of mines, a few orchards, and a litany of other enterprises."

"I see," she said. *Why do men have to always talk about what they own? As if they would take their possessions with them to Amarna.*

"One day, all of that will be mine," Mertca said. "Maybe ... *ours*?" he added, flashing her yet another rotted smile of questionable intention.

Dina laughed uncomfortably in reply. "So, tell me about your interests, Lord Malasi." Maybe they would find something in common to talk about.

"Please," the lordlet said, gesturing dismissively, "call me Mertca. Or Merty, if you like." He winked. "May I call you Dina?"

Dina was taken aback by his crude forwardness. "You may call me Dina, Mertca," she said. Even if the Gods threatened to damn her soul for eternity, she would still refuse to call him *Merty*.

"Ah, very well then," Mertca said cheerfully. "Well, Dina. I am an avid hunter!"

Dina perked up a little. *Maybe the lordlet was not as puffed up as he seemed.* But then again, everyone hunted. In the hinterlands, children old enough to shoot an arrow hunted. "O," she said, feigning awe, "what is your preferred game?"

"They are a wily bunch," Mertca said. "Even if you corner them with arrow nocked," he gestured as if holding a fletching to his cheek, "they can still get away from you! Very fast!" He let go of his imagined arrow.

"Foxes?" she asked. She had gone foxhunting a few times and they could sure give one the slip.

"No." The lordlet's face took on a serious expression.

Dina's interest was piqued. "If not foxes, then what?"

"Quail!"

Dina was surprised at her ability to suppress the bellowing laugh that threatened to burst out. Her chest and stomach hurt from the strain of holding it in. Quail! Birds that preferred to run away instead of fly? Birds that stayed so bunched up together that one arrow could easily skewer three? "My word!" she exclaimed, "that sounds incredibly …" She searched for something that would sound heroic, but came up with nothing. "That sounds incredible," she said finally.

"Yes," Mertca said, moving a little closer to her. "I could take you sometime and show you how to use a bow," he added in a low, breathy tone.

"I know how to use a bow, Mertca," Dina said, politely sidestepping in an effort to put a little space between them.

"You Arinol women are indeed something different, are you not?" the lordlet added. "So … wild. None of the other noblewomen even know how to hold a bow. Though a woman hunting is considered unbecoming."

Dina felt herself tense.

"But. I like it."

Abruptly, Dina felt a hand smoothly slide across her buttocks, eventually resting on her hip. She looked over at the lordlet and found his rotted smile staring at her crudely.

In a flash, she grabbed his wrist and swung herself under his arm, spinning and twisting it behind his back. As she spun, she felt his wrist pop under her grip.

Merty screeched.

Six veiled men in white Regent Guard uniforms, with bows readied, popped up around Dina and the lordlet. A lone Regent Guard with gold trim on his veil jumped in front of the lordlet.

Dina pushed the surprised and whimpering excuse of a man into the Regent Guard who had appeared in front of them. "I am fine, Captain Sadi," she said, still fuming at the lordlet's pass.

"She broke my wrist," Mertca whined, holding his wrist gingerly. "That bitch broke my wrist!"

"You better watch your tongue before I cut it out of your mouth," Captain Sadi threatened through his veil before shoving the man aside.

Mertca stumbled over to his bodyguards, who had barely had any time to react to the sudden appearance of seven men. "You witnessed what happened!" he said gesturing toward the captain and Dina.

Captain Sadi regarded the man who appeared to lead the body-guards and slowly shook his head. The bodyguard mimicked the captain. "No, I have not witnessed any such thing," he said.

Mertca reached down, grabbed a handful of dirt and flung it at his bodyguards. And missed. With obvious frustration, he beckoned Hernel to bring the carriage over. "The Regent will hear of this!" he yelled, still cradling his wrist. "This is not how you treat a respectable lord!"

"And touching me inappropriately is how you treat the Heiress Regent?" Dina fumed. The gall of that man! She was livid enough to break his other wrist.

"Lies!" the lordlet exclaimed as his carriage pulled up beside him. He stepped in, shut the door, then popped his head out the window, like a turtle sticking its head out of its shell. "Lies!" he exclaimed again. "Take us home, Hernel!"

The carriage started to roll awkwardly along the hillside. Dina watched, still furious, wishing that the carriage would topple over. But Hernel and the horses did not deserve that fate. Men were pigs, plain and simple.

"You need to hold yourself back a little, Heiress," the captain said. "Breaking lords' wrists is a bad habit to get into." He chuckled. "Maybe I trained you too well."

"I barely did anything, Nekmi," she protested. "It is not my fault his bones are as hollow as a bird's."

"Maybe you do not know your own strength," the older man murmured.

"No, I do."

"Then you broke his wrist on purpose?" Nekmi asked, unveiling. His face held a strange expression of judgmental pride.

Dina did not answer but simply smiled, then turned to watch the lordlet and his entourage disappear into a clump of trees. The sound of hooves and carriage slowly gave way to the pleasant melodies of nature.

Chapter Six

Why did I let Rein talk me into this?

Yesterday, Adir met Rein at his home as neither had ventured to graze their cows. The memories of recent events were still too raw. They sat in silence, drinking spiced lemon water by Rein's cowshed. Eventually, they switched to some wheat ale that Master Maranda had brewed from last harvest's grain, and their tongues loosened. They spoke of many things, except the pastures, till their conversation settled on the Regional Games.

"If nothing else, it'll be a step toward normality," Rein had said, in an attempt to convince Adir to compete in the Games. For some reason, that had resonated with Adir. He knew that he wouldn't be able to put everything behind him if he didn't give his mind other things to focus on.

After his visit with Rein, Adir had met Tia on their usual hilltop. He had been reluctant to talk to her about the pasture, as he wanted to protect her from that. But, like always, she had been able to pull it out of him, like removing a painful thorn from his mind. At first, she'd but gently felt at it, then had prodded and poked till it was visible, finally pulling it out and giving his mind some much needed relief. In the midst of that conversation, he had mentioned that Rein wanted him to compete in the Games. Tia had thought it was a great idea.

Sometimes I think I should just marry that girl. She knows me! But for some reason, he still felt that he needed more time.

"NEXT!" a voice bellowed.

Adir broke out of his daydream as a flood of sights and sounds rushed in. He was standing in a queue that led to a brown canvas tent where officials were registering competitors for the Staff Tournament.

Around him, the whole place was buzzing. Adir heard hawkers selling knickknacks, food, and drinks. Competitors ran through their warmup routines, and thousands of people were shuffling about. Folks from neighboring Akkasha and Nagra had come to Marafel for the Regional Games. Everything felt normal, perhaps even jovial. No one seemed to be talking about Tamaar or the rakhor, at least not openly.

"NEXT," the voice bellowed again. "We don't have all day!"

Adir looked forward and realized that he was at the front of the line. A little embarrassed, he stepped up to the registration table. The official seated behind the table looked at him with obvious frustration.

"Name?"

"Adir Nathar."

"Residence?"

"Marafel."

"Fee?"

Adir fished around in his purse and pulled out a few coins, handing the official his fee of fifty crowns. It was a pretty steep price, one he wasn't sure he wanted to pay. But it seemed worth it for some peace of mind.

The official put the coins into a metal box then pulled out a long strip of white cloth. Subsequently, he dipped a thick paintbrush into an inkwell and painted the number fifty-two on the cloth. After blowing on the numbers a few times, he handed it to Adir. "Once this dries," the official instructed, "tie it onto your left arm. Make sure the number is visible. Thank you for registering. Good luck. NEXT!"

Adir took a moment to process what the official had told him. "Thank you," he said to the man. "May the Gods favor you."

"They will, once you let the next person come up and register."

Adir's temper rose. *There's no need to be that rude. I should give him a lesson on manners!* But what would he gain from that? With effort, he held in his anger, which made his chest feel like it was about to burst. *Is this what it feels like to be a man?* Shooting the official a dirty look, Adir stood at the table for a few moments longer, just to annoy him, before walking away.

As Adir made his way over to the staff section, he spotted Rein in the midst of other archers, stringing his bow confidently. Adir envied him; confidence was something he severely lacked at this moment, unsure that he'd even make it past his first fight. Approaching the staff section of the grounds, he surveyed his competition. And of course, the first person to catch his eye was Boar Sayarna. The short ball of muscle was hard to miss.

Adir had seen Boar fight at the Regional Games three years before and had been awed by his combat skills. The man seemed to have a talent for the staff. *That's why he placed second at the last Daroongaamen.*

Boar appeared to be practicing attack sequences. He spun, slashed, jabbed, and dashed, making Adir even more nervous and less confident than he already was. He forced himself to look away, lest he decide to quit out of sheer intimidation.

But what he saw around him dropped his confidence even further. The competitors who were warming up displayed a combination of strength, speed, and skill, none of which, Adir was sure, he possessed. Quite a few of them were spinning their staves from side to side, swapping hands. Grunts and shouts rang through the air in perfect harmony with complicated and precise movements.

"How many competitors are there?" Adir heard a voice ask behind him.

"Sixty-two," replied another voice.

Adir turned around and spotted two men with officials' badges talking.

"Sixty-two!" exclaimed the first official, disappointed. "That will take all day!"

"No, it won't," said the second. "We'll pair up the novices and weak ones against the more experienced and stronger ones. The bouts will be over quickly." Both men shared a laughed.

Which are the novices and weak ones? Adir thought in confusion. None of the competitors he'd seen so far fit that description. He unstrapped his staff from his back and began mimicking what the other competitors were doing, hoping he wouldn't make a fool of himself.

"Adir!"

Adir recognized that voice. Tia! Adir turned and spotted her running to him, hands full of crumbcakes. She looked beautiful in a simple green dress, her straight black hair swishing untethered behind her shoulders. As she got closer, Adir met her eyes—pools of black that were all too easy to get lost in.

Wrapping her arms around him, Tia held Adir in a tight embrace. Then she raised herself onto her toes and kissed him gently on his cheek. The kiss sent a warm chill down Adir's spine. "Thank you," he said. "I'm glad you came."

"I wouldn't miss a chance to see you compete," Tia said excitedly. "I may not see you win," she added with a teasing smile, "but at least I'll see you compete."

"That's a mean thing to say," Adir said, stung by her words.

"You know I'm just joking," Tia said. "Here"—she handed him three crumbcakes—"you're going to get hungry between bouts and these will help."

"Crumbcakes?" Adir said, a little surprised but accepting them nonetheless. "And three of them? We're not supposed to eat too many in one sitting or we'll get a stomachache." He smiled, remembering the warning every mother gave her child.

"You still believe that?" Tia laughed. "Are you still a child, Adir Nathar?"

"No, of course not." Adir huffed and gazed elsewhere.

At that moment, several calls went up for the competitors and crowd to head to their respective tournament grounds.

"Looks like the Games are about to start," Adir said. A flutter started up in his gut.

"Good luck, Adir. Make me proud!" Tia said. "I'll find a good spot to watch." She planted another kiss on his cheek, then headed off to the section's perimeter.

Popping a crumbcake into his mouth, Adir followed his fellow staff competitors to where three officials stood. Two of them were the officials he had overheard earlier, and the third was Captain Marwar—Adir's *staff trainer*. They didn't exactly have a formal student-teacher relationship, but the captain had given Adir a few basic lessons.

"Gather around," said one of the three officials, a burly man. "We have some rules to go over." The competitors tightened around the officials. "Welcome to the Regional Staff Tournament," he began. "The winner of this tournament will represent Naven in Daroongaamen!"

Everyone cheered.

"The tournament," the official continued, "has three elimination phases and then the final fight. In the first phase, each of you will be paired against a random competitor. Each fight in this phase will have three bouts. Win two out of the three bouts and you move to the second phase. The loser is eliminated. The second phase is a free-for-all melee, which will end when you are down to eight competitors. Finally, in the third phase, each of the eight competitors will be paired against a random opponent—just like in the first phase. The eight will be eliminated down to four and four down to two. You will have to win three of five bouts in these fights. The final fight between the last two competitors will have seven bouts. You win the final, you earn your place in the Naven Daroongaamen team along with the winners from the other Regional Games in Naven!" He paused for a long moment, as if expecting some cheering or at least a bit of applause. But none came.

"Now!" a frail official said. Paired with the burly one, the two made quite the antithetical pair. "If you successfully land a hit on your opponent's body, you win the bout. If you step out of the ring, you forfeit the bout. If you take a step or attack your opponent before the fight is called to a start, you forfeit the bout. Hits above the shoulders or to the groin will get you disqualified. Everywhere else is fair."

"Injuries are bound to happen," Captain Marwar chimed in, "but we ask that you try not to hurt your opponent." He paused for a moment. "For the first phase, we will have two fights at the same time. Good luck!" He met Adir's eyes and nodded.

The officials walked to a tent as the competitors lined themselves around the ring. A row of wooden benches split the large oval into two smaller rings, yet each side could still easily fit fifty cows.

A short while later, Captain Marwar and the frail official emerged from their tent and approached the ring. The captain took his place in the smaller ring closest to the tent, while the other official walked over to the far side of the benches.

The captain pulled out a piece of paper and read, "Daicon Trestall. Nagra! And … Bendell Jetmot. Akkasha!" He looked up. Two men walked into the ring, staves in hands.

"Muhain Shaptel, Nagra, and Adir Nathar, Marafel!" the frail official bellowed.

Adir jumped at the mention of his name. He knew he would be eliminated in his first fight, but he hadn't expected it to be the very first fight of the tournament! *This is going to be embarrassing! Everyone is going to remember the first fight.*

Adir crossed to the center of his ring, his stomach churning at the sight of the approaching competitor. He'd always thought that Boar Sayarna's arms were the size of his thighs—well, Muhain's arms were the size of Boar's thighs. That was perhaps a bit hyperbolic, but his arms were surely massive!

"Any questions about the rules?" the frail official asked. Adir and Muhain shook their heads. "Good. Give me a clean fight. When I call halt you break off. Understood?"

Both men nodded.

The official pointed at Adir's left arm. "Where's your number?"

"Number?" Adir asked, confused. "Oh! The number!" Hurriedly, he pulled out the strip of cloth from his pocket—he had forgotten all about it—and tied it around his left arm, number visible.

"Good," said the official, then he walked to the edge of the ring.

Muhain held his staff about a third of the way up and casually placed its other end on Adir's shoulder.

Adir immediately swatted the staff off. It hit the ground with a blunt thump. "That's a disqualification!" he cried.

Muhain looked surprised. "We haven't begun yet," he said. "I'm just proving the distance."

Adir knew that phrase—*prove the distance*. Captain Marwar had once mentioned that before the start of a bout, the fighters were supposed to place their staves on each other's shoulders, thereby proving they were within striking distance. *Great!* Adir thought. *I forget about the number and can't even remember how to start a bout!* He looked around, hoping no one had noticed his folly, when he spotted Tia jumping and waving at him.

"Right!" Adir said, turning back to Muhain. He proved the distance and assumed his ready stance. With staff held in both hands, shoulder-width apart, his body turned outward, and he met Muhain's gaze over his shoulder.

The large man's eyes displayed a mild boredom that was born of the knowledge of an eventuality. Muhain knew he would win.

Suddenly, Adir's forehead, armpits, and palms broke out in a cold, slippery sweat. He looked up at the sun as if to blame it for his sudden dampness.

"FIGHT!" bellowed the official.

In a situation like this, a normal person would do … something. Attack, defend, or simply strafe. Adir, however, did nothing; he stood frozen in his ready stance, watching, as Muhain shifted his grip to one end of his staff and spun. But just as Muhain's staff was about to make contact, awareness returned at the sudden prospect of pain. Though Adir's mind pictured a block, his body hopped backward.

Muhain's swing was a feint. The muscular fighter shifted a step forward, converting his swing into a thrust.

The rounded metal ferrule at the end of Muhain's staff met Adir's ribs, knocking the wind out of him and staggering him onto the ground.

"HALT!" cried the frail official. "First bout goes to number thirty-nine!"

The crowd cheered and applauded. One section was particularly boisterous. It had to be a group from Nagra.

Adir lay on the ground, clutching his chest and gasping for air, pondering the flexibility of his ribs. Fortunately, nothing felt broken. He was just in intense pain. A man could handle pain. Forcing himself to his feet, he walked over to one of the benches dividing the large ring and sat down. The frail official eyed him but didn't say anything.

"He's strong but slow," came a gruff whisper.

Adir looked over and realized that Captain Marwar had seated himself next to him.

"Yea," Adir began, "but he's—"

"Shh. I'm not supposed to talk to you while I'm officiating," whispered the captain. Then he stood up and walked away.

True enough, Muhain was strong. *Very strong!* But what the captain had said was also true. Muhain *was* slow. His swing seemed all too easy to follow. *And did I see a twitch mid-swing? Is that why I jumped back instead of blocking?* If Adir had blocked instead of dodging back, he would have had a few broken ribs ensuring his end at the tournament.

"Are you forfeiting?" The frail official was standing in front of Adir.

"No," Adir replied.

"Then let's get going. There are many more fights to be fought." With that, the official turned and strode to the edge of the ring.

Adir stood and made his way to the middle of the ring where Muhain waited, lazily holding himself up with his staff. "I'm ready," Adir said to him.

"Finally! Let's get this child's play over with!" Muhain sneered.

Child's play? Adir thought, as the two proved the distance. *I'll show him child's play!* Adir assumed the ready stance, searching his mind for attack sequences. Nothing! He'd never had this problem when he had fought shrubs. *Shrubs?*

"FIGHT!" yelled the official.

Muhain spun once again, swinging his staff horizontally. But his grip didn't seem appropriate for the arc he was cutting. *Another feint,* Adir realized as his eyes followed Muhain's slow dance. The real blow was going to be an uppercut.

Adir had guessed correctly. As he sidestepped the plane of the expected uppercut, Muhain's staff passed inches from his left leg. Adir turned and pictured Muhain as a … shrub—a very large shrub! An attack immediately formed in his mind.

Muhain moved forward, swinging. Adir ducked under the arc of the staff, hopped left, then transitioned into a lateral thrust. With all his strength, he slammed his staff into Muhain's side as the large man spun past Adir, propelled by his own momentum.

The recoil that shot through Adir on making contact with Muhain flared the pain in his ribs from the previous bout. Muhain, who took the full force of Adir's attack, merely grunted.

"HALT!" bellowed the official. "Second bout goes to number fifty-two!"

A few in the crowd, Tia being the loudest, cheered. It wasn't much, but the cheers felt good. Adir's heart raced, though not with nerves. No, his heart was thumping from the adrenaline of fighting and beating another person in a staff bout. He had not expected to win any fights, but here he was. Maybe his practice had paid off to some extent. Maybe he had finally graduated from shrubs.

Adir spotted Captain Marwar seated on one of the benches. He sat within earshot and stealthily regarded the man.

"I see you understand," the captain whispered while watching two competitors spar in his ring.

Maybe I do understand, he thought, scanning the crowd. Amidst the myriad faces, he spotted two he was quite familiar with. Arvan was in the crowd, watching. And Athvan was with him. He'd assumed that his akka and brother wouldn't come to the Games. After all, the other day, when he'd talked to Arvan about competing, Arvan had brushed it off, calling it a childish fancy. "There are more important things than the Games," Adir remembered Arvan saying. *Like milking cows?*

Despite that, his father was here. Watching him fight. Their eyes met and Arvan flashed a quick, short smile. *Akka smiled?* Adir didn't know what to think of that. He wanted to accept his father back into his life, but there was a lot Arvan had to answer for. But at the same time, Adir was afraid to say what was on his mind—afraid that maybe his father's responses wouldn't be what he expected.

"Let's get the third bout started," said the frail official.

Adir stood, his mind snapping back to the moment, and again walked to the center of the ring. All he had to do was focus on his instincts and pretend Muhain was a shrub, and he might stand a chance. Muhain walked up, eyes determined, but Adir was not perturbed. He felt a strong determination within himself. Something in him seemed to have clicked.

As Adir proved the distance and assumed the ready stance, a surge of energy radiated through him, ready to burst out. He could hear his heart beating. He could feel the staff in his grip. He could smell the dirt underneath his feet. He dug in his front foot.

"FIGHT!"

Adir charged forward, pushing off his front foot, staff raised. As he closed in on Muhain, he brought it down in an overhead strike. Muhain spun, sidestepping the attack, swinging his staff around him, almost hitting Adir's thigh. With an awkward jerk, Adir abruptly changed direction, hopping away from the incoming staff. Landing a few paces away, he spun around and faced Muhain. They paused.

Muhain looked *surprised*, his earlier arrogance slowly draining away. Then his face hardened. He let out a roar and charged at Adir, lashing out with a flurry of quick jabs and short swipes. However, Adir had no trouble tracking each attack. Muhain certainly was strong, but all that bulk came at the price of speed. Who knew being lanky could be an advantage?

Adir dodged and parried successfully as if he knew exactly what Muhain was about to do. None of Muhain's attacks succeeded. However, each attack did push him closer to the ring's boundary, eventually pinning him against it. If he stepped out, it'd all be over.

Again, they paused for a moment. Adir stood his ground, staff held defensively, blocking his chest. Listening to his breath.

Muhain leapt forward, guiding his staff in a downward diagonal arc from the left. Adir ducked and threw himself to his left. He felt the air stirred up by the whipping staff cool his scalp. Crashing onto the ground, he rolled away.

Muhain, carried forward by the momentum of his unsuccessful charge, now teetered at the ring's boundary. The tables had turned— one step and Adir would win.

Muhain strained against himself, arching backward, arms outstretched and flailing, desperately attempting to keep himself from crossing the boundary. Anxious murmurs spread through the crowd but were soon hushed as Muhain started to tip outward. But just before he tipped beyond the point of no return, Muhain kicked off and, with the grace of a drunk toddler, managed to tumble backward, falling into the safety of the ring. The crowd let out a collective breath.

Realizing that the bout wasn't over, Adir swung and struck Muhain's arm.

"HALT!" bellowed the official, and some of the crowd broke out in cheers and applause. "Adir Nathar moves on to the melee!"

THE MUGGY AFTERNOON made Arvan crave the cool shade of his veranda. Sweat drenched his shirt and gave him a general sense of discomfort as the sun sat stubbornly overhead. Athvan fidgeted beside him, munching on a crumbcake and sipping spiced lemon water out of a conical leafcup.

"Athvan," Arvan said, annoyance slipping into his voice.

"Yea, akka," Athvan said, crumbcake in mouth and looking at the sparring ring.

"Could you stand still, lad? You've bumped into everyone here."

"Sure, akka." Athvan stopped. A few moments later though, he started up again.

Arvan sighed.

"When are they going to start the final fight?" Athvan asked.

"When they are ready," replied Arvan, wiping sweat off his brow, only to have a fresh batch pool up.

"Do you think keta is going to win?" Athvan sounded excited.

And why shouldn't he be excited? Arvan thought. Athvan looked up to Adir, mimicking his older brother in every aspect. When Adir grew his hair long, Athvan had done the same. When Adir began carrying a staff, Athvan found a stick and called it his staff. "I don't know, lad," he said candidly.

Athvan's adulation was one of the reasons why Arvan pushed Adir so hard. But Adir was oblivious of his influence on his younger brother, not realizing how his behavior could shape the boy. Maybe Adir's defiance wouldn't rub off on Athvan, but things didn't look too promising on that front.

"He will. I know he will!" Athvan said, his voice cracking as he began bouncing in place.

Arvan looked over at his older son sitting on a bench at the other edge of the ring, scratching at his staff. Next to him sat Boar Sayarna. Boar said something to Adir, who stiffened.

The Daroongaamen victor, who was much larger and far better with the staff than Adir, had tried to knock Adir out in the melee, after ganging up with another competitor. But with a little luck, Adir had managed to survive the melee, though the way he'd done it seemed to skirt the edges of honor. Adir had attacked an unwitting competitor from behind, reducing the field to eight and thereby ending the melee. Arvan wasn't sure if his son had earned that victory.

After the melee, Adir had fought twice more. In these fights, however, he'd certainly earned his victories.

Adir's first fight in the third phase had been against Bruca Dannar, the blacksmith. The large man had fought well, but Adir had displayed a surprising fluidity with the staff. His son's movements bore an instinctual grace with which he'd defeated Bruca in the first three bouts and advanced.

After Bruca, Adir had sparred against Fetwin *something* from Akkasha—Arvan couldn't quite remember his family name. Fetwin was the one who had ganged up with Boar during the melee. Fetwin's combat style had been an exercise in fancy footwork with unexpected kicks and dodgy shuffles sprinkled into his attack sequences. The Akkashan had defeated Adir in the first bout with a kick to the gut.

In the second bout, Arvan had noticed that Fetwin was performing the exact same attack sequence as in the first bout. Adir seemed to have noticed it too, for he easily evaded Fetwin's attacks, defeating the Akkashan in the second, third, and fourth bouts.

Captain Marwar walked toward Boar and Adir, said something to them, then returned to his tent with Boar. Arvan knew Kremmon Marwar well. He'd known him ever since he'd been a footman under his command. He'd been glad when he'd learned that Kremmon was giving Adir lessons on staff combat; Kremmon was a seasoned warrior with relative expertise in all weapons—one couldn't rise to captain in the Navengaard without such knowledge. But more than that, Arvan was glad for the mentoring that Kremmon provided to Adir. The boy needed someone to be a father figure. *I certainly wasn't there for him.* He wasn't sure why he still felt guilty about that. His past actions couldn't have been avoided. He'd done what was best for his family. But maybe he could have done more, or done things differently. Wishing things were different was a futile exercise, but still, he couldn't help but wish.

Boar returned to the bench, then Adir stood and walked over to the captain's tent.

"What are they doing? Are they about to start?" Athvan's impatience was beyond bothersome.

"I don't know, lad." Arvan let out a long breath. *A little bit of shade would be nice.*

"Master Nathar," Tia said, sliding in between a couple of onlookers. "How are you doing today?"

"I'm doing well, Tia. Have you sold many crumbcakes today?"

"O yea! Mama says that she might need to run home and fetch the reserves we didn't bring this morning." She looked at the ring as Adir returned to his bench and sat down. "Good! They haven't started yet!"

"Hey, Tia," greeted Athvan, smiling at her through quick glances. Arvan was convinced Athvan had a crush on Tia.

"Hey yourself! I haven't seen you in a while."

"Well, here I am now!" Athvan said. His voice cracked and he flushed slightly.

"Do you think Adir is going to win?" Tia asked.

"You bet!" Athvan asserted, taking a bite of his crumbcake. "Though I'm sure it will be a tough fight. Keta is fighting Boar Sayarna." Athvan's mood fell abruptly.

"I'm sure your keta can handle himself against Boar," Tia said, placing a hand on his shoulder. "He made it to the final fight, didn't he?"

Arvan smiled at the care and tenderness with which Tia lifted Athvan's spirit. Tia was a decent girl, and a pretty girl. Marcy had done a wonderful job raising her, and that too without a father. But he didn't quite like Adir's relationship with her, not that he'd voiced this to Adir, however. Though Marcy was a good woman in many ways, she'd whelped Tia out of wedlock. *And they're Faithless.*

The Faithless weren't bad people, but their morals and values were far different from those of the Annadi. He was concerned that Tia's influence would corrupt Adir, though he had no real reason to suspect that.

"They're starting!" Athvan shouted. He was practically vibrating with excitement.

Adir and Boar walked to the center of the ring where they were joined by the burly official. The thin official and Captain Marwar walked to opposite sides of the ring.

After saying something inaudible to Boar and Adir, the burly official regarded the crowd. "Ladies and gentlemen. Welcome to the final fight of the Staff Tournament in the Regional Games. Before me are two competitors, one of whom will have the honor of representing Naven in Daroongaamen!" He threw his hands up in the air.

The crowd cheered. Shouts of "Akkasha forever victorious!" and "Marafel, Marafel, Marafel!" rivaled each other, as if their intensity would decide the outcome of the fight.

"Here"—the burly official swept an arm toward Adir—"we have Adir Nathar from Marafel!" Shouts, whoops, and applause sounded from the crowd. "And here"—he pointed at Boar—"is the second-place winner in the Staff Tournament at the last Daroongaamen in Ostarium —Boar Sayarna from Akkasha!"

The crowd erupted in loud cheers and thunderous applause. Arvan was sure that every single person there—even the ones who cheered for Adir—was cheering for Boar.

Boar stepped up and basked in the adulation. He dropped his staff to the ground a few paces in front of him. Then he cartwheeled over the staff, picking it up in one smooth motion and landing perfectly on his feet. Staff twirling in his right hand, he bowed and casually walked back to where he had been standing. The crowd went wild.

"The first to win four bouts wins the tournament!" announced the burly official.

The two competitors proved the distance and assumed their ready stances. Arvan noticed that Boar's ready stance wasn't the typical one that he'd used all morning—the basic, chest-blocking defensive stance that offered a variety of offensive transitions.

Boar gripped his staff at one end, as if holding a sword by the hilt. It was held above his head, parallel to the ground, and pointed at Adir. Bending his knees, Boar lowered himself into an almost-crouch, giving him the appearance of a taygar about to lunge on its prey.

The crowd went silent.

"FIGHT!"

Boar leaned back, then lunged forward with his staff, expertly threading it through the hole between Adir's arms and staff, jabbing him in the chest. Adir went down, clutching his chest.

"HALT!" called the burly official. "The first bout goes to Boar Sayarna!"

The crowd cheered.

This is why I didn't want that boy competing! Arvan thought. He was concerned for his son. Boar Sayarna had moved with such speed and precision that Arvan had barely seen his attack before Adir hit the ground. How was Adir to fight against that?

Aided by his staff, Adir got to his feet, signaling that he was fine.

The competitors proved the distance for the second bout and assumed similar ready stances. Adir seemed to be staring his opponent down. Then he took a step!

"HALT!" bellowed the burly official. "Adir Nathar moved before the fight was called to a start and forfeits this bout. The second bout goes to Boar Sayarna!"

While most of the crowd cheered for Boar, quite a few curses were hurled at Adir. Some of the Marafellens weren't too happy that their staff competitor "didn't know which end of the staff to use." It was a clever insult, Arvan realized, but he didn't appreciate that it was directed toward his son.

"I heard the official call fight," Athvan said, defending his older brother.

"I think so too," Tia said with well-feigned skepticism, disappointment in her voice. "But the official has the final word."

Athvan turned away, scowling.

Adir looked rattled and ashamed as he proved the distance and assumed his ready stance. *Get a grip on yourself, lad!* Arvan thought. He'd only lost two of seven bouts. He could still win.

"FIGHT!"

Adir leapt backward. Boar stepped forward slowly. Then the two circled each other like taygars about to fight over a fallen prey.

Suddenly, Boar threw his staff at Adir. Adir dodged, spinning. Boar's staff zipped by his shoulder. Boar charged while Adir was mid-spin, then leapt toward Adir with his feet out. Adir sidestepped, managing to somehow dodge the attack. Boar flew past him and landed next to his fallen staff. They paused.

Picking up his staff, Boar muttered something. Something Adir didn't like, for Arvan saw his son stiffen again. *He is so easily rattled,* Arvan thought with a familiar frustration. For some reason, the boy didn't seem to understand that a person can't think in anger.

Adir puffed out his chest, narrowed his eyes, and gritted his teeth. Swinging his staff, he attacked Boar, but Boar simply dodged back. Adir attacked again and Boar dodged to the side. Adir took a long, determined step forward swinging his staff at Boar once again. But Boar simply ducked, stepped inside Adir's reach, and struck Adir's shoulder with an elegant, ascending arc. It was pure dynamic finesse.

"HALT! The third bout goes to Boar Sayarna!" bellowed the official.

"Let's keep going!" Adir yelled loud enough to be heard over the crowd's cheers.

"Good!" Boar exclaimed even louder. "We'll get this done quickly then!"

"Just prove the distance!" Adir extended his staff and clenched his jaw.

The two competitors proved the distance and assumed their ready stances. Arvan could plainly see the anger bubbling in his son, ready to erupt at any moment. And anger always led to hasty actions.

"FIGHT!" the official bellowed.

Adir attacked, shifting his grip to the middle of his staff. He spun his staff in figure eights from side to side, slowly picking up speed till a whirling barrier of hardwood surrounded him.

Arvan was impressed. Till now, all Adir had displayed was nothing but rudimentary staff combat—swings, thrusts, dodges, and occasional parries. But this! This needed a certain level of skill and precision that took time and patience to build.

"BEAT HIM, ADIR!" Athvan shouted, fidgeting furiously. By this time, people had learned to give Athvan a wide berth.

The staff and Adir advanced as one cohesive unit, forcing Boar to retreat from the incoming barrage. Adir pressed forward, pushing Boar nearer the boundary. But before he could be pinned, Boar hopped left.

Either Adir had reflexes quicker than a mongoose fighting a snake or he'd anticipated Boar's evasion, for he immediately ceased his figure eights. The staff slid through his hands, but he gripped it just as it reached its end. Crouching, he spun with staff extended, striking Boar on his shin. Boar tripped and hit the ground.

"HALT!" the burly official called. "The fourth bout goes to Adir Nathar!"

Arvan found himself cheering loudly along with Athvan, Tia, and the rest of the crowd.

"He just needs to win the remaining three bouts," Athvan said confidently. "Then he'll go to Daroongaamen!"

"That would be great, wouldn't it?" Tia's level of excitement seemed to be approaching Athvan's.

At the center of the ring, Arvan spotted an unfriendly exchange of words between Boar and his son. Boar turned and walked away. Though he couldn't hear what was said, Adir's posture and gestures told him all he needed to know.

Abruptly, Adir charged Boar and shoved him from behind, hard enough to stagger the solid man. Boar steadied himself with his staff, then turned, face red with anger. He threw himself at Adir. But at that moment, the burly official grabbed Boar from behind, temporarily saving Adir broken bones or worse.

But Boar was just too strong. He moved toward Adir, dragging the burly official behind him. Seeing his companion unable to contain the massive fighter, the frail official joined in to help, finally managing to cease Boar's advance. In the meantime, Captain Marwar ran up to Adir's side, disappointment all over his face. Boar struggled for a moment, then stopped and shook the officials off.

"Adir Nathar is disqualified from the tournament for dishonorable conduct!" the burly official bellowed through labored breaths. "Boar Sayarna will once again represent Naven in Daroongaamen!"

The crowd was silent for an awkward moment, turning and looking at each other. Then someone took up the cry of "Boar! Boar! Boar Sayarna!" and the crowd erupted into cheers, shouts, and applause.

Arvan didn't cheer, shout, or applaud. Not because Adir lost— every loss taught a valuable lesson—but because of how he lost. Those who lacked self-control lacked honor.

Athvan slumped on the ground next to him, a picture of disappointment.

"There's always next time," Tia said, attempting to console the boy.

Adir seemed to take notice of Athvan and Tia, then he looked over at Arvan. Arvan met his son's eyes for a short moment before the young man dropped his gaze and walked away.

Chapter Seven

The Aurora, resplendent in hues ranging from violet to red, had begun its wispy dance in the northeastern sky, wrapping chromatic fingers through tall, distant peaks of the Bahzenelyn range. A few stars, defying the setting sun, speckled various parts of the heavens, resembling tiny ivory tears in a vast curtain of orange and purple. A breeze blew just strong enough to incite the leaves of the lone almond tree on the hilltop to a soft whisper.

How did that tree get there? Tia thought. *Someone had to have planted it there.* That had to be it. There were no other trees around, let alone almond trees.

Adir was lying down beside her, his head on her lap. The two of them frequented this hilltop on the northern edge of the Daaman Woods, especially on warm evenings. The vantage of the hilltop gave a clear view of the Village Square to the south, where lamps were being lit. Tia looked into Adir's eyes, but he seemed to be staring at the sky, unfocused. Veyka snorted nearby as she grazed.

After getting disqualified, Adir had disappeared from the tournament grounds. Tia didn't blame him for that though. She'd want to be alone too had she made such a fool of herself. She hadn't joined Arvan and Athvan in searching, for she knew she'd find him on this very hill-top. Once she and her mama had finished selling their crumbcakes—and Adir had sufficient time to settle himself—she'd made her way here and had found him lying on the grass. Silently pondering.

"What's on your mind?" Tia asked, running her fingers through Adir's thick black hair. The silence had stretched on long enough.

Adir sighed and met her eyes. "Nothing."

"You don't sigh like that unless you are thinking of something." She cocked her head to one side. "Is it about the tournament?"

"No," Adir said, then broke his gaze with her, staring off at the sky once again.

Tia, of course, didn't believe that. She knew him too well. After all, they had spent a fair amount of time together growing up. Also, she was pretty good at reading people. She didn't know why, but ever since she was little, people had fascinated her, prompting her to observe them closely in an effort to understand their mannerisms and motivations. She'd come in contact with many different types of people, as she'd spent most of her life selling crumbcakes with her mama at the Village Square.

Once, when Tia was a little girl, her scrutiny had inadvertently revealed a clandestine affair. She'd been so excited at being right that she blabbed about the affair to anyone who would lend her an ear. Needless to say, that had landed her in some hot soup. But that defeat hadn't dissuaded her from her self-assigned mission. She considered herself a student of the human mind. That was why she loved fairs, Worship nights, village dances, and the Games—plenty of people to watch. Over time, she'd catalogued enough experience to where she could reasonably predict a person's action. The lower their smarts, the easier it was for her to predict. Though people still surprised her more often than she liked to admit.

"I know you're lying to me, Adir," Tia said, accusingly. "You always look away when you lie, even when you're just fibbing."

"Hmm ... I'll have to remember that." A small fleeting smile touched the edges of Adir's mouth. After a brief moment of silence, a serious expression shadowed his face. "Sometimes"—he sat up—"I do things believing that what I'm doing is right. But when I think about it later, my actions just seem foolish." He brought his knees up to his chest and wrapped his arms around them.

"You mean your fight with Boar?"

"That … and other things."

"Like what?"

"It doesn't matter."

Tia grew exasperated. "Gods save me, Adir! Sometimes you can be mopier than a juvenile girl!"

Adir didn't look pleased at the comparison. But her statement still stood. However, chiding someone wasn't the best way to get them to open up. It often led to unnecessary arguments.

"I'm sorry," Tia said, reining in her exasperation. "What happened with Boar earlier today?"

"He besmirched my honor, Tia," Adir said, meeting her eyes. "He called me a coward!" he added in a whisper.

That's it? He got himself disqualified because of name-calling? Adir had previously confided in Tia about how Arvan always treated him like a child and, frankly, she could see why. In many ways, Adir was more a boy than a man. Though based on what her mama had told her—and her own observations, of course—all men were merely boys, just physically larger. They just used words like honor and duty to justify their childish impulses.

But Adir was *her* boy. She loved him, and she wanted to spend the rest of her life with him, despite his puerile nature. Not to mention how fascinating a person he was. He was stubborn but usually right, which only encouraged his stubbornness. He was prone to rash actions but agonized over them later. He could be one way one moment, then the exact opposite the next. She was not sure how he handled swinging from one extreme to the other and still seem somewhat put together.

STOP IT! Don't analyze him like you do everyone else.

"Did you hear what I said?" Adir asked, sounding a little annoyed.

"Yea," Tia replied. "That was wrong of him."

That wasn't exactly what she thought, but she'd spoken the truth—or at least a part of it. Boar should have been more honorable than to resort to name-calling. However, Adir had certainly overreacted. She wasn't going to tell him that though—he was the sensitive and defensive sort, which made for an explosive combination.

"Exactly!" Adir said, apparently pleased that she had agreed with him. She looked at his nose and saw that his nostrils were flared. That usually meant he was trying to control his temper. "And all those people laughing at me as Boar and Fetwin chased me around during the melee." Adir shook his head. "Boar called me a coward because I snuck up on that competitor during the melee and jabbed him in the back. Did you think that was cowardly?"

"No," Tia said. She'd probably have answered the same even if she thought he had been cowardly.

"That wasn't cowardly!" Adir exclaimed. "It was brilliant strategy! By doing that, I avoided getting beaten up by Boar and his crony!" He paused. "And ended the melee at the same time!"

Tia decided to change the subject, hoping to avoid steepening Adir's downward spiral. The man was getting too worked up. "Rein won the Archery Tournament." She leaned back onto her elbows. "Did you know? He's going to Cayan!" However, that didn't work. Adir simply nodded and took to staring back at the sky, lost in a world where his poor ego needed to be soothed.

Tia looked up at the darkening sky and spotted the Chariot of the Gods. The bright white star zipped across the dimming evening sky as if with a purpose. Like it did every night. "Adir, what do you think the Chariot is?" she asked, trying to pull Adir's mind out of its foul mood. "Why is it the only star that moves much faster than the rest?"

"The Word says it carries the Messenger of the Gods," Adir said. "He travels the skies and watches over our world. If harm is about to befall Leakarha, the Messenger will come down and warn us."

"Who do you suppose the Messenger is?" she asked. Talking about the Messenger seemed to be doing the trick.

"I'm not sure. He's just the Messenger."

"So he's not a God?"

"No, there are only seven Gods, Tia." Adir sighed. "He's the Messenger. He may not be a God, but I'm sure he has some divine power."

"Is that what you really think?" Tia knew that Adir wasn't the type of person to take the Word literally. After all, he'd previously revealed some doubts about the reality painted by the Sanctum. She was Faithless and didn't subscribe to the Annadi ways, having been raised by her mama to believe in what she felt was right. For a time, she had flirted with the idea of becoming one of the Faithful, as most of her friends were Annadi, but she didn't appreciate the rules and restrictions that came with it. Besides, growing up Faithless had awarded her the ability to see the world more freely. She hated that word though—*Faithless*.

"I don't know," Adir said. "It is what it is. Why does it matter to us?" He paused for a moment, then looked directly into her eyes, face hard and nostrils flaring. "What matters to us are things like Boar Sayarna calling me a coward!"

Before Tia could say anything, Adir stood up in a huff, straightened his shirt, and pulled his sleeves down. "It's getting dark," he said. "We should head back."

Tia brushed dirt and grass off her green dress, watching Adir as he walked over to fetch Veyka.

Adir was a man of passion, and if she were to be his wife, she would have to learn to deal with his outbursts. It would be a long while before he let this incident with Boar pass, and he'd be agonizing over it all the while. She wanted to tell him that he was overreacting and should just let it go, but what if Adir didn't appreciate what she had to say? He might spurn her, acting in the heat of the moment as passionate people often did. And even if he later realized that he'd spurned her unintentionally, he would stick by his decision out of sheer pigheadedness. No, it was best to just let him sulk for a while. Saying something right now would only exacerbate the situation.

Adir returned with Veyka and stopped in front of her. "I know I shouldn't have shoved Boar," he said, voice soft. "But ... I had to! I can't let someone call me a coward and get away with it." He paused. "Yet by shoving him, I got disqualified and brought shame on myself and my family."

"I don't think you brought shame on your family," Tia said reassuringly, though she was growing ever more tired of his self-pity. "Or yourself. You did what you thought was right and there is no shame in that."

"Yea," Adir agreed. "In my mind I was right, but that's not how everyone else will see it."

"You can't control what people think, Adir," Tia said. "You shouldn't worry about what others think, especially when you know you're right." Again, she wanted to tell him he was worrying over nothing, but invalidating his concerns wouldn't end well.

Adir didn't speak further and Tia decided to leave him with his thoughts.

◉

TIA IS A VERY SUPPORTIVE GIRL, Adir thought as he led Veyka home on a silent, meandering dirt road. He'd just escorted her to the Village Square from where Tia had returned home with her mother.

Although the whole fiasco with Boar and his disqualification from the tournament was a result of him defending his honor, he'd felt foolish for how events had unfolded. However, Tia had unconditionally stood by what he'd done. He wondered if her reassuring nature was the quality of a good wife. The Word sure said so—in fact, being supportive was essential for a woman to live a Worthy Life. He knew he'd certainly appreciate it.

But if the support was truly unconditional, then what if he were about to do something incredibly foolish? Would Tia stop him? He'd like to think that she would, since she didn't follow his ways. She was Faithless after all, and Faithless women could be more … *challenging*.

Or maybe the Word was wrong about wives needing to be unconditionally supportive of their husbands. There certainly were some rather large inconsistencies between what the Word dictated and how the world actually seemed to work. The Book said that Daroon had sealed off the rakhor at the Precipice, but that wasn't true.

As if on cue, the scene from the pastures began playing in Adir's mind, but this time he was able to stop it without much effort. The brief resurgence of those memories, however, combined with the darkness, sent a cold shiver down his spine. He fumbled in his saddlebag for the torch, which he pulled out and lit. But the light didn't allay his unease very much. Gripping Veyka's reins a little tighter, Adir continued down the road.

The road made its serpentine way to the south, eventually coming to a fork. Adir led Veyka onto the thin trail through open fields—a short and direct route to the farmhouse compared to the more circuitous road. A light breeze blew, bending the tall grasses that grew on either side of the trail. He wasn't too far from home. And once he got there, he was sure Arvan would be waiting for him.

Arvan, unlike Tia, would be anything but supportive. His father had warned him on many occasions about his short temper and how a man should learn to control it. And, as the Gods as his witness, he did try to control it. *No matter how hard I try though, akka will never see it!*

Adir could already imagine how the impending argument with Arvan would go. Arvan would chide him for *acting like a child*, and Adir would say that Boar had deserved it. Arvan would argue that no matter how much Boar had deserved it, Adir had acted dishonorably and had brought shame to himself and the Nathars.

Maybe his father was right. He shook his head. *No, I shouldn't care about what he thinks*, he thought. But this was Naven. Faith and honor were the foundations of its culture.

Abruptly, Adir heard movement behind him. A visceral fear radiated from his gut, rendering him immobile. *Gods save me! What if it's a rakhor?* His heart was pounding harder than a hammer forging metal. He waited for a long moment, listening intently. Nothing.

Adir took another step. A rustle behind him. Closer this time. As if someone, or something, was walking through the tall grass. With a lot of effort, Adir's muscles managed to overcome his dread and turned around. He raised his torch high.

A short dark figure was walking up the trail behind him.

That's no rakhor, Adir thought, relief washing over him. All he could see was a dark silhouette, but it certainly wasn't a rakhor. According to the stories, they were supposed to be much taller than men.

A small suspicion kindled. These fields lay far enough from the

Square that only those who lived nearby ever walked through them. Most didn't wander them at night. The best thing to do would be to hop onto Veyka and ride home. The short figure didn't have a horse and Adir could easily outrun him, if he meant him harm. Shifting Veyka's reins back over her head, Adir prepared to mount. He lifted one foot into a stirrup.

"Took you long enough to spot me, *coward!*"

"Boar?" Adir dropped his foot back onto the ground.

"Yea."

"Have you been following me?" Adir asked, though he obviously knew the answer.

"Yea, since the Village Square. You really are oblivious, aren't you? Perhaps that's why you are a coward."

"Stop calling me a coward!" Adir yelled. He'd had enough of that kind of talk.

Boar laughed derisively.

Adir's anger flared hot, like a branding iron just before contacting cattle flesh. He wanted to unstrap his staff from Veyka's side and slam it into Boar's nose, but then what? Boar wouldn't just walk away. *Maybe I am a coward. An angry coward!*

"We have some unfinished matters to take care of," Boar said, drawing closer. The torchlight illuminated his face and revealed a nasty smile.

"We don't have any unfinished business!" Adir said, fighting to control his unsettling mix of anger and submission. "You won!"

"Yea. That I did. That I did. But we still have to settle the matter of your cowardly shove from behind." He half raised his arms in a shrug. "I didn't get a chance to retaliate."

"I got disqualified for it," Adir said, starting to understand the predicament he was in. He should have just jumped on Veyka and ridden away when he had the chance. "Isn't that enough?"

"No." Boar was still wearing his nasty smile, but now he was unstrapping his staff.

"So you want to fight me?" Adir asked, his breath quickening.

"Yea," Boar replied calmly. "Yea, I do."

Could he fight Boar without any officials, without any rules? Adir hesitated, pondering.

Boar didn't hesitate. He leapt into the air with his staff raised.

Somehow, Adir reacted in time. Instinct forced him to throw himself to the side, dropping his torch and Veyka's reins. Fortunately, the tall grass cushioned his fall.

Boar landed between Adir and Veyka, his staff hitting the ground with a loud crack, spraying mud and grass about. The crack echoed hollowly across the field, startling Veyka. The mare squealed and took off in the direction of the farmhouse, leaving Adir behind.

My staff! Adir thought, panic-stricken. It was strapped to Veyka and she was gone. He was defenseless! Scrambling to his feet, Adir tried to run away, only to get tackled again by Boar. The heavy man straddled Adir, pinning him to the ground. Thick, muscular fingers wrapped around his throat and squeezed.

"I detest cowards!" Boar hissed. "I detest cowards!"

Adir started to feel light-headed as Boar's fingers squeezed more tightly around his throat, cutting off his air. Desperately, he tried to pry Boar's hands off his neck, but Boar was just too strong. He tried to knee Boar in the back, but he didn't have the right leverage to make it effective.

A blackness began to creep in from the edges of Adir's vision, like blinders on a horse. Boar squeezed harder, cutting off even the smallest trace of air his gasps had managed to salvage. Adir struggled but failed miserably at countering with any meaningful resistance. He needed air! He had to get Boar off him! His eyes darted left and right, searching for something solid he could smash into Boar's head. Through his peripheral vision, Adir spotted Boar's staff. He stretched his arm out, trying to will his fingers to extend and grasp the staff, but it was just out of reach.

Suddenly, an incapacitating numbness blossomed in his extremities as his chest burned from lack of air. The numbness slowly advanced up his legs and arms till, finally, his whole body went limp. His body had given up. The black around his vision crept in further, leaving only a small circle of hazy sight.

Is that the Aurora? A rainbow-colored hue had swished into Adir's residual vision, dancing about in playful patterns, as the Chariot of the Gods sped across the night sky. *What is the Aurora doing down here?*

The black crept in further, reducing his vision to pinpricks. Peace washed over him. *Am I dying?*

A loud explosion shook the ground. And all went black.

WHAT WAS THAT?

Arvan pulled the pipe from his mouth and sat up sharply. He looked out the window of the sitting room, trying to pinpoint the source of the loud noise. It had sounded somewhere from the north, like a booming cannon. Not too far away either.

Was Marafel under attack? With rising worry, he peered out the window for another moment but saw and heard nothing. *I should go take a look.*

Kirsch burst into the sitting room. "Sir, did you hear that?"

"Yea," Arvan replied. "I was about to take a look."

"I suggest you arm yourself, sir. In light of recent events."

Arvan nodded. He stood up, exited the room, and strode rapidly down the hallway—Kirsch close behind him—then turned into his study and approached the left wall. A display case at its center exhibited Arvan's medals and captain's pin. To the left of the case hung two steel swords, crisscrossed behind a slightly convex steel shield. The swords' slight curve at the tips and hand-guards professed its Naven origin; the shield had four circular bumps, patterned as four points of a square, protruding off its face—a trademark of Naven shields. Two crisscrossed spears were affixed to the right of the display case.

Arvan smoothly pulled one of the swords out from behind the shield. It slid out, rasping slightly as the blade brushed against the shield's handle.

"Haven't seen you hold a sword in years," Kirsch said from behind him.

"I was hoping I'd never have to use it again." Arvan regarded his sword. His arm felt complete. Lamplight glinted off the blade, turning it gold for a fleeting moment. "Come on! Let's find out what that explosion was about." He picked up one of the scabbards that hung below and sheathed his sword.

In the sitting room, Arvan found Nilane and Misuma looking out the windows and conversing quietly. "Stay here and keep the doors shut till I return," he said.

"Yea, sir," Misuma said.

At that moment, hurried footsteps clattered down the main staircase. Athvan came bounding into the room. "Are you going to see what that noise was, akka?" His long brown hair was disheveled.

"Yea," Arvan said. "Stay here, lad. Kirsch and I will be right back."

"No, I want to go with you!" Athvan protested.

"Athvan"—Arvan's patience was slipping—"I don't know what's out there, lad. It could be dangerous."

"I'll go get my staff!" Athvan darted upstairs.

"Athvan!" Arvan called, but Athvan was gone. *I'm not going to convince him to stay behind. He's turning out to be just as stubborn as Adir and Morena.* He didn't like that prospect, but couldn't help smiling as he was reminded of his own stubborn younger days.

"Let's head out before he gets back," Arvan said to Kirsch. He turned to Misuma. "Shut the door as soon as we leave and do not let Athvan out!"

"Yea, sir. We'll make sure the young master doesn't leave."

Arvan stepped out into a cool, moonlit night. He pointed his sword northward, toward where he believed the explosion had originated. Kirsch acknowledged with a nod. Arvan took careful steps as he crossed the courtyard and made for the front gate. As he opened it, he heard Athvan yelling at the housekeepers, demanding that he be let out.

"I hear hooves!" Kirsch exclaimed. He darted forward, a long dagger in his hand. A horse galloped toward them on the road from the Village Square. "I don't see a rider, sir!" Kirsch exclaimed, craning his neck for a better look.

As the riderless horse got closer, Arvan recognized its features. "It's Veyka!" And Adir wasn't riding her. A bottomless pit formed in his gut.

Kirsch grabbed Veyka's reins as she passed by. The mare responded violently, kicking and pulling forcefully against her reins.

"Whoa, Veyka! Whoa, girl! Calm down," Kirsch said soothingly, trying to stop her panicked plunging.

"I need to find Adir," Arvan said.

"I'll be right with you, sir!" Kirsch replied. He cajoled Veyka over to a sturdy fencepost, tied her off, then nodded to him.

Arvan took off running north on the road, in the direction Veyka had come from, the direction the explosion had sounded from. Myriad different scenarios played in his head, each one magnifying his trepidation.

Could Adir have been attacked by bandits? No. Marafel hadn't seen bandits in decades. Was the village under attack and Adir caught in the onslaught? No, if Marafel were under attack, there would have been repeated cannon fire, not just one shot.

At the back of his mind was a persistent thought, like a tethered bull raging to break free. He didn't want to entertain the idea that Adir could have been attacked by rakhor. They certainly could have done something to cause the explosion—no one quite knew what they were capable of.

Arvan had only seen a rakhor once, back when he trained with the Watchmen. While accompanying a squadron on patrol, he'd spotted the demonic creature a few dozen yards away. It'd been walking away, moving unnaturally. Six protruding spikes ran down the length of its back, three on each side of the spine, like the remnant skeleton of what might have once been wings. Occasionally, the creature faded to complete invisibility, then slowly reappeared.

What other supernatural abilities do they have? The Word spoke it true; the rakhor truly were demons. But if a rakhor had hurt Adir, nothing would deter him from hunting down the creature!

After a long while, a narrow trail shot off the road through some fields with knee-high grass that rippled in the light breeze. Unsure of which split to take, Arvan stopped and searched the surroundings. Some of the tall grass had been recently trampled. *Veyka must have run through here.* "This way." Arvan pointed with his sword and broke into a run. He could hear Kirsch's pounding footsteps close behind.

The two had covered a few dozen yards more when Arvan spotted something in the middle of the trail. He cursed at himself for not bringing a torch as a cloud began moving over the moon. Arvan stopped, then carefully approached the dark lump. As he closed in, the lump took on a familiar shape—

"Adir!" Arvan yelled, racing to his son, his shout echoing across the wide and silent fields.

Adir lay sprawled in a slight depression in the ground. Dirt, grass, and other debris were strewn around the depression, as if blown outward. Arvan crouched beside his son. Kirsch came to a stop behind him, dagger in hand, eyes searching the area.

"He's breathing," Arvan said, feeling a faint flow of air under Adir's nose. He looked at the few drops of dried blood on Adir's cheek. It didn't appear to be Adir's though; there were no cuts that he could see.

The cloud completely swallowed the moon, leaving Arvan only faint starlight. Unable to see anything clearly, he examined Adir's limbs and torso by palpation. "Nothing's broken either," he concluded.

"The Gods are watching over him," Kirsch said, walking farther north on the trail.

The fact that Adir appeared completely unhurt perplexed Arvan. The tiny crater Adir was lying in seemed to have been created by the explosion he'd heard earlier. But if Adir had been in the explosion, only the Gods would have been able to find his remains. Arvan had seen the destructive power of a cannon's explosion firsthand. He scanned the area. There was no sign of a cannonball. *Then how? Could he have fallen into this depression after the explosion?*

Deciding to focus on the fact that Adir was safe and sound, Arvan leaned over to pick his son up when he noticed some marks on Adir's neck. *Is that dirt?* He hefted Adir onto his shoulders.

"Sir!" Kirsch called. "You should come take a look at this!" The steward sounded grave.

Arvan, carrying the unconscious Adir, walked to where Kirsch was standing amidst the tall grass. The cloud, completing its eclipse of the moon, moved away on its destined path. Soft white moonlight illuminated the night once again.

"What is it?" Arvan asked. Then his eyes fell on what Kirsch was pointing at and he felt his own eyebrows rise.

Boar Sayarna lay dead in the grass, his thick limbs twisted at odd angles. His massive chest had been caved in as if smashed by a heavy boulder.

"GODS!" Arvan exclaimed. "What is going on in this village?"

Chapter Eight

Ekren walked down a windowed hallway on a floor laid with yellow and white tiles, trailed by Ferrith and two Regent Guards. Dina walked next to her, straightening her white, flower-worked bandana.

Ekren hadn't been too happy with Dina's dealings with Lord Malasi's son. Her daughter had actually broken his wrist. But based on Dina's version, that lecher deserved much more than a broken wrist. Ekren wished she could hang the man for laying his filthy hands on her daughter, but that would be seen as an abuse of her Regency. Dina had certainly proved she could take care of herself, yet Ekren hoped that one day Dina would let a worthy man take care of her. Everyone needed someone to lean on.

"How do I look, mara?" Dina asked, running her fingers through her auburn hair.

In a red tunic with a gold-embroidered neckline, white salwar, and her white bandana, Dina looked every bit the Regent she would one day become. "Regal for court," Ekren responded, then lightly flicked her hair.

"Mara!" Dina said, her voice indignant. "Please do not do that!"

Ekren laughed then let out a long sigh. "Sometimes I forget you are no longer my little Dinana anymore." That was what Dina used to call herself as a toddler, dabbling in words for the first time, playing with various sound combinations.

"No, I am not," Dina said crossly, but then she smiled warmly. Abruptly, she grimaced, placing her hands on her stomach.

"Did you not have any breakfast?" Ekren asked.

"No."

"You should go get something to eat. You can join me at court another time."

"No, it is all right." Dina straightened up. "I will wait till after we are done."

"You should really get—"

"Mara! I will be fine. I am not your little Dinana anymore, remember?"

Ekren smiled. "As you wish, daughter." But she knew it wouldn't be long before the hunger started to consume Dina's thoughts, making it hard to focus on matters of court. Ekren knew because she herself had attended court on an empty stomach, when she was being groomed by her father for her elevation to Regency.

It had been a tenuous time back then, as the powerful houses of Ostarium were worried about having a woman as a Regent, given the disastrous rule of Ilka Torkul. Though Ilka had been Regent a long while ago, she had left Ostarium in shambles, and her own generals had felt obliged to wrest the Regency from her hands. Since then, Ostarium had heavily favored men as Regents.

But the Arinols were different. Ekren's father had believed in her. Garron, her late husband, had believed in her. And she believed in herself. Armed with this belief and fueled by determination, she had won the support of most of the houses, thereby consolidating her Regency. Still, every day was a new battle to prove that she was just as good as, if not better than, her predecessors. She had built a great legacy, but would that be enough to ease Dina's elevation to Regent?

A pair of large wooden doors at the end of the hallway, each carved with the Ostark seal of two clasping arms, marked the private entrance to the Court Chamber. The two guards in front of the door saluted by thumping spear butts on the floor. The familiar murmur of courtiers and petitioners could be heard on the other side of the door.

"Lords and ladies! Servicemen and citizens!" the announcer bellowed on the other side. The murmur faded, the guards opened the doors, and Ekren entered followed by Dina, Ferrith, and the Regent Guards. "Entering the chamber is Lady Ekren Arinol, the Regent of Ostarium!" bellowed the announcer.

Someone in the crowd cheered as if they were at the games and all heads turned toward the sound. Ekren, however, ignored it. Court was a place for all, even those citizens not well versed in court decorum.

The spacious chamber had a domed ceiling that displayed a mosaic of sky dotted with clouds. The wide windows that lined either side of the chamber let in enough light that a quick glance at the ceiling gave the illusion of being outdoors. Lords and ladies, generals and their aides, and common citizens from all strata of society—at least two hundred people, in Ekren's estimation—filled the chamber, yet the chamber was far from claustrophobic.

On the dais, Ekren seated herself in the Regent's Chair. It was an intricately carved, gilded, and well-cushioned piece of furniture that was more a throne than a chair—a remnant from the days when men ruled as Regents. Dina sat beside her on a more sedate chair, holding herself decorously. Ferrith stood in front of the dais, to the side, holding two sheets of paper that contained the list of petitions for the day. *Two scrolls!* Ekren thought. *It'll be a long day.*

"For the first petition of the day, the Lady Regent shall hear the dispute between Remzi Dalmeen and Saami Tabka," Ferrith announced.

A few moments of shuffling later, two men emerged from the crowd. Though both wore a jubba and salwar, their similarities ended there. One was clean and well kempt, his clothes laundered, rings adorning his fingers—clearly a merchant of some sort. The other was stained, shabby, and shoeless and appeared as if he had just bathed this morning, for the first time in a while. Unfortunately, the bath had not been enough to wash away years spent in meager conditions.

"State your names," Ferrith demanded.

The shabby man looked to the well-kempt one beside him in obvious deference.

"Remzi Dalmeen, my lord," the merchant said, bowing deeply and speaking with polished words. "May the Gods favor you."

"May the Gods favor you as well," Ferrith replied with an acknowledging nod, then regarded the shabby man. "And that would make you Saami Tabka," he said, a slight disgust in his voice. Ferrith was not always kind to the misfortunate. He viewed them as a drain on Ostarium.

"Yes, m'lord," Saami said. His country accent, thick enough to fill the room, confirmed his humble status. He'd most likely moved to Lanmeria looking for work.

"Very well," Ferrith said, turning to Remzi. "What is your dispute?"

Remzi shook his head. "I have no dispute, my lord. Tabka here is the one with the grievance." He made a dismissive gesture. "This is all a waste of time, if you ask me."

Ekren exchanged a look with Ferrith. It was not often that a lowly citizen took a wealthier one to court.

Ferrith turned to Saami. "Please state your dispute."

"It is very simple, m'lord," Saami began. "Master Dalmeen killed m'goat. I had saved for a while to buy that goat. I was to take it home to Boloppa. For m'mara. She's old and the goat could give her milk."

"Did you witness him killing your goat?" Ferrith inquired.

"No m'lord. But, one of his men, I saw him do it."

Ferrith nodded, then turned to Remzi. "Your defense?"

Remzi turned to look at the crowd then back toward the dais with an expression that seemed to say his story would straighten things out. "My lord Vice Regent," he began, his words smooth as silk, "as a true Faithful, I do not lie. And as such I am compelled to say that yes, one of my men did kill his goat. Yet I did not do any wrong."

"And why is that?"

"He says m'dog killed his chickens," Saami interjected.

"I will speak to you if I wish for you to speak," Ferrith snapped.

"Sorry m'lord," Saami said, kowtowing.

"Stand up!" Ferrith was plainly annoyed. Saami sprang to his feet. Ferrith again turned to Remzi. "So, his dog killed your chickens?"

"Yes, my lord," Remzi said. "You see, Tabka here works on my meat farm. I sell a variety of meats"—he paused and looked around at the crowd again—"at very reasonable prices." Looking back at Ferrith, he continued. "Tabka had been living in the farmhands' quarters by my chicken coops, as he could not afford a place of his own. One day, he shows up with a goat and a dog. Now, I am not sure where he got the money from to buy a goat ... he could have stolen it from me, I suppose."

A few gasps escaped the crowd.

"But I am a good Annadi. I do not presume ill. Anyways, I warned him that if his dog caused any damage, he would have to pay for it. And, Gods smite that dog, he killed my chickens. When I confronted Saami about it, he said he was not responsible since it was the dog that killed the chickens and not him personally. But even if he had accepted guilt, he would not have been able to pay me. I doubt the man had a penny's worth of crown on him. So I told one of my butchers to kill his goat and use its meat as payment." Remzi turned his gaze onto Ekren. "Lady Regent, you and I as Faithful Annadis know that the Word says it is only just to pay back in kind."

"I don't care what the Word says," Saami snorted. "I don't live by it!"

"This is your last warning, Master Tabka," Ferrith reprimanded. "If you speak again without my leave, I'll recommend that the Lady Regent dismiss your petition." Saami's admission that he was Faithless did not help his standing with Ferrith. "Is there anything else you would like to add, Master Dalmeen?"

"No, my lord Vice Regent."

Ekren considered the case for a moment as she studied the shabby man. She knew what verdict she wanted to pass, but decided she would consult Dina on the matter. After all, Dina had to learn to wade through such matters and deliver a fair judgment. She turned to her daughter, "Heiress Regent," she said formally, "what say you about this matter?"

Dina looked at Ekren with an appreciative smile, then turned to the petitioners. "Master Tabka," she said, sounding gracious yet firm, "you've clearly testified that *your* dog killed Master Dalmeen's chickens."

"Yes, m'lady," Saami replied, dropping his gaze to the floor.

"And how many chickens did your dog kill?"

"He killed three," Saami said, eyes still glued to the floor. "But I cannot control what a dog does."

Dina simply nodded. "And based on the fact that you are here claiming justice for a dead goat, I assume you did not give Master Dalmeen permission to use your goat as payment." Saami nodded assent. Dina turned to Ekren. "Lady Regent, both parties are at fault here. Since Master Tabka has admitted he owns the dog and the dog killed the chickens, he is responsible for the dead chickens, owing Master Dalmeen the cost of three chickens." Dina turned to regard the meat merchant, who looked pleased. Remzi moved as though to bow, but Dina continued. "However, that does not give Master Dalmeen leave to kill Master Tabka's goat. Thus, Master Dalmeen owes Master Tabka the cost of the goat. Since the cost of a goat is far more than that of three chickens, Master Dalmeen will owe Master Tabka the remainder." She turned to Ekren and gave her a small triumphant smile.

Ekren's chest swelled with pride. Her daughter had proved yet again that she was well on her way to regency. She faced the petitioners. "The Heiress Regent is wise."

"But, Lady Regent," Remzi chimed in protest. "I did nothing wrong. I but followed the Word of the Gods."

"Master Dalmeen," Ekren said, feeling her anger rise, "in Ostarium, a person's beliefs do not translate to societal law. If I were to pass judgment based on the Annadi faith, then I would be placing our faith ahead of the rest. But in our lands, we value all faiths or lack thereof equally and are ruled by the law of man." Regarding Ferrith, she said, "Lord Vice Regent, what is the punishment for wanton destruction of property?"

"The guilty has to pay the cost of damages and spend no less than ten days in prison," Ferrith said matter-of-factly, although he looked confused. He certainly had not expected a judgment in favor of Saami the Faithless farmhand. Ferrith was a pious man.

"Now, Master Dalmeen. In light of this information, would you rather I hand you the full punishment or the more lenient judgment of the Heiress Regent?" She leaned forward in her chair and looked directly into the meat merchant's eyes.

Remzi wilted. He looked at Dina, who smiled sympathetically at him. He turned his head toward Ekren but did not meet her eyes. "The Heiress Regent is a wise woman," he said sheepishly. "Her judgment is fair."

"Then it is settled," Ekren said. "Master Dalmeen shall pay Master Tabka the difference in cost between a goat and three chickens." She paused. Something did not feel right. Ekren did not think that Remzi would learn a lesson from such a light punishment. The amount he had to pay would hardly hurt the meat merchant's purse. Ekren faced Saami. "Master Tabka, I presume you are no longer employed with Master Dalmeen."

"No, m'lady," Saami said. "I've been sleeping in an alley since I left the job."

Ekren nodded. "In addition to the payment for the goat, Master Dalmeen shall pay ten scepters as severance. So shall it be!"

Remzi's face flushed red, but he did not say anything. He bowed, though only barely, then spun and disappeared into the crowd.

"Thank you, m'lady," Saami said, bowing repeatedly, hands clasped in front of him. He looked like a filthy bird searching the ground for edible tidbits.

Ekren raised her palm, signaling him to stop. "I suggest you find yourself another employer. And pick a better one this time. You may leave." Saami bowed once more and shuffled out.

The morning stretched on. Petitioner after petitioner stepped up with their grievances and disputes. While she passed judgment on most, Ekren involved Dina in some to sharpen her skills. The Heiress Regent had been attentive and fair, despite her worsening hunger grimaces.

After a long while, Ferrith put aside the first sheet. Ekren turned to Dina. "You are hungry, are you not?" she asked.

"Yes," Dina replied, "but I am all right."

"There are many more petitioners to listen to," Ekren said, glancing at the scroll in Ferrith's hand. "There's another whole sheet. It'll be a long while before it's done."

Dina sat pensively for a moment. "All right," she said hesitantly, "I will go get something to eat. I will meet you back here."

"Why don't you wait for me in my study? Things will be winding down here by the time you are done."

"If that is the case, then I am staying," Dina said in an annoyed whisper. "I don't want to miss out on the second half, mara."

"There will be plenty of other opportunities for you, daughter. And you did very well today." Ekren felt a fond smile span her face. "Besides, how would it look if the Heiress Regent fainted from hunger? We do not want to appear weak in front of our subjects."

Dina considered that for a moment. "You are right," she finally said grudgingly. "I'll meet you in your study after I get something to eat." She stood and gave Ekren a deep curtsy. Ekren dipped her head in acknowledgment.

When Dina exited through the private doors, Ekren turned to Ferrith who had waited patiently through the whole exchange. "Let us get on with it."

◍

DINA SAT in a capacious leather chair at the Regent's Desk waiting for Ekren to arrive. Warm sunlight bathed the room through wide-open windows. Her mother always kept windows open, preferring a gentle breeze to servants fanning her. This preference led to several open windows throughout the palace, much to the dismay of the Regent Guards who worried about assassins entering through them.

She'll be finishing up with court soon, Dina thought. She had not been too happy with having to leave court after just a short while and was trying to determine if she should give her mother a hard time about it. Her mind was split on the matter. On the one hand, Ekren had *made* her leave court early, but on the other hand, she had been hungry. Ravenously so! Maybe she'd let this one go. She could make this one concession given all the concessions her mother had made for her.

Ekren had been very patient as Dina rejected every suitor arranged for her, especially with this last lordlet, seeing how she had broken his wrist and all. The fact that Ekren wanted her to marry someone and have a child was certainly no secret. But Dina did not see herself following that path, though securing her lineage would be her duty as Regent. She felt trapped. How was she to ever break that news to her mother?

At the thought of her impending Regency, Dina looked up and eyed Ekren's chair. It was austere but regal, with supple black leather and minimally carved wooden arms. She wondered what it would be like to sit in that chair as Regent. Before she knew it, she found herself seated in it. Leaning back, she stuck her elbows out to rest on the chair's arms. It felt right, but she had a lot to learn from her mother still.

Dina leaned forward and perused the items on the desk. Her eyes immediately fell on a book that sat in its center, as if Ekren had been reading it recently.

On the book's leather cover was a two-toned metal symbol about the size of her palm. She ran her fingers over it and felt it warm to the touch. Seven sinewy strands of a silvery metal emanated from a single source at the bottom of a dark—almost black—metal ring. The silvery strands, resembling wisps of smoke or licking flames, fanned out across the ring, three pairs of strands perfectly reflecting each other about a straight central strand. Words in a strange language—or at least she assumed they were words—were inscribed below the symbol.

Curious, Dina opened the thick book to a random page in the middle, half-expecting to find it written in the same language as the inscription, but it was not.

> *... these aberrations are usually unable to control themselves.*
>
> *A telltale sign of a venna is a haze that surrounds it. The haze is a mixture of the colors of a rainbow—more specifically, red, orange, yellow, green, blue, indigo, and violet ...*

Dina felt a chill pass through her. She rubbed absentmindedly at the coldbumps on her arms. "Venna?" she mouthed softly. She closed the book to look at the inscription more closely, when a thought struck her. She grabbed a sheet of paper and a pencil from a drawer then placed the sheet of paper over the inscription and scribbled over the sheet-covered inscription with the pencil, resulting in a rubbing of the inscription on the paper. Dina peered at it then stuck the paper into a pocket in her tunic's sleeve. She had just opened the book again to continue reading when she heard the familiar thump of spears on floor.

Dina froze. Ekren was back and Dina was reading a book on her mother's desk without her leave. Ekren tended to be very private about the things in her study, and Dina feared she had crossed a line.

A moment later, the door opened and her mother strode through in her long white Regent's robe, banded at the waist by a broad yellow sash. Ekren paused for an instant upon noticing Dina behind her desk.

"Imagining what it would be like to be Regent?" she said affectionately.

"Something like that." Dina smiled and slowly stood to walk around the desk as casually as she could, then took a seat in the leather chair she'd been sitting in before. She left the book open, hoping that Ekren would think she had left it open from her last reading. Closing the book would have looked ... *suspicious*.

Ekren walked behind her desk and took a seat. Dina panicked as Ekren gave the book a long look then closed it, turning her eyes on Dina. They seemed accusatory. Dina held her breath as a still silence descended on the room.

"I need to send the Herran messenger back with something," Ekren said finally, eyes still on Dina. "If it were you, what would you write back?" She leaned forward and rested her elbows on her desk, fingers laced.

Dina let out a sigh of relief. Either her mother assumed that she had left the book open or did not mind her reading it. She struggled to collect her thoughts for a moment as her mind jumped between her relief, Ekren's question, and what she had read in the book. Finally, her thoughts coalesced. "I'd send a positive response," she said, then looked out the window, giving Ekren's question stronger consideration. "However, I'd keep it vague. Promise them aid, but not specifically what or how." She paused for a moment. *That would keep King*

Dooghlas on a leash, she thought. But the rebel leader would still be a liability. She looked back and found Ekren intently watching her. "I also think we should enter into talks with the rebel leader," she said gingerly. "Possibly assist them as well."

"That would not sit well with Dooghlas." Ekren leaned back in her chair.

"Well, he does not need to know about it," Dina said. "We do not know if the rebel leader's claims are unjust. That is for the Herrans to deal with." She paused, her proposed course of action feeling foul. "Though," she added slowly, "I feel it would be very dishonorable for us to play both sides like that."

"Let the historians worry about what is or is not honorable," Ekren said emphatically. "We act in the best interest of our people, in the moment. And in the process, we will write our own history."

Dina studied her mother. She could see a few more strands of silver in her curly brown hair. Her mother always spoke ostentatiously. But that was Ekren. The Regent of Ostarium believed every word she said and Dina did not doubt that Ekren would sacrifice her life for her beliefs. "So, that is how we proceed then?" Dina asked.

"Yes," Ekren replied. "For now, I will send a message promising aid as you suggested. And our spies are already busy searching for the rebel leader." She looked away, her eyes unfocused.

Dina sat patiently, but her eyes kept sliding to the book on her mother's desk. She wished she had more time to read it. Maybe she could ask Ekren for the book. But she could not fabricate a believable pretext to need it. As far as Ekren was concerned, Dina had no idea what was written in the book.

After a while, Dina's patience began to wane. "Well, if there is nothing else, mara"—she stood—"I will take your leave."

"Very well, daughter," Ekren said, as if just realizing that Dina was still in the study with her. "May the Gods watch over you."

"And you as well," Dina replied, then kissed Ekren on her cheek and walked away.

Venna! She needed to find out more.

PART II
ANDANTE

Chapter Nine

"Ah, you're back!" said the clerk. The old lady's smile belied the lines of age streaking across her face. "Did you hear he was awake?"

"He's AWAKE!" Tia exclaimed, her heart bursting with joy.

It'd been four days—*four long and horrible days*—since Master Nathar had found Adir unconscious. After being rushed to the Healing House, he'd been thoroughly checked for external wounds and internal troubles. Fortunately, none had been found, which utterly perplexed the sarawaan as to the cause of his coma.

"I'm just going to pop in for a visit then," Tia said, trying to gather herself. Her Adir was awake! She took a step around the clerk's table and headed to the door that led to the patients' rooms.

"Not yet, dear," the clerk said. "His father and Mayor Alameah are with him right now. You'll have to wait till they're done."

"O, all right," Tia said, deflating a bit.

She wandered over to an empty chair in the waiting room. There was a sense of sickness to this place. Some of those seated around her didn't seem to be faring too well. Looking down the hallway in between patients' rooms, she spotted the two constables of the Village Watch standing guard at one of the doors.

Tia still couldn't believe that Boar Sayarna had been found dead near Adir. Demanding justice, the Sayarnas had descended upon Marafel, claiming to the Arbiter that Adir had killed Boar. To be safe— *apparently*—the Arbiter had ordered guards posted by Adir's door at the Healing House, lest he try and escape.

What foolishness! Adir would never have killed Boar. He was an honorable man, and killing someone wouldn't even have crossed his mind. Well, he did have a temper, but that just resulted in harmless outbursts. *Like they say, barking dogs seldom bite.*

Honor aside though, Adir tended to act quite hastily sometimes, Tia admitted. Could this have been one of those times? By Adir's own admission, Boar knew how to rattle him. And Adir was someone who was easily rattled. *No!* she thought. Her poor Adir had been through a lot in this last week. She'd stay by his side, no matter what.

The news of Boar's death had spread faster than a flash of lightning. That, coupled with the possibility that a murderous rakhor was roaming their lands, had the Marafellens on edge. While selling crumbcakes at the square, Tia had overheard quite a few rumors that spoke of rakhor. Some were of sightings along the foothills and Daaman Woods, while others connected Adir and Boar to the rakhor in myriad ways. Some of the *true* Faithful seemed to believe that the rakhor portended the damnation of people's souls.

That's if people have souls. As Faithless, Tia didn't quite believe in a life force that dwelt within a person, demanding morality and controlling their actions.

None of it was true of course. Well, there may be a rakhor this far south; the Watchmen—clad in fur-lined green-and-brown leather armor and cloaks to match—had arrived a few days ago and were maintaining regular patrols. But the other rumors? *Preposterous!* Yet all of these events seemed to have a depressing effect on the village folk.

"All right, I'll schedule a hearing with the Arbiter for three days from today," a voice said. Master Nathar and Mayor Alameah were walking down the hallway from the patients' rooms, heading toward her.

"That should work," Arvan said. "Sarawaan Bremman thinks he's healthy enough to leave tomorrow." Arvan paused for a moment.

"He'll have an additional day to recover at home. Then we can put all this behind us."

Tia stood as the two men approached.

"Tia." Arvan nodded to her with a smile. "May the Gods watch over you."

"Thank you," Tia said. "How is Adir doing?" She suddenly felt apprehensive.

"He's a strong lad. He seems to have made it out without a scratch." Arvan paused, as if considering something. "He says he feels fine, which, in a way, validates the sarawaan's assessment that Adir is healthy. I guess she got something right after all. Now if only she can do the same with cows."

Cows? Tia decided to ignore that. "Do you think he's well enough to see me?"

"I think he'll be happy to see you," Arvan said with a smile. He turned to Laraan. "Have you met Tia Ellar, Laraan? She is a ... *friend* of Adir's."

"No," Laraan said, stepping forward with his hand extended. "I haven't had the pleasure yet. I'm Laraan Alameah. It's a pleasure to make your acquaintance, Tia."

"It's a pleasure to make your acquaintance as well," she responded, shaking his hand while desperately trying to contain her awe at meeting the mayor. She didn't know the man, but stories of his altruism were often repeated in Marafel. Everyone knew about his rebuilding efforts after the Great Snowmelt Flood that wiped out acres of farmland and left many without a home. Some even spoke of a calming effect he had on those around him. Now, standing next to the man with brown hair and eyes, she could feel that effect.

Abruptly, Laraan started to cough. With watering eyes and a red face, the mayor coughed with his whole body. A vein popped up in the middle of his forehead, bulging threateningly every time he coughed.

The clerk was next to him in a short moment with some water. "You should have the sarawaan take a look at that cough," she said to Laraan, sounding grandmotherly.

"No," Laraan said in between bouts, "it's just a cough. It'll go away."

"We've been seeing a lot of people with coughs lately," the clerk said, looking concerned. "Something may be spreading and you may have it. You shouldn't delay treatment."

Laraan coughed some more, but eventually the cough trickled down to just one or two intermittent hacks. "If it gets worse"—he took a sip of water—"I'll get it checked out." He smiled as he handed the cup back to the clerk. "Well," he said, turning to Arvan, "we better get going. I have a few more matters to attend to." He waved to Tia. "I'll see you around, Tia. It was good to meet you."

"You can go see him now, dear," she heard the clerk say.

"Thank you!" Tia quickly stepped through the doors to the patients' section, delighted at the prospect of hearing Adir's voice once again.

During the four days that Adir had been in a coma, Tia had engaged in a lot of introspection about her relationship with him. At the end of it all, she had come to realize what she had always known. She loved him in more ways than she could describe and didn't want to lose him again—she'd been so petrified that he would never wake from his coma. Life without Adir would not be worth living.

I am going to marry that boy, she thought, feeling determined. Life was fleeting and she knew she wanted to spend hers with him. And she knew that Adir felt the same way.

With a skip in her step, Tia bounded down the hallway, feeling her face stretch into a broad smile.

⚜

"Open your mouth," Sarawaan Bremman said.

Sitting upright, Adir obliged. He watched the sarawaan over the tip of his nose as she peered into his mouth.

"All right, you can close it." She picked up an odd-looking device—a metal tube with conical ends that spread outward; one of the ends was larger than the other. Holding the larger end to Adir's chest, she pressed her ear to the smaller end.

When she put the device away, Adir asked, "What were you doing, Sarawaan Bremman?"

"What?" the sarawaan responded absentmindedly. "O, yea. I can listen to your heart quite clearly with this"—she pointed at the device —"and detect any irregularities."

Adir glanced at Tia, who looked concerned. She had arrived a short time ago and had been patiently waiting for the sarawaan to be done with her poking and prodding.

"Well," Adir said, regarding the sarawaan, "did you find any ... irregularities?"

The sarawaan smiled. "No. No irregularities. You seem absolutely fine to me. How do you feel?"

"I feel fine," Adir said truthfully, though that surprised him.

"Good. Like I told your father, we'll keep you here for another day and check on you regularly to make sure nothing's changed. If things remain the same, or Gods' favor, improve, you can go home."

"That sounds great! Thank you, Sarawaan Bremman." Adir was relieved. Though he'd come to know that he'd been in the Healing House for four days only a short while ago, he was already itching to go home.

"Call me Charika, Adir," the sarawaan said, giving his arm a gentle nudge. A playful smile danced across her lips. "You always called me Charika when I apprenticed with your mother."

"You weren't sarawaan back then, Charika," Adir said, feeling mildly indignant, though he certainly had called her Charika back then. He remembered the pretty, brown-eyed girl who would come to the farmhouse to study under his mother, her long brown hair neatly tied back by a ribbon. He also remembered having a crush on her— he'd been very young and she had paid attention to him.

Charika laughed. "I'll be back to check on you in a few hours. I'd prefer if you stayed in your room, but you're well enough to walk around if you want." She stood then walked to the door, pausing by Tia. "I'm sure you're glad he's awake," she said, placing a hand on Tia's shoulder.

"Yea! I am very happy," Tia said, smiling broadly.

"She's been here every day, Adir," Charika said, looking back at him. "She even spoke to you while you were in your coma. You should consider yourself fortunate that the Gods have graced you with her." With that, Charika left the room.

Tia was blushing when Adir met her eyes. She walked to his bed and sat next to him. For a long moment, she just sat there silently, staring at him. Then she abruptly threw herself onto him, wrapping him in a tight embrace. "I'm so glad you're all right!" she said. She looked up and planted a passionate kiss on his lips.

Adir reciprocated in kind. All was right once again.

When their lips parted, Tia looked at him anxiously. "So ... what happened?"

What *had* happened? Adir wanted to know that himself. He remembered Boar choking him. He remembered drifting away. He remembered seeing the Aurora. Then ... *nothing*.

Earlier, Arvan had unexpectedly asked Adir about an explosion. Adir had no knowledge of it. Maybe he had heard and felt something like an explosion, but his mind had been all fuzzy from strangulation.

"Well," Adir began, "Boar apparently had been following me from the Square. He—"

"After you dropped me off?"

Adir felt a cloud of annoyance puff up at being interrupted, but he quelled it. "Yea." He paused, waiting for another question. When none came, he continued. "Anyways, I spotted him while in the fields I usually take to get home. He said he wanted to fight me because of what I did at the tournament."

"And you fought him?" Tia asked, worry marring her perfect face.

Why was she concerned? Obviously, he was all right. "No. He attacked me without warning. Then strangled me." He could still feel Boar's fingers around his throat. Noticing Tia look at the choke marks on his neck made him a little self-conscious.

"The marks have faded quite a bit," Tia said, as if sensing his mood. "They'll be completely gone soon." They fell silent for a moment. Then she spoke again. "I overheard something about a hearing?"

Adir nodded. "Laraan will schedule one with the Arbiter in three days' time." He glanced at the guards standing outside his door. He was still in disbelief that he was alleged of committing murder, even though Boar had been the one who attacked him! The allegations were ludicrous, of course.

"I think the Sayarnas are taking a big leap blaming Boar's death on you," Tia said. "Anything could have happened while you were unconscious."

"Yea," Adir agreed. He looked out the window and watched a robin glide effortlessly to perch on a banyan branch with thick gnarled roots hanging off of it. Sometimes, he wished he could just lift off and fly away to somewhere else.

"Adir," Tia said softly, "I know this is a silly question, but did you hear me while you were ... asleep? The sarawaan said that you might have heard me."

No, Adir thought. And he was unconscious not asleep. But admitting that would only serve to hurt Tia. And so he lied. "Yea, I did hear you. Although I didn't know it was you. I remember feeling eager to hear that voice again."

Tia beamed. She embraced him tightly once again. When she pulled back, she looked at him lovingly through those eyes as black as midnight. He could feel her gaze holding him. "Adir," she began, "when you were unconscious, I wasn't sure whether you would ever wake up. I was so afraid I might lose you. It ... well, it made me see things in a new light. I have come to understand that time is precious and that we shouldn't waste any of it." She looked away for a moment, black hair swishing slightly, then held him with her gaze once again. "What I'm trying to say ..." She trailed off as her eyes welled up. "I didn't know it would be this hard," she said, chuckling suddenly. She wiped off the tear and continued. "I don't want to lose you again, Adir. I want to marry you. Today. Now!" She smiled and looked at him expectantly.

Adir certainly hadn't expected to have this conversation right now. Yea, he loved Tia. Yea, he wanted to marry her. But now wasn't the time. He had things he had yet to take care of before he could devote his attention to a wife. "Did you just ask me to marry you?" he asked, looking for a way out. Changing the subject outright was not an option.

"Yea," Tia said, nodding. "I believe I did."

"The man is supposed to do that," Adir said, hoping she'd find his comment amusing.

And she did. She burst out laughing and Adir joined in, relieved. The laughter went on for some time, longer than an average laugh, then degraded into individual grunts.

"Tia, I really do want to be the one to ask," he said. "And I will!"

"You better," Tia said, still smiling, though her smile had lost some of its luster.

Chapter Ten

The Judgment Hall stood a few dozen yards ahead, at the end of the dirt street. Though he had passed by this place many times, this was the first time Rein would enter it and witness its proceedings. Most folk in Marafel kept their children out of matters of law and politics till they came of age, and the Marandas were no different. *Rein, these are adult matters and the Hall is no place for young children,* his father had once said. Well, he was no longer a child.

Yet his father had argued against him attending this hearing. Eli considered Adir to be a bad influence on Rein. True, Adir was the one who'd always got them in trouble, ever since they were little. He'd been caught peeping on girls, stealing from peddlers, and had once accidentally set fire to a hay pile. Each time, though Adir was the sole culprit, Rein was dragged in with him. Rein cared for none of that, of course. Adir was his closest friend, a brother. Not even the Gods themselves could stop him supporting his friend. However, given recent events and Adir's colorful past, Rein could see his father's reasoning.

Rein walked through the front doors of the plain grey building, entering a large chamber filled with wooden benches. The seal of Naven—a yellow, three-headed taygar on a circular field of crimson—was affixed to the far wall. Below it was a dais, atop which stood a wide wooden desk. As he stepped into the chamber, a few eyes turned to openly stare at him, while some others tossed furtive glances and whispered to those next to them. Ignoring them, he looked around for Adir.

Since finding Tamaar's body and his victory at the Regional Games, Rein had acquired a notoriety he didn't quite care for. Well, he did want to be recognized, but not like this! Rarely did people congratulate him on his victory; most regarded him with suspicion or sympathy.

Ahead, Rein spotted Adir seated in the front row, conversing with Laraan. Morena and Arvan were seated there as well. Rein had expected to find Tia at the Hall, though oddly, she was nowhere to be found. Making his way up to the second row, he shuffled past a couple of people and seated himself behind Adir.

"Hey, Rein!" Adir said, turning to face him. "What are you doing here?" Then he abruptly added, "Not that I am not glad to see you." He smiled, though it was stiff and somehow … different.

"Yea, well. It's been godsforsaken difficult to track you down." He smiled back at his childhood friend.

Adir laughed. "I've been a little, uh, busy," he said, his laughter fading quickly. "So busy, in fact, that I haven't had a chance to congratulate you on your win!" he added, smiling awkwardly. "You're going to Cayan, my friend!"

Despite Adir's stiffness, Rein felt himself smile broadly. "Thanks! I guess you owe me money now. You promised to pay my fare."

"I did no such thing!" Adir said defensively.

"Of course you did!" Rein replied. "At the pastures, when—" Abruptly he felt a lump form in his throat. Every time he thought of the pastures, the lemon-sized ball spontaneously bloomed. However, he'd learned to push through it.

"How are things out there?" Adir asked, his expression concerned. "I've been unconscious. But you've been around. Talking to people."

"It hasn't been that bad," Rein said, trying to sound reassuring.

Adir nodded. "I've heard there are rumors circulating about me," he said.

"What have you heard?" Unlike the stories surrounding Rein, which were mostly benign and factual, those surrounding Adir were more insidious. Some seemed to think that Adir, Boar, and Tamaar were servants of the rakhor who had crossed the demonspawn in some way.

"I don't know. No one's telling me." Adir pouted a bit.

Rein simply nodded in response. "I'll tell you later," he promised, though he knew he wouldn't. He'd always been bad at delivering bad news.

The bailiff walked in. "Please rise for his wisdom, Arbiter Rabinar." Everyone stood as a grey-haired man in a long crimson coat strode in through a back door and seated himself behind the desk on the dais. "You may be seated," the bailiff said.

"Let it be recorded that the hearing in the matter of Master Adir Nathar has commenced," the Arbiter proclaimed. A scribe in a corner began scribbling in a book. "Is Master Adir Nathar present?"

"Yea, your wisdom," Adir said, standing.

The Arbiter nodded. "You may sit, lad." He paused as Adir seated himself. "Just so we are clear," the Arbiter said, his gaze sweeping those assembled, "this is a hearing, not a trial. Master Nathar here has not been legally charged with any crime, though he has been alleged of one. Our sole purpose today is to determine whether or not there is sufficient evidence to charge him with the crime of murder."

A few murmurs rose in the crowd, but the bailiff quickly got a handle on things.

"Is Master Syfis Sayarna present?" the Arbiter asked.

"Yea, your wisdom," came the reply from a stocky, balding man a few benches to Rein's right. The man stood maybe as high as his shoulders but was built like an ox.

"Who's that?" Rein whispered to Adir, careful not to speak too loudly.

"That's Boar's brother," Adir said, loud enough to be heard all the way in Akkasha. That earned him a nudge and an angry glare from Arvan.

"Master Nathar," the Arbiter said as if speaking to a delinquent child, "might I remind you that we're in the Judgment Hall deciding your fate?"

Adir dropped his gaze to the floor as if embarrassed, but Rein noticed him clenching his jaw. "I apologize, your wisdom," Adir said with a forced sincerity.

The Arbiter turned back to Syfis. "Master Sayarna, you may begin."

"Thank you, your wisdom," Syfis said, dipping his head. Then he shot Adir a look full of reproach and hate and pointed at him. "Your wisdom, I charge that Master Adir Nathar killed my brother Boar Sayarna." He walked across the floor and halted in front of Adir's bench. "On the ninth day of Marayi, this man started an altercation with my brother at the Regional Games that was witnessed by many. Then later that day, my brother is found dead next to this man. It doesn't take a scholar to put those two facts together and ascertain that Adir Nathar undoubtedly murdered my brother in cold blood!" His words carried a furious passion. Staring daggers at Adir, Syfis returned to his seat. The tense silence that followed was somehow exacerbated by the soft scribbles of the scribe.

"Master Sayarna," the Arbiter said, "it's hard to lose a loved one and it's only natural to want answers. But be wary of jumping to ill-conceived conclusions. They often lead to more harm than good." He then regarded Adir. "Master Nathar, what do you have to say?"

Adir shot to his feet, his face flushed. "Boar accosted me that night, your wisdom!" he shouted. The Arbiter gave him a stern look.

Rein knew all about Adir's short fuse. In his experience, the more pressure Adir felt in a situation, the shorter his fuse got. And the shorter the fuse, the quicker the outburst. He was convinced that Boar had fallen victim to Adir's short fuse at the Games.

"I was on my way home," Adir started over, seemingly more in control of himself, "and Boar Sayarna followed me from the Village Square. He said he wanted to fight me, since he didn't get to settle matters at the Games." He paused for a moment. "The altercation at the games … was an unfortunate incident."

"All right," the Arbiter said, scrunching his eyebrows together, "but how did Boar Sayarna die?"

Adir did not reply for a long moment. "I don't know, your wisdom." He appeared a little shaken.

"You must know something, lad"—the Arbiter held up a scroll—

"the Village Watch report says that you were found mere paces from Boar."

"The last thing I remember is being choked by Boar," Adir said, then added more softly, "I thought I was going to die." He grabbed his shirt by the collar and pulled it down slightly, exposing fading red marks that wrapped around his neck.

"So you know nothing of how his chest was crushed?"

Boar's chest was crushed? Rein hadn't known that.

"No, your wisdom."

The Arbiter nodded. "That certainly is very odd. The Village Watch report says that nothing was found in the vicinity of the scene that could have crushed Master Sayarna's chest."

"Your wisdom, if I may speak?" Syfis said. The clean-shaven man was red in the face.

"You may."

"Adir Nathar could have killed my brother elsewhere, and on his way to get rid of his body, the murderer fell unconscious. The Gods themselves must have smote him!"

"Master Sayarna," the Arbiter said, "your arguments require a lot of assumptions to be true. And we're not in the business of putting a man's life on the line based on assumptions." He regarded Adir's father for a moment. "Master Arvan Nathar?"

"Yea, your wisdom," Arvan said, standing.

"You were the one who found your son and Master Sayarna. What did you find?"

"My son was unconscious, your wisdom," Arvan began, "but otherwise he seemed fine, save for the choke marks on his neck." He turned to Syfis and added, "And they were indeed choke marks." Facing the Arbiter again, he continued. "Master Sayarna had already passed away by the time I found him." He paused for a moment. "I know I am not under oath, your wisdom, but I speak the truth when I say that neither I, nor my steward Kirsch Nayal, disturbed the scene, save for picking up my son. I immediately dispatched Kirsch to get the Village Watch once Master Sayarna was found."

"And what about this explosion?" The Arbiter questioned. "The report says you stated you went to search for your son after you heard it. Several folks in the village say they heard it too. Did you find anything?"

"Save for a depression in the ground in which my son lay, I found no signs."

The Arbiter gave a reluctant nod. "Thank you, Master Nathar. We all know you're a man of your word." He tapped his finger on his desk for a while. "Let me ask you this, however," he said eventually. "Do you think your son could have killed Master Sayarna?"

Without hesitation, Arvan replied, "I apologize, your wisdom, but I'd rather not answer that question. My thoughts on the matter would be biased and would frankly add to irrelevant speculation. I believe the evidence speaks for itself."

The Arbiter simply smiled and nodded. Rein spotted Adir smoldering at his father. "Fair enough," the Arbiter conceded, then he spoke to everyone in the Hall. "We have few facts and much hearsay. And the little that we do have isn't enough to charge Master Nathar with the most heinous of crimes. At most, Master Nathar would be a person of interest. Even if we were able to prove his culpability in Master Sayarna's death, Master Nathar's account of the night makes a strong case for self-defense. Additionally, there are no witnesses to refute Master Nathar's story. As such, he is free to go."

A few gasps rose from the benches. Adir didn't seem as excited as Rein had expected him to be. He simply sat nodding, with a small smile on his face. Syfis, on the other hand, stood up as if ready to charge the Arbiter. An old man seated next to him grabbed his wrist, coaxing him back down. Syfis sat grudgingly and glared at Adir.

"However," the Arbiter continued, "the investigation is far from over. The Village Watch is to continue investigating Master Sayarna's death till they are convinced they can go no further." He looked at Adir. "If the Village Watch finds anything incriminating, Master Nathar, we'll be revisiting this case. Do you understand?"

"Yea, your wisdom," Adir responded. Seemed like he wasn't entirely off the hook.

"Good. Let it be recorded that the hearing in the matter of Master Adir Nathar has concluded."

The entire assembly stood as the Arbiter vacated the dais and left via the door he'd entered through. Laraan and Morena gave Adir some words of encouragement, while Arvan waited quietly, face tense.

As he scanned the Hall of shuffling people, Rein spotted Syfis stomping toward them and nudged Adir with an elbow.

"This isn't over, Nathar," Syfis said, stopping so close to Adir that a strand of hair could barely fit in the space between them. Adir, to his credit, stood his ground.

"Are you threatening my son?" Arvan said, stepping up. Laraan and Morena stood as well, surprise splashed on their faces.

"I can handle my own battles, akka!" Adir said sharply, giving his father an irritated look. He turned back to Syfis. "I think it's over," he said.

Rein could feel the tension between the two, taut as a drawn bowstring.

"As long as I breathe, I'll not rest till I find justice for my brother," Syfis said in a growl.

"SYFIS!" came a gruff, commanding voice from behind Rein. He turned and saw the old man who'd held Syfis's wrist earlier. "It's time to go," the old man said more softly. Syfis glanced at the old man then gave Adir a long, hard look like a hungry taygar eyeing its meal. Without another word, Syfis lumbered away.

Rein found himself agreeing with Syfis, though for Adir's sake he didn't want to admit it. *This certainly isn't over.*

Chapter Eleven

Adir made his way down the main stairs of the farmhouse wondering where Tia had been. Her absence from the hearing was odd.

The last time he'd seen her had been at the Healing House three days before, after which he'd holed up in the farmhouse, avoiding everyone, especially his father. That had been difficult, but he'd managed by claiming he needed some rest. Today, he'd hoped to see Tia at the hearing, but she wasn't there. Sight of her somehow made the world seem all right.

Adir entered the sitting room and found Arvan in his customary chair, writing in his diary as wisps of vapor steamed from a cup of tea on the small table in front of him. Adir slowed his pace, walking casually through the room, adeptly avoiding his father. He held his hand out to grasp the latch.

"Adir." Arvan's voice was as cool as fresh snowmelt and surprisingly emotionless.

Adir paused but didn't bother turning. "Yea?"

"Where are you headed?"

A fierce annoyance gripped Adir. "Not that it's any of your business," he spat, turning and meeting his father's eyes, "but I'm going to meet Tia."

"It looks like it's going to rain," Arvan was seemingly unbothered by Adir's curt response. *What game was he playing now?*

Adir looked out the window and gauged the distance of the clouds. "They look far enough that it shouldn't be a problem," he said, calming himself.

Arvan nodded, then pointed at the chair opposite him. "Have some tea with me, lad," he said, leaning forward and flipping over an empty cup next to his own. "We need to talk."

Speaking with Arvan right now was the last thing Adir wanted to do. He'd much rather go see Tia, though he wasn't sure she'd be at their usual spot. "If you're right and it rains soon," he said, keeping his voice as calm as he could, "I should get going." He turned and slid the latch open with a click.

"Take a seat, lad." Arvan's voice was still cool, but Adir viscerally felt the command.

Grudgingly, Adir slid the latch closed, then took a seat opposite Arvan. His father handed him a cup of tea, which he accepted without a word.

Picking up his cup, Arvan leaned back in his chair and sipped at his tea. "Did you kill Boar?" he asked a few moments later, without any preamble.

At first Adir was a little taken aback by the bluntness of the question, and incredulous that his own father didn't trust him. But then his anger bubbled up with an intensity he hadn't felt before. This was an anger he didn't care to suppress—couldn't suppress even if he wanted to. He'd put up with enough! He was done playing the submissive child.

"Is that why you didn't defend me at the Hall?" He glared at Arvan as his chest swelled and caved with heavy breaths. "Your own son!" He spat each word at Arvan slowly, his voice dripping with loathing.

"It would've been wrong to give *my opinion* of you at Judgment Hall during a *hearing*." Arvan was defensive, his voice no longer cool. "If it were a trial, of course I would have defended you!"

"Hah!" Adir scoffed. "You were the one who told me that how a person behaved yesterday is how he will behave tomorrow. So you expect me to believe that you would defend me at a trial, seeing how you didn't do that very thing when the opportunity presented itself?" He paused, his mind splitting into thousands of tiny parts, each unearthing and replaying all the wrongs his father had ever committed toward him. "And why do you think you have the right to fight my battles?" he added. "You should have stayed out of the business with Syfis!"

"I was merely preventing the possibility of disgrace to our family," Arvan said. "I didn't want matters to get out of hand."

"Disgrace?" Adir was seething. "That's what you've always thought I am, isn't it? A disgrace! Where do you get the right to call me a disgrace? I'm not the disgrace. You are!" Before Adir realized what was happening, all those things he had been afraid to say to his father rushed out. The gates that once held them at bay were flung open. His mouth merely followed the unhindered torrent of thoughts. "You left your wife and three young children and went off with the Navengaard! If that was the life you wanted, you probably should never have married mara." Thoughts of his mother caused tears to threaten. He fought them down, focusing on his anger. "And after she was gone, you still didn't return! You left your children to raise themselves! What kind of a father does that?"

The question hung in the air for long, uncomfortable moments, but Arvan didn't respond. He sat with a blank expression on his face.

Typical, Adir thought, anger still burning hot. "*That's* disgraceful!" he spat.

Abruptly, a thought occurred to him, which Adir knew would, if spoken, stab at his father. The thought wasn't necessarily true, merely dark speculation. He considered not saying it, but only for a fleeting moment. As the words came out of his mouth, it fueled his rage. "Is that why mara left you?" he asked accusingly. "You were such an uncommitted father. An uncommitted husband. She was a sage for staying with you for so long."

"ENOUGH!" Arvan roared, eyes narrow, face red, and voice so far from its usual cool that Adir wasn't even sure it was his father's voice.

Arvan's hands clenched into fists. "Do not speak of things that are beyond your understanding!" His gaze burned a hole through Adir.

Adir realized that he'd never seen his father truly angry before. He looked dangerous, and for a moment Adir suspected that if he hadn't been Arvan's son, he might not live to take another breath. However, he was not about to be outdone.

Slamming his cup onto the small table between them, he stood. His father continued glaring at him but didn't say another word.

"The truth often hurts," Adir said as he unlatched the door and stalked out.

Chapter Twelve

The moon hung low in the sky, close enough to touch. The birds had ceased their song, the wind had ceased its flow, and a mild chill had descended upon the night. Tia wrapped her wool shawl a little tighter. Had she known they'd be out so late, she wouldn't have worn a blouse without sleeves.

Staying out this late is just foolish, she thought, looking at the man passively forcing her to be foolish. Adir had fought with his father and was now refusing to return home. She'd offered to let him stay at her place, but he'd refused that too.

The lamps in the Square were flickering out one by one. And due to recent events, the village folk were being very wary at night. "It's dark and cold," Tia said. "It's fully night."

Adir, who sat next to her chewing on a length of grass, looked up as if noticing the night for the first time. The Chariot of the Gods passed overhead as usual. "O," he said, "so it is."

Tia wondered what was going through his head. The poor man had almost died, then been dragged through a public hearing and, by his account, his own father had entertained the possibility that his son could have killed another man. Yet a part of her felt as though she shouldn't care, as this was the same man who had rejected her not three days ago.

Did he reject me because he was still reeling from his coma or ... The alternative wasn't very appealing. The seed of doubt, however, had been planted, which was why she hadn't attended his hearing. She hadn't been able to bring herself to go, as her mild doubt about their relationship had suddenly become her focus. Though afterward, she was thoroughly guilt-ridden.

When Adir was in a coma, she had promised herself to stay by his side through thick and thin; she loathed those women who abandoned their men in their time of need. How quickly she had forgotten! She cursed herself for it. No! She hadn't forgotten—it had merely been a lapse. These things took time to learn. *Didn't they?*

This evening, she found herself hurrying to the hilltop hoping that Adir would come. And now that he was here, she'd stay with him as long as he needed—though she sincerely hoped he'd decide to leave soon.

"Tia," Adir said softly, "when I was at the Healing House, I wasn't really thinking straight." He paused, letting out a small breath. "I'm not sure I still am. With everything that has happened, I feel like the Gods are punishing me for something I did. But I don't know what. I don't know where to go. I feel ... trapped. " He looked at her through eyes weary with burden, not speaking for a long moment. "I need to get away from it all," he said finally.

"You're being very vague, Adir," Tia said, trying to understand what he meant. "And I'm always here. You can come to me."

Adir smiled, but there was no warmth in it. It seemed strange on his handsome, troubled face. "I don't intend to be vague," he said, sounding apologetic. "It's how I feel." He fell silent for a few breaths. "I just wish things were different."

What was she to say to that? How could she understand what he'd gone through to make him feel trapped? Make him feel things were different? And if she couldn't understand him, could she truly be there for him? "You just do your best and I know you'll figure it out," she said gently, quashing her unpleasant thoughts. For all the pride she felt at being able to read people, she found herself utterly incompetent in being able to help her Adir.

Suddenly, Tia felt a drop of water strike her forearm. A light drizzle began, prompting her to wrap her shawl over her head.

Adir looked up, annoyed—more annoyed than one could reasonably get at rain. "We should get going," he said. "I'll stay at the Rainbow Inn tonight." He stood, picking up his staff and strapping it to his back.

That was something new. A habit he'd picked up ever since his coma. Usually, he strapped his staff to Veyka's saddle. Tia couldn't blame him for fearing another attack, if that was what was prompting the constantly present staff. She herself had started carrying a belt knife ever since the inexplicable deaths began plaguing Marafel. Just in case.

Walking silently side by side, the two made their way toward Veyka, who stood grazing farther down the hill by a clump of trees. Halfway to the mare, Tia's skirt got snarled on some thorns, and she stopped to free it. "I'll just be a moment," she said, bending to pull her skirt off its anchor. Adir carried on down the hill.

After some careful effort, Tia managed to free herself and looked up just in time to see two men run out of the clump of trees toward Adir and Veyka. The drizzle had turned into a light shower, yet the moon shone bright in the sky.

"I told you it wasn't over," Tia heard a male voice say. She stayed silent, crouching, hoping they hadn't seen her. She began inching toward them when she noticed a third person, this one slowly walking toward her, sword at his hip. She froze as a fear she had never felt before gripped her from within.

"Do all Sayarnas sneak up on unsuspecting people?" Adir asked. Tia sensed some fear under his irritation.

"The Village Watch won't investigate," the man said, ignoring Adir's question. "Boar wasn't a Marafellen, so why should they care? And your father was a mayor of this godsforsaken village." He paused then added, "But I will do my own investigation." The two men began closing in on Adir, each holding a weapon of some sort in their hands. "And pass my own judgment."

No! Tia thought, panicked. Adir was in trouble! And the man who was walking up to her was only a few yards away! What could she do?

"Look," Adir said, a tremor in his voice, "I didn't kill your brother."

Suddenly, Tia remembered her belt knife. Dropping her shawl, she pulled out the palm-size blade and charged at the approaching man, completely unsure of what she was going to do. The man hesitated for a moment then grabbed the hilt of his sword. Running as fast as she could, Tia reached the man before he could draw his weapon and slashed at him, cutting a gash across his chest and arm. The man clutched at his wound, cursing loudly, but she kept running. She had to get to Adir!

The cursing drew the attention of the others, who turned to face uphill. A short, sturdily built man stood facing her just a few yards away. Acting out of pure instinct, Tia threw her knife at him. The knife cut through the air, spinning end over end, only to harmlessly hit the man's chest, hilt first.

But the distraction bought Adir enough time to unstrap his staff. He swung it down from overhead, striking the sturdy man between his neck and shoulder. The man went down, bellowing in pain. Immediately, Adir hopped onto Veyka and the mare began galloping uphill. "Tia!" Adir yelled, extending his free arm.

As Veyka passed her, Tia grabbed Adir's arm and swung onto the horse's back. As soon as she was on, Veyka sped up.

Cold droplets of rain pelted her face as Tia bounced behind Adir. She held on to him as tightly as she could, pressing her chest against his wet back. He was shaking—whether from cold or fear she could not tell. But somehow she knew that they were both wondering what was to come next.

THE STABLE SMELLED STRONGLY of horse dung and hay.

Wrinkling her nose at the pungent odor, Tia stood cold and wet as Adir tied Veyka off. They'd escaped their assailants, though she feared that since they'd found Adir so easily earlier, they might know where he lived.

The rain had let up shortly after they'd descended from the hill-top, but Tia's clothes had soaked up a lot of water, making for a very uncomfortable ride. And to make matters worse, Adir had been silent the whole time, despite her best attempts at getting him to speak.

"What's going on, Adir?" she asked. She was cold and scared and wanted answers.

"Shhhh. Keep your voice down," he whispered curtly. "We don't want to wake anyone."

From the path they'd taken, she'd guessed correctly that they were headed to the Nathar farmhouse. And based on what she'd heard on the hilltop, she had gathered that their assailants were Boar's brother and his cronies. Other than that, she knew nothing.

"Why not?" Tia asked, matching Adir's whisper. "You were almost beaten to a pulp, if not worse. We should be going to the Village Watch!" Her voice rose as she spoke.

"Be quiet!" Adir whispered harshly, his anger clearly visible in the dim light. He looked away, then let out a long, audible breath. "I'm sorry," he said in a calmer whisper.

"I need to know what's going on, Adir," Tia managed to say softly, though turmoil wracked her inside.

Adir breathed in deeply. "Syfis is out for blood. That's Boar's brother."

Tia nodded. She knew that much.

"He thinks I killed Boar, and though the Arbiter judged I was free to go, he's still not convinced. I don't think he'll ever be convinced." He laughed as if just understanding a joke he'd heard a while ago. "First Boar, then Syfis," he said shaking his head. "The Sayarnas won't let me be."

"We should tell your father and go to the Village Watch. They can help you."

Adir let out a derisive laugh. "No they can't. What will they do? Trail me wherever I go? Post guards at my door every night? No, they won't do that. They can't do that." He paused. "Syfis will eventually get me. And I don't want to be around when he comes."

"What are you saying?"

"I need to get out of Marafel, Tia," Adir said almost immediately. "I can't live my life constantly looking over my shoulder."

"But this is your home, Adir." Tia wasn't quite sure whether he was joking. "Your family is here. Your friends are here … *I* am here! We can keep you safe."

Adir smiled that cold smile again. "I know you and Rein would try to protect me, but I can't burden you with that." His face took on a dark expression—the darkness only enhanced by the shadows of night. "Home?" he scoffed. "What kind of a home is it where a father doesn't trust his own son? I'd much rather not have a home at all." His eyes held a panicked determination. "Come with me, Tia," he said—no, pleaded. "I have no one but you."

"I'll go with you," she found herself saying without hesitation. *What? Why?* This was a huge mistake. But now was not the time to walk away from him. Not when she was all he had. "Where are we going?"

"Meneres. I doubt the Sayarnas would look for me there. I doubt anyone would look for me there. And even if they do, the city is too large for them to find us easily."

"Meneres." Tia brought up imagined images of a sprawling metropolis. She'd only heard of the capital from travelers. "I've never been outside of Marafel before," she admitted. "And won't the Village Watch find it suspicious that you left without telling anyone?"

"It'll be fine," Adir said reassuringly, though she wasn't sure whom he was trying to reassure. "They may find me leaving suspicious, but I didn't kill Boar. They won't find anything to implicate me in his death." He paused. "We'll get to Meneres. Find some work. A place to live. Together."

Tia found herself smiling as the fantasy of a life with her Adir took hold. They'd go to work each morning, return home in the evening. She'd cook him dinner, and the two would relax the night away or go drink at taverns—she'd heard there were more taverns in Meneres than stars in the sky. And maybe a few children when he was ready. Best of all, she would have him all to herself. It would be just the two of them. A fearful excitement blossomed in her. "You're right. It will be fine."

Adir nodded. "Wait here. I'll go into the house and grab some supplies for our journey."

"Could you find me something dry to wear?" Tia asked, suddenly aware of her sodden clothes. Adir nodded and left, leaving her with her thoughts in the dark stable.

For a long while, Tia waited excitedly, wringing her clothes dry. But as soon as the last drop hit the stable floor, her excitement withered and she began doubting herself. What had she been thinking? She was about to leave everything she knew for a man who'd all but rejected her not three days before. What if he leaves her when they're in Meneres? *He wouldn't do that, would he?* And what about her mother? She couldn't leave her all by herself.

Adir returned a few moments later carrying two saddles, two packs, his staff, and a bundle. He dropped his burden next to Veyka, then handed Tia the bundle. "Morena's riding clothes," he said. "I've also packed some of her other clothes so you have something to wear on the journey. Just till we get to Meneres and I can buy you some proper clothes."

"That's thoughtful of you," Tia said, walking into an empty stall with the bundle. She put aside her misgivings for the moment in favor of getting dry. Pulling off her wet clothes, she slipped on Morena's. Though the shoulders and bust on the blouse felt a little large, the clothes fit well enough.

"I've also packed clothes for me, food, some water, cloaks, and sleeping rolls," he said, pointing at the packs. "And money. I have some money. Thirty-two scepters and some crowns."

"That's a lot of money," Tia said, stepping out of the stall. It would take her and her mother months to save up that much, and only if they were being very frugal.

Adir shrugged. "It's my pay for these last few years." He began unstrapping the saddle that was on Veyka. "Besides, we need it. We'll be able to stay at an inn in Nagra and have enough left to hold us over at an inn in Meneres. By the time we run out of money, we should have found jobs and a place to stay."

"It sounds like you've been thinking about this for a while," Tia said, realizing that Adir wasn't just running away from Boar's brother.

He was running away from his past. Adir shrugged but didn't say anything. He picked up a different saddle and slung it over Veyka's back.

"Keta?"

"Athvan! What are you doing up so late?"

"Sleep doesn't usually come till much later. Besides, I heard someone moving around the house."

"Gods! How loud was I?"

"Not very. I just heard you because I was awake." Athvan looked at the items on the stable floor then back up at Adir. Though Tia could not see his face, she heard the surprise in his voice as clear as Temple bells. "Where are you going?"

"Away," Adir said.

"I'm coming with you," Athvan said immediately, then added eagerly, "I've been looking forward to an adventure!"

"Athvan, no!" Adir said firmly. "You can't go."

"Is Tia going?"

"Yea."

"Why does she get to go and I don't?" Athvan pouted. He seemed to be picking up his keta's habits. "Are you two eloping?" he asked suddenly.

Adir seemed taken aback by the question. "Where did you hear that word?" he asked.

"I heard it from Nikal," Athvan said nonchalantly. "He said his aunt eloped with one of their butchers. His father is furious about it." He paused, his head swiveling back and forth. "Are you going to marry Tia?" he asked, a sly smile cutting through his voice.

"Yea," Adir said.

Was that an answer to appease Athvan or did he really mean it? Tia couldn't say for sure. Whatever the case, she felt slightly comforted.

"But," Adir continued, "you have to stay here and cannot tell anyone. Promise me."

"If you tell me where you're going, I won't say anything," Athvan negotiated, "I promise."

"All right," Adir conceded, "we're going to Meneres." Tia was surprised that Adir was truthful.

"Meneres, huh?" Athvan mulled. "I really want to go with you, but I guess I'll just wait till you guys get back."

At that, Adir looked at Tia then back at Athvan. "We're not coming back," Adir said slowly. "At least, not for a while."

"You're not coming back," Athvan repeated slowly. She could hear the tears in his voice. "Then I'm going with you!" he added adamantly.

"Shhhh!" Adir hushed, running to the door and scanning the surroundings. Turning back to his brother, he said consolingly, "I'm sorry, Athvan, you can't come. I really wish I could take you. But for now, could you do me a favor and keep an eye on things here?"

Athvan shook his head mulishly.

"You already promised." Adir's voice was heavy with brotherly warmth.

Athvan looked up at his older brother for a long moment, then nodded. "Are you leaving because of akka?" he asked.

"Yea." Adir sighed. "Among other things." He walked back to Veyka to finish packing up.

"He's not that bad." Athvan picked up the last saddle and pack and walked over to a smaller horse. "You can have my horse, Tia," he said as he slung the saddle over his horse's back. "Her name is Mira."

"That's a pretty name." Tia came up next to him and gave him a light kiss on his cheek. For his young age, Athvan often acted more maturely than Adir. "Thank you, Athvan. I'll keep Mira safe."

"You better," Athvan said, forcing a laugh while tightening the saddle. Then he wrestled the pack into position behind the saddle and secured it. Finally, he bridled Mira, grabbed the reins, and walked to the door. Tia followed.

Adir led Veyka out of the stable as Athvan helped Tia onto Mira. He stopped next to Athvan and gave him a tight hug. "Take care of yourself, Athvan," he said. It was bright enough outside that Tia could clearly see Adir struggling to hold back tears. He kissed Athvan's forehead, then mounted and gave Tia a long look. He smiled his new, cold smile. "Ready?" he asked.

Was she ready? Tia didn't know for sure. Nevertheless, she said, "Yea." *I'm all he's got.*

Chapter Thirteen

"The first time Daltaar called for independence from the Gronelle Empire," Bilgan said in his nasal voice, gesturing expansively with his pudgy hands, "only a few answered him. Life was bad for the Ostarks, but they did not know any different after having lived under the Empire for centuries. But what the Empire did next brought about its collapse." He cast his large eyes upon Dina. "Can you tell me what that was, Heiress Regent?"

Dina pretended to think for a moment, just to play the part of the good student. That was what these tutoring sessions were all about. The independence of Ostarium and fall of the Gronelle Empire weren't new topics to her. She wasn't even sure why they were talking about it. "It was the Malmanad Massacre," she answered. Every Ostark man, woman, and child knew of the massacre. "The Empire brought in soldiers at a gathering of the freedom fighters and killed a great number of them."

"Three hundred and seventy-nine to be precise," her preceptor added. Bilgan paused, as if allowing her time to process the number. "As we all know, Daltaar managed to escape with his life and thereafter made another call for independence. This time, all of Ostarium stood behind him, leading to the independence of Ostarium in sixty-five forty-seven."

"Preceptor Koray," Dina said, trying to sound respectful while hiding her frustration, "we've talked about the independence a number of times already. So why are we discussing it again?"

"So far, Heiress Regent," Bilgan said, "we've only discussed those events from the standpoint of Ostark independence." His arms flowed about with his words. "We regarded the massacre as the spark that lit the fire of freedom in people's hearts. However, we have never looked at it from the standpoint of the Empire."

What does that mean? Dina thought.

Bilgan seemed to sense her confusion. "Put yourself in the mind of the Gronelle Emperor," he said, opening a palm toward her. "Let's look at the events from his standpoint. Thousands were openly rebelling. Causing unrest. Trade and commerce suffered. And one of the duties of any ruler is to provide stability to his people."

"Are you saying the massacre was justified?" Dina asked, horrified by the thought. "All those people and their families!"

"Of course not!" Bilgan said matter-of-factly. "Killing innocent people is never justified." He paused for a short moment. "But one day, Heiress Regent, you may find yourself in a position similar to that of Emperor Rimul Kanuk. And if that day comes, it would be beneficial, at the very least, to know where you stand. As opposed to erring by acting out of passion."

Dina met her preceptor's eyes as she mulled over his words. Her studies had shown that empires and governments rose and fell. But could her nation—*her rule*—fall prey to that? It seemed unlikely, for the Ostarks had struck a good balance between lineal continuity and the will of the citizens. "Preceptor," she said, "under Ostark law, if the citizens are unhappy with the Arinol Regency we would be deposed. The citizens would then elect another Regent. There would be no need for rebellions or toppling of governments." As she finished speaking, a thought struck her. *Did Bilgan have them discuss the Herran rebellion at their last session as a prelude for today?* That was clever.

"True," Bilgan nodded, his loose-fitting, sky-blue jubba shifting back and forth with each bob of the neck. "The citizens could depose you. But if they did, would you step down from the Regency?"

"Of course!" Dina answered without hesitation. The alternative was unthinkable.

"Even if you truly believed that you at the helm of Ostarium would be best for its people? You would have the might of the military at your disposal." He paused, displaying a smile that one often saw on those who knew something you did not. "Remember, a good ruler provides stability to her people."

Dina found herself devoid of words. She did not want to admit that Bilgan had made a good point. A long silence ensued as she mulled over what to say. "A ruler must also uphold the laws she swears to protect," she said finally. "And our laws say that I must step down if deposed. And I shall!" She sounded as ostentatious as her mother.

"I hope age doesn't wither your idealism," Bilgan said, "but I have no doubt you will do right by your people."

Dina wasn't sure what Bilgan meant by that but decided not to push it. "Thank you, Preceptor," she said respectfully.

Bilgan Koray was a learned man, an encouraging man. It was hard to believe that this educated, worldly person had once been a Sage of the Temple of the Seven Truths. By his account, though he'd found that life spiritually awakening, it had lacked something. From what she could remember him telling her a long time ago, he had purchased a book on something called hydrodynamics from a peddler during his days as a Sage and had found it fascinating. From then on, he read many more books on a variety of topics such as history, geography, political theory, science, and many others, expanding his mind and making him question his worldview. Eventually, he renounced the saffron to pursue a life of learning, spending many years at the universities in Cayan and Ostarium, till one day he landed at her mother's court.

Maybe he knows about venna, Dina thought suddenly. But should she bring it up? Dina doubted that Ekren would want such things shared. But her curiosity got the upper hand. "Preceptor Koray," she said hesitantly. "Have you ever come across the word venna?"

"Veena?" Bilgan asked, looking puzzled. "That's a ... type of stringed instrument, isn't it? From Naven, I believe. It's usually accompanied by percussion on that round drum. Now what is that drum called?" Bilgan tapped his nose. "Ah! A defele!"

"No, not veena. Venna. Ve, not vee."

"Venna?" Bilgan pondered, massaging his chubby face with his fat fingers. "Venna. Venna. No. I don't believe I've ever heard that word before. Where did you come by it?"

Dina felt a little disappointed. "I overheard it in the city somewhere," she lied. "When I first heard it," she said, continuing the lie, "I thought they were saying veena too. But they said it a few times and they were definitely saying venna." She paused, remembering her futile search in the palace library. "I spent many hours in the palace library over the last few days, searching for references to the word. But I came up empty-handed."

Bilgan remained pensively silent for a while. "Well," he said, tapping his lip, "we could go to the Lanmeria Library."

Of course, the Lanmeria Library! How had she been so dense as to not think of it herself! "That is a splendid idea!" She almost clapped. "I'll have my carriage brought around."

DINA WAITED PATIENTLY for the door to be opened after the carriage came to a smooth stop. Bilgan sat opposite her, his mouth curved up in a smile. "I do not think I have ever seen you this excited, Preceptor," she said.

"It has been a long while since I flexed my research muscles," Bilgan said, a boyish smile spanning his face. "And we are at the Lanmeria Library—the largest library known to man!"

That it certainly was. The mile-long structure contained two-stories-tall bookshelves with books that spanned nations and time. The library was rumored to hold all the knowledge in the world. Master Jazacki, the Master Archivist, had once given her a personal tour of the enormous building while regaling her with stories of famous scholars who had made use of the library's vast collection to further their works.

The door opened and Nekmi held out his hand. "Heiress," he said.

Dina stepped down onto a gravel pathway that encircled a large fountain. At the center of the fountain stood a statue of Hrenwaldt, arms raised in exultation as water arced out from his palms like glistening drops of diamonds. The statue of Hrenwaldt at the front of the library had always seemed odd to Dina, for she felt that a statue of Berron, the God of Wisdom, would have been more appropriate. Though, she admitted, Hrenwaldt was the God of Water.

On the other side of the pathway was a flight of wide stairs, gleaming white in the early evening sun. The stairs were wide enough to accommodate fifty carriages lined from tip to tail, horses and all. Folks in acolyte and adept robes strode up and down the stairs with the hurried pace of university students. Atop the stairs stood the library with its pristine white facade, preceded by an arcade of thick columns.

"What? I do not get a hand to help me out the carriage, Captain?" Bilgan said nasally as he stuck half his body out the door.

Dina laughed silently. Bilgan, for some reason, loved to tease Nekmi, and the captain always took the bait. One would think that after almost five years, Nekmi would have learned to not fall for Bilgan's goading.

"Are you the Heiress Regent?" Nekmi said venomously. He did not even bother to turn and face Bilgan—a sign of disrespect. Ostark culture dictated that one young of age must always face their elder when speaking.

"No," Bilgan replied.

"Then you can step down yourself." The captain made his way up the stairs.

Dina turned toward her preceptor and shrugged with an amused sympathy, then followed the captain. Six guards—veiled and garbed in the white of the Regent Guards, with swords on hips—fanned around, encircling her in a protective bubble. Some folks looked on with curiosity, while most acknowledged her with some form of greeting, be it a simple head nod or a deep bow. Yet all seemed to give her and her guards a wide berth.

At the top of the stairs, the captain entered the library through one of the large wooden doors, gesturing the rest to wait. He returned after a few moments and held the door open for everyone to enter.

Down one of the aisles between shelves, Dina spotted an average-sized man with a bushy mustache making his way toward them. The Golden Book pinned to his chest marked him as the Master Archivist, but it was not Master Jazacki. This man was much younger, somewhere in his late middle years. "Heiress Regent," he said, bowing deeply, "may the Gods favor you."

"And you as well, Master Archivist," Dina responded. "I don't believe I have met you before."

"I am Cassail Tymanol, Heiress Regent," the Master Archivist said. "I took over the duties of Master Archivist after Master Jazacki passed away."

Dina felt sorrow for the loss of Master Jazacki. "He was a good man," she said. "He used to pick out fables for me when I was a little child." She fondly remembered the bearded old man escorting her through the shelves of books, giving her a small yet thrilling introduction to the book he had picked for her.

Cassail nodded in agreement. "That he was. That he was." He paused for a moment. "What brings you here today, Heiress Regent? If I had known you were coming, I could have made better preparations."

"It was a last-minute decision," Dina said reassuringly.

"Fair enough. So, did you have a particular book in mind?"

"Well, I do not know what book I need, I am afraid. All I have is an obscure word and an overheard conversation."

Cassail scrunched his brows and cocked his head. "What is the word?"

"Venna," Dina said. "And before you ask, no, I am not referring to the Naven instrument."

The Master Archivist's mustache flared out with his smile. "Thank you for the clarification," he said, sounding amused. "I may be able to help you, but I need to rummage around the shelves for a while." He gestured to one of the side walls. "If you would allow me to escort you to one of the reading chambers, you could wait there while I search."

As they walked across one end of the gargantuan library, they passed shelf upon shelf of books with intricately carved ends. A globe of the known world stood in front of each shelf. Librarians and patrons alike moved about silently or spoke in hushed tones.

Eventually, turning right along a side wall, they came upon a row of private reading rooms. Stopping at the first empty room, Cassail opened the door and let them in. "I shouldn't be too long, Heiress Regent," Cassail said. "I shall return shortly after your refreshments arrive."

"Thank you, Master Archivist," Dina said as she entered, followed by Nekmi and Bilgan. The other six Regent's Guards stood outside.

The shelf-lined, windowless room was not very large and contained only a small table and two chairs. Dina sat in one while Nekmi took the other seat, leaving Bilgan to stand.

"You will not even offer me a seat, I see," Bilgan accused Nekmi.

"The way I see it, you have two perfectly good legs." Nekmi eyed Bilgan. "And it certainly looks like you could use the exercise," he added in a manner that could be construed as a joke or an insult.

"The way I see it," Bilgan said, sounding suddenly serious, "a captain of the Regent's Guards might want to be standing *alert!*" He paused then added more softly, "Since you are to protect the Heiress Regent and all."

Nekmi shot Bilgan a look of violent intent. "If the Heiress weren't here, I—"

"That is enough, you two!" Dina was exasperated and wanted their unfriendly banter to stop. If she did not put an end to this now, it would only devolve into something much worse later. "I will stand as long as you two stay quiet! We are in a library after all!" She stood, glaring at them both, then walked over to one of the shelves. It contained an unreturned book. The title read *The Faithless Revolt and the Rise of Empires.* She opened the medium-sized, leather-bound book, flipping pages till she came upon the introduction.

In the year of 6350, the very foundation of civilization known to man was shaken to the core. For many decades before, an idea had begun spreading that challenged the doctrines of the Sanctum of the Seven. An idea that questioned why one lived the Annadi way. In that fateful year, the idea had gained enough momentum that it lashed out at the world proclaiming that the Gods are not real.

The Faithless Revolt, as it came to be called, cast the rule of the Sanctum into chaos, paving the way for cunning nobles of the time to seize lands and peoples away from the Sanctum; some still aligned with the Sanctum while others openly shunned it. The rule of God was replaced by the rule of man, giving rise to the empires of Cayan, Gronelle, and Narenath.

This book delves deep into the propagation of the Faithless philosophy and the Faithless Revolt and attempts to shed light on the events that led to the rise of the empires we know today. The bibliography at the end —

The sound of the door opening pulled Dina's attention away from the book. One of the library's peons stepped in holding a tray. He placed a pitcher of iced tamarind sherbet on the table, along with three tall glasses. Filling each glass with sherbet, he handed them out. Dina thanked the man as she accepted her glass. He smiled and bowed deeply, then exited the room leaving the pitcher behind. As she enjoyed her cool refreshment, the door opened again and Cassail walked in holding a book, which he then handed to her.

"The bookmark is at the spot where you will find the word venna," the Master Archivist said. "It is quite interesting."

Dina examined the book's cover. Brown and leather-bound, the title read *A Collection of Poetry and Fables for the Young. Children's stories?* She was disappointed. She almost did not want to read it, for what truth could she find in a fable? Yet the Master Archivist had personally fetched the book for her when he could have easily had one of the many librarians in his employ accomplish that task. She opened the book by the bookmark and read.

> *Go To Sleep, Little One*
> *A Cautionary Poem from Kheryne*
> *When the sky goes dim as night falls.*
> *When the sky goes dim as night falls,*
> *Close your eyes, little one.*

Listen to the sounds of the last bird's calls.
From harm your dreams will shelter you.
From harm your dreams will shelter you,
Keep you safe, little one.
Lest it appear shadowed in a rainbow hue.
For tonight, the venna freely roams.
For tonight, the venna freely roams,
Looking for awake children, little one.
To take them away from their homes.

Dina looked up at Cassail and smiled. The book was not exactly what she had expected. She had hoped to find a book like the one in her mother's study. Something that she could have perused for a little longer than the time it took to read a poem. Something that had more substance. All hope of quenching her curiosity flowed out of her.

"What does it say?" Bilgan asked.

"It is a poem about venna," Dina replied. "It is from Kheryne and it scares little children into going to sleep. I am surprised those savages are sophisticated enough to have poetry." Not much was known about those that lived on the other side of the Bahzenelyn, but what little she knew of the lands of Kheryne seemed to indicate that they were nothing but bloodthirsty savages who pillaged and plundered each other.

"May I see it, Heiress Regent?" Bilgan asked, reaching out. "Thank you, Heiress Regent," Bilgan said, accepting the book, then promptly turned his attention to reading.

"That book is a copy of a compilation some three hundred years old," Cassail said with a pedantic air befitting a Master Archivist. "And that poem is said to be a few thousand years older, possibly from the time of the ancient Farrakhans." He looked at Dina with a curious expression. "And the word venna is very obscure. Most of the librarians I asked did not know of it. Where did you hear this word, Heiress Regent?" His curious expression turned to one of concern. "Did you happen upon any Kheryne?"

"No, no. I did not run into any of those savages in the city. And I am sure the City Watch would take care of things should any show up." Dina paused, her mind racing to create a believable story as to how she had heard the word. The moment stretched long, till finally the silence turned uncomfortable. Unable to fabricate a story on her feet, she finally said with a dismissive gesture, "I just happened to overhear it somewhere in the city. Who knows why people discuss the things they do? And in Ostarium, one shouldn't care either. Folks are free to speak their minds." She sounded ostentatious again. Preparing for Regency was turning her into her mother.

"That is very true," Cassail replied, stroking his mustache.

"There's some good information here," Bilgan said. "Looks like the venna were creatures that glowed with a rainbow-colored hue. Very dangerous, by the sounds of it. Though a scary villain was typical to fables. When I was little, my maromara used to tell me stories of a scary horned creature that cut off children's thumbs if they did not fall asleep … O, grandmothers and their tales!" He let out a little chuckle. "The story did not scare me to sleep. It kept me awake instead! There was little Bilgan lying huddled in his sheets, cowering, clutching his maromara, hoping the horned creature didn't cut off his thumbs. Thing is," he placed the book on the table and waggled his thumbs, "I still have my thumbs." Nekmi let out a small groan.

"Heiress Regent," Cassail said, "are you satisfied with this poem?" He tilted his head to one side. "I get the feeling that you were looking for a little more? You wouldn't have come all the way here otherwise."

Dina nodded. "I was hoping for something more substantial."

"Well, fear not, Heiress Regent," the Master Archivist said, sounding like a warrior coming to her rescue. "I will have my librarians search the archives and I am sure we will find something to your liking."

"Thank you, Master Archivist!" Dina said as hope blossomed once again.

"I must warn you though," Cassail said, "the search will take time. As I mentioned earlier, the word *venna* is quite obscure."

"That is quite all right. I am in no rush."

Chapter Fourteen

The fact that Tia had never been outside of Marafel became abundantly clear as Adir watched her gawk at the sights and sounds of Nagra. Back in Marafel, the Village Square was considered a busy place, with its few shops, stalls, and inhabitants. But this street that they were on, in an obscure corner of Nagra, had more shops, more stalls, and scores more people than his entire native village. He tried remembering what it'd felt like the first time he had visited this town—new smells and colors, the increase in ambient sounds, the sense of mild claustrophobia. That was a long time and many trips ago.

The street was crowded enough that they had decided to dismount and lead their horses through town—though the townsfolk still shot them unpleasant looks. Tia didn't seem to notice however, lost in her reverie of the town.

Frankly, Adir had been surprised that Tia had so easily agreed to leave Marafel with him, but he was glad that she had. The journey would have been quite a bit more taxing alone. They'd stayed clear of the road from fear of being ambushed, instead navigating through pastures and woods. Riding through the night and the next day, they'd stopped only long enough to take a short nap. Through all that, Tia had been a good pair of eyes, but she'd been far from a soothing companion. For some reason, he couldn't help but feel that she had been a little distant, a little lost, on their whole journey to Nagra. *Or is it me who is distant and lost?*

The last ten days had been a string of unexpected events. He'd found Tamaar's decapitated body, almost been killed by Boar, then ambushed by Syfis. And to top it all, his own father suspected that he could have killed Boar. What was going on? Why were the Gods punishing him? Or didn't they care? And how had Boar died?

That last question had plagued Adir ever since waking up at the Healing House. How *had* Boar died? After all, Adir was the one being choked. Involuntarily, he moved his free hand to his neck and remembered how helpless he'd been, struggling desperately to free himself from Boar's clutches, all the while unable to breathe. Then there'd been the Aurora.

Ahead, Adir spotted the familiar tan building with its thick oak door. A sign jutted from the facade that read 'The Soft Pillow.' His father and he had stayed at this inn a few times, while in Nagra on business. "It's right up there," he said, pointing. Tia didn't seem to hear, her eyes and mouth open wide as she stared at a large produce shop. "Tia!"

"What?" Tia met his eyes.

"I said the inn is right there." Adir pointed again. "You didn't hear me?" he added, quite amused.

"No," Tia said, eyes as wide as a surprised rabbit's. "It's so loud here."

Adir laughed. "It'll be quieter inside the inn. I'm exhausted and hungry. I could use some good food and drink."

"And a wash," Tia added. "I'm filthy."

As they approached the front door of The Soft Pillow, a disheveled, thin rail of a boy around Athvan's age walked up to them. "Looking to stay?" he asked.

"Yea," Adir replied.

"Well, we have rooms," the boy said, then looked at the horses. "It'll be two crowns each to stable the horses for a night. Three crowns each for two nights. How many nights you staying?"

"Just tonight."

The boy counted on his fingers, then said, "Four crowns, then. You pay that to me. You pay Master Hirnar for the room." He held up his palm.

"All right," Adir said, reaching for his coin purse, when he remembered something. "Hey, I don't recall Master Hirnar ever charging separately to stable horses. It was always settled when we left."

The boy's eyebrows almost jumped off his face, but he brought them back down quickly. He swallowed hard, shifting from foot to foot. "It's new," he said, sounding entirely unsure. "It's uh … uh …"

At that moment, the door to the inn slammed open as if a battering ram had struck it. A fuming Master Hirnar emerged, wielding a baton. "You little swinespawn!" he yelled, shaking the baton at the boy. "When I catch you, you'll be sorry your godsforsaken sow of a mother ever whelped you into this world!"

The blood drained from the boy's face and he scurried away like a scared mouse, disappearing into the crowded street. Master Hirnar chased after him, yelling, shouting, and putting on a fierce display, but gave up after a few paces.

Red-faced and panting, the innkeeper walked back toward them. "My apologies," he said, clasping his hands together, still clutching the baton, and bowed. "We're having trouble with some hooligans who have been swindling good folk."

"It's a good thing you showed up when you did, Master Hirnar," Adir said. "I almost handed him four crowns."

The innkeeper straightened and studied Adir, his brow furrowed, then he switched his gaze to Tia, then back to Adir. A moment later, recognition dawned on his face. "Master Nathar!" he said exuberantly. "Haven't seen you in these parts for some time. O! Let's get you all taken care of." He looked over to the side of the inn. "Thirith! THIRITH! Come take these horses!" He turned back to Adir. "Why don't you grab your packs and meet me inside? I'll get rooms ready for you." Master Hirnar turned and made for the inn, but stopped mid-step. "Rooms? Or *room*?" he asked with a flat expression.

"Just one room," Adir replied. He had to be as frugal as possible till they found work in Meneres. Out of the corner of his eye, he caught Tia smiling.

"Very well, Master Nathar." Master Hirnar paused for a moment, as if picking his next words carefully. "I hadn't realized you were married. Please introduce me to your lovely wife."

"This is Tia," Adir said. "We've only been married a short time," he lied. It was best to not contradict the innkeeper, lest he ask unwanted questions.

"It's nice to meet you, Mistress Nathar," the innkeeper said, bowing.

"You as well, Master Hirnar," Tia responded.

"I'll see you folks inside." The innkeeper turned and bustled into the inn.

Thirith came by and relieved them of their horses. The two picked up their packs and walked into the entry chamber of the inn, where the innkeeper instructed one of the maids to lead them to their room on the second floor. The room was decently sized and contained a bed, a couple of chairs, and a few hanging lanterns, with enough floor space for a traveler's effects. Adir thanked the maid and tipped her a crown, then dropped his pack and staff on a bed.

"I like being Mistress Nathar," Tia said with a broad smile, after the maid left. "There's a nice ring to it."

"I didn't want Master Hirnar asking any questions," Adir said, walking over to the basin. He splashed some water on his face then looked at Tia. She was no longer smiling. *What have I done now?* Grabbing a towel, he wiped his face dry then tossed Tia the quickest of glances. She was frowning now. That was always a bad sign. Walking back to the bed, Adir grabbed his staff. "I'm going to the common room. I'll get us some drinks while you wash up." Without waiting for an answer, he left the room. It seemed best to leave her alone.

The common room was quite a bit larger than the one at the Rainbow Inn but felt empty with only a few patrons. Adir found an empty booth that was easily visible from the stairs to the rooms above, placing his staff next to him.

Shortly, a serving girl walked up. "What'll you be having?" she asked with a sultry voice and looks to match.

"Two wheat ales, please," Adir replied.

"I'll bring them right up." The serving girl smiled at Adir with a look that made him a little giddy.

"What's your name?" Adir found himself asking.

"If you tip me well, I'll tell you," she replied, then walked off to the bar, hips swaying.

While Adir waited for the drinks, Tia arrived and sat opposite him. She remained silent for a few moments then took a long breath. "Adir," she said, "we're going to get married someday, right?" She paused, though not long enough for him to respond. "I've just left everything I know for you. And I'd like to think that it was for something. I'm worried that one day I'll find myself alone."

"Tia, you are the only one for me," Adir replied earnestly, "and I will—"

"Here are your drinks," said the serving girl, in a voice that made him forget what he was about to say. She placed two full mugs of ale on the table. "Now. How much is my name worth to you?" She held out her palm.

Adir looked at the serving girl, who oozed sensuality, and handed her two crowns. She looked at the coins then tilted her head with an expression that implied her name was worth more than that. He dropped another crown, then another, at which she finally smiled.

"My name is Waari," she said and winked, then turned to Tia. "And what'll you be having, gorgeous?"

"I'm fine," Adir heard Tia say. He wasn't looking at her. His gaze was fixed on Waari's curves.

"Suit yourself," Waari said over her shoulder as she swished her hips away.

Adir found himself smiling as he looked over at Tia, but the smile faded as soon as he saw her expression. She looked angrier than a bear whose cub had been threatened.

"So I'm the only one for you, am I?" Tia spat.

The appropriate response would have been to apologize—even if he thought he was in the right—yet he found himself matching her agitation. He was tired from the long journey and fearful for his life.

He could do without her jealousy. "Am I not allowed to talk to other women?" he spat back.

Tia recoiled as if slapped. "No, but you don't have to ogle them."

Adir picked up one of the ales and began gulping it down, eyes fixed on Tia. *Does she think she can control what I do?* He finished about half of the ale and continued drinking, feeling hot under his clothes. *Does she not trust me?* He emptied the mug, thumped it on the table, then lifted the second mug to his lips, eyes still holding her gaze. *Does she think that just because she came with me, I owe her something? No! Coming with me was entirely her choice!*

Adir thumped the second empty mug down on the wooden table and wiped his mouth with his coat sleeve. "Well," he said, standing up and grabbing his staff. He needed to get away from here before things took a wrong turn. "You'll just have to deal with me ogling women then." He tried to keep his voice as cool as his father's, but that had never worked.

"Where are you going?" Tia's eyes were wide with anxiety.

"Out."

"But I don't know this town at all."

"Don't leave the inn then!"

As soon as he stepped out into the night, all of his warmth left him. However, the wheat ales—much stronger than he was used to—had begun to take effect. That, combined with the fact that his last meal had been hours before, made the cold a distant sensation. Strapping his staff to his back, he picked a direction and wandered off—his mind getting mushier and more vulnerable to his increasingly foul mood.

Tia had always been a very supportive girl. What had changed? Or had she always been like this and her support was just an act? Did she really think that he would abandon her? *I would never do such a thing,* he thought indignantly. He wasn't his father. Sure, yea, he could be a little flirtatious, he admitted. But that was harmless. Why couldn't Tia see that? After all, he'd asked her to run away with him. Didn't that imply he wanted to start a life with her? Didn't that mean anything to her? His mind was plagued with too many questions and not enough answers.

Abruptly, he found himself in a dark, dimly lit alley, with buildings rising up around him. Everything seemed … *slightly off*. Hesitantly, he walked down the alley and made a few turns. A few moments of wandering later, he admitted that he was lost and decided to retrace his steps, but it all looked unfamiliar. With no other option he kept walking, hoping to find his way back, when he came upon three men in a dark corner.

"Give it up, you unworthy bastard!" said one of the men, who had a lilting accent. He was clutching another man's collar in one hand while wielding a knife in the other. A third man stood and watched.

"I did not *steal* it! He *gave* it to me!" cried the captive man.

"Do not lie, you swinespawn!"

"I swear by the names of the Miakos. He gave it to me!"

The third man still just stood and watched.

Adir wasn't sure what came over him. Maybe it was his anger and he just needed to let it out. Or maybe he understood how the captive man felt; after all, he had been ambushed a couple of times himself. Whatever the reasoning of his drink-addled mind, he unstrapped his staff and charged.

The man who'd been watching noticed Adir and whirled around, pulling out a knife of his own. However, knives were a poor defense against the long reach of a staff. Adir whipped his staff sideways, cracking the man in the skull, who dropped to the ground, motionless.

The man who held the captive by his collar was startled by the sudden attack and shoved his captive to the ground. The captive lay on his stomach, face cupped in his hands as if trying to shut out his current plight.

Adir felt a surge of energy course through him as he pulled his staff back, preparing for a thrust. He lunged, briefly catching a look of horror on the man's face, and thrust his staff square into the man's chest. The impact sent the man flying a few paces before he slammed into a wall and slumped to the ground.

For a moment that lasted one flap of a bee's wing, Adir saw a rainbow-colored haze on his hand, creeping up his arm. Fearfully, he jerked his hand to his face for a closer examination, but the haze was no longer there.

The once-captive, now-free man looked up from his prone position and surveyed the scene, then stood. "Thank you, master," he said, bowing and scraping. "I am forever in your debt."

The man's words seemed to tumble out of his mouth in a clatter, or maybe Adir couldn't understand him on account of being severely drunk. "What did you steal from them?" Adir asked, eyeing the man suspiciously, his inebriation fueling his paranoia. Sure, he'd saved the bearded man, but that didn't mean the man was harmless.

"I did not steal anything, master," the man said, still pronouncing every word oddly.

Adir looked at him, trying to force his eyes to focus. "All right," he said, realizing that he'd do nothing even if the man admitted to stealing something. All he really wanted to do was get back to the inn and sleep. "Do you know the way to The Soft Pillow?" he asked, trying and failing miserably to strap his staff onto his back.

"Ya, master," the man replied with enthusiasm. "I will take you there."

<hr>

WHAT AN UNEXPECTED FIND, Uaqui thought. Had he really seen it? He wasn't sure, as it had only lasted for a short while. He looked down into the alley at the two men on the ground. Both had been motionless a moment ago, but one had started to writhe around. Lifting up onto the balls of his feet, Uaqui moved to the other side of the roof and scanned the alley below. Empty.

Making his way back to his original spot on the roof, Uaqui considered whether it was wise to jump down to the alley below. Not because he was almost fifteen feet above the ground. Such a jump was child's play. But if he were spotted by anyone, curious looks would be the least of his worries. Though, he decided, confirming what he thought he had seen would be worth the trouble.

Uaqui landed on his feet, light and silent as a spider. He swiftly moved up to the motionless man, crouched, and felt for a pulse with two black-gloved fingers. The man was still alive. Uaqui pulled out his short dagger and sliced the man's throat in one fluid motion. He cleaned his blade on the man's shirt then sheathed it. He glanced at the second man who lay writhing in pain and moaning softly.

As Uaqui neared, the man called out softly. "Help," he pleaded, his voice barely above a whisper.

"Of course," Uaqui replied, crouching. He palpated around the man's chest and found a few broken ribs. *That was a powerful thrust!*

Uaqui looked into the man's eyes. "Brother," he said, "will you answer a question before I carry you to a Healing House?" The man looked puzzled, but he nodded as he clutched his chest and took shallow breaths. "Did you see a rainbow-hued haze around the man who attacked you? Like the Aurora?" He pointed to the northeastern sky.

The man's face went white, like the moon. Slowly, he nodded.

"Thank you," Uaqui said. "Now for my end of the bargain." He leaned forward with open arms, as if to grab the man by his shoulders, but instead grabbed his head and gave it a sharp twist. The snap was satisfyingly audible.

Casually, Uaqui stood. He had taken care of two of the possible three liabilities. The man who had been rescued was still at large and had to be silenced, though he wasn't sure how much that man had seen while cowering on the ground like a scared dog. Yet the last thing Uaqui wanted was for stories to spread. Ensuring that they didn't was part of his duties. However, the Khasir had to be informed of what he had just witnessed. No time could be wasted on that.

Chapter Fifteen

"I'm sorry," Adir said from behind, as Tia strapped her pack onto Mira's back. "I said things I shouldn't have. And I shouldn't have left you by yourself."

"I was quite all right without you," Tia replied calmly. "A few gentlemen were kind enough to buy me food and drinks, seeing how you'd left with all the money."

Adir stiffened at the mention of *a few gentlemen*, but Tia didn't care. She tied off the ends of her pack to Mira's saddle to keep it from sliding. He could have helped her with her preparations, but he just stood around after he was done with his. He could be very inconsiderate. Like stomping into the room in the middle of the night with no effort to be quiet. Though she was quite pleased with herself for having taken the entire bed. She'd left him a bedroll, of course; she wasn't cruel.

"You could have just put your food and drinks on our room's tab," Adir said, as if stating something obvious.

Well, it hadn't been obvious to Tia; she'd never been anywhere but Marafel before, so how was she supposed to know the subtle intricacies of how an inn worked? Sure, there was the Rainbow Inn in Marafel, but she'd never stayed there! She glared at him in response.

"But I shouldn't have left you alone in the first place," Adir said. "I'm sorry."

"And?"

"I shouldn't have lost my temper like that."

"And?"

Adir gave her a quizzical look. "And? And? That's it," he said, shrugging.

Tia found herself getting worked up again and turned to face the man-child. "And what about you ogling that serving wanton?" she said, fighting the urge to slap Adir across the face.

"Not this again!" Adir said, nostrils flaring.

Where did HE get the right to be angry?

Adir must have noticed her expression, as his face softened. "I wasn't ogling," he said, his voice calm yet adamant. "My eyes might have lingered a bit, but I wasn't ogling."

For a moment, Tia considered his explanation. But only for a moment. "Your eyes did more than linger," she retorted.

Adir let out a sigh. "Look, Tia," he said, "I don't think I did anything wrong. No matter how much you kick and scream, nothing's going to change that. But in the future, I'll take your feelings about ogling into consideration." He smiled a smile warmer than those of the previous few days.

Tia couldn't help but return that smile. "Thank you," she said. Had Adir just shown a hint of maturity? Sure, it wasn't exactly the outcome she'd hoped for, but it was something. However, she found that her insecurities about their future still remained.

"See, we're good at working things out," Adir said. He helped her mount Mira. "I'm going to go settle up with Master Hirnar and then we'll be on our way." Tia nodded in response and Adir walked into the inn.

Looking around, Tia gathered in the morning awakening of the street. It was still fairly early—shops were barely opening their shutters, hawkers and beggars were fighting for prime locations, and a few townsfolk moved about on their business. A few yards down the almost empty street, she spotted a scraggly man with a head full of curly red hair and a bushy beard to match. He wore a long, loose-fitting, buttoned shirt that may have once been white. The shirt hung down to his shins, below which dark pant legs were visible. With a wool shawl draped around his neck, he carried a cloth-wrapped bundle on his back. Passing by, he acknowledged her with a nod, walked up to the front of the inn, then dropped his bundle onto the ground and sat atop it. She found her eyes glued to this man; folks outside of Marafel were quite strange.

The bearded man simply sat, not doing much. At one point, he ate some dried meat from his bundle, after which he rinsed his mouth with water from a skin. However, instead of spitting the water out, he swallowed it. Most people would have found that sort of behavior disgusting. But not Tia. She wanted to know why he'd picked up that habit.

The door to the inn opened and Adir reappeared, securing his purse onto his belt. He had taken but two steps when the man jumped to his feet and bowed. "Master!"

Adir looked baffled. "Do I know you?" he asked. But as the man rose, he exclaimed, "O, it's you!"

That was interesting—Tia hadn't realized Adir had friends in Nagra. Though the two of them didn't act like friends. Maybe they were merely acquaintances. But why had the man called Adir master?

"Ya, master," the man replied. "I had to come see you and offer up my services." His accent sounded like someone was shaking a stone in a brass pot, yet his sentence ended with a pleasing lilt. The way he held himself displayed a strong reverence toward Adir. *Why?*

A look of surprise spread across Adir's face. "As I told you … uh … I didn't catch your name last night."

"I am called Ghareeb, master."

"All right, Ghareeb, but you don't owe me anything. I'd rather we just carried on with our lives."

Ghareeb pondered for a moment as he ran his fingers through that thick red beard of his. "Are you sure, master?"

"Absolutely," Adir said.

"You are very generous, master," Ghareeb said, bowing. "But if you ever need anything, please call on me."

"Thank you. I will," Adir said dismissively, turning toward Veyka.

Ghareeb squinted. "Are you leaving today, master?"

"Yea." Adir swung a leg over Veyka's back.

"When will you be returning, master?"

"I don't know."

Ghareeb gazed down the street in an unfocused way for a moment. "If you do not mind telling me, master, where are you headed?"

"I do mind," Adir snapped, not looking back. He paused for a moment, then added more calmly, "I don't see how that's any of your business, Ghareeb."

"You are correct, master," Ghareeb said apologetically. "It is none of my business. But if you are leaving, I was wondering if you could do me a favor."

Adir turned Veyka around dramatically, forcing Ghareeb back a step. "I don't have any money to spare," he said curtly.

"No, master"—Ghareeb shook his head—"you misunderstand me. I do not want your money. Just your company. I figure that since you are headed out of town, I could join you. I have been meaning to get out of Nagra for quite a while, and last night all but made my decision for me. But I would not dare do it alone. I know the roads are safe as long as you can make it to an outpost before night, but I do not have the stomach to travel alone, even during the day."

Ghareeb's words only increased Tia's apprehension about this journey to Meneres. She'd been so caught up in Adir's rush to get out of Marafel that she hadn't considered the possibility of a perilous journey. Hearing about bandits, wild animals, and other dangers of the road from peddlers and travelers was one thing, but to have to deal with it yourself? She found herself fervently wishing for a smooth journey to Meneres.

Adir didn't speak for a long moment. "I'm sorry, Ghareeb. But I'm afraid you will only slow us down since you don't have a horse." He pointed at Veyka and Mira. "And we need to make good time."

Ghareeb looked crestfallen, his expression tugging at Tia's heartstrings. He looked at his bundle and wrung his hands. "I could run—" he began, but ceased speaking immediately and instead stood shaking his head. He looked at Adir, then at Tia, and then at their horses.

Suddenly, a smile spread across his face. Slinging his bundle over his back, Ghareeb said excitedly, "I will be back soon! Please wait for me!" Then he took off running in the direction he'd come from, almost knocking into Mira. The mare snorted.

"What was that all about?" Tia asked Adir, amused. *This morning just got interesting.*

"I'll tell you later," Adir said, shaking his head. "Let's just be on our way. I want to be as far away from here as possible before he gets back."

⬤

"So you just charged into a fight?" Tia asked, unable to comprehend Adir's idiocy. The two rode west on the road toward Meneres.

"Yea," Adir said, nodding. "He needed help."

"But you were drunk!" *This foolish man could have been killed!*

"I wasn't that drunk," Adir protested, shaking his head, then he paused. "Maybe I was," he conceded, "but I was fine."

Whether Adir was brave or utterly foolish, Tia couldn't truly tell, but she inclined toward the latter. What would she have done if Adir had been killed? And after what Ghareeb said about dangers on the road, she didn't quite like the idea of traveling back to Marafel alone and heartbroken. She shook her head to banish the thought. "So, obviously you saved him. And then what happened?"

"He took me back to the inn. And I came into our room to find that someone had taken the entire bed." Adir frowned. His slightly flared nostrils told Tia that he was annoyed.

Not wanting to deal with another one of his outbursts, Tia swung the conversation back to Ghareeb. "We could have let him come with us. It wouldn't have hurt to have another pair of eyes. And arms."

Adir shook his head. "No. That would've been a bad idea. I don't want to leave even the remotest possibility of being found. So the less people know of who we are and where we're headed, the better. I just want to pop up in the middle of Meneres as if I were placed there by the Gods themselves."

"But you took us to the inn where Master Hirnar knew who you were," Tia said delicately, hoping not to rile him.

Adir didn't respond for a long while. "Fair enough," he said finally.

"MASTER!" came a holler from behind.

Tia turned and spotted Ghareeb careening up the road toward them on a sturdy donkey. He rode bareback, his bundle now fashioned into a makeshift pack that was slung over the donkey. He whipped at the animal with a thin cord, which seemed to do the trick as the donkey was galloping, at least as much as a donkey could gallop.

"Gods save me!" Adir whispered under his breath. Tia suppressed a smile. She found herself amused at his plight. He glanced at her and signaled to keep moving.

"I am glad I ran into you, master. I was afraid you would have been long gone." Ghareeb was now only a few yards from them. As he inserted himself into the group, he said, "I found a donkey."

"Good for you," Adir acknowledged dryly.

Ghareeb seemed not to notice Adir's demeanor and beamed an appeasing smile at Tia. "I am Ghareeb, my lady. May the Gods favor you." He made an effort to bow atop his donkey.

Tia returned his bow. "Thank you," Tia said. "And I'm no lady. So please call me Tia."

"I couldn't do that," Ghareeb protested. "You're the master's lady and I could never call you by your name."

"I'm not your master's lady"—Tia looked at Adir, who sheepishly looked away—"yet." *That man will marry me one day.*

"Very well, Tia," Ghareeb said politely. "Where are you folks headed?"

"Meneres," Tia replied. Adir huffed and shook his head disapprovingly.

"Meneres, huh? May I join you?"

"Absolutely," Tia said. The red-haired man, who appeared to be a decade or so older, would make great company on their journey. He seemed like an interesting specimen for her observations, and robbers and bandits would think twice before attacking three people. *Wouldn't they?* At the very least, Ghareeb would make a good buffer when Adir got into one of his moods.

"I think you meant absolutely not." Adir sounded very annoyed.

"No," Tia said shortly. He really was irritating. "That's not what I meant at all. Besides, Ghareeb has a donkey," she added. "Your earlier complaint was that he didn't have an animal."

"Yea, but it's not a horse," Adir argued.

"No. But it's something he can ride to keep up with us."

Adir's nostrils couldn't flare any wider. Turning to Ghareeb, he barked, "Where did you get the donkey?"

"From a friend," Ghareeb replied, though he wouldn't meet Adir's eyes when he said it.

"We'll be galloping quite a bit," Adir said, looking steadily at Tia, "and a donkey cannot keep up with a galloping horse."

Tia didn't know how to respond to that. Sure, a horse was certainly faster than a donkey, but she didn't think that they'd be galloping all the way to Meneres. They hadn't galloped so far. But she didn't know for certain. Like most folk, she'd never owned a horse or a donkey; it was far too expensive to feed and shelter a person, let alone an animal.

To her relief, Ghareeb chimed in. "Master," he said, reverence apparent in his voice and posture, "Meneres is a few days' ride away, and it would be inadvisable to work your horses too hard. You don't want them dying from exhaustion."

Adir scowled for a long moment. "Fine!" he said finally. "You can go with us, but I need your word that you'll not reveal where we're headed to anyone. Better yet, just let me do the talking!"

Ghareeb looked perplexed, but nodded. "As the Gods as my witness, I give you my word, master."

Adir nodded, though he seemed far from satisfied.

The trio continued riding west as the sun stood directly overhead. Tia was grateful for the large trees that lined either side of the road and provided a tunnel of shade, letting in only slits of sunlight through the latticework of leaves.

"Where are you from, Ghareeb?" Tia asked. "I don't think I have ever heard an accent like yours before. Though, truth be told, I've only heard one accent all my life."

Ghareeb smiled. "Well, my lady," he began, then immediately corrected himself, "I mean, Tia. I am from all over and from nowhere."

That was an interesting way of putting it, Tia thought. "What do you mean?"

"You see, I was born in Peleria," Ghareeb said, "but spent a long while in Cayan. My accent is a mix of the two."

Peleria. Cayan. Faraway lands that Tia knew only through rumors and stories. "You're a long ways from home," she said, then realized that she might never see her home again.

"Ya and no," Ghareeb said. "For me, home is not really a place." He was silent for a moment, his eyes unfocused. "It is all in your mind. If you believe that where you are is home, then you are home."

Tia grew confused. "I'm not sure I understand. Marafel will always be home to me." Adir shot her an angry look but said nothing.

Ghareeb smiled warmly. "For a lord, his house and lands are home. It is one place. But for a traveler like me, anywhere can be home, even the road." Tia found herself nodding and feeling oddly better about her current situation. "Now, do you mind if I ask you a question?" Ghareeb asked.

"Not at all," Tia replied. "In fact, the more we converse the easier our journey will be."

"That is very true." Ghareeb nodded. "Anyways, I mean no offense, but you are not one of the Faithful, are you?"

"No," Tia said. "I am not an Annadi."

"I thought so," Ghareeb said, snapping his fingers. "You said *thank you* when I greeted you in the Annadi fashion."

The appropriate Annadi response to Ghareeb's greeting of 'May the Gods favor you' would have been 'And you as well.' Or something along those lines. However, she'd never used the proper responses to Annadi greetings because they weren't her greetings.

"It doesn't matter to me, of course," Ghareeb added hurriedly. "I was born and raised in Peleria, where someone's faith or no faith was their business alone, as long as they kept it within the walls of their home."

"I wish that's how it was in Naven," Tia admitted. Though she'd just met this man, his demeanor had a sense of familiar comfort. "There were only a handful of families in Marafel that were not Annadi. And though the Faithful were friendly and neighborly enough, we Faithless never quite felt like we belonged. Peleria sounds like a place I could see myself living in."

Ghareeb nodded as if he understood exactly what Tia was saying. "Peleria is a great land, though it is not without its faults. However, Tia, I must say that Naven is not that bad. It is certainly not Cayan. There, if they find out that you are Faithless, you are pretty much shunned from society. I have seen Cayani stand by and watch someone's house burn down, though they could have helped. But they didn't just because those that lived in that house were Faithless."

"That's awful," Tia said. How could someone turn a blind eye to someone else's calamities? "And all that in the name of the Gods. And that's if they even exist."

"You don't think the Gods exist?" Adir asked out of nowhere. She'd almost forgotten that he was with them.

"Not exactly," Tia admitted. "Truth be told, I'm not sure."

"And you're fine with not knowing?"

"Yea, I don't see the point in agonizing over something I know I can never know," Tia said, poking fun at Adir's tendency to brood, though he didn't seem to notice.

"You know," Ghareeb said, "there was a Pelerian philosopher who believed that he had proof the Gods do not exist."

"Really?" Adir turned in his saddle to look at him.

Ghareeb nodded. "Well, according to Erogat, everything we know of is created. Trees create leaves and fruits, animals create or birth young ones. And as we Annadi know, the Word of the Gods itself says that the Gods created us to begin with." He paused exchanging thoughtful looks with her and Adir. "So," he continued, "if everything is created, then that means that the Gods must have been created too. And being created goes against what it is to be a God."

"But the Gods have always existed," Adir said.

"We, the Faithful, believe that," Ghareeb said, "but even the Word does not specifically mention that the Gods have always been."

Adir's curiosity seemed to turn pensive as he swayed on Veyka's saddle. Then he shook his head. "It seems like a pretty weak argument to me."

"I agree, master," Ghareeb said, smiling. "As one of the Faithful, I believe that the Gods exist. But I also think that Tia is right. We will never truly know."

Tia smiled at Ghareeb's affirmation. Having Ghareeb join them seemed to be working out quite well.

Shielding his eyes, Ghareeb looked up at the sky. "It is way past noon!" he exclaimed. "I should have had lunch ready for us." Before Tia could say that they had some food in their packs, Ghareeb leapt off his donkey and handed her the reins. "I will not be gone too long," he said over his shoulder as he disappeared through the trees by the roadside.

"We should just leave right now," Adir said, a determined look on his face.

"I'm not going to leave him behind," Tia responded firmly, then added, "again."

Adir threw Tia a disapproving look. "I don't want to risk you telling him more than you already have." His voice was as sour as the expression on his face.

Tia's annoyance matured into a thorny anger. She'd had enough of his condescension. "I'll tell him what I please," she said. "I don't remember promising to obey your every command when I agreed to accompany you to Meneres." She held his gaze.

At first, Adir's silence gave Tia a sense of victory that filled her with a smug confidence. But as the silence drew longer, her insecurities began to creep in. Just a slow trickle barely enough to notice at first, but soon she found herself wracked with worry. Had she been too harsh on him? Was he considering leaving her behind like he wanted to do to Ghareeb? No, he'd promised he wouldn't do that. But then again, he had wandered off in Nagra, leaving her alone.

"Fine!" Adir said finally. A warm relief flooded into Tia, washing away her apprehension. "We'll wait for him," he added. "So far, he's been harmless, I suppose, if you don't include his chatter."

Tia smiled. "It's entertaining. And you seemed quite interested." Adir simply nodded his head.

A nearby rustle in the underbrush drew her attention to where Ghareeb had disappeared into the woods. A few short moments later, the red-haired man walked out from the trees holding two dead rabbits, one of which was fairly large.

Tia glanced at Adir, whose eyebrows were raised so high in surprise that they almost disappeared into his hair. She herself was astonished that Ghareeb had managed to catch two rabbits in such a short time. "That's impressively fast!" she exclaimed.

"Thank you," Ghareeb said. "When you've lived as long as I have, you learn a few tricks. And besides, I had to be quick as the master must certainly be hungry." He looked at Adir. "I hope you are pleased, master. Shall we rest and roast these?" He held up the rabbits. "I think I have some salt and red chilies," he added.

Adir gave Ghareeb a stern look that gradually lost its intensity. "Yea, let's take a break for lunch," he said finally. "But only if you promise me one other thing, Ghareeb."

"What is that, master?"

"Call me Adir."

Chapter Sixteen

Arvan knocked on the door and waited. A few moments later, he heard the shuffling of feet from inside. The door opened a crack; it was barred from opening completely by a door chain. Morena's brown eyes peered through.

"Akka?" Morena asked, sounding surprised. He didn't often visit his daughter at her home.

"Hello, Morena," Arvan said. "May the Gods favor you. May I come in?"

"You as well," Morena replied, then she shut the door. Momentarily, Arvan heard the rasp of the door chain sliding and the door swung open. Morena stood in the doorway in a light yellow dress. "What is it?" she asked without inviting him in.

"Have you seen Adir?"

"No," Morena replied slowly. "What's going on? Is he in more trouble?"

"Truth be told," Arvan said, fervently hoping Adir hadn't gotten himself killed, "I don't know. He hasn't been home for a day and a half."

At first, Morena looked puzzled, but then her expression grew dark. "Gods save me! A day and a half? And you are only telling me now? Why didn't you come any earlier?" Panic laced her voice.

Arvan shook his head. "Adir is a grown man. Old enough to do as he chooses. I didn't think anything of it when he didn't come home the night before last. But when no one at the farmhouse had seen him yesterday, I went to the Marandas and spoke to Rein. He hasn't seen Adir since the hearing."

"Why wouldn't he come home?" Morena asked, squinting suspiciously at Arvan. She was quite aware of his relationship with Adir.

"I don't know," Arvan answered, though that was far from the truth. He strongly suspected that Adir's absence was related to the harsh exchange they had after the hearing. However, mentioning it to Morena would only worsen his already ruined relationship with his daughter. "You know how he can get sometimes," he added.

During that *exchange*, Adir had said some hurtful things, no matter how untrue. Though, Arvan admitted, he'd once entertained that very notion—that Malia had indeed left him. Hearing it from Adir had been unexpected, ripping open old wounds.

Morena nodded at that, seeming a bit calmer, but Arvan knew better. No matter the tribulations in her life, Morena was always capable of keeping herself in check. In that way, she was a lot like him. But that commonality wasn't enough to make up for years of not being a true father to her. By the time he'd returned home, Morena was all grown up and betrothed to Laraan. She didn't need her father anymore. Arvan doubted that Morena even considered him her father.

"I'll let Laraan know," Morena said. "He can have some of the Village Watch help search."

"I don't think that's necessary. I'm sure the Village Watch has their hands full dealing with other matters. I have Rein helping me look for Adir. In fact, he's gone to talk to Tia. Hopefully, she'll know where Adir is."

"That's all well and good, but we should get the Watch involved," Morena insisted. "My little brother is missing."

"If you're adamant about it, there's nothing I can do," Arvan said, knowing full well how stubborn Morena could be once she put her mind on something. "But Adir's not so little anymore. The Watch is going to assume he merely left home for greener pastures. Things like this happen quite often. The Watch may assign a constable to look into it because the mayor asked, but one constable can't do much."

"All right," Morena said. "I won't go to the Watch. Yet. But I'm going to tell Laraan. If he decides to go to the Watch, that's up to him."

Arvan nodded. Sure, Morena herself wouldn't go to the Watch; she would keep her word. But she'd cleverly left an opening in the form of her husband—Laraan was wrapped so tightly around her finger that Arvan sometimes got the feeling that Morena was the real mayor of Marafel.

"I better get going," Arvan said. "I told Rein I'd meet him at the Square. Let me know if you hear anything. It was good to see you, daughter."

"May the Gods watch over you, akka," Morena said, a small sympathetic smile touching her lips.

Arvan's heart skipped a beat. It'd been a long while since he'd seen Morena smile at him. "You as well, daughter."

The door shut behind him as Arvan walked to his horse. He swung himself up into the saddle and rode down the tree-shaded dirt street that meandered through the Alameah estates, then turned south onto a road. With the evening sun to his right and a light breeze at his back, he passed by some jute farms, then a few houses till finally he arrived at the Village Square.

Though there were a few more hours of light left, the Square looked sparse. A few people wandered around, buying goods from stalls and handcarts, and some Faithful milled around the Temple. An unusual silence permeated the area. The only real sound was that of Bruca working his hammer—a sound that usually blended in with the Square's ambiance. But right now it rang louder than the Temple bells ever had.

Tamaar's death, Boar's death, and a few unconfirmed rakhor sightings had sucked the life out of Marafel. Folks left their homes only if they absolutely had to, with most seeking shelter before dark. No one had outright asked Arvan about Adir's involvement in Boar's death, but he spotted the furtive glances and hushed whispers when people saw him. Where was that boy?

Ahead, Arvan spotted Ellyn Kalathar standing beside two constables. She was speaking to a group of peculiarly dressed people who were clustered a few yards from the inn. There were maybe a dozen or so of the outlanders, men and women ranging from sprightly squirts to slow seniors.

The outlanders all wore a thick woolen fabric that resembled a large coat that fell all the way to their ankles. However, unlike a coat that was buttoned down the middle, the left side of the garment was wrapped over its right side with a single button holding its upper corner in place. Older folk had broad sashes tied across their waist, while children had cords with tasseled ends. Their boots appeared thick and woolen as well, with upturned toes. Some carried fur-lined hats. Broad curved swords, bows, and a quiver of arrows hung at the hips of a few of the able-bodied—men and women alike. Though he'd been many places during his service, he'd never come across folks dressed such as these. Wherever they were from, it must be a cold place.

As Arvan studied the outlanders, Rein rode up beside him. The young man had an uneasy look to him.

"Master Nathar," Rein said, halting his horse next to Arvan's. Rein fidgeted with the reins and refused to meet Arvan's eyes.

"Spit it out, lad," Arvan said.

"I just spoke with Mistress Ellar." Rein said hesitantly. "She hasn't seen Tia in a day and a half."

Gods save me! "Did she say anything else?"

"Just that the last she knew, Tia had gone to meet Adir." Rein paused. "Do you think they ran off together?" he said slowly.

"That seems plausible," Arvan said. "But you know more about Adir and Tia's relationship. Were they that serious?"

"I know that they love each other," Rein said, "but Adir always said he wasn't ready to marry yet."

Arvan nodded. That certainly sounded like his Adir. His son was foolhardy enough to leave home, especially after their recent disagreement. However, he felt an irrational urge to blame Tia. Had Tia taken advantage of his fight with Adir and convinced Adir to leave home? Maybe. What did the Faithless know about home and family? But, no matter who was to blame, Adir was still gone. How could he have not seen this coming? "Thank you, Rein," he said. "I'll come to you if I need anything else."

"You're welcome, Master Nathar," Rein replied politely, yet a mild sorrow could be heard in his voice. "I'll continue to ask around. They couldn't have got far," Rein said with an optimism all too common in those young of age. "May the Gods watch over you."

"You as well, Rein."

Rein gave a quick nod, then spun his horse about and rode out of the Square.

Arvan knew that there was no point in Rein asking around for his son and Tia. Two people who were determined to leave home and make a new life could prove hard to find. Besides, Adir had made a choice to leave Marafel, and maybe it was time for Arvan to respect that. All he could do was hope that his son would return one day. Abruptly, he felt an overwhelming sense of loss overcome him, threatening to wrack him with deep sobs. He steeled himself and nudged his horse south toward the farmhouse, where he could deal with his emotions more privately.

As Arvan passed the Rainbow Inn to his left, he glanced over at Ellyn. She looked at him and smiled. He smiled back as he continued riding, but stopped reluctantly when Ellyn began walking toward him. He had a lot on his mind and wasn't quite in the mood for a conversation.

"May the Gods favor you, Arvan," she said as she approached. She wore a white dress and dangling earrings, her black hair flowing freely behind her. She was a beautiful woman.

"And you as well, Ellyn." Arvan gestured to the group of outlanders. "Who were you just talking to?" he asked, trying to focus his mind on anything but Adir.

Ellyn turned her gaze to the group. "They're Kheryne Khuun."

"Kheryne!" Arvan was shocked. "What are those savages doing here? They are nothing but trouble."

"I don't think so," Ellyn replied. "They're not here to cause trouble."

"Are you sure about that?" It was hard to look past the Kheryne's reputation.

Ellyn nodded in response.

Arvan wasn't convinced however. "It wouldn't hurt to be careful. They should be kept under guard."

"The Council already has that under control. They'll be kept under watch till we figure out what to do with them."

"When did they get here?"

"Early this morning. A group of Watchmen found them on one of their patrols of the foothills. They were then escorted to the Village Watch and the Council was notified. But don't you worry yourself about it. You're not mayor anymore." She gave him a teasing smile.

"That's true enough," Arvan said, her smile blossoming a pleasant flutter in his chest and causing him to loosen up a bit. However, letting his guard down immediately brought back that overwhelming sense of loss. "Anyways, I better get going," he said, steeling himself once again.

"O, all right," Ellyn said. She furrowed her brow. "You're looking very gaunt, Arvan. Have you been ill?"

"No," Arvan replied, "just … busy."

"Well, you should come over sometime and I'll cook you dinner," Ellyn said, smiling. "They say I'm a pretty good cook."

"Thank you, but I couldn't possibly trouble you like that," Arvan said. "I promise to take better care of myself."

"All right. But I'd still like to cook you dinner one night."

"I couldn't."

"It's no trouble."

"But—"

"Arvan!"

Ellyn's persistence wore Arvan down. "All right," he said, resigned. "You can cook me dinner one night."

"Good," Ellyn said, looking pleased. "It'll be one of the best dinners you've had," she added.

"I'm looking forward to it," Arvan said. "May the Gods favor you, Ellyn."

"You as well, Arvan." With that, Ellyn turned and walked back to where the Kheryne congregated.

Arvan nudged his horse and headed home. Ellyn was a wonderful woman and dinner with her would be a pleasant experience. However, right now, he needed to deal with the loss of his son. *First Malia. Now Adir.* The Gods were playing a cruel joke on him.

Chapter Seventeen

"I do not care what Lord Malasi thinks," Ekren said, looking straight into Ferrith's eyes, livid. "As far as I am concerned his son should consider himself fortunate to have walked away alive."

"Yes, Lady Regent"—Ferrith smiled ingratiatingly—"but Lord Malasi is very powerful. Their family's support is of some import to your Regency. And one day, his son Mertca will inherit that power. Do you not think it would be wise to make a peace offering"—he gestured respectfully toward Dina—"for the sake of your daughter's Regency?"

Though Ferrith had made a fair point, Ekren found it difficult to believe that the loss of Malasi's support would upend her rightful Regency. "I am not worried, Ferrith," she said, calming herself as she regarded her daughter sitting in a chair opposite her, glowing in the afternoon sun. "The citizens love the Arinols, and Dina most of all. Our family has served as Regent of the most powerful nation for over a century now. Houses have left us before, but we've endured."

"Yes, Lady Regent, but would it not be beneficial to ensure that there is a peaceful transition of power from you to your daughter? Especially after all the hardships you had to endure to secure your own Regency?"

"I have already done that, Ferrith. None of the powerful houses oppose a woman in the Regent's Chair. Those days are far behind us."

Ferrith was persistent. "They may not today, but what will happen after you are gone? I doubt Lord Malasi will let this go. He will try to gain support from other houses to upend the Arinol Regency."

"If that day comes, Ferrith, Dina will know how to handle it. She is a very capable young woman."

"Very well, Lady Regent," Ferrith said, face impassive, though his voice betrayed his true sentiment.

A knock at the door drew Ekren's attention. "Enter."

The door opened to let in a lean young man in a scout's uniform. Sweating from head to toe from the late spring humidity, he stood at attention next to Dina's chair, eyes straight ahead. He stomped his foot and said, "Lady Regent!"

"What news do you have, soldier?" Ekren asked.

"Lady Regent," the young man said, meeting her eyes, "Captain Altrana sent me with instructions to deliver this message." He paused, then as if speaking from memory, continued. "A raid at Ghatirodh by Sorcha Camran weakened King Dooghlas's forces enough that they were forced to retreat. However, the rebel leader is currently unaware that the region is unguarded." He paused once more. "That's all, m'lady."

"Thank you, soldier," Ekren said. "Now go get some food and rest. You must be weary from your travel."

"I am, m'lady, but if you need me to ride back with a message this moment, I will," the scout said emphatically.

Ekren could not help but smile at the duty and loyalty displayed by her scout. If Lord Malasi—or anyone else for that matter—tried to wrest the Regency from Dina, Ekren was sure her soldiers would die before they let that happen. "You have done well, soldier. Now I order you to go get some rest."

The scout stomped his foot in salute, swiveled on a heel, and exited the room.

"That message couldn't have been timed better," Ferrith said.

Ekren stood, nodding, then walked over to a set of drawers and pulled one open. Inside were several long thick scrolls of paper.

Rummaging through them, she read the names at the edges of the scrolls. Finally she found the one she was looking for: Ghatirodh, the region that was at the confluence of Ostarium, Phucao, and Herraland, the same region that was now unguarded by the Herran forces. It was time to extract payment for the debt the Herrans owed the Ostarks.

Ekren carried the map back to her desk. "Dina, do you mind clearing some space?"

Unfurling the map, Ekren weighted it down with a couple of books, then pointed at a heavily wooded, hilly area. "That is Ghatirodh," she said. She turned to her daughter. "What do you see?"

"It appears to be a very strategic region," Dina said after studying the map for a few moments. "Looks like all trade from Herraland travels through this region," she added, pointing to the only major road that led west from Herraland.

"It is also a rich source of copper and iron with a staggering amount of working mines," Ferrith interjected.

"What in the world made King Dooghlas pull his troops out of there?" Dina asked. "If I am reading these contour lines correctly, the whole region sits in a valley that appears very defensible. Even with a small force."

"You are right, Dina," Ekren said. "Kierand must be desperate if he gave up that region. And since the rebels do not know that Kierand has pulled out, it is the perfect time to *lend our aid* to our Herran neighbors."

Ferrith nodded in understanding, but Dina furrowed her brow. "What do you mean? Are we to send some of our forces to reinforce Ghatirodh for the Herrans?"

"Yes," Ekren replied, "but not for the Herrans. We are going to annex Ghatirodh."

"So, we go in and never leave?"

"In a manner of speaking," Ekren replied. "The local folk of Ghatirodh—or anywhere for that matter—do not care who rules them as long as they have peace and stability. Without the protection of the Herran forces, Ghatirodh will fall into chaos. That means unsafe roads, which means travel and trade become hard. And when trade dwindles, people go hungry and die. Do you see what I intend?"

Dina nodded. "The folks in Ghatirodh will blame Kierand for the hard times that befall them."

"Exactly!" Ekren said. Dina's mind was well suited for Regency. "But we will go in there and give them the stability they need. We will tell Kierand that our goal is to hold Ghatirodh for him while he strengthens his forces. But by the time that happens, the local folk will want Ostark rule over Kierand's and they will beg for us to stay."

"And that is how you invade bloodlessly," Ferrith said. "It is a good plan."

"Thank you, Ferrith," Ekren said with satisfaction. Though she did not need Ferrith's approval for matters of state, she did appreciate it. After her husband's death, it was this bony old man who had taught her the subtle intricacies of politics. And much more.

"What if the rebels get to Ghatirodh before us?" Dina asked.

"That is a possibility," Ekren admitted. "We'll just have to get there quicker." She looked down at the map, trying to work out the logistics in her head. "Dina," she said, glancing up at her daughter, "what do you think our force's composition should be?"

Dina looked at the map. "Where are you planning on setting up?"

"Around here." Ekren pointed to an area a few miles from the road, lined by hills to the southeast and forests to the north.

Dina studied the map for a long moment. "An archer-heavy force would be the most efficient." Pointing at some contour lines, she said, "You can take advantage of the high ground here." Then she moved her finger toward a tree-lined border. "You could line a contingent of mixed cavalry here to flank any ground assaults that get close, and have a few ranks of swords as well."

Abruptly, Ekren heard a faint buzz, like a distant hovering fly. Annoyed, she looked at Ferrith, who nervously shifted the armlet on his forearm.

Dina didn't seem to notice the buzz and continued poring over the map. "You could also take a few cannons with you and place them in these spots." She pointed at a few locations, all of which would defend vital spots. "How does that sound to you, mara?"

"You are as clever as any seasoned general, Heiress Regent," Ferrith said before Ekren could answer. "In a few years, none will be your match," he added, then gave Ekren a quick glance.

Ekren caught something in that glance. Something urgent. "I agree with Ferrith," she said, peeling her eyes away from her Vice Regent. "I will take your advice into consideration, daughter. Now, would you mind excusing us?"

Dina looked up at Ekren, puzzled. Clearly, she hadn't expected to be asked to leave. "All right, mara," she said, rising. She walked gracefully to Ekren and kissed her on the cheek. "May the Gods keep you safe," she said.

Ekren watched Dina leave. She found it odd that her daughter had not put up much of a fight; usually she hated being asked to leave.

When the door shut and the guards thumped their spears, Ekren turned to her Vice Regent. "Your armlet should not have gone off right now," she said, letting out her annoyance. "This is why we gave them specific times to call on us. Thankfully, Dina was preoccupied and did not take notice."

Ferrith simply shrugged. He walked over to the door and bolted it from the inside. Shaking her head, Ekren stood and moved to one of the alcoves in the corner of the room. Ferrith stepped in beside her, then stepped on two tiles on the circumference of the alcove's floor.

The floor began to shimmer with a rainbow-hued haze. The haze rose up from the floor, creeping up Ekren's feet, then knees, then waist, then chest, till she was completely covered in it, unable to see or hear anything. Momentarily, the haze began to descend as vision and hearing returned.

Ekren looked into a large room of brown stone. A brown marble desk and a chair stood in front of a far wall. On the opposite wall was a thick wooden door. This room was a stark contrast to her study—no windows, no breeze, no sunlight, though she did not need windows to tell the time. She knew it would be close to midnight. However, the room was well lit by two lumenotes that floated on opposite walls.

Ekren walked over to the imposing desk, then grabbed her brown robe from a peg and donned it over her tunic and salwar. She hated having to do that, as the multiple layers of clothing made her feel uncomfortably warm.

Ferrith walked to the door, unlocked it, and stepped out as Ekren seated herself behind the desk. Shortly, Ferrith returned with a veiled operative clad in black, two swords strapped to his back and a dagger at each hip.

"Khasir," the operative said, dropping to one knee and resting his forehead on his right fist. His Phucak accent was unmistakable—it sounded as if he were speaking through a mouthful of thick molasses.

"Rise, operative," Ekren said. "What is your name?"

"Uaqui, Khasir," the man said, standing. He unveiled. A thick white scar ran down from his left eyebrow to the cheekbone. His nose was crooked from multiple breaks.

"What was so urgent that you had me summoned at this hour?" Ekren asked in a practiced, harsh tone.

Uaqui stood his ground, unfazed. "I've found a venna, Khasir," he said flatly.

Ekren felt the blood drain from her face. She turned to Ferrith who looked as if he had just seen a ghost. "Are you sure?" she asked, looking back at the operative. A venna had not been found in over two centuries.

"Yes, Khasir," Uaqui said. "I saw the rainbow glow myself and also had it confirmed by a witness." He paused. "The witness has been dealt with."

"Where did you find it?" Ekren asked.

"In a small town in Naven, some four days ago."

Ekren calmly nodded in response, but her heart and mind were anything but calm. Simply put, venna spelled destruction. Though she had not seen the destruction first-hand, she had read about them extensively in the vast archives here at Mount Schinay. With effort, Ekren brought her thoughts under control, but her heart thumped louder. The creature had to be killed. But not before it served its purpose. "Does it know what it is?" she asked.

"I don't know, Khasir," Uaqui answered.

"Take a few other operatives and anything else you need with you, Uaqui," Ekren ordered. "Track this vile creature down and bring it back. Alive!"

"As you command, Khasir." Uaqui saluted, dropping to one knee, fist to forehead. When he rose, Ferrith escorted him to the door and shut it behind him.

"What do you make of this?" Ekren asked.

"What is there to make of, Khasir?" Ferrith said. "Figuring such things is beyond us. We merely heed Daroon's Warning and keep the Staff safe."

Ekren nodded ascent. "For humanity's survival."

PART III
MODERATO

Chapter Eighteen

"There!" Ghareeb said, pointing. "The eastern wall!"

Adir paused his conversation with Tia and looked up. Some distance ahead rose a tall, gleaming wall that cast a long shadow against the setting rays of the sun. Seemingly built of one solid slab of stone, the wall spanned a great distance to either side of a large wooden gate built into it.

"What are those?" Adir asked, pointing at black dots that appeared at intervals along the top of the wall.

Ghareeb squinted. "Cannons. The walls all around the city have cannon housings built into them."

"Ah." Adir looked at the red-bearded man. Ghareeb had proven to be quite resourceful, despite his initial misgivings. Aside from his talent for hunting meals, Ghareeb was a storehouse of knowledge. He knew how far they could travel in a day to make it to outposts for the night, or when they should seek shelter from approaching rain. Furthermore, the man who was bowing and scraping not five days ago had suddenly transformed into someone bold and confident; a stark change that Adir found utterly odd. Not only that, since Ghareeb had joined them, Tia's mood had changed for the better. Those two had enjoyed chatting about all manner of things throughout their journey, much to his dismay, as he'd wanted to be as inconspicuous as possible. Tia's roiling laughter upon hearing funny stories from Ghareeb hadn't much aided in that. Though Tia not being sour toward him was a plus.

That was not to say that all Ghareeb spoke of was jokes and hilarity. He had quite a rambling philosophical side as well—one that he attributed to his previous Cayani employer. Apparently, the old Cayani man taught Ghareeb to read using various books, most of which dealt with philosophy. During one of his rambling monologues, Ghareeb had spoken of a philosopher who claimed that the Gods had created man with a purpose, but given humanity's fleeting memory, folk had forgotten what that purpose was.

Unbidden, two memories stirred in Adir. One of the night when Boar had strangled him and the other when he'd saved Ghareeb—the two nights he'd seen a rainbow haze. The memories shifted in and out of each other, coalescing into one yet staying distinct. *Was I the source of the haze?* he thought for a fleeting moment. No, that was preposterous! His mind had been addled on both nights, be it from lack of air or abundance of drink.

Ghareeb fell back with his donkey, and the three rode side by side as they passed through the large recessed gate. Two sentries posted there gave them long, studying looks but didn't stop them from entering. Adir returned their looks in kind.

"There is a decent inn closer to the middle of the city," Ghareeb said. "I will escort you two there."

Adir peeled his eyes away from the sentries and caught sight of the city of Meneres. Now it was he who gaped at the city as Tia had back in Nagra.

Adir had thought that Meneres would be like Nagra, just bigger. It certainly was bigger, but it was much more than that. Tall buildings with perfectly straight lines bordered the street they were on. The care and attention that had been given to the construction of each structure was evident even in the doors and windows, all designed precisely. The street itself was wide, filled with people, horses, and carts. However, it didn't feel crowded as in Nagra. Horses and carts rode in the center section of the street, edged by evenly spaced trees, while pedestrians walked on the sides. People were dressed in brightly colored and well-laundered clothing. It seemed like everyone in Meneres was quite prosperous.

"Where are all the shops and hawkers?" Tia asked, her eyes darting every which way.

"I do not think I have ever seen a hawker in Meneres," Ghareeb responded, "but there are plenty of shops in the two shopping districts."

"What's a district?" Tia asked with furrowed brows.

"It is a part of a city that has its own characteristic," Ghareeb said.

"O, like the Village Square in Marafel?"

"Ya, something like that."

Adir turned to the older man. "Now that we're in Meneres, Ghareeb, what are your plans?"

Ghareeb fidgeted with his reins. "Truth be told, Adir," he began, "I do not have any plans. I just needed to get out of Nagra."

Adir nodded. He understood what that was like. He himself was running away from somewhere. And someone. "You could stay with us if you wish," he found himself saying. Over the course of their journey he'd started to feel a certain kinship with Ghareeb.

Ghareeb's face lit up with a smile. "O, thank you, Adir! I would love to stay with you two." He paused, eyeing them with an amused smile. "Just for a little while though," he added with a burst of laughter. "I do not want to come between you two."

Adir chuckled, though he felt a little indignant. "Now where's that inn?"

Ghareeb led them through the wide streets of the capital. As they rode their animals on the middle cart lane, they passed several fine buildings and statues of Naven heroes. They passed by apothecaries, bakeries, cheese houses, and taverns. They saw a library and an amphitheater—the amphitheater had a fountain at its entrance, spraying water into the air. He'd never seen such a thing before. From time to time, when he snapped out of his reverie, he glanced at Tia who was staring at everything in her field of vision with a wondrous curiosity.

Eventually, weary and exhausted, they made it to the Drink and Dreams. The inn didn't look like any inn Adir had ever seen before.

With clean white plastered walls, the three-story building was a long structure with three rows of curtained windows lining its sides.

Two grooms in matching uniforms relieved them of their rides and packs. They were told to go through two sets of doors and get their room arranged by the receptionist. Their effects would be sent to their room.

Adir dismounted and grabbed his staff off Veyka. Followed by Tia and Ghareeb, he led the way through the first set of doors into an entry chamber, then walked through the second set of doors into a spacious room containing a large table. The room held a quiet elegance. Two shaded chandeliers hung from the ceiling, bathing the room in soft yellow candlelight. Seated behind the table were two attractive women. Careful not to stare, lest Tia misconstrue, he fixed his sight right between the two women and approached the table.

"Welcome to the Drink and Dreams," one of them said in a soft, hushed voice. A pleasant smile left deep dimples in her cheeks. "How may I be of service?" The other woman was lost in work, poring over some books.

"We'd like to get a room," Adir said in a similarly hushed voice, not wanting to ruin the ambience of the inn.

"Just one?" the receptionist asked, eyeing Ghareeb and Tia.

"Yea," Adir replied, a little embarrassed at the notion of what this woman would think of renting one room to two men and a woman. *But it's none of her business,* he thought. "A large room, preferably with two beds," he added.

"Very well." The receptionist opened a thick ledger. "How many nights?" she asked, placing one finger on a particular line.

Adir pondered. First, they needed to find jobs, then save enough to hopefully rent a room somewhere in the city. He didn't know how long that would take. "I'm not sure," he said. "At least a month?"

The woman nodded. "We can give you a discounted rate for a room with two beds for the extended stay. But the discount will only apply if you stay the whole month."

"How much per night?" Adir asked

"Fifty crowns a night," she said. "The room has a copper tub for bathing, but the rate doesn't include laundry services or any food and drink you might get from the common room."

Adir pondered for a moment. *For thirty-five nights in a month, at fifty crowns a night …* he'd end up spending a total of seventeen silver scepters and fifty copper crowns. "That sounds reasonable," he said. If the rooms were half as nice as this reception area, fifty crowns a night was a decent bargain.

"You'll have to pay for the whole stay up front."

"Very well." Adir fished out seventeen scepters depicting the Scepter of Naven and fifty crowns, and handed them to the receptionist. That left him with eleven scepters and a few crowns.

"Thank you, sir." The receptionist handed him a key in exchange for the coins. "You'll be in room three-two-zero. It's on the other side of the inn on the third floor." Pointing to a door behind her, she said, "To get to your room, you'll have to go through those doors, cross the courtyard to the other side, and take the stairs to the third floor. It'll be a few minutes before we have the room ready for you, so why don't you folks relax in the common room?"

"We will. Thank you." He turned, expecting to find Tia and Ghareeb behind him, but neither was there. He scanned the room and spotted Ghareeb standing in a doorway, waving him over.

"The common room's through here," he said rather loudly, which earned him unpleasant looks from the receptionists.

Embarrassed, Adir muttered a quick apology then hurried through the door.

The common room was the liveliest Adir had seen so far. Several tables filled the room, with patrons eating, drinking, and conversing. Others sang along as a man and a woman on a raised dais entertained with music and song. The man played a veena as the woman sang 'Don't eye your brother's wife,' while rhythmically rolling her fingers on a round defele producing a triple beat.

"Tia's at the bar," Ghareeb said, pointing.

When Adir took a seat next to her, she met his eyes with a wide smile. "This is exciting!" A giddy laugh escaped her. "The music, the people, the revelry!"

"There's a lot more to this city than this inn," Ghareeb said. "I'll show you around."

"Before we spend all our time sightseeing, we need to find jobs," Adir chimed in. "I just paid the receptionists almost eighteen scepters for our stay."

"I can pay you my share," Ghareeb said, "though I don't have much on me right now."

"We'll deal with that when the time comes," Adir said, not really expecting Ghareeb to pay much. "But for now, do you think you can find us jobs? You know a lot more about this city than Tia or me."

"We could just ask the bartender," Ghareeb said matter-of-factly.

"A bartender? Really? Why would a bartender of all people know about jobs?"

Just as Adir finished speaking, a bartender came up to them. "What'll you be having?" he asked.

"Three wheat ales." Adir hoped the man hadn't heard what he'd said. He didn't want to offend anyone unnecessarily.

"I'll bring them right up," the bartender replied. He grabbed three mugs from a shelf then poured wheat ale into each from a tapped wooden keg. "Here you go," he said, placing a mug in front of each of them.

"Thank you," Adir said, relieved. He took a sip.

Ghareeb nudged Adir. "Ask him if he knows of any jobs."

"Fine," Adir said, exasperated. "I guess it wouldn't hurt to ask." He took another sip. "Excuse me," he said to the bartender, "but would you happen to know if there are any jobs in the city for folks like us?" He gestured at the three of them.

"Hmmm ..." The bartender tapped his lip and stared off for a moment. "Ah, yea. I heard a few days ago that Lord Preschad's steward was looking for a few extra hands to help out around the manor. Not sure if they found anyone yet."

Adir tossed a quick glance at Ghareeb who was trying to hide a smug smile behind his mug. "I'll do that," Adir said, then realized he had no idea who Lord Preschad was or where his manor was located. "How can I get to the manor?"

"It's pretty simple," the bartender said, wiping some dampness off his bar. "Follow the east wall north, then take the path that goes up the hill to the Palace district. Once you get there, one of the sentries can point the way."

"Thank you," Adir said. "Your help is much appreciated." The bartender nodded then busied himself with another patron.

Ghareeb held up his mug. "To a new city, new prospects, and good friends!"

Chapter Nineteen

Adir walked up the narrow servant's staircase, bumping along its sides as he maneuvered an awkwardly large wicker laundry basket balanced against his hip. As if the annoyance of stubbing his knuckles on the railing or scraping his elbows against the wall weren't enough, he had to endure all that wearing a ridiculous black smock!

Stop complaining, Tia's voice said in his head. She'd been glad that all three of them had found work at Lord Preschad's manor. Gods' favor, Master Steward hadn't found any *reliable help*. Of course, Tia had nothing to complain about—she was to work as a serving maid. Even Ghareeb had been assigned a more enjoyable job in the stables. Adir, however, was told to help with the laundry—and wear a smock. Ghareeb and Tia would be breathless from laughter if they saw him in this ridiculous garb.

Stepping onto the second floor landing, Adir opened the door and clumsily maneuvered through, entering a long, windowed hallway. Recessed into the wall opposite the windows were doors to guests' quarters. His eyes wandered down the length of the hallway identifying dirty clothes—expensive dirty clothes—piled to the side of some doors. A few piles were neatly stacked, but most seemed to have been tossed out of the room as if discarded. He'd always heard that nobles had no regard for the value of things, and that certainly seemed to be true.

Just pick up the clothes outside the door, Dhara, the laundress, had said. Don't knock on any doors. We don't want you disturbing the guests. If you run into any of them, put your head down and back away toward a wall. It's best to stay out of their way. You don't want to land your ass in prison, do you? Adir walked down the hallway, collecting the piles and depositing them into his basket.

Tia is right. I shouldn't be complaining. He was away from Marafel, away from Syfis, and away from his father. He was starting his own life and was going to live it in his own way. Though collecting laundry wasn't what he had in mind when he'd thought of work, but for now it was income. He could always find something better later. What would he do though? Dairy farming again? Did Meneres even have a dairy industry? It must, as they did pass by a few cheese houses on their way to the inn. However, the thought of returning to his previous way of life didn't feel right. It was time to let go of the past, let go of all the anguish and turmoil he'd endured while in Marafel.

As Adir passed an open door, he reflexively looked inside and saw a woman with brown hair sorting through her clothes. The woman looked up, meeting his eyes, and Adir felt his lips curve upward. Abruptly, he remembered Dhara's words of caution. Immediately lowering his gaze to the floor, Adir hurriedly walked away from the door, hoping that the woman hadn't noticed him smiling at her.

"You! Launderer!" the woman called out.

Gods save me! I can't seem to stay out of trouble! Why in the world had he shown his teeth to her? Sighing deeply, Adir walked back, determined to adhere to the proprieties and not get tossed in prison. As he turned into the doorway, eyes on the floor per Dhara's instructions, he felt something soft slam into his face. He caught it before it fell to the ground.

"Does that smell dirty to you?" The woman had a lilting accent.

Adir looked at what he held in his hand. A stocking. Did she really expect him to smell her dirty stocking? But he figured he had to smell it if he were to stay out of trouble. Holding the silky material up to his nose, he took a whiff. Surprisingly, it didn't smell. "No, my lady," he said, looking up. "It doesn't smell dirty."

That was when Adir really saw the woman who stood before him. His breath caught somewhere in his throat. Garbed in a dress of red and green that accentuated the curves of her hips, she had straight brown hair that fell to below her shoulders. Her hair framed an oval face that was fair and stunning and kind. With eyes a mesmerizing hazel of pale brown and sparkling green, and perfectly shaped, rose-pink lips, this woman gripped his attention so fully that Adir was incapable of looking away. Among the Gods, Menera held the mantle of the most beautiful, but this woman would put Menera's beauty to shame.

"Well, good," she said. "I do not have any laundry for you then. You may leave."

At first, Adir didn't quite hear what she'd said, still suffering as he was from the lingering effects of his enthrallment. Then reality slowly crept in. He'd walked into this room expecting to be punished for his breach of the proprieties, but that didn't seem to be the case. A bit emboldened by relief, Adir asked as coolly as he could, "Where are you from, my lady?"

The woman's eyes narrowed, but her annoyed expression only served to make her more beautiful. She considered him for a moment, then a small smile touched the edges of her perfect mouth. "I am from Cayan," she said. "Do you know where that is?"

"Somewhere there?" Adir said uncertainly, pointing west. "That's all I know," he admitted. "What are you doing in Meneres, my lady?"

"You are quite forward, aren't you?"

"I'm sorry, my lady," Adir said, suddenly fully aware of what he was doing. He was such an ass. "I meant no offense," he added hurriedly.

The Cayani noblewoman smiled. "It is all right. It is nice to talk to someone who is not a stuffy noble. Akka has some matters to attend to with Lord Preschad and King Taschari, and he brought me along."

"Your father must be a very important man to gain an audience with the king," Adir said, thoroughly impressed. Maybe he could find a job at court. Maybe he'd become a noble himself.

It's time to give up on childish fancies, he heard his father say in his head.

The woman nodded. "He is a close friend of the muslar."

"What's a muslar?" He'd never heard that word before.

"That's what we call our king in Cayan," she said. "He's more than just a king though. His right to rule is blessed by the Miakos of the Sanctum of the Seven." She paused and tilted her head to one side. "You should come visit Cayan some time," she said, nodding. "It is a wonderful place."

Adir laughed. "First, I need to see Meneres and some more of Naven before I can go to Cayan," he said.

"O." She delicately wrinkled her brow. "You have not seen much of this city? Haven't you lived here all your life?"

Adir hesitated. "Not quite, my lady. I grew up in a small village called Marafel. It's a few days' ride to the east. I came to Meneres looking for work, and since I arrived, I haven't had a free moment to explore the city." That was the truth, though he may have been vague about the timeline. *Why am I telling her any of this?*

"Meneres is a beautiful city," the noblewoman said. "It is worth finding a free moment." A warm smile touched her eyes.

"Habya," a soft male voice called from outside.

Shortly, an older man with a balding head, wearing a long buttoned shirt and pants, strode into the room. His attire was similar in style to that of Ghareeb's, except this man's clothing was worth more than all the money Adir had ever seen in his life.

The man bumped his shoulder on the doorframe and stumbled forward a couple of steps before catching himself. He stood erect then brushed off his clothes as if they'd somehow been dirtied by the doorframe. Tossing Adir a sharp look, the older man turned toward the noblewoman. "Habya," he chided. "Do not speak to the servants. They are not much better than mopra."

Habya folded her arms across her chest. "We speak to some mopra," she said.

The look on Habya's face pulled on something in Adir, filling him with a strong urge to protect her. "I was the one who started speaking to her, my lord," Adir lied.

The older man turned his gaze onto Adir and squinted. "Did I give you leave to speak?" he spat.

Adir's heart began to race. He was getting quite adept at gaining the ire of those around him. "No, my lord," he said, heeding Dhara's advice and dropping his gaze to the floor.

"Had my daughter given you leave to speak?"

Gods save me! This man is Habya's father and is a close friend of the Cayani king! "No, my lord," Adir answered fearfully. He'd really stepped in a pile of dung this time.

"Then why did you open your mouth?" the nobleman asked, voice dripping with disdain.

"I'm sorry, my lord," Adir said hurriedly. "I meant no offense. I … I … was merely inquiring about laundry."

"You do not need to *inquire* about laundry. You only need pick it up and walk away." The nobleman's squinted eyes were smoldering angrily. "I should have you whipped!"

"I beg your pardon, my lord," a smooth voice interjected. "What seems to be the problem?"

Adir turned and found Master Steward standing in the doorway. The grey-haired man had an air of precise nobility that would put most of the nobles to shame, despite not being one.

"You would do well to keep your help under control," the nobleman said. "This one seems to think he can shoot his mouth off to anyone."

Master Steward gave Adir a stern, scrutinizing look. "My apologies, Lord Si'Pyaara," he said, bowing deeply. "He is one of our newer hires and is unaccustomed to the proprieties. I hope you can show him some mercy."

Lord Si'Pyaara huffed. "Keep him away from here!" he ordered.

"As you wish, my lord," Master Steward acceded. "I shall ensure that this man doesn't cross your path for the rest of your stay. And I apologize for his insolence." Master Steward bowed yet again. "Now, if I may have your leave?" Lord Si'Pyaara gave a curt nod. Turning to Adir, Master Steward said curtly, "Come with me."

Adir followed the old man out into the hallway. They walked

toward the servant's staircase in silence, till they were far enough away from Habya's room.

"First day and you're already causing me trouble," Master Steward said softly, yet the look on his face was harder than stone.

"I'm sorry, Master Steward."

"There you go again! Speaking without permission!" Master Steward scolded. "Are you going to continually create trouble for me?"

"No, Master Steward." Adir wanted to say more but thought it best to keep his mouth shut. Maybe working for a noble wasn't what he was meant to do. But he needed the money.

Master Steward didn't respond immediately. "Punishments are the best lesson," he said after a few moments, gazing down the hallway. "Since you've never worked here before and since this will be your *only* offense, I shall be lenient. But next time ..." he trailed off.

"There will be no next time, Master Steward," Adir said. "I give you my word."

Master Steward seemed to ponder something for a moment, then said, "You will be docked today's pay."

Adir nodded as a sense of relief washed over him. Though he didn't like the idea of not being paid for the day, it was better than losing his job or getting whipped or being thrown in prison. "Thank you, Master Steward. I promise I will be on my best behavior."

"*Expected* behavior," Master Steward corrected. "After what happened, I don't trust your judgment of best behavior. And since Lord Si'Pyaara doesn't want to see you anymore, I'm going to have you work in the stables." He gave Adir a stern look then added very seriously, "Hopefully, you won't offend the horses."

Chapter Twenty

The smell of dung in Lord Preschad's stable wasn't as pungent as the one back at the Nathar farmhouse, though that was to be expected. As soon as a horse relieved itself, a stableman was there to clean it up with shovel, broom, and bucket.

These horses are treated better than most people, Adir thought, pushing a wheelbarrow full of hay from stall to stall as Ghareeb forked some into each. Master Steward had instructed the stable master that Adir was not to have any contact with the nobility, and so Adir was put to work in the back stables. At least he didn't have to wear that ridiculous smock.

After getting back to the inn yesterday, Adir had told Tia and Ghareeb of how he'd been barred from the manor and docked a day's pay. He'd also told them the why of it. He'd expected Tia to be furious and Ghareeb to laugh in his face. However, the exact opposite had happened. Tia, though she'd been upset with him for losing his pay, had let out one of her roiling laughs upon hearing his mishap with the Cayani lord. She warned him that only ill would come of ogling other women, especially noblewomen. Ghareeb, on the other hand, had taken on a serious expression and seemed to want to avoid the topic of Lord Si'Pyaara and Habya.

That reminded Adir of something.

"Ghareeb," he called.

Ghareeb stopped forking hay and looked at him. "Ya?" he said, wiping sweat off his brow.

"Is mopra the Cayani word for servant? Or attendant?" Adir asked. He figured that resourceful Ghareeb would surely know what a mopra was; after all, he'd lived in Cayan for a while.

Ghareeb's face took on the same serious expression as the day before. He scrunched his eyebrows, forming lines of worry across his forehead. "Why do you want to know?" he asked curtly before forking some hay into the stall. Then he rather abruptly signaled for Adir to move on to the next.

"Lord Si'Pyaara spoke of it yesterday," Adir said, confused by Ghareeb's ill temper. Living in Cayan must have been awful based on his reaction every time the Cayani nobles were mentioned. "The way he said it," Adir continued, "made it sound as though he was referring to servants." He paused, recalling the bald man's exact words. "Though what he said was that servants are not much better than mopra."

"Servants in Naven," Ghareeb said slowly, "are not *better* than mopra, but they certainly are treated much better." He didn't yell or shout, yet the cold softness of his voice placed a certain emphasis on his words.

"How so?" Adir asked.

Ghareeb let out a long breath. "If you and I wish to leave the service of Lord Preschad, we are free to do so. We are our own men. But mopra—they are not free. They are considered *unworthy* property. Their cheeks are branded like cattle with the sign of the mopra. To be done with as *true-blooded* Cayani please."

"Aren't the mopra true-blooded Cayani?" Adir asked.

"No." Ghareeb shook his head. "They are born in Cayan, but they are not considered Cayani. They are mopra."

Adir didn't quite understand the difference. Anyone born in Naven was a true-blooded Navenite, be they king or pauper.

The conversation flagged as they moved down a few stalls. Though Ghareeb had answered his questions, Adir couldn't help but think that the man was being reticent. It was usually quite difficult to keep Ghareeb from squawking incessantly, like a parrot. "You mentioned that the Cayani can do what they please to mopra," Adir said, then paused, unsure if he should proceed. "Like what?"

Ghareeb remained silent for a few moments, mechanically performing his job. "Anything that comes to their sick minds," he finally replied. "The lucky mopra are put to work. In the house, in the fields, in slaughterhouses, cleaning gutters. Everywhere really." Then his voice took on a dark tone. "But the unlucky ones ... they can be maimed, hanged, burned alive ... *buried alive.* They know nothing but fear."

"That's horrible!" Adir knew how it felt to be fearful of one's safety. But to live like that all their lives, with no hope of escape, seemed inhumane. "That's just wrong!"

"Ya, it is," Ghareeb said with disgust. "The Cayani are bad folk!"

"Lord Si'Pyaara and his daughter Habya didn't seem like bad people," Adir said, remembering, not for the first time, his pleasant conversation with the brown-haired Cayani noblewoman. "In fact, the lady was quite genial."

Ghareeb forced a chuckle. "She may not seem bad, but a person tends to be a victim of their environment and culture. If it came down to it, I am sure she would act just like every other Cayani."

"Did your previous master treat mopra badly?" Adir asked. "He was a true-blooded Cayani, wasn't he?"

"He was different," Ghareeb said defensively. "He was one of the good ones."

"Ah! Then can't Lord Si'Pyaara and his daughter be different from the rest of the Cayani?"

"Maybe," Ghareeb said, plainly irritated. "Look, all I am saying is that one conversation is not enough to judge someone's character." Ghareeb angrily forked some more hay into the stall, then signaled for Adir to move.

Adir pushed the wheelbarrow forward. The two continued moving down the long stable in silence, forking hay into each occupied stall. Though Adir had come to trust Ghareeb over the previous week, he couldn't help but feel that the red-bearded man's assessment of the Cayani noblewoman was far from the truth.

A short while later, the stable master approached. "You there. Laundry man," he said with a mocking smirk. "Lady Si'Pyaara is here looking for you." He studied Adir. "What did you do now?"

"Nothing," Adir said as the familiar flutter of panic came alive in his gut. "I've been here all morning!"

"Well," the stable master said, "I told her you were busy, but she insisted that you go see her at once. She's at the front entrance. You better get your ass over there now before you get into more trouble." He laughed.

Adir didn't see the humor in the situation, as his mind was trying to determine what he'd done wrong. But he couldn't think of anything. He'd come straight to the stables from the inn and hadn't seen or spoken to anyone all morning except Tia, Ghareeb, and the stable master.

Dropping the wheelbarrow, Adir turned to run, when Ghareeb grabbed his wrist. "Do not do anything to offend her," he warned. "Do what she says and get away as soon as you can."

Adir nodded and took off. There was wisdom in Ghareeb's words. Though he didn't truly believe that Habya was capable of the brutality that Ghareeb attributed to all Cayani, he realized that he didn't want to test it. He barely knew her. And besides, even if Habya were decent, her father might be a whole other matter.

Swinging around some stacked bales of hay, Adir approached the front entrance and spotted Habya. Her mere act of standing still held all the beauty and motion in the world. He ceased sprinting and slowed to a casual walk.

"My lady," Adir said, bowing. Though the proprieties dictated that he keep his eyes fixed on the ground while in the presence of nobility, he found it impossible to not look into her eyes of sunlit sand and dew-laden grass.

"Launderer," Habya said, her pink lips curling up in a smile. "Or maybe I should call you groom."

Adir returned her smile. "My name is Adir, my lady."

"Ah," she said. "May the Gods favor you, Adir." Adir was

enchanted by her lilting accent that added a pleasant sweetness to her voice.

"How may I be of service?" Adir asked.

"I am in need of a horse," Habya said.

"I can certainly help you with that," Adir replied, relieved. "I'll go fetch one for you."

"Also," Habya said before he turned away, "I am in need of an escort. Akka says I am not to leave the manor ground unescorted."

"Master Steward will be the one to arrange that, my lady," Adir said, unsure of whether that truly was the case. "Or maybe the stable master."

"*You* can escort me."

Adir hesitated. He was flummoxed. Lord Si'Pyaara had caused him to be banned from the manor for merely speaking to his daughter. "I don't think your father would like me to be your escort," he eventually said.

Habya waved her hand dismissively. "He will never know. Akka is as blind as a bat and has no clue what you look like. If he sees us he will not know it is you. And I doubt anyone will tell him. So, will you escort me?"

Acting as an escort to nobility wasn't part of his job responsibilities. Even if Lord Si'Pyaara didn't find out, he was sure that Master Steward wouldn't approve. However, he couldn't very well deny a command from a noblewoman. "It'll be my honor, my lady," he said.

Adir started back toward the stables to fetch two horses when he spotted the stable master and Ghareeb intently watching him. As soon as he met their eyes, they immediately looked away and began a quiet conversation, tossing furtive glances at him.

When Adir approached them, the stable master asked, "What trouble are you in now?" His voice sounded serious and concerned, but his face displayed an amused smile.

"No trouble," Adir said nonchalantly. "She wants me to escort her on a ride."

"And you're going?" Ghareeb asked, sounding incredulous. "Did you forget what we just talked about?"

"I have to," Adir said, making it sound as if he really didn't want to go. "But she commanded me."

"This is very unusual," the stable master said, "but you're right. We cannot disobey commands from the nobility." He gestured at the stable. "Let's go get you a couple of horses."

Adir followed, with Ghareeb at his side.

"Be careful," Ghareeb whispered as he followed Adir into the stable.

"I will," Adir said dismissively. "I'm sure I'll be fine."

"I hope so." Ghareeb's voice was grave. "You have no idea what the Cayani are capable of."

A LIGHT BREEZE, stirred up by riding, pulled at the tails of the long silk scarf draped around Habya's neck, providing some relief from the typical Marayi humidity. The low chime of her anklets in rhythmic time with the clops of hooves produced a swirling cadence to the slow ascent of the midmorning sun. It was hard to believe that they were still within the city limits of Meneres, as the landscape gave no hint of it. Devoid of houses, shops, and crowds of people, the downhill path was lined with bushes, trees, and wildflowers of pink, yellow, blue, and red. She wished that Omanna had such picturesque refuges within the coastal city. The best she had was a garden at her villa, large and abundant though it was.

The path eventually led to a peaceful, panoramic hollow, at the center of which sat a small pond. Upon hearing their approach, frogs sitting atop wide leaves of an aquatic flower began to croak. She was told the flower was called a lotus. With petals of white and pink, several lotuses floated atop translucent waters. Some were fully open, drinking in the yellow rays of the sun, while others were yet waking from the slumber of the night past. She had only visited this place once before, but it had taken her breath away.

Reining her horse to a halt, Habya dismounted and turned to face her escort. "What do you think of this place?" she asked.

Adir hopped off his horse, looked around, and shrugged. "I've seen ponds before," he said, sounding utterly unimpressed. "There are a few in and around Marafel."

"How can you be so blind to this beauty?" Habya asked, disappointed at his reaction though she tried her best to keep it from her voice.

"I don't know," Adir replied. "You see one pond, you've seen them all." Her expression must have betrayed her emotion, for he added, "But I suppose it is beautiful. Though it doesn't compare to you."

Habya felt herself smile involuntarily and quickly turned away to hide it. *It is very unbecoming of a Cayani woman to smile at the advances of a man,* her mother had said. Especially one who had not been approved by her father. The man could mistake that smile for interest. But she was not interested in Adir. Was she? *No.* This lanky young man was merely her escort. However, she had to admit she did find him quite intriguing. No lowborn person had ever spoken unbidden to her father before.

Walking down to the edge of the water, she bent down and reached out to grab a lotus, but it was just out of her reach. She entertained the idea of stepping into the water but decided against it in favor of keeping her silks dry.

"Let me get that for you." Adir removed his shoes, pulled his pants up to his knees, and stepped into the pond. A small school of tiny silver fish skittered away from their feeding ground in the shallows. "You have to twist the flowers off," he said, grabbing the stem. "If you try to pull it out, you'll end up pulling up the roots, which could extend far below." He spun the flower around in one hand till the stem snapped. Stepping out of the water, he presented it to her. "For you, my lady."

"How gallant of you," Habya said half-jokingly as she accepted the flower.

Adir did not seem to pick up on her humor. "Thank you, my lady," he said formally with a bow.

With Adir by her side, she began walking around the circumference of the pond. "How do you like working for Lord Preschad?" Habya asked, gently rubbing one of the wide lotus petals between her thumb and forefinger. The smooth petal with mild ridges running along its length felt oddly gratifying.

Adir chuckled. "I wouldn't know. This is only my second day." Abruptly, his amusement faded and he looked around shiftily. Then he added, "It's a fine job, but it's just temporary. I'd rather be doing something else."

"Ya? Like what?" Habya smelled the pink lotus and at once her nose was filled with a sweet fragrance. *What a wonderful flower!*

Adir pondered for a moment, gazing into the distance. "I don't really know. Something that will make a good living, I suppose," he said. "Honestly, what I do for work isn't very important to me."

"Really?" Habya said in surprise. In Cayan, words like those could be very detrimental to one's reputation. It was a sign of someone lazy. Someone who wouldn't amount to much. "What you do for a living defines who you are," she said.

Adir nodded. "Maybe for some. But I think it's how you live your life that defines who you are. Not what you do for work." His handsome, high-cheekboned face had a look of determination. "What's important to me is to live by my word. Be a good friend, a good father." He turned his eyes, the shade of burnt wood, onto hers and said, "A good husband." He held her gaze.

Habya had not realized that she was holding her breath till she let it out in one long exhalation. "You may have a point," she said. She laughed a bit nervously as she grappled to determine if Adir was hinting at something, then she decided to let it go. "But I do not think my mothers will be convinced."

Adir's face scrunched. *"Mothers?* You mean mother."

"No," she said. "Mothers."

"You have *more than one mother?*"

"Ya," she said, nodding. "I have three."

"THREE!" His voice went up an octave. "That's ..." He trailed off.

Habya laughed. "Ya, three."

"Do you have three fathers as well?"

"That's just silly," Habya said. These Navenites knew nothing of the world outside. "In Cayan, we follow the true tenets of Annadism. And as such, a man can marry more than one woman."

"Did your father bear children with all your mothers?"

"Ya. With my mother Barika, akka has two children. My first sister Nabila and myself. Then there's my second brother Munaam and my second sister Sumaiyah. They were birthed by my mother Phawzia—akka's second wife. And my mother Rahaya is pregnant with my third sibling. I hope she gives birth to a girl!"

Adir shook his head. "I mean no offense, my lady, but all that sounds very strange to me."

Habya could not help but release her amusement in laughter. "I can see how it seems strange to a Navenite with only one mother."

The incredulity disappeared from Adir's face, giving way to something dark. Had she offended him some way? *Well done, Habya! First I get him into trouble*—she had almost forgotten about that!

"Adir," Habya said, "I feel bad for what happened yesterday. I wanted to say something, but things got out of my control too quickly." She paused. Her father had mentioned that Adir had been docked the day's pay, opining that it had been too lenient a punishment for a mouthy degenerate. "You came to my aid, however foolish or unnecessary that may have been, and got punished for it. For that, I am sorry."

"O. Don't worry about it." His voice was somewhat somber.

"So," Habya continued, "I thought I would make it up to you and show you some parts of Meneres, since you mentioned that you have not explored this city before." She looked around. "But you weren't as dazzled by it as I thought you would be." She gave him her best devilish smile, hoping—*no, wanting*—to lift his spirits.

It worked. Adir cracked a small smile, which broadened and touched his eyes—his dimples added a boyish charm.

"You could take me somewhere else next time," he said.

"Next time? You are quite presumptuous!" But for some reason beyond her grasp, she found that she rather liked the idea of seeing this man a next time.

Chapter Twenty-One

Tying off his horse to a fencepost, Arvan walked through the dark, wrought-iron gates at Ellyn's house and entered her courtyard. It had been almost a month since her dinner invitation in the Square. There had been plenty more invitations since then, but he'd always found an excuse to dodge her offers. However, the last invitation spoke of a Council meeting at her house, where his input on village matters *would be greatly appreciated*. He couldn't refuse that.

Up ahead, the wooden doors to Ellyn's house swung open and a peculiarly dressed woman walked out. It was one of the Kheryne. Instinctively, Arvan put himself on military alert and surveyed the surroundings with his peripheral vision—the way he'd been taught in the Navengaard. Why was this woman walking out of Ellyn's house?

"Arvan Nathar?" she asked, her grey eyes questioning. Her *R*s rolled as smooth as marbles, but her *T*s popped like raindrops pelting a metal roof. She was garbed in the Kheryne fashion—long coat with overlapping sides, wool sash around her waist, and woolen shoes with upturned toes. In addition, two leather straps tightly crisscrossed her chest.

"Yea," Arvan replied hesitantly. "I'm Arvan Nathar."

The Kheryne woman dipped her head. "May the Gods aid your soul."

The greeting took Arvan by surprise. He hadn't expected the savages to believe in the Gods. Or souls. They were savages after all. However, this woman didn't seem savage. Come to think of it, the Kheryne in Marafel hadn't lived up to their reputation at all. The ones he'd seen talking to Ellyn at the Village Square, and another group that had wandered in a few weeks later, had quietly faded into the population. News from Akkasha had spoken of Kheryne showing up there too. But there were no reports of Kheryne killing and pillaging the village folk as Akka Hallen sermonized. At least not yet.

"May the Gods favor you," Arvan replied.

The woman smiled. "Ellyn is upstairs and will be down shortly."

Arvan dropped his guard, but just a bit. "Am I the first to arrive?" he asked.

Giving him a puzzled look, the Kheryne woman said, "Yes," but she sounded unsure. "Come in and make yourself comfortable," she added, then turned to lead the way.

A toddler, fast asleep, was strapped to the woman's back in a snug cloth pack. His limbs and head swayed from side to side as his mother walked into the house. The woman led him into the sitting room, then to a specific chair, then said, "Sit." It wasn't quite a command, but it certainly wasn't a polite offer of a seat either.

"Thank you," Arvan said, seating himself. "Might I ask you for your name?"

The woman, who'd seated herself at the very edge of another chair, gave him another puzzled look, "Yes," she said. "Why do you need my permission to ask me for my name?"

"It's a way of asking for someone's name politely," Arvan replied. An awkward unease settled over him. "I didn't mean any offense," he added.

"I am not offended," the woman said nonchalantly. "I thought Ellyn was polite when she asked me my name outright." She shrugged and tilted her head slightly, raising her eyebrows.

"Very well, then." Arvan was getting slightly irritated. In some ways, the Kheryne were savages. But he kept his voice level when he asked, "What is your name?"

"I am named Barma," she said. Raising her right hand, she touched the tips of her fingers to her forehead, then extended her arm toward him, palm turned toward her.

"It's nice to meet you, Barma."

"Barma," she said, emphasizing the roll in the *R*.

"Barma," Arvan tried again. Barma simply shook her head in disapproval and Arvan thought it best to change the subject. "What brings you across the Bahzenelyn?" he asked.

Barma's expression changed slightly. "I decided to move," she said, pointedly not meeting his eyes.

"May I ask why?" Arvan asked.

"You do not need my permission to ask, Arvan," Barma said, referring to him very informally, but she didn't answer his question. She looked uncomfortable.

"You can tell him, Barma," came Ellyn's voice. The roll in her *R* when she said the name was as smooth as polished stone. Arvan stood as she entered the sitting room. "Please sit, Arvan," she said as she took a seat on a sofa, resting her side on its arm. She turned to Barma. "Arvan was the last mayor of Marafel," she said. "It's all right if he knows. You won't be breaking your word."

Barma gave Ellyn a nod, then turned her grey eyes to him, her expression darkening. "Four full moons ago," she began, "I was awoken by my husband in the middle of the night. He had heard some movement outside our gehr. He took his sword and stepped out. For a while, there was silence." Her round young face tensed. She was no older than Morena. "Then I heard a loud scream, then another and another. Batby"—she pointed with her thumb at her son—"awoke and started to cry. I did not know what was happening, so I covered his mouth and pulled out my sword and waited in the dark for my husband to return. There were more screams. After a few moments, it was as if my whole yiria was screaming. Everyone and everything was screaming. The goats, the horses, the chickens, the people!" She paused and took a long breath, then audibly let it out. "My husband had not returned. I worried the worst, thinking that a rival yiria was raiding mine. But Kheryne Khuun do not attack in the deep of night. We are no cowards! We raid when our enemies can see us coming.

"So I decided to go find him. I strapped Batby to my back, and with sword in hand, I left the gehr. My husband …" Her eyes welled up, but she immediately wiped it off and hardened her face. "A rakhor held my husband by his neck. His feet were off the ground, kicking. When he saw me, he said something that I could not hear. I ran toward the rakhor with my sword raised, hoping to save my husband, but it was too late. The rakhor threw him to the ground and stepped on his head. May his soul fulfill its desires. I thrust my sword into the rakhor's heart, but he was unhurt." She gritted her teeth as anger spread across her face. "Then I cut off its head and it simply faded away."

"You killed a rakhor?" Arvan said in disbelief.

Barma nodded. "But there was more than one. I looked around and people were being slaughtered by the rakhor. Most used their claws to slash and stab, but some choked and crushed. I knew if I stayed to fight, I would only be ensuring the death of my son." She lowered her gaze to the floor. "So I ran. To save my son's life.

"I traveled south and west for many days and came upon another yiria and was surprised to find only a few bodies, crushed and dismembered. The rest—I do not know what happened to the rest. By the grace of the Gods, I hope they escaped. I searched in their gehrs but they were all intact. It was as if the rakhor just wanted to kill the people.

"I packed as much food as I could and found a horse and rode for several more days. My food and water ran out and I had to kill my horse and use its meat. Then even the meat ran out and we began to starve. Because I was not eating and drinking much, I did not make much milk for Batby. I was sure we were going to die.

"But just when I was about to lose all hope, some Kheryne Khuun who had themselves been chased off by rakhor found me. They were not of one yiria, but of many. They spoke of several raids close to the Source and had decided to travel west through the Bahzenelyn. I joined them. A few days later, we found three more Kheryne Khuun, who joined us. Together, we crossed the Bahzenelyn and came here." She looked up and flashed a forced smile.

"I'm sorry," Arvan said. "After all that, crossing the Bahzenelyn must have been hard." No one in their right minds would ever cross the treacherous mountain range filled with seen and unseen dangers. *Unless they were desperate.*

Barma shook her head. "No. We Kheryne Khuun live with nature and only know a life of movement with the seasons. At other times, we go where our hearts please."

From what little Arvan had heard of the Kheryne, he knew that they were a nomadic people. "What do you think of Marafel?"

"For us it is simply a new land. It is a strange land, but it is soil, air, and water. And Ellyn and other members of the Council have been more than generous in sheltering us." She paused. "Though I do not know how you lowlanders stand living only in one place," she added with a smile.

Batby began to stir behind Barma, sticking his arms out in a satisfying stretch. Then he let out a long wail full of hunger. "All right, all right," Barma said, her voice gentle and loving. "I better tend to him," she said. "He gets very hungry when he wakes. May the Gods aid your soul, Arvan." Without waiting for a response, she stood and left the room.

"Shall we get some dinner?" Ellyn asked, standing.

"You cooked dinner for a Council meeting?"

Ellyn didn't reply.

Arvan followed her from the room and into a hallway. "What does the Council want to discuss with me? Is it about the Kheryne?"

"The Council ... couldn't make it," Ellyn said, walking through a door toward her veranda.

"O?" Arvan said as he followed her out. "Were they—"

Arvan's unspoken question was answered as soon as he saw the small wooden table set for only two. Each place had a plate, cutlery, and an empty glass. A couple of covered pots, a wine bottle, and two candles sat at the table's center.

"There was no Council meeting, was there?" Ellyn had tricked him into having dinner with her. He hadn't expected something like that from her, but he had to admit that he was pleasantly surprised.

"No, there was," Ellyn said, her expression impassive. "They were all busy." She flashed him a sly smile.

"Very well," Arvan said, amused, "they were all busy."

Ellyn gestured for him to sit and took a seat herself. She poured wine for each of them and served some steamed rice and lamb stew. Holding up her glass, she said, "Here's to putting some meat on your bones." She laughed, a pleasant, melodious laugh, throwing her head back slightly. Her black hair, hanging loose, flared and swayed in the light breeze.

"It's very kind of you to give Barma a home," he said, spearing a piece of lamb.

"It's the least I can do." Ellyn's brow creased slightly. "That poor woman has suffered enough. Losing her husband and loved ones and being all alone. Besides, I have a large and empty house."

"What did she mean by yiria?" Arvan asked. "Does it mean family?"

"Not exactly," Ellyn said. "I'm not sure of the exact translation, but I think it means clan or tribe. Though from what Barma says, the Kheryne Khuun in a yiria are closer to each other than families in Naven. It has something to do with the Gods and their purpose in life."

"And gehr?"

"That one I know. It means house. Apparently their houses are made of animal skin over a frame of light wood. Barma says the light construction makes it easy to transport the gehrs when they leave one place for another."

"And when she mentioned the Source, did she mean the Precipice?"

"Yes." She paused to take a sip of her wine. "The Kheryne are a strong people and so far quite unlike what we've thought of them," she added.

Arvan nodded in response, his mouth full of Ellyn's delicious food. "Akka Hallen must be in shock," Arvan said after swallowing. "Every one of his sermons had some message related to how the savages live the most unworthy of lives."

Ellyn laughed at that though Arvan hadn't meant it as a joke. "You know," she said, "there are many more Kheryne looking for homes. Would you be able to shelter some, at least till we find them something more permanent?"

Kheryne living in the Nathar farmhouse? Arvan didn't like the sound of that. They may seem tame now, but that could change at any time. "Maybe," he said. "By the way, you are a fantastic cook!"

Once dinner was over, Ellyn led him to a cushioned swing on the veranda that faced the western pastures. The wildflowers were all bent in sad farewell as the early-summer sun of Akkayi slowly sank beneath the horizon, cooling the world below. She topped off each of their glasses with wine, emptying the bottle, then sat next to him. They spent a couple of moments in silence, sipping their wine. Ellyn lightly rocked the swing with her foot.

"How are you doing, Arvan?" Ellyn asked. Her voice held tenderness.

"I'm doing well," he answered flatly, looking out over the pastures and completely unsure of whether to respond to the question or her tone.

"I heard about Adir."

Arvan simply nodded, trying to keep his face impassive. It had been thirty-four days since he'd last seen his son. He sighed. "I guess I have been better," he said, and sent a quick prayer to the Gods for Adir's safety.

"What happened?" Ellyn asked softly.

Arvan wasn't sure why, but he found himself opening up to Ellyn. "Adir and I had a fight the day he left. It had been difficult dealing with the boy since I returned from the Navengaard. Though I can't say I blame him much." He looked into her eyes and found them listening deeply. He let out a long sigh. "Sometimes I wish I hadn't joined the Navengaard."

Ellyn gave him a quizzical look. "You don't mean that."

"No, I do," Arvan said. "Adir blames me for being absent from his life. He blames me for not coming back home after Malia went missing." He paused for a brief moment, then added, "He told me right before he walked out that Malia left me because I was an uncommitted husband." That thought left his mouth bitter. He watched a butterfly flitting across the pasture, blown by the breeze. "You know," he said after a moment, "Malia was the one who urged me to follow where the Navengaard took me. She told me she'd take care of the children and the farmhouse. And she did. She was … is a wonderful woman." He missed his wife. "When she went missing, I didn't hear about it for a year. By the time I did find out, my duty stopped me from returning home immediately."

"I understand," Ellyn said with a sympathetic smile. "My husband would have done the same. Duty was above everything. But his duty cost him his life."

"Do you blame him for that? For choosing the Navengaard over your marriage?"

"Sometimes," Ellyn answered. "But that's just my self-pity. When I married Lakesh I knew the Navengaard was his life and that he'd be away from home a lot, but I didn't truly understand what that meant till we started living it. But I loved him and had made a commitment. And isn't that what marriage is? Commitment?" She paused. "How then could I truly blame him?"

Though Ellyn's answer was comforting, it wasn't enough to absolve Arvan of his guilt. "By the time I finally got back, Adir was already grown and full of anger. I couldn't tell him that I'd left because of his mother's encouragement and support. He would never have believed me." He shook his head in defeat. "I have failed my wife and my children. I wish things were different."

A smooth hand slid over Arvan's and gripped it. He met Ellyn's eyes and found them regarding him with a warm tenderness. "He'll come back one day," she said. "You'll get your chance to make things right."

Arvan wrapped his fingers delicately around Ellyn's hand. He nodded, smiling, then took a sip of wine as his eyes followed the lone butterfly still flitting across the pastures. Blown by the breeze.

Chapter Twenty-Two

Being a serving maid was no different than selling crumbcakes, except that Tia didn't have to sell the food she was serving. And it certainly beat standing in the Village Square sweating under the midsummer sun in the month of Suguni, hoping that the crumbcakes didn't dry up too much. And to make matters even better, she could do her job in the company of like-minded, fun-loving women.

"Did you hear," Preya said with raised eyebrows, "the Daroongaamen competitors will be in Meneres in a few weeks!" The young woman of an age with Tia was in a perpetually good mood. "King Taschari will be hosting them for a dinner at the palace."

"Yea," Ramika said as she finished peeling a potato and tossed it into a bowl. "And I bet you're going to try and bed each and every one of them."

"If you weren't an old hag, some of the competitors would bed you too, Ramika," Preya shot back. She had a knack for such snappy retorts.

Ramika huffed. "Who says they don't want to bed me? Men prefer a woman with some experience in the bedchamber."

"I'm sure your husband would have something to say about that." The two women shared a laugh.

Such was the camaraderie between serving maids under Lord Preschad's employ. They loved teasing each other and Tia loved to observe their interactions. They were so much more colorful than those in Marafel.

"What about you, Tia?" Preya asked. "I'm sure a beauty like you could easily snag a few big strong competitors."

Tia couldn't help but smile. "No, I'm all right," she said. Big men were not her preference. Tall and lanky were more to her liking.

"You're such a liar," Preya accused. "I have yet to find a woman who didn't want to bed a Daroongaamen competitor."

"You have now," Tia said. "But I am looking forward to seeing my friend Rein Maranda again. He's an archer."

"An archer?" Preya sounded disgusted. "Archers aren't much fun in bed."

"Is that all you think of?" Tia asked, finding the insinuation distasteful. "I don't want to bed Rein. He's a friend from back home in Marafel."

"You're from Marafel?" Ramika asked. "I didn't know that. I thought you were from Meneres."

What did I do? Adir didn't want me telling people where I'm from. But it was too late. "Yea," Tia admitted, realizing there was no way out.

"So what brought you to Meneres?" Preya asked.

"I came here looking for work," Tia said. She did not want to reveal any more than she already had.

"Tia," Ramika said, looking straight into her eyes, "I've lived long enough to spot a lie from afar. No woman leaves her home to come to Meneres looking for work."

Tia swallowed the lump that had formed in her throat. It seemed that she wasn't the only one with the skills to see the truth behind a person's words. "I eloped," she said softly.

"Now there's the truth," Ramika said triumphantly. "Where's this man of yours?"

Tia had adeptly maneuvered herself into a corner. But she could trust Preya and Ramika; after all, they didn't care about her past. "His name is Adir. He works in the stables here."

"He must be one lucky man," Preya said, eyeing her up and down. "I wouldn't mind eloping with you." She winked.

Tia felt her cheeks turn red hot as Preya's words rendered her speechless.

Ramika scrunched her eyebrows. "Did you say your man's name was Adir?"

"Yea," Tia said. "Do you know him?"

"I don't know him, but I know of him," the older woman said. "My husband who works in the stables has told me about him. Tall man, long hair?"

"Yea," Tia said. "That's him. But I wouldn't go telling him that I told you about us. He's … very private."

Ramika nodded slowly. "Is he now? Makes sense."

"What do you mean?" Tia asked, grabbing a potato from a basket in between the three of them.

"Gods save us, but when a man keeps his dealings private, it means he's trying to hide something," Ramika said with the surety only seen in those who know how life works.

Tia's breath caught. She'd revealed too much. For someone who prided herself in understanding human nature, she sure had a loose tongue. "No, he isn't hiding anything from me." But Ramika didn't look convinced. "What do you think he's hiding from me?"

"I don't know," Ramika said as she cut into another potato. "Did he tell you about the Cayani noblewoman?"

A sense of relief washed over Tia. *Good,* she thought. Their secret was still safe. "Yea," she replied. "He told me how he got in trouble for speaking to her without leave. He got docked a day's pay for that."

"Is that all he told you?"

"Yea. What else is there?"

"I think it best that you talk to him about it, but—"

"But what?"

Ramika sighed. "My husband tells me that the Cayani noblewoman has been taking rides into the city with your man as her escort. Her *only* escort."

The doubts that Tia had about leaving Marafel with Adir exploded back to the surface. She struggled to push them to the recesses of her mind. "Isn't that part of a groom's duties?" she asked, wrestling with herself to give Adir the benefit of the doubt.

"Yea," Ramika said, "but every time the noblewoman wants to go into the city, she specifically asks for your man. From what I hear, they've been all over the city."

Tia felt her heart sink and her stomach hollow out. This is what she'd been worried about ever since he ogled the serving girl in Nagra, ever since he left her by herself at the inn, alone and afraid. Did Adir actually love her?

"Be quiet, Ramika!" Preya chided. "You are such a gossipmonger." Ramika simply shrugged. Preya placed a hand on Tia's shoulder. "Don't listen to her. She's from a different time and doesn't know how things work today."

"Is that so?" Ramika asked. "How many times have you been out alone with a man and not ended up bedding him?"

Preya didn't answer for a long while. "That's different," she said finally. "All those men were unattached."

"All right," Ramika said, "but I know what men are like. I've lived—"

"Yea, we know," Preya interrupted, "you've lived long enough to know. I'm sure Adir is different than the men you've known."

Is Adir different than other men? Tia's emotional heart said yes, but her analytic mind didn't agree.

Chapter Twenty-Three

Uaqui had dreaded the thought of returning to the Khasir empty-handed. The Khasir was not known to tolerate failure. But by the time he got back to Nagra, the creature was gone, and all that the idiot innkeeper could say was that the creature, who was from some village called Marafel, had gone west. Days had turned into weeks as he and his worthless team of operatives unsuccessfully scoured every village and farmhouse west of Nagra. The creature had simply vanished.

As the weeks ran past a month, their money began to run thin. Uaqui knew it was only a matter of time before he would have to return to Mount Schinay to resupply his funds. Everyone would know of his failure then. He would probably be executed, but he would gladly accept it to end the heavy shame of failure. However, by the grace of Daroon, a soldier at an outpost had mentioned a man with a staff, traveling to Meneres with a woman and a strange, red-haired man wearing a long buttoned shirt the Cayani called a seherwani. Finally! Uaqui knew he had found the venna. And it seemed that his third liability was traveling with it.

"You have been quiet, Uaqui," Afzar said. Though the ox of a

Cayani—physically and mentally—behaved as bluntly as a Herran, this Shadow operative knew how to follow orders.

"I am thinking," Uaqui replied.

"What are you thinking about?" Rhonea, the Herran operative asked in an accent typical of that nation, clipping the last letter of each word. She sat on the bed, trimming her toenails with her khari. Herrans had no respect for their weapons. The khari was not just any short dagger; it was imbued with the blessings of Daroon, as were the other three blades of every Shadow operative.

"I am thinking why it is that we are not at Aedenin right now with the creature captured, when it has been three days since we spotted it gallivanting with the Cayani woman?"

Afzar and Rhonea looked at each other but said nothing. This was what he had to deal with—unmotivated, idiotic people. It was only the fate of the world that was at stake. He let out an exasperated breath.

"We are all waiting for your orders," Rusane said from a chair in one corner of the room. "Since you are the one charged with its capture."

Uaqui detected a veiled ridicule in Rusane's voice. He looked into the Kheryne operative's eyes. "Yes, it is my charge, but I would like to hear your ideas. You are operatives too."

"We could take him when he is on his way to the inn," Afzar said. "Plenty of spots for an ambush." The clean-shaven man scratched the back of his head. "Besides, I have not ambushed someone in a while. Feels like it is time."

"Are you mad?" Rhonea exclaimed. "What if it unleashes its powers? What if it forces us to take him to the Staff? Are you willing to risk death and destruction because you haven't ambushed someone in a while?"

Afzar seemed to shrink a little. "The venna does not know about the Staff of Beckoning. Does he, Uaqui?"

"I do not think it knows it is a venna," Uaqui said, giving serious consideration to Afzar's plan. "We could knock it unconscious before it has a chance to realize what is happening. We could be in Aedenin by nightfall."

Rusane laughed from his corner and Uaqui's patience began to fade. That Kheryne had been nothing but a pesky rock in his boot. If it were up to him, he would upend his boot and let the rock fall out and crush it till it was nothing but dirt. But he was under orders from the Khasir herself to keep this rock in his boot. And so he did, despite sharp reminders of its existence. Like when a traveler had unwittingly crossed their path while they were garbed in their uniform. No mere man, except the godsforsaken Kheryne Khuun, had ever seen an operative and lived to tell about it. But what did Rusane want to do? Let the fool go with a promise he would keep his mouth shut. Who wouldn't tell the tale of running into four people donned in black in the middle of the forest?

"What is so funny?" Uaqui asked, trying to control his rising anger.

"This whole situation. Do we even know if this man is a venna?"

"Are you calling me a liar?" Uaqui asked. The whole world lied, but Uaqui's words were always true.

"Are you one?" Rusane asked coldly.

"I know what I saw," Uaqui said slowly, holding Rusane's gaze. "That thing is a venna." Abruptly, he realized that his hands were clenched into fists. "Are you willing to disregard Daroon's Warning on your false hunch that I might be wrong?"

"My hunch may be false. But right now, without any solid evidence, my *false* hunch is as true as what you … *saw.*"

"What do you propose we do then? Let it go?"

"No. But we should make sure he is a venna before we accidentally kidnap an innocent man."

Uaqui shook his head. Rusane did not get it. "If we capture this creature and it turns out that it is not a venna, then the world loses just one man. But if it escapes again, it will not be long before the allure of the Staff pulls the vile creature toward it. What if it manages to get its hands on the Staff? If that happens, we won't lose just one man, but the whole world! We might as well piss on the God of Courage and his Warning."

A deafening silence fell upon the room. No one spoke—Afzar kept his eyes glued to the floor, while Rhonea stared unfocused with an expression of discomfort. Rusane and he, however, continued staring at each other—Rusane's face hardening with each passing moment.

"Fine," Rusane said. "We will take the creature. But not in an ambush in the city. We are the Khasmia Shadow. We can be more subtle than that."

Chapter Twenty-Four

Tia sat at the edge of her bed taking stock of her relationship with Adir. She had left her mother, her friends, her home, all for him. Not to mention suffering through his childish outbursts and his flirtatiousness. *And he shows his gratitude by chasing after some noblewoman?*

The first time Adir had mentioned that wench, Tia had thought nothing of it. After all, he'd been in trouble, which made her think that Adir would have learned his lesson. Even after Ramika told her about Adir's frequent rendezvous with the Cayani wanton, Tia had given him the benefit of the doubt.

But what happened yesterday was the blow that felled the tree. Upon Adir's return from the manor, well after his duties had ended, Tia found two small flowers stuck in his hair. At first she was puzzled, but then she realized that Adir was acting like a fool. And men only acted like fools when they were either drunk or with a woman they wanted to bed. Tia could no longer turn a blind eye to what was happening. *Ramika was right.*

The knob turned and the door opened. Adir walked in with a smile for all the world to see. When his eyes met hers, however, his smile abruptly faded. "Hey, Tia," he said, then seated himself in a chair and started pulling off his boots.

Adir's casual tone sparked a flame of annoyance in her. "Hey," she said. "Long day?"

Adir nodded. "The stables are full of surprises."

"I'm sure they are." She paused for a short moment. "Ghareeb must really be shirking his duties then."

"No, he's doing fine," Adir said. "In fact, the stable master gave him more responsibilities today."

"O!" Tia said, feigning surprise. "Did you get more responsibilities too?"

"No," Adir said from inside his shirt as he pulled it off.

"Hmmm … that's odd, don't you think? You clearly work a lot more than Ghareeb."

Adir shrugged. "We work about the same."

"That's not possible," she said, forcing a smile. Her spark of annoyance was now a raging fire within her. But instead of letting it out, she stoked the flames. "Ghareeb has been back at the inn at least an hour before you every single day since we started working here. In fact, he's been in the common room for a while now. There's no way he's working harder than you."

Adir didn't answer. He walked to a chest of drawers and rummaged around for a shirt, which he then donned.

The door opened and Ghareeb let himself in. "Adir," he said, his speech showing signs of drink. "A runner came from the manor with this." He thrust out his hand holding a waterskin. "You forgot to take this back from the Cayani lady."

Adir grabbed the skin from Ghareeb. "Thanks for your help," he said in an apprehensively sarcastic tone.

"Are you coming downstairs?" Ghareeb asked.

"I'll be down soon."

"You better, or I may have found myself in the company of that rather charming serving girl," Ghareeb said with a smile as he closed the door behind him.

Tia noticed how Adir didn't look at her as he made his way back to the chest to fish out a pair of pants. "Why did the Cayani noblewoman have your waterskin, Adir?" she asked, trying to keep her voice level.

"Lady Si'Pyaara got thirsty while I was escorting her and so I gave her a drink."

"O. Seems like you've been *escorting* her quite often," Tia said, her voice rising.

Adir paused for a moment. "It's part of my job."

"I heard that she asks specifically for you. Why is that, Adir?"

"I don't know, Tia," Adir said shortly, his nostrils flaring. "I'm simply obeying commands."

Tia felt a sudden pang of betrayal that catapulted her raging fire into an explosion of fury. "Do you think I don't realize what's going on?" she asked through gritted teeth.

"What do you think is going on?" Adir asked, raising his own voice, as if challenging her to accuse him.

And so she did. "You're chasing after her!" Tia spat. "How could you do this to me!?"

Adir shook his head. "This again!" He plopped into a chair. "We can't keep doing this every time I have to deal with a woman. Gods save me! Stop being so jealous!"

"You know this is different."

"How? How is this different?" He paused. "I work in the stables and as such, if one of the nobility asks me to do something, I have to oblige."

"This is more than just you fulfilling your duties. I've seen you after you've spent time with her. You have this ... this look on your face." She stopped speaking in order to hold back a sudden urge to cry. Her eyes began to well up.

"What look?" Adir asked, his face a mask of anger.

"The look you had when you chased after me," Tia said, swiping at her tears.

An expression that Tia couldn't interpret passed across Adir's face, then he sat silently for a long moment. Tia feared for what that silence meant. "That's just your imagination," he said eventually, looking away.

It very well could have been her imagination. But she knew it wasn't. Adir wasn't the only one on whom she'd seen that look. She'd seen it many times before, and she knew full well what that look meant. It was a look that was all too apparent on those who were swooned by the charms of another.

At that moment, all her fury faded away, leaving not a single trace behind. She felt numb. "Do you love me, Adir?" she asked slowly.

Adir looked at her. Those dark brown eyes gazed into hers. "Tia," he began, "you know I care about you very much."

Care? she thought. *Care isn't love.*

Chapter Twenty-Five

Aftr a long day of backbreaking hoof cleaning in the midsummer's heat, Adir was glad to be back at the Drink and Dreams. Pulling out the key from his pocket, he inserted it into the keyhole, turned the knob, and pushed the door open. *Good! She isn't here*, he thought. He was glad to have some peace and quiet, especially after the previous day's awkwardness.

Adir pulled out a clean set of clothes from the chest and donned them. Then he splashed some water on his face from the basin and slicked his hair back with his wet hands. Seating himself in a chair, he stuck out his legs in a satisfying stretch. His thoughts settled on Habya.

Over the past few weeks, Adir had escorted Habya to myriad places throughout Meneres. Though he was actually the one being escorted. Aside from places of *scenic beauty* that Habya seemed to prefer, she'd also taken him to the more expensive of the two shopping districts, the Meneres harbor on the Penner, some place called a museum where they displayed old relics, and a few eateries. She had a taste for Naven food. Who wouldn't? It was the most flavorful food one could find.

Each outing had only made Adir want to spend more time with her. Her smiling face was etched into his mind. She made him feel as if he could soar higher than birds, yet she also had a way of making him feel grounded and still. But their time together was coming to an end. Habya was to return to Cayan in a few days. Leaving him behind. He'd known this day would come, yet he longed for her to stay.

His eyes wandered the room and landed on the bed he shared with Tia, though they hadn't done so last night. He abruptly sat up for a closer examination. Tia's pack and saddle were missing. Adir hurriedly got to his feet and walked over to the bed. Dropping to his knees, he bent down to peer under the bed. His pack and saddle were there, but not Tia's. As a pulse of worry shot through his body, he scanned the rest of the room. Everything else seemed to be in place.

His eyes fell upon a folded piece of paper on his chest of drawers. He'd completely missed it while grabbing his clothes. Sprinting across the room, he picked up the note and unfolded it.

Adir,

I have come to realize that you don't love me. You think you do, or you want to, but you don't. I don't blame you for that. You cannot help whom you love.

In a way, I'm angry with myself for letting things go so far. I had thought that if I ran away with you, giving up everything I know and love, you would see how much you mean to me, and I hoped that you would come to love me as much as I love you. But that was a foolish thought. A childish fantasy. Loving someone out of mere gratitude or obligation is not true love.

Still, I deserve better. I deserve someone who will recognize the sacrifices I make for him and love me for it. I deserve someone who will make his own sacrifices for me and I will love him for it. Not someone who takes me for granted.

So I am leaving. I hate to have to leave a note, but I don't trust myself around you—I seem to make bad choices. I have taken Mira and my travel pack. I hope you don't mind. I'll drop them off at your farmhouse. And don't worry. I won't tell anyone where you are.

Goodbye. I hope we both find what we are looking for.
Tia.

Adir looked around the room unseeingly as a strange amalgam of anger and sorrow washed around inside him.

The sorrow was for Tia. How had he been such a mule and not realized what she was giving up for him? Yet another person had been added to the ever-growing list of those who couldn't stand him.

The anger was for himself. Had he destroyed what he had with Tia for a fleeting fancy? What chance did he have with a noblewoman, and a noblewoman from another land, at that? He should have been more forthright with Tia about Habya. Maybe then she would have stayed.

But then again, there was a reason why he had been so secretive. Adir felt something for that Cayani noblewoman. Something grander than what he felt for Tia. A heavy blanket of guilt smothered him for having that thought, though it validated Tia's worries.

At that moment an unpleasant thought worked its way out. Was he the cause of his own turmoil? Was Tia right that he was too self-absorbed and took people for granted? Did he do the same with his father … ? *No!* But he'd certainly made Tia feel that way. Annoyed by the ill temper generated by his thoughts, Adir tried to turn his mind elsewhere, but he couldn't. The guilt was too overbearing.

The door opened and Ghareeb strolled in. He seemed a little inebriated, which had become something of a habit for the red-haired Pelerian. "Adir! What are you doing sitting up here alone? Come join me in the common room. I need some help with this blonde singer." He gestured with cupped hands in front of his chest, face held in an expression of awe. "Gods, are they magnificent!"

Adir let out a breath. "Tia's gone."

"What? When? Why?"

"I don't know when," Adir said, gazing at the letter. "I don't know why either." Well, that was a lie. What would Ghareeb think if he found out the real reason? "I think she may have been homesick." He crumpled the note and stuffed it into his pocket.

Ghareeb nodded. "Or maybe Tia left because you have been spending an inappropriate amount of time with that Cayani lady," he said, catching Adir by surprise. His inebriation had given him a loose tongue. "I heard what she said last night." Ghareeb paused. "I didn't stay around to listen of course," he added hurriedly, "just heard something on my way down. She wasn't very quiet."

"Why didn't you say anything to me earlier?" Adir asked, anger flaring inside him.

"It was none of my business," Ghareeb protested, his speech slurring slightly. "I learned a long time ago to stay out of lovers' quarrels."

"But I could have—" Adir realized he was grasping at nothing. He was just looking for someone to blame. He deflated with a sigh. "You're right," he admitted.

"I know I am," Ghareeb said, completely unsympathetic. "I told you the Cayani are nothing but trouble." He paused, giving Adir a long look, and his expression grew soft. "And I know you're falling for the noblewoman," he added gently.

"Am I that obvious?"

"It doesn't take a scholar to see what is happening."

"Tia saw that too. You know what the worst part of it is?" Ghareeb shook his head. "I don't feel like I should find Tia and bring her back. I don't know whether it's because I think she deserves someone better or because I don't feel as strongly for her as I do for Habya." A bitter taste formed in his mouth. "I don't know what to do, Ghareeb," he admitted.

"If I were you, I would go get Tia," he said. "She's right for you. And besides, you have no future with that Cayani."

"Tia doesn't think I'm right for her. And I think she's right." As the words came out of his mouth, Adir felt a deep sorrow that he hadn't felt since his mother disappeared.

Ghareeb sighed gently. He walked over to Adir and placed a hand on his shoulder. "Well then, young master," he said consolingly, "all I can say is that things will heal in time."

Chapter Twenty-Six

Adir felt something brush against his arm. Sleepily, his barely open eyes scanned the darkness for a moment before shutting again.

He felt the brush again, then heard a light creak of the floorboards. This time his eyes opened fully. A shot of wakefulness passed through him, accompanied by a surging tide of irritation at being woken. His head felt heavy from the sudden waking. He hated that feeling. He sat up. "Ghareeb? Is that—"

A hand slid over Adir's face then pressed down hard, cutting off his speech and breath. At the same instant, an arm looped around his neck, choking him.

Devoid of air once again, Adir's mind shot back to the night Boar attacked him. He felt the same way now, his lungs grasping for air. He tried to kick and struggle, but the numbness set in much faster than the last time.

"Adir?" he heard Ghareeb's voice. "Did you say something?"

A cloud must have moved, as moonlight broke the darkness in the room. Unable to speak, move, or breathe, Adir watched as a silhouetted Ghareeb sat up in his bed then remained still for an excruciatingly long moment.

"HELP!" Ghareeb yelled. "HELP! HELP!"

Shouts of concern and anger rose up from various parts of the inn. At that moment, the pressure on Adir's face and neck vanished. He took a long breath of air then coughed uncontrollably. He heard soft, hurried footsteps make their way to the window, then nothing.

The next instant, Ghareeb was by Adir's side. "Are you all right?" he asked.

Adir continued coughing in between gulps of air. Holding up a finger, he nodded. "I'm,"—he coughed—"fine." After a few more bouts of coughing and labored breaths, he began feeling somewhat normal. "I'm fine," he repeated. The shouts around the inn faded.

"Here. Have some water." Adir accepted the proffered cup and sipped from it. Ghareeb walked over to the window and peered out. "There's no one down there," he said. "He jumped down three stories and escaped?" Astonishment was plain in his voice.

"I'm sure he's badly hurt," Adir said through intermittent coughs. The back of his throat felt all scraped up.

There was a knock at the door. Adir and Ghareeb looked at each other.

"We heard shouts for help from this room," a voice called from outside. "Are you folks all right?"

Ghareeb opened the door cautiously. A wall of light penetrated the room through the open door, and two men, one holding a lit candle, entered.

"Someone broke in through the window and tried to kill my friend," Ghareeb said.

The two men strode over to Adir, shoving Ghareeb aside. As the men got closer, Adir noticed that they wore the uniforms of the inn's peons. "Is this true?" the peon holding the candle asked.

Adir nodded in response. "He may have been here to rob us and got startled when I awoke." But he had a sinking feeling that that was not the case. Syfis Sayarna had found him! Was there nowhere he could be safe?

The peon looked at his companion. "Where is he now?" he asked.

"He jumped out the window," Ghareeb said.

"From the third floor?" The other peon sounded as astonished as

Ghareeb had been. He hurried to the window and peered out. After a few moments, he pulled himself back in. "We'll search the area around the inn," he said, sounding unconvinced that a man had climbed up three stories, then jumped out a window and escaped. "Would you like to report this to the City Watch?"

"No," Adir replied immediately. Getting the authorities involved wouldn't be to his benefit.

"All right," the peon with the candle said hesitantly. "I suggest you keep your window barred." With that, the two men exited the room, their fading light pulling a sheet of darkness over the room.

Ghareeb lit a candle and moved closer to Adir. "Do you really think we were being robbed?' Ghareeb asked.

Adir nodded.

"Well then you are a fool!" Ghareeb said emphatically. "I don't think that man was a robber. No common thief can jump three stories down." He paused, regarding Adir with his brown eyes. Adir could see the reflection of the candle flame in his eyes. "Did you offend the Cayani noblewoman in any way?"

"No," Adir said indignantly. "Even if I had, Habya would never do such a thing."

Ghareeb's expression must have meant to convey disbelief, but the shifting candle flame gave him a menacing look. "You don't know Cayani," he said. "This is exactly the kind of thing they do."

Adir wrestled with himself. One part of him wanted to let Ghareeb think whatever he wanted to. That way, Adir wouldn't have to tell him about Boar's death, Syfis's ambush, and his escape from Marafel. But another part of him—a much stronger part—couldn't bear to hear untruths spoken about Habya.

"Ghareeb," he began, "there is something you need to know." He pondered for a moment, searching for the right words that would only reveal as much as necessary. "Back home, I got tangled up in something, and a man named Boar Sayarna ended up dead."

"Boar Sayarna? Why do I feel like I have heard that name?"

"He was one of the staff tournament victors at the last Daroongaamen."

"Ah," Ghareeb said, nodding. "You killed him?" His tone was grave but not accusatory.

"No! No. I didn't kill him. In fact, he tried to kill me after an unfortunate incident at the Regional Games in Marafel. The last thing I remember of that night is being choked unconscious by him. But somehow he ended up dead. And I was found near his body." He almost raised his hand to his neck but stopped himself. "The Village Watch in Marafel and the Arbiter concluded that there wasn't enough evidence to hold me responsible for his death. But Boar's brother, Syfis, is convinced that I killed Boar and swore revenge. That's why I had to leave Marafel. And now I fear he's found me."

Ghareeb stayed silent for a few moments, the candlelight casting various shapes on his bearded face. "I can certainly understand your reason for leaving your home," Ghareeb said, "if you recall our first meeting. But," he paused, "do you really think it was this Syfis who just tried to kill you?" Ghareeb's tone indicated that he still thought Habya was at the bottom of it.

"Who else would it be? Syfis himself told me that he would not stop till his brother was avenged."

"Maybe. But can this Syfis jump out a window three stories high and walk away?"

"Yea," Adir said defiantly, though he knew that was far from the truth. But he would rather be struck down than believe that Habya wanted him dead.

Ghareeb let out a long breath, causing the candle flame to angle horizontally. "So what are you going to do now? If what you say is true, or for that matter, if what I say is true, you cannot stay here."

"No, I can't." Adir hadn't foreseen this eventuality. He'd expected to be safely lost in a city as large as Meneres. What was he to do? Go live with the mountain tribes in the north? That wasn't a valid option.

A thought sprang up in Adir's mind. He pondered it. "Maybe I'll go to Cayan," he said slowly.

"Cayan!" Ghareeb's face looked stunned in the candlelight. "I thought you'd move to another part of the city or somewhere else in Naven. But Cayan? Have you been deaf to what I have told you about that nation?" Ghareeb eyed him for a moment. "You want to go there chasing after the noblewoman, don't you?" he said, his voice now saturated with accusation.

"Maybe," Adir replied, feeling quite defensive. "But Cayan is very far away. It'll be a while before I'm found there—that's if I'm even found."

"Gods save your soul!" Ghareeb said. He let out another long breath. "You just refuse to listen to advice. But it's your life. If that's where you want to go, then go. I hope she wasn't the one who—" He paused as he must have seen Adir's anger rise. "Are you planning on leaving with her?" he asked.

"Yea, that makes the most sense. There's no reason to risk traveling the roads alone, especially now that I'm being hunted again."

"Isn't she leaving tomorrow?"

A lump formed in Adir's throat as realization blossomed. He'd left his home. Tia had given up on him. And now he was going to leave Ghareeb. He looked at the red-haired man, who was far more intelligent than he pretended. Ghareeb had grown on him, despite their rocky start. He breathed in deeply to allay the sorrow he felt rising up in him—the same sorrow he had felt when saying his goodbyes to Athvan. "Do you want to come with me?" he asked. "We've had a great time together so far."

Ghareeb smiled a knowing smile and patted Adir's back. "I am sorry, my friend," he said. "But I am doing well here in Meneres. For the first time in my life, I feel as though I can make something of myself. You know, settle down in one place for a while. Soon I'll be able to afford a place to rent. I want to see how things turn out."

Adir understood that. He'd hoped to do the same in Meneres. But it seemed the Gods had another plan for him.

Chapter Twenty-Seven

Cayan was the last place on Gods' Leakarha that Ghareeb wanted to be. Yet here he was riding atop his donkey making his way west to that very nation. With Lord Si'Pyaara's party nonetheless. And they were all Cayani. *Wonderful!*

There was no one to blame for this but Adir. If it had not been for him, Ghareeb would have been working in Lord Preschad's stables right now. This was what he got for agreeing to accompany Adir to see Habya for one last goodbye. After all, Adir was a good friend and Ghareeb wanted to wish him well for the future, no matter how foolish his notion of going to Cayan was. How was he to know that they would rope him into traveling to Cayan with them?

Ghareeb had to admit, though, that Habya's plan to get Adir and him admitted into their travel party had been quite cunning. Taking advantage of Lord Si'Pyaara's poor vision, Adir had been passed off as a merchant's second son who wanted to find his fortunes in Cayan. The Cayani lord had agreed to let Adir join their party at the behest of —or badgering from—his daughter, albeit reluctantly. However, the only flaw in the plan was that Ghareeb had been introduced as Adir's attendant who had left home with him. After that setup, Ghareeb could not very well refuse to go with Adir. The whole ruse would have fallen apart and both of them would have been severely punished. Besides, he knew he would be dead right now had Adir not saved him in Nagra. Furthermore, ever since joining Adir he had begun feeling like his old, confident self again. And so he had decided to be a good friend and return to Cayan.

The wagon in front of them came to a halt, subsequently causing the entire party to stop. The door opened and Lord Si'Pyaara stepped out. Habya stuck her head out, shaking it in annoyance. Then she turned to Adir and flashed him a smile.

Lord Si'Pyaara strolled up to the captain of his guards and spoke to him for a few moments. Ghareeb couldn't hear what they were saying, till finally Lord Si'Pyaara exclaimed, "Excellent! Get some men ready!" While the captain conversed with some of his men, the Cayani lord walked to his wagon and opened a large box fixed to its back, from which he pulled out a bow and a quiver of arrows.

"Is he going hunting?" Adir asked, leaning over to Ghareeb.

"It seems that way."

"He's almost entirely blind."

"Ya. So? He's a lord. They can do whatever they want, whenever they want."

The captain appeared next to Adir. "Do you fancy an elk hunt? Lord Si'Pyaara says he heard one calling for a mate from over there." He pointed toward a rocky section of the woods.

"Absolutely!" Adir responded.

"Good," the captain said, then he looked at Adir's staff. "You're not going to kill an elk with that. We have a couple of palmas the two of you can use."

Two of you? Did the captain think that Ghareeb wanted to go hunt an elk? He did not voice his objection, though—attendants did not negate their master's wishes. At least, not openly.

"All right," Adir said, dismounting. "Let's go, Ghareeb!"

Hoping that the slow pace of his dismount would hint at his lack of interest, Ghareeb slid from his donkey. When the captain turned and walked away, he said in an urgent whisper, "Elk are large and dumb and I do not want to go hunt it."

"My attendant has to go where I go," Adir replied as they followed the captain. "It'll be fine."

After grabbing palmas from the captain, Ghareeb and Adir joined the rest of the hunting party. All in all, there were nine. Ghareeb rolled the shaft of the palma in his hand. The sword-like blade at the end of the polearm weighted the weapon in a strange way. He'd never held a palma before; the most dangerous weapon he had ever used was a knife—and that was for cutting food.

"Watch where you step," Lord Si'Pyaara advised. "We don't want to startle the beast by making unnecessary noise. Once we get close, we'll surround it and take it down." He paused and squinted around, and Ghareeb wondered what exactly the blind lord saw.

The party made its way through the woods as silently as nine men could. At random times, Lord Si'Pyaara stopped and said, "Listen," then picked a direction. Sometimes it was the same direction they had been walking in, but not always. Eventually, the party approached a large crag where the elk, with its massive body and wide antlers, was rubbing its side against the rock face, scratching at some itch.

"In the name of the Gods!" Adir whispered to Ghareeb. "He found it by hearing alone."

Lord Si'Pyaara signaled and his men spread out and around the elk, pinning it against the crag. As the party crept around, the Cayani noble stepped up next to Adir.

Pulling an arrow from his quiver, Lord Si'Pyaara nocked it to his bow, *aimed* it at the elk, and let it fly. The arrow cut through the air and struck the crag some ways wide of the elk. Seemed like the lord needed his vision for hunting after all.

The elk, startled, perked up its ears. It turned its great head toward them.

"GET IN CLOSER!" Lord Si'Pyaara shouted. His men cautiously hurried to close in on the animal. The lord pulled out another arrow and shot it. This time it hit, sending the elk into a terrible frenzy.

Ghareeb watched as the elk first walked, then trotted, then acceler-ated into an all-out charge, heading straight to where Lord Si'Pyaara stood. The Cayani lord, who had unsurprisingly not noticed the charging elk, stooped to pull out another arrow. The elk closed in with a speed Ghareeb had not attributed to the lumbering beast. As it neared the nobleman, the elk dropped its head, angling its antlers for the attack.

"MOVE!" Ghareeb yelled, but Lord Si'Pyaara simply nocked his arrow.

Just as the elk was about to ram into the Cayani lord, Adir leapt and tackled him to the side. At that moment, Ghareeb realized he was holding a palma in his hands. Drawing back, he thrust the polearm into the elk's side, but the elk did not fall. It did not even stumble. It harmlessly thundered by, unable to rein in its momentum, the palma sticking out from its side.

"Get him out of here!" Adir shouted, pulling the lord to his feet and shoving him toward one of his guards, who hurriedly escorted the nobleman to safety.

All this while, Ghareeb was watching as the elk slowed and turned, then prepared for another charge. This time toward Adir. "Adir!" he bellowed, warning his friend of the incoming danger.

Adir turned and his eyes widened as the elk plowed toward him. Seemingly panicked, he threw his palma at it, but the heavy weapon did not make it very far. The elk continued to bear down on the lanky man. Ghareeb, weaponless, had no way to help.

Adir whirled around and ran away from the charging elk, leaving Ghareeb puzzled as to why he had not simply jumped to one side and avoided the elk as he had before. Adir zigzagged through the trees with the elk in close pursuit.

Before long, Ghareeb could no longer see Adir or the elk. Knowing that following Adir would be futile and unwise—especially unarmed—Ghareeb cast around, looking for a tree to climb in hopes of catching a glimpse of his friend. Finding one that looked suitably easy to climb, he scampered up to the highest branch that could safely support his weight and surveyed the area. He spotted a few of Lord Si'Pyaara's guards running in the direction Adir had taken.

Some distance farther, Ghareeb caught sight of Adir. His friend had trapped himself by running into an area surrounded on three sides by large rocks. The elk was cutting off his only escape. Ghareeb's heart plummeted as he realized what was about to happen.

But suddenly, and to Ghareeb's utter astonishment, Adir's whole body was covered in a colorful haze, revealing only a silhouette of his friend. *It looks like the Aurora*, Ghareeb thought. The haze swirled in wispy patterns, brightening its splendor as the elk closed in on Adir.

Just before the elk rammed him, Adir jumped. He shot up into the air, easily clearing the elk's height, arced over the large beast, and landed right behind it. The elk had run itself into the rocks behind Adir and seemed dazed, shaking its head and staggering slightly. In one smooth movement, Adir turned, pulled Ghareeb's palma from the elk's side and jammed it through the brown beast. The palma tore right through the animal and poked out the other side. The elk dropped motionless to the rocky ground.

"Gods save us! How can this be?" Ghareeb said to himself. He watched as Adir started to walk away, then stopped. Raising his arms, Adir turned them about, as if examining the rainbow glow. Then Adir lifted his head and looked directly at Ghareeb. After a long moment he looked away, took another step, and the haze faded. He swayed, then collapsed to the ground.

ADIR OPENED his eyes and stared groggily at the ceiling. As wakefulness slowly returned, he realized that the ceiling wasn't one he'd seen before. This was not the room at the Drink and Dreams. *Where am I?*

Panicked, Adir sat up. Immediately, his head began to spin. He tried closing his eyes, but that just made it worse, so he opened them again and tried to focus.

"Praise the Gods, you are awake!" Ghareeb said from somewhere in the room, relief plain in his voice. "We have all been worried sick! Especially Habya."

"She's Habya now?" Adir asked through rotating vision that gradually slowed to focus on Ghareeb sitting in a chair.

"You were right." Ghareeb grinned sheepishly. "She is not so bad."

His grin widened. "She has genuine concern for you. She has been checking on you incessantly since we got here."

"Here? Where's here?"

"We are at an outpost along the road to Cayan," Ghareeb replied. "Lord Si'Pyaara was so grateful that you saved his life that he stopped at the first outpost we came by to have you looked at."

Abruptly, it all came back to him. Leaving Meneres with Habya, the hunt, the elk chasing him, and—. He could no longer deny what he had seen. Was he going insane? *No!* But normal people didn't see themselves covered in the Aurora. Adir brushed the thought aside. "How long have I been asleep?"

"All afternoon and some of the evening." Ghareeb paused for a moment. "When the sarawaan checked you, he found nothing wrong and was perplexed by your unconsciousness." Ghareeb tossed him a knowing look. "I told them you collapsed from exhaustion."

Adir held Ghareeb's gaze as he remembered the moments just before he lost consciousness. He'd spotted Ghareeb perched on a tree branch. "Right before I"—he began slowly—"collapsed from exhaustion, did you see anything?"

Ghareeb's expression grew cold enough to suck the heat out of the room. "Well, I saw you cornered," he said. "That was utterly foolish."

"I didn't realize I was going to get cornered," Adir said. "I hardly had time to think. I was being chased by an enraged elk."

Ghareeb nodded. "Ya … well, then you glowed like the Aurora, jumped twice the height of the animal, landed behind it, and killed it."

Adir's heart raced. Fear and paranoia ran rampant through his mind as he realized that he truly wasn't insane. Reality itself seemed to be unraveling before him. "I … I—"

"You know," Ghareeb interjected, "I once came upon a children's song that Kheryne mothers sang to their children to get them to sleep. The song was about a creature who glowed with a rainbow hue." He paused and pointed at Adir. "Much like yours." He paused again. "That creature was called a venna."

Venna? Adir wasn't sure he wanted to know, but he asked anyway. "What's a venna?"

"I don't know for sure," Ghareeb replied. "The song does not say much about it other than the rainbow-hued glow."

"How come I've never heard about this creature?"

"Maybe because it's part of Kheryne folklore?" Ghareeb sounded entirely unsure. "No one knows much about those savages." He shrugged. "I do not truly know."

Adir let out his frustration. "Then what do you know?" Was this a joke to Ghareeb?

"Honestly, not much at all," Ghareeb said calmly, then he looked away as if pondering something. "Now that I think about it though, the song did mention something about the venna stealing children who were not safely guarded by their dreams."

"So, it's a demonspawn?" Adir asked, even more perturbed. "Like the rakhor … ? Gods! Am I a demonspawn?"

"Maybe. But you do not look like much of a demonspawn to me." Ghareeb paused, then added with inappropriate amusement, "At least not right now."

"But you think I'm this … this venna?"

Ghareeb shrugged. "I don't know, Adir. But even the most fantastical of fables have some shred of truth behind them. And since I do not know what else to call what I saw you as, venna is as good a word as any."

"Ghareeb, if anyone else hears about this—"

"You do not have to worry, young master," Ghareeb said. "I will not tell anyone."

"I need your word, Ghareeb," Adir pushed. He had no idea what was happening to him, but he knew that no one could ever find out.

"You have my word," Ghareeb said, nodding vigorously. Then he let out a long breath. "And I suppose that since I know your secret, it is only fair if you know mine." He paused for several long moments as a still silence descended upon the small, windowless room. Eventually, he shook his head in clear frustration. "I am a mopra," Ghareeb blurted in a loud whisper, throwing his arms up. He sighed. "So now you know."

"You're a mopra?" Adir asked slowly. Where had he heard that word? Then he remembered what Ghareeb had told him when they'd first started their jobs at Lord Preschad's stables. Mopra were Cayani slaves!

"Then why are you going to Cayan?" Adir asked, the implications of Ghareeb's revelation becoming horribly apparent. "Won't they kill you if they find out?"

"I am not planning on telling them," Ghareeb said. "I hope you won't either," he added with a tense smile.

"Of course not!" Adir was indignant. Ghareeb was a good friend. Despite the danger to himself, Ghareeb had decided to accompany him to Cayan. Ghareeb was not only intelligent, but loyal and brave as well. Adir felt a deep sense of gratitude toward the man. Sure, he'd saved Ghareeb's life, but it looked like that debt had been paid twice over. "But weren't you born in Peleria? So how can you be mopra?"

"While growing up in Peleria," Ghareeb began, "I was quite the thief on the streets of Port Rathawia. There was nothing I could not steal, if I wanted to, but I mostly stuck to small valuables that fetched a decent price, and I stole only at night. When everyone was fast asleep." He paused and sighed. "But being young, no older than ten, also meant being foolish and prideful. I started to show off. I started taking unnecessary risks by stealing things too big for me to carry, as long as they got me a hefty price. I began stealing during the day, because nighttime got too boring, too easy. And one day I was caught. Unfortunately, the man who caught me was a Cayani. That was that. He brought me to Cayan and branded me as a mopra. That is why I have this beard." Ghareeb said, pulling at the bushy fur that lined his face. "To hide my mark."

"But I thought that your previous master was a good man."

"My previous master wasn't the first. I was sold many times before he bought me."

"So, those men who attacked you in Nagra. Who were they?"

"They were my master's sons. They were nothing like my master. Till I met Habya, I had thought he was one of a kind." A scowl spread across his face. "The old man had taken me to Nagra with his sons and a few others for a business dealing. His sons hated me for the attention their father paid a mopra. On the journey there, he took ill. Shortly after we got to Nagra, he passed away. I knew that if I stayed my life would be miserable, if not over. So I gathered some of the books he had given me and ran away, but they found me. You know the rest." He leaned forward in his chair with a smile. "We make a good pair, do we not?"

Adir smiled. "Yea. We do."

A knock at the door drew Adir's attention.

"Probably Habya," Ghareeb said.

At the mention of Habya, Adir felt a broad smile span his face. "Come in," he said.

The door swung open, but much to Adir's disappointment, Lord Si'Pyaara strolled in with the captain of his guards.

"Look at that, Sinain!" Lord Si'Pyaara exclaimed, clapping his hands together, "my savior is awake!"

Adir stood. "My lord. May the Gods—"

Before Adir could finish what he was saying, the Cayani noble had grabbed him by the head and kissed each of his cheeks, an act that Adir found most disturbing. "If not for you, I would be dead," Lord Si'Pyaara said fervently. "How are you feeling?"

"I feel fine, my lord," Adir said. "Thank you for stopping at the outpost for me."

"No need to thank me," Lord Si'Pyaara said with an airy wave of his hand. "I am forever in your debt. May the Gods watch over you." He paused. "Now, I know I can never fully repay you, but I hope you will accept a small token of my appreciation."

"I don't need any reward, my lord," Adir said.

"It is not a reward, per se," the Cayani lord said. "And I have to say, I will actually end up reaping the benefits of this token."

Intrigued, Adir asked, "What is it, my lord?"

"How would you like to be one of my guards? I know you will watch out for me. Gods favor you, you have already risked your life for mine." The lord beamed. "And this can be your path to the fortunes you hoped to find in Cayan. What do you say?"

Adir thought for a moment. "That is most generous, my lord. And I accept. Gladly." He had to accept of course. Working as Lord Si'Pyaara's personal guard would allow him to be around Habya!

"Excellent!" Lord Si'Pyaara beamed again. He appeared to be in a fine humor. Then turning to the captain of his guards, he said, "So, what do you think, Sinain? Will he make a good recruit?"

Sinain scrutinized Adir, then nodded. "He took down an elk single-handedly," he said with a lilting Cayani accent that stood in stark contrast to his muscular build. "He certainly has potential."

Chapter Twenty-Eight

"Come in," Dina said. The door opened and a servant in yellow-and-white livery entered her bedchamber, which was warmly lit by the late-summer afternoon sun.

"Heiress Regent," the servant said, bowing and holding out a scroll and two books, "the Master Archivist sent a scribe with this."

A burst of excitement shot through Dina as she perused her delivery. It had been almost three months since her visit to the Lanmeria Library where the Master Archivist, Cassail Tymanol, had promised her more books on the subject of venna. Since then, she had exhausted the collection of books in the palace library. It had been tedious, boring work—opening books, skimming introductions or the first chapter, then disappointedly tossing them aside. Frustrated, she had given up on her search. That was, until now.

"Thank you," Dina said, accepting the items. The servant bowed and exited the room.

Using her long thumbnail, she carefully peeled the seal off the scroll and unrolled it, revealing three sheets of paper. She began reading the very first sheet.

Day 2 of Pagirai, 6996

Lady Dina Arinol, Heiress Regent …

Dina skimmed through the honors and pleasantries, then a heartfelt apology followed by rationalization for the wait—Cassail had some of his scribes work up detailed summaries of the two books.

The first book, titled 'Life of the Kheryne Khuun,' contains the accounts of an explorer who crossed the Bahzenelyn—a feat most rarely attempted and only accomplished by him, so far—to live with the Kheryne savages for a time. He mentions that the savages practice a corrupted version of Annadism called 'Adis Vilgaan.' Though the philosophy of that religion is nothing but barbaric, it is interesting to note that it contains a prophecy that places the venna right at its center.

Dina looked up from the scroll, mulling over what she had read. Clearly the Kheryne had something that resembled culture. Could they then rightly be called savages? But civilized folks did not believe in prophecies.

Without any warning, the door opened and Ekren strode in.

A warm elation filled Dina at the sight of her mother. It had been almost two months since Ekren had left for Ghatirodh, hoping to secure the region for Ostarium.

"Dina!" Ekren said with a broad smile, her arms outstretched.

Hurrying to her mother, Dina wrapped her arms around Ekren in a tight embrace. She loved her mother and had missed her dearly. Ekren was all she had known since she had been old enough to remember anything. Dina's father had died in a fire while trying to save her when she was but a babe. But Ekren had never made her feel the lack of a father. To her, Ekren was both her parents.

"The Gods heard my prayers and kept you safe," Dina said. "How was the journey?"

"Hmph, tiring," Ekren said. She made a face. "Though my mind feels as young as ever, my body is rebelling. My back is killing me from sitting in a saddle for days. Saddles are not made for a woman's behind." Ekren's green eyes smiled with her lips. Though her mother was in her middle years, she still held the beauty of years past.

"You should have just ridden in a carriage, mara." Dina felt slightly annoyed. How many times was she and the sarawaan supposed to badger Ekren till she got the point?

"This was a military expedition, Dina," her mother said, suddenly sounding like the Regent. "It would have been inappropriate for me to ride in a carriage. If it had been a diplomatic mission, then perhaps."

"Fine," Dina said in exasperation. She knew her mother would not see any sense till she was crippled in her old age, but even then Ekren would stubbornly refuse to ride in carriages. She decided to change the subject. "How did the troop placement go?"

"It went well," Ekren said, nodding. "We had to make some changes from the initial plan that you and I discussed. That reminds me, our maps will need to be updated. But we were able to secure vital points around Ghatirodh. In fact, we have secured it so well that Sorcha Camran sent over a messenger asking us to leave. *Asking!*" Ekren laughed a melodious yet ominous laugh.

The Ostarks did not have the largest force in the world—that honor fell to Naven—but they did have the most powerful force. The rebel leader could do no more than to ask the mighty Ostarks to leave.

"Would you parley with her?"

Ekren shook her head. "There is no need. The fact that she has not raided our forces since we set foot on that soil makes me think that her forces are not very large." She, very indelicately, scratched under her nose. "She could be buying time to strengthen her forces, I suppose. But by the time that happens, our reinforcements should be in place."

"When do we plan to send reinforcements?"

"Maybe in a few months. If we send in too many troops too soon, Kierand could see that as an act of invasion. We certainly do not want that. Also, if and when Sorcha strengthens her forces, Kierand himself will beg us to send more troops." Ekren paused, glancing at the clock on the wall. "Anyway," she continued, "I better get going or Ferrith will scold me in that calm way he always does. I hate that. Just raise your voice once in a while." She laughed. "But I have been away so long that I am sure I have quite a lot of state-related matters to attend to, and I need to get washed up before I get to it."

"You do smell quite pungent," Dina said with a chuckle. "Proper Ostark women should not smell so foul." Dina clamped her nose shut and smiled.

"You better show some respect to your Lady Regent," Ekren chided affectionately. Then she lightly kissed Dina on her cheek. "I will see you at dinner and you can tell me everything you have been up to these last two months."

Dina could feel the books and scroll on the table behind her, but she was not about to tell Ekren about her findings. At least, not yet. "Of course," she said. "I will see you at dinner. May the Gods watch over you, mara."

"And you as well, daughter." Flashing Dina a warm, motherly smile, Ekren turned and exited the room.

Once the door was completely shut, Dina returned to her seat and picked up the scroll, eyes scanning to find where she had left off reading.

The second book, titled 'Of The Shadow' is not of much academic worth as a few of the author's works were found to be fraudulent, which in turn had the effect of discrediting all of his works. But I thought this book might be of interest to you since it delves into the inner workings of a secret society called the Khasmia Shadow, who hunted venna. Apparently, the goal of this society was to capture the venna's supposed powers in a weapon called the Staff of Beckoning, but it does not mention why or how. I would approach this book with a sense of caution given the author's reputation and the fact that no other record of this society or the staff has ever been found, though not from lack of searching. This could very well be another one of his fraudulent works.

After wishing her well, the letter ended with the Master Archivist's graceful signature. Dina sifted through the other sheets and found that they were the detailed summaries the scribes had worked on. Putting the sheets aside, she picked up each book and idly flipped through the pages. The explorer's book was thin, and the pages bore large letters, while the book about the secret society was thick with small, exquisite penmanship. Within the first few pages of the latter book, however, Dina spotted the same symbol she had made a rubbing of in Ekren's study almost three months ago. The sight of the two-toned metal symbol with seven sinewy strands atop a dark ring further elevated her excitement. So far she had found a poem, a savage prophecy, the ravings of a supposedly discredited author, and the book in her mother's study. She certainly had her work cut out for her if she were to get to the bottom of this.

Chapter Twenty-Nine

The gardens that bordered the villa's west end were a burst of colors from the late summer blooms of pink stonecrops, white daffodils, and chrysanthemums of a variety of shades —Pagirai was always a beautiful month. Though the flowers put a smile on her face, Habya found herself wishing for the lotuses from Naven—they had been so majestic. Unfortunately, she was unable to bring any back with her to Omanna. She had, however, brought something else back from that land, though he was no flower.

Over the course of their two-week journey to her homeland, Habya had only increased her liking of the lanky man. Well, it was more than a liking. And since Adir was now one of her father's guards, the two had found some time every day to enjoy each other's company. Adir had a charm that was irresistible. Even her mothers and siblings had fallen prey to it. Everyone except Nabila.

"He is late," Nabila said impatiently. Her long blonde hair swished from side to side as she shook her head in frustration.

"He will be here soon," Habya said. They had been meeting in the gardens after lunch for a few weeks now, as her father usually napped after gobbling down a large meal, thereby freeing Adir from his duties.

"Soon is still late," Nabila said. "I have other things to do, you know, not just keep an eye out while you two whisper sweet nothings to each other."

"Thank you, keki," Habya said.

"You owe me," her older sister said with a fond smile.

And she certainly did. Though Habya hadn't told Nabila of her interest in Adir, her older sister had somehow figured it out. Upon being confronted by Nabila during one of their garden rendezvous, Habya had admitted to her feelings for Adir. Surprisingly, Nabila had been quite understanding, though she had been skeptical about Habya's future with Adir—he was lowborn, after all, and not a Cayani. But despite her skepticism, Nabila seemed to encourage their relationship; it had been Nabila's idea that she keep watch while Habya and Adir met, lest someone else spot them.

Habya did not even want to think about what would happen if she and Adir were ever caught. She certainly would be disowned by her family. And Adir would be executed, if he was lucky, or worse—he could be made a mopra.

"Here he comes," Nabila said. "He looks like he's starved. I will not be surprised if we find out one day that the wind blew him away to sea."

"Do not say such things," Habya said, irritated. "It might come true." She muttered a quick prayer asking the Gods to disregard her sister's words, then added, "Besides, I like him the way he is."

Nabila chuckled. "Of course *you* would say that."

"Hello, ladies," Adir said cheerfully as he arrived, palma strapped to his back. His smile touched his eyes.

"Took you long enough to get here," Nabila chided.

"I apologize, my lady." Adir bowed his head. "Your father kept me from getting here on time."

Nabila gave Adir a sharp look. "Likely excuse."

"Keki, leave him alone," Habya said. Nabila, like Adir, had a bit of a temper. "Now, are you going to waste more of your precious time scolding him for something he had no control over?"

Nabila gave Habya a long, menacing look. "Fine!" she finally said indignantly. "Go!"

"Thank you, keki." Habya gave her a smile over her shoulder as she strode into the garden with Adir.

Walking side by side, they made their way down the stone path. A few bees buzzed about busily, hopping from flower to flower. To their right stood a peacock, tail feathers fanned in splendor. The bird had been a gift from the muslar to her father.

"Why did akka keep you?" Habya asked once they were far enough away from Nabila's hearing.

"He wanted to tell me that I was to join him at the Grand Council meeting preceding Daroongaamen," Adir replied.

"That is a great honor." Sinain had been the only one, so far, to accompany her father to such events. But her father held Adir in high esteem—after all, Adir had saved his life. She did not doubt that that fact had a lot to do with why Adir had been so easily accepted into her household. However, if her relationship with Adir was ever discovered, she was convinced that Adir's brave act would not count for much.

"Absolutely!" Adir said excitedly.

"I have to admit that I am a little jealous. I have begged akka to take me to Grand Council events, but he never has." Of course, Cayani women did not involve themselves in such matters, but Abdel had taken her on other diplomatic missions, despite staunch opposition from her mothers.

"You have no reason to be jealous," Adir said with a laugh. "You're his favorite!"

Habya felt herself smile at that. Adir knew how to make her smile. "Maybe," she conceded.

Turning around a hedge, they came upon morningdew bushes arrayed on either side of their path, running down its length. She bent down and plucked one. Its blood-red, yellow-streaked petals lay spread open, tips curling in on themselves. She showed it to Adir. "Do you know what this flower is called?" she asked.

Adir examined it closely. "Yea. It's a red flower, right?" Then he burst out laughing.

Habya smacked him on the shoulder, but he just laughed louder.

"I'm sorry, I'm sorry," Adir said, reining himself in. "What is it called?"

"Morningdew." She huffed.

"The name does the flower justice," Adir said. "Is this your favorite flower?" he asked sweetly.

"No, but it is an important flower in Cayani culture."

"Why?"

Habya looked into his dark brown eyes. They held a certain optimism, despite what he had endured in his past. Adir had been very open about his life before her. About the disappearance of his mother and his relationship with his father; about how he had almost been killed by someone named Boar then blamed for that man's death; about his escape from Marafel and the attack on his life in Meneres; about Tia—he had been surprisingly honest about Tia, down to the details of his reticence to marry and the reason for that woman's departure. In light of that, she wondered whether it was wise to mention the importance of morningdews.

"Well," Habya began, deciding to tell him the truth. His honesty about his past revealed a certain weight to their relationship. "In Cayan, when a man wants to ask a woman to marry him, he brings her three morningdews and lays them at her feet, then gets on both knees and asks for her hand."

Adir smiled at her. "Three, huh?" he said. "Why three?"

"That is a good question." Habya was pleased that Adir was interested in her customs. "One for the man, one for the woman, and one for their life together."

"Ah! That seems … appropriate."

"Of course," Habya said as a sobering thought crept in, "before all that, the man and the woman need their parents' blessings." Something she knew was impossible in their situation.

"I don't think that would be a problem," Adir said calmly. He grabbed the morningdew she had plucked from her hand and placed it behind her ear, then smiled.

Habya smiled, imagining her father accepting Adir's proposal. His optimism was infectious. But in Cayan, when optimism and reality clashed, reality always won.

That worry was for another day though. For now, Habya was happy with what she had.

Chapter Thirty

Adir walked down the crowded street, looking up at the tall buildings on either side with their colorful domed roofs. Even the stalls and handcarts had some fashion of domed roofing atop them. He didn't quite understand the fascination, but it was a stark reminder that he was not in Naven anymore.

If the domed roofs weren't enough of a reminder, then the sight of the tall, humped creatures called dromeds that the nobility rode on certainly did the trick. When one of those brown creatures ambled toward you, it was best to get out of its way, not to avoid getting trampled—dromeds were very gentle creatures—but rather to avoid earning the ire of a Cayani noble.

Folks also dressed quite differently in this land, though strictly speaking, he was the one who was oddly clothed. Men mostly donned seherwanis—the long, buttoned shirt that Ghareeb always wore—with loose-fitting pants, while women clothed themselves in silken skirts, long blouses, and translucent veils—the veils were only worn in public. Cayani women held an elegant beauty Adir hadn't encountered before. And none was more beautiful than his Habya.

The Cayani noblewoman had a firm grasp on his mind and soul. Her smile played pleasant melodies with his heartstrings. Her gaze gently pierced through his persona and caressed his true inner self. She was understanding and kind, but she also told him exactly when he was being foolish.

Adir was glad that Habya had come into his life, though he couldn't help feeling guilty for how quickly it had all happened. He hadn't realized that he was falling for her while he had, in some way, promised himself to Tia. But he couldn't change the past. And of all places, he found solace in Tia's words. *You cannot help whom you love,* she had written. For that and many other things, he would forever be in Tia's debt.

As Adir turned a corner, he noticed a sizable crowd gathered ahead, in front of a busy bazaar. Upon getting closer, he heard shouts for mercy emanating from the center of the crowd, amidst the heaving sobs of a child.

"Please, m'lady! Spare this worthless soul!" a woman's voice cried out. Then he heard a blunt thump, instantly followed by screams of pain.

Adir walked up to the edge of the crowd and lifted up onto his toes to see what was happening, out of a morbid curiosity. But he was unable to catch even a glimpse.

"YOU DON'T DESERVE MERCY!" another woman's voice cried out, full of hate and venom. Then he heard another blunt thump and the screams stopped. Then more thumps followed in quick succession. An excited murmur rose among those gathered, but Adir felt a rotten pit form in his stomach as the child's cries wailed on.

The dense crowd shifted and Ghareeb squeezed his way out—cheeks the same fiery red as his hair, eyes stained red by tears.

"Ghareeb!" Adir called out. Ghareeb met his eyes, but the Pelerian man wasn't looking at him. "Are you all right?"

Ghareeb stared at him blankly for another moment, then asked, "Where are you headed?"

"I'm going to spar with Sinain at the gymnasium."

"I will walk with you." He gestured for Adir to lead the way.

Adir obliged and the two began walking down the street away from the still-enthralled crowd. Ghareeb walked in unusual silence.

"Are you all right?" Adir asked again.

"No," Ghareeb replied in a gruff voice. "No, I am not all right." His tone was uncharacteristically harsh.

"Because of what happened back there?"

Ghareeb stopped in his tracks, leaving Adir to walk a few steps ahead before he realized. He stopped and turned to face his friend— the bottom of his shirt following the afternoon ocean breeze. People shuffled by the two, tossing them annoyed looks. Abruptly, Ghareeb realized the attention they were attracting and walked on to join him. The two continued on their way.

"Do you know why that woman died today?" Ghareeb asked, but before Adir could respond, he continued. "Do you know why that child lost a mother today?"

"No," Adir replied truthfully.

"Because the true-blooded Cayani woman did not think the mopra got out of her way quick enough," Ghareeb said with a cold disgust. "What is quick enough?"

"I … I don't know," Adir said.

Ghareeb shook his head. "I do not know either." He gave Adir a quick look. "Remember when I told you that all Cayani are monsters? You see how that is true, do you not? No one in the crowd even lifted a finger as a woman lost her life in front of their eyes." Ghareeb dropped his head and scoffed. "I did not do anything either."

"But you couldn't," Adir said. "If you intervened and they found out that you are—" He quickly looked around to see if anyone was listening. "You know what I mean."

Ghareeb's lips twisted up in a smile, but there was no mirth in it. "That is how they keep us where we are. They make us fear for our lives." He paused for a long moment. "But all our lives are forfeit the day we are born."

Adir could feel Ghareeb's pain as they walked in silence. Ever since they had stepped foot in Cayan, Adir had noticed a change in Ghareeb. The once-boisterous man was suddenly reserved. What could he say about it though?

The mopra were made to do all the jobs that the Cayani considered themselves too good for, and they got killed for it or they lived a life of misery. He did not understand why a whole group of people would be subject to such mistreatment. Life as a mopra wasn't something he could relate to, but he wasn't blind to it. He could see the fear and apprehension in every mopra's eyes. Knowing that they could be killed at any moment, despite following the unjust rules set forth by those in power, withered away a part of them. Was such a life worth living?

The silence stretched on till they approached an intersection.

"I have to go do something," Ghareeb said abruptly. "I will see you later."

"What do—" Adir began, but Ghareeb had already turned left. "May the Gods watch over you!" he yelled from behind as Ghareeb walked away.

Adir carried on straight through the intersection and made his way toward the gymnasium where Abdel's guards trained in the afternoons. A brisk ocean breeze slightly broke the humidity of the late-summer afternoon, but Adir barely noticed. His mind was busy mulling over Ghareeb's view of the Cayani.

Were all Cayani monsters? From what Ghareeb had said and what he'd seen since coming to this land, Adir couldn't deny that there was some truth to it. The treatment of the mopra was inhumane to say the least. Though scenes like the one earlier were not commonplace, neither were they uncommon. And who could say what happened behind the walls of a Cayani's dwelling? Yet the Si'Pyaaras didn't seem like monsters. Sure, they could treat their mopra better—let them live free lives—but, given the culture and circumstances, the Si'Pyaaras' mopra were far from being treated ill. Even Ghareeb had agreed with that.

Shortly, Adir arrived at the gymnasium. It, too, had a domed roof, painted in swirling colors of red and green. Turning in, he walked through a couple of hallways and entered the sparring ring. Sinain was already there, warming up. Lord Si'Pyaara's Captain of the Guards had taken him under his wing for three reasons.

The first—and possibly the most important—was that Adir had saved Abdel's life. The Cayani nobleman was well loved by those who worked for him. Even the mopra.

The second reason was that according to the captain and a few other guards, Adir had exhibited an exceptional talent with the staff. He had Captain Marwar to thank for that, of course. Sinain's goal was to take that talent and apply it to the palma. The odd staff with its broad and slightly curved blade at the end had been fairly easy to learn. The basics were the same as a staff, except, unlike the staff, thrusts to the chest ended with a twisting of the blade. *For a quick and painless death*, Sinain had said.

The third reason was that Adir had single-handedly killed an elk. Though Sinain was in the dark concerning the details of what had occurred during the hunt.

Venna. That's what Ghareeb had called him.

Wrapped in a haze resplendent with the colors of the Aurora, Adir had felt transformed. He'd been able to see each strand of hair on the elk move as the animal charged. He could hear its every breath despite the much louder thumping of its hooves. The strength he had felt within himself was unimaginable. He had jumped so effortlessly over the elk that he hadn't realized how high he'd jumped till Ghareeb described it to him. That state of being was intoxicating, beckoning him to take it up again. It was like nothing he had felt before! But no matter how hard he tried, he hadn't been able to do it again, though that maybe a good thing, he realized. He also realized something else: he had killed Boar, though not intentionally.

How long can I keep this secret? Adir wondered. Every time he'd transformed, it had come about abruptly and without his will. What if he transformed when he was with Sinain? Or walking down a street? Or worse, when he was with Habya? Though he'd been very candid about his past to his love, he couldn't get himself to tell her about this *condition*.

"Sinain," Adir called out, pushing those thoughts aside. "May the Gods favor you."

Sinain, a man of an age with his father, stopped his warmup routine. "Adir! May the Gods favor you as well. Are you ready for some sparring?"

"Of course," Adir said excitedly, as they only sparred with weapons on one day of the week. Three days were devoted to hand-to-hand combat, while the other three days were spent training with the palma, honing his movements and control of the weapon. There were no rest days, as, according to Sinain, *We can rest when we die.*

Adir walked to the weapon rack and grabbed a training palma—the sword at the end was made of wood—then made his way to the middle of the ring.

"Do you remember everything we talked about in the last few sessions?" Sinain asked, eyeing him with a smile.

"Yea," Adir said politely.

"Good. Perform a few admaars and shirmaars to get warmed up and then we will start."

Adir obliged and walked to one side of the ring to go through the exercises. He brought his legs together and stood with a straight back. With an adjacent grip, he held the palma about two-thirds of the way from the sword tip and began performing shirmaars. He brought the palma down in overhead arcs, first from his right side, then his left, looping their motion together in figure eights with increasing speed. When the motion of the palma began guiding the motion of his wrists, he widened his stance by stepping out with his left leg. The change in his position shifted his balance, giving him a moment of instability that immediately flowed into an equilibrium as he swirled the shirmaars into praars, palma swinging overhead and cutting a wide frontal arc through the air.

"The boy looks good, Sinain!" Zaal's voice called out. "I think I am going to put my money on him today."

"I will take that bet, since you are so keen on losing your money," Fini said.

Adir really liked the sound of that, but he held back any outward expression of it and continued his warmup. Bringing his feet together, he smoothly transitioned from praars to admaars by looping figure eights of upward arcs. The figure eights slowed, and he brought the palma to a stop.

"Good," Sinain said, then cuffed Adir at the back of his head. "I did not ask you to perform any praars."

Adir rubbed at his hurt. "Sorry. But I thought I needed more of a warmup."

Sinain raised his arm as if to cuff Adir again, but held back and smiled. "All right. Show me what this additional warmup did." With that, Sinain threaded his palma between Adir's legs and pulled, tripping him to the ground.

Quickly, Adir rolled away. The Cayani didn't believe in opening rituals like proving the distance. If two warriors were in proximity, the fight had already started.

Adir sprang to his feet and took a few steps back. But Sinain was on him in a flash. Adir swung to put some distance between the two, but the man bent backward like a willow in strong winds. The moment Adir's swing arced away, Sinain looped his palma behind Adir's and clamped it to his chest. Adir held on to his palma tightly and was pulled toward the brawny man. In the next instant, Adir felt a foot on his stomach pushing him away with enough force to send him staggering to the ground, leaving his palma in Sinain's clutches.

Sinain tossed Adir's palma to the side and closed in on him. Adir got to his feet, unarmed. He eyed his polearm, but there was no way he could get to it. His only recourse was to get inside Sinain's reach and disarm him.

Palma swinging, Sinain attacked. Adir ducked and the palma harmlessly passed over his head. He lunged toward Sinain, arms outstretched. But Sinain took one perfect step to the side and Adir flew by him, crashing to the floor. The next moment, Sinain had his palma pointed at his throat.

"Pay up!" Fini said from the other side of the ring.

"Fine," Zaal replied. "You let me down, Adir," he called out.

Fini laughed. "Did you really think he stood a chance against Sinain?" Zaal did not respond.

Sinain withdrew his palma. "If you had remembered what I have been telling you so far," he said, extending an arm out to Adir, "I would not have bested you so easily."

"I thought I did well," Adir said, taking Sinain's arm and standing.

"If you lost, you did not do well," Sinain said bluntly, and Adir felt a bitterness form in his mouth. "Your movements are still choppy. You focus too much on yourself and the now. You react. Remember, it is all about Continuity. Every movement of your body, every twitch of your muscles, every breath should be part of your Continuity."

Continuity was the essence of Cayani martial arts. Utilizing Continuity meant that a fighter's every move, every breath, was to flow seamlessly and unperturbed. Like a river that didn't care about the rock in its path and simply flowed around it. But fights were so chaotic, especially against a seasoned opponent like Sinain, that Adir hardly found time to react, let alone go on the offensive or breathe consciously. In theory, Continuity felt simple, but in practice, it was quite another thing. Sinain himself had acknowledged that it took years of practice to hone one's perception and skill in Continuity.

"Yea, I get that," Adir said. He'd heard this lecture multiple times a day for many weeks, ever since he'd accepted Lord Si'Pyaara's offer to work as one of his guards.

"Then apply it! Knowledge unused is useless."

"But when you attack, you disrupt my Continuity."

Sinain shook his head. "Do not think of your opponent as an invasion of your Continuity. Rather, see him as part of it."

Adir nodded, but he had no idea what Sinain was talking about. Still, he felt confident that he'd get the hang of it soon. After all, he did have a talent for this kind of thing. Then one day, he would surprise Sinain in a spar. "I'll work harder to apply what I've learned," he said.

"If not, I will literally hammer it into you," Sinain said with a smile, then he walked over to a watertable and began drinking handfuls of water.

For some reason, Adir didn't doubt that. The man had some unorthodox ways of teaching. When Adir had first arrived in Omanna, Sinain and the guards had taken him to an eatery. After an enjoyable meal, the serving girl had brought everyone bowls of hot water with lime slices in it. Sinain had told him that the lime water was to aid in the digestion of their meal, and so Adir had squeezed the lime into the water and had drunk it. The whole table burst into laughter. Sinain had then confessed that the bowl of water was meant to be a wash bowl.

Despite his unorthodox methods of teaching, Sinain had taught Adir many of the Cayani ways and always welcomed questions. So far, Adir had stayed away from topics that he found uncomfortable to broach—like mopra. But the mopra were everywhere and their plight was hard to ignore, especially after the incident he'd heard that day.

"Sinain," Adir began, unsure of whether he should continue.

"Ya?" Sinain's blond hair was matted down with sweat.

"Why are the mopra treated the way they are?" Adir hoped he hadn't crossed the line.

"Because they are mopra," Sinain said with the nonchalance that was displayed by those discussing mundane affairs like weather. He didn't seem the least bit offended.

"But why are they mopra?"

"O. Well, because they are unclean and unworthy souls."

"You mean they are like the Faithless?"

"No," Sinain said, shaking his head. "The Faithless have simply lost their way. They just don't know any better. But the mopra are unworthy souls cast aside by the Gods themselves for reasons that are beyond our understanding."

"So if we don't understand the reason why their souls are unworthy," Adir probed, "how do we know that someone is truly a mopra?"

"You can tell that a fruit is bad by just looking at it, can you not?" Sinain said. "Sometimes the tree the fruit comes from is diseased. At other times, they simply turn bad. It is the same with mopra. If you are born a mopra, your soul is already unclean. If you commit rotten acts, that means you have an unworthy soul and will be branded a mopra. And those with unworthy souls will only beget others with unworthy souls."

Adir swallowed at the implication of Sinain's words and the lightness with which he spoke. It felt wrong to him that an innocent child born to mopra parents was instantly branded a mopra. A child who didn't understand what it meant.

What will happen to the child who was orphaned this afternoon? Adir thought. But who was he to question the Gods or millennia of humanity's knowledge. Maybe the mopra were unworthy, though Ghareeb didn't seem so. The more he saw of life, the less sense it made to him. Why did people blindly follow the will of the Gods? Couldn't they think and feel for themselves? It seemed no matter where he went, no one truly understood the mind of the Gods. *How can people believe in something without understanding it? How could the Gods let some of their own creations be treated in such a manner?*

Sinain seemed to have noticed Adir's pensive mood. "Do not worry yourself about this, Adir," he said. "Mopra are mopra. Their lives are of no importance to Faithful like you and me."

Chapter Thirty-One

Ghareeb was uncertain as to why he was sitting in this familiar banyan tree, overlooking a Cayani's flower garden. It had been years since the last time he had climbed it—an action born of a child's promise made with a child's understanding of love. *I'll wait in this tree every day till you return,* he had told her. She had not returned. But watching the mopra woman get bludgeoned to death this morning brought back memories of her, along with an irrational fear for her safety. He did not know where she was or if she was even alive. However, he had to come back here, despite the futility of the gesture.

The door on the second-floor balcony swung open and a woman walked out holding a watering pot and a heavy bucket. Ghareeb pulled his legs up onto the branch he was perched on and crouched, holding on to the tree trunk. Getting caught would not end well for him. He should have left as soon as he realized that the once-empty house was now occupied, but his mind was lost in fond memories.

Awkwardly, the woman carried her burden down a set of stairs from the balcony into the small garden below. She filled the watering pot from the bucket and began watering, one potted plant at a time.

When the watering pot was empty, she refilled it from the bucket and continued with her task.

Careful not to rustle leaves, Ghareeb scooted toward the tip of the branch to get a better look, while holding on to another branch for balance. As he got farther out, the branch under his feet bent and let out a small cracking sound.

Ghareeb froze as the woman looked in his direction, but not before leveraging his weight onto the branch he was holding. After a moment, the woman returned to her task and Ghareeb felt like he could move again. Taking a couple of steps back to where the branch was thicker, he leaned toward the garden.

Immediately, he spotted the mark of the mopra on the woman's cheek. His eyes traced the outline of her face and he squinted as if willing his eyes to see better. *Could it be?* It was! Only, she was older. She wasn't the girl he once knew, but rather a new woman.

Ghareeb's heart beat faster than dromed toes on race days. Before his mind could determine the right course of action, his body jumped into the garden. Slowly, he walked the few steps toward her, approaching her from behind. She must have sensed him as she stopped her watering and turned her head slightly, seemingly focusing on his shadow.

"HEL—"

Instinctively, Ghareeb covered her mouth with his hand and pulled her close. Her cry ceased immediately and, unsurprisingly, she did not struggle. This was how mopra were conditioned to react to assaults. Give up! What if their assailant was a true-blooded Cayani? Giving up might mean living … just to give up another day.

Ghareeb released her, ashamed by his reaction. But the woman did not turn or run away; she simply stood. Frozen with fear. Ghareeb knew that if she could, she would force the breeze from shifting a single strand of her short blonde hair.

"Aiysta," Ghareeb said softly.

At the sound of his voice, the woman's shoulders visibly relaxed. Slowly, she turned and faced him. As he looked into her eyes the blue of ocean water, he first saw shock, then recognition, then tears.

"My Pelerian Ghareeb," Aiysta said, matching his tone. When she smiled, it was as if no one else existed but the two of them.

"Does this count as me keeping my promise?" Ghareeb asked, then moved to embrace her, but Aiysta stopped him with a palm.

"Someone might see us," she whispered, wiping away her tears. "Come with me."

Grabbing his arm, Aiysta led him to a corner of the small garden, where stood a wooden shed. She pulled him into the space between the back of the shed and the wall that surrounded the house. While Aiysta's slender figure easily passed through the small space, Ghareeb found himself somewhat squeezed. He wasn't a big man, but he had broad shoulders.

When they were safely hidden, Aiysta threw her arms around him and the two embraced for a long while. Then she abruptly pushed him off her. "You should leave," she said. "M'lord will be back soon."

Ghareeb did not respond. Instead he looked at every inch of her, trying to memorize the new Aiysta. She was much taller than before, merely a hand shorter than he. Her face that was once slightly chubby was now lean and angled in a most pleasing way. Yet her eyes still held the sorrow he had seen so long ago. Right where her ears met her face was a fresh purple bruise, just above her mark. Gently, he touched it with his fingertips.

"Your master hits you?" Ghareeb asked, managing to keep the anger out of his voice.

Aiysta's rough hand grabbed his and moved it away. "Do not worry yourself over it."

"Aiysta," he said gently, "tell me."

Aiysta gave him a look of mild annoyance, then said in a normal tone, "After m'lady passed away a few years ago, m'lord called me into his bedchamber one night and used me to cure his loneliness." She paused, looking away. "He still gets lonely sometimes. Sometimes, he gets a little rough."

"He defiles you and beats you? I—"

"This is why I did not want to tell you," Aiysta scolded in a whisper. "You haven't changed at all, have you? Still believing that our masters treat us unjustly. M'lord is not a bad person. This is simply the life of a mopra."

"It does not have to be."

Aiysta shook her head. "But it is."

"I can take you away from here."

"Do not speak such blasphemy. You may not understand because you were made a mopra. But I was born a mopra and have lived long enough to realize that this is how things are." She paused for a moment, took a deep breath, and let it out slowly. "The Gods have forsaken us," she said calmly, "why shouldn't man?"

"Because the Gods have not forsaken us."

Aiysta waved her hand dismissively. Ghareeb was glad to see that she still used that haughty gesture, despite her status in life. "How can you be so sure?" she asked.

"Because I escaped from my masters and the Gods have not struck me down." He said it more harshly than he intended.

"Is that why you have the beard? To conceal your mark?" Her eyes were wide with surprise. Ghareeb nodded. "How did you escape?" she asked.

"I had some help," Ghareeb said as his mind raced back to the night of his rescue, which was also the night he'd met Adir for the first time. The same man responsible for him being in this godsforsaken land. "My last master, a kind Cayani, had taken me to Naven on some business. He passed away while we were in a town called Nagra and I became the property of his sons, who were like every other red-blooded Cayani. Monsters. Needless to say, I could not stay with them, Aiysta. If I had, I would not be alive today."

"You should not have left, Ghareeb. That is not our way."

"No man or woman should be treated the way mopra are treated," Ghareeb protested. "We deserve better!"

"We are living the lives we deserve." Aiysta touched his face gently.

Abruptly, the sound of screeching metal interrupted their conversation. "M'lord just got home," Aiysta said, panic plain in her voice. "You need to go. Now!" Aiysta's expression held the fear that every mopra felt for their masters. She pushed him out of the tiny space. "Climb over the wall and leave. Please!"

Ghareeb heaved himself onto the wall then straddled it. "I will be back, Aiysta," he said.

"I know," Aiysta said with a strained smile.

Ghareeb jumped down into the narrow street on the other side of the wall and walked away from the house that was Aiysta's prison. It was worse than a prison—people could get out of prison once they'd served their sentence. But Aiysta could not. He would not let her live like that. There was a better life for her, and he was proof of it. He would get her out of there, even if it was the last thing he did.

Chapter Thirty-Two

"We are sheltering almost three hundred Kheryne refugees," Ellyn said. "And all of them say that they were driven out of their homes by the rakhor."

Arvan turned the wine in his glass then sipped at it, idly using one leg to sustain the swing's slow motion on Ellyn's veranda. He sensed the fear that Ellyn held at bay so well. Maybe he didn't sense it, but rather knew it was there. Everyone was afraid, but not many liked to show it or even admit it.

That one dinner, almost two and a half months before, had turned into several, and Arvan found himself enjoying the food and her company; the latter more so than the former. Maybe it was because Ellyn reminded him of Malia, or maybe it was because when he was in her company he was able to breathe a little easier. "That's quite a lot of people. How's the Council handling it?"

"Poorly." Ellyn laughed. "Gray and Niman want to send them back. They think that the Kheryne Khuun are gathering their numbers in Naven before they attack and take over. They also think that the Kheryne will corrupt our youth with their Adis Vilgaan philosophy and recruit them into their ranks." She shook her head. "Those are such preposterous notions that I feel like the only reason they're doing it is because those two enjoy being the thorns in our feet." She paused. "Worst part is that quite a few villagers seem to be adopting their paranoia. I don't see why. The Kheryne are assimilating well."

Arvan nodded. "Gray and Niman have always been that way. I don't understand how they keep getting re-elected."

"I don't know." Ellyn huffed. The conversation lulled for a few moments. "What I am more interested in," she went on, "is how similar the stories of the Kheryne refugees are. And they all seem to say that *bands* of rakhor raided their yirias. I have never heard of rakhor roaming in bands. Have you?"

Arvan shook his head.

"That's what I thought."

"But just because we've never seen more than one or two at a time doesn't mean that the demonspawn don't gather in larger numbers." The Navengaard had taught Arvan to consider every eventuality, no matter how unlikely the situation. It was always better to be prepared than get caught off-guard. "Do you have any reason to doubt the Kheryne?"

Ellyn shrugged, then sipped at her wine. "I'm glad that the Watchmen are here."

"If what the Kheryne say is true, we'll need more Watchmen."

"I agree." Ellyn nodded. "Laraan has sent word to King Taschari. Akkasha has done the same." She paused for a moment. "How are the Kheryne at your farmhouse faring?"

Arvan smiled, remembering the first day he had brought Tegeth, Erebi, and Nugai to the farmhouse. A family of Kheryne—it was rare for a family to cross the Bahzenelyn intact. Nilane and Misuma had been afraid enough to ask for farmhands to stay by their side while the Kheryne were present. But as the weeks went by, Nilane had taken a liking to little Nugai, a sweet five-year-old girl with the most courageous soul. Tegeth was a great help with farm chores and his wife, Erebi, helped the other maids around the house. "They're doing quite well," Arvan replied.

"That's good to hear. And I knew you would be a good person to give them hope."

Hope? Arvan thought. How could he, a man unable to keep his family together, give hope to others?

Finishing off the rest of her wine, Ellyn placed her glass on a small table beside the swing and laid her head on his shoulder. Arvan smiled; he hadn't felt this closeness to a woman since Malia.

"Do you think you'll marry again?" Ellyn asked.

"I hadn't thought about it," Arvan admitted.

"I hadn't either," Ellyn said. "Till you came around." She looked up and smiled. Her eyes seemed to invite him to her lips.

Arvan leaned in and kissed her. "I think marriage sounds like a wonderful idea. Now that you've come around."

"SINCE THEY WERE SO CHEAP," Kirsch said amidst the calls of night creatures, as he leaned against the veranda's railing, "I bought ten cows." A cool evening breeze blowing across the Nathar farmhouse broke the heavy humidity of this late-summer night. "Nine to replace the ones we lost and a calf."

"Good, good," Arvan responded, but his mind was still with Ellyn. How was it that he could spend hours with that woman and still feel like only moments had passed?

"You seem a little distracted, sir," Kirsch said. "Is everything all right?"

"Of course," Arvan replied. "I was just thinking of something else. But anyway, you were saying that you purchased ten cows."

"Yea, sir." He paused for a moment, then continued, "Master Hirnar at the Soft Pillow said he saw Master Adir and his wife."

Arvan's heart soared. "Adir was in Nagra? With a wife?" This was wonderful news.

"Yea, sir. I believe Tia Ellar was his *wife*."

"Did you find them?"

"No, sir. Master Hirnar saw them about three months ago, but said they'd left the next day."

"Did he say where they went to?"

"Just that they headed west."

After all these months of searching, this was the first glimmer of hope Arvan had found. How he longed to see his son and reconcile. But, alas, it was not to be. Disappointment clenched his chest, but he fought it down with the practiced ease of a man who had mastered the art of burying his pain. *At least he's married Tia and I hope the two lead a Worthy life.* He forced his thoughts elsewhere. "By the way, did the sarawaan ever figure out what was ailing our cows?"

"No, sir. But apparently cows on other farms are also showing the same symptoms. She worries that we may have an—"

Kirsch gagged, then raised his hands to his neck, where a blade stuck out. The blade slid back out and blood oozed from the steward's mouth and neck wound.

"Kirsch!" Arvan cried out, leaping from his seat, but he was forcefully pushed back down onto the bench. The sharp edge of a blade rested against his throat.

A figure dressed all in black climbed up the steps to the veranda, sliding a long dagger into a sheath on the hip. A short, curved blade was sheathed at the other hip, while two sword hilts protruded over each shoulder. The approaching figure's face was covered, except for a horizontal slit that barely showed the eyes.

"If you answer my questions, you do not have to get hurt," the man said as he climbed the last step.

Arvan placed the man's accent. He was a Phucak—a thick-tongued Phucak. "You expect me to believe you after you killed my steward?" Arvan said. His military training had kicked in and he began listening to his breath in an effort to keep calm and collected.

"He was a liability," the man said. "Like those two women I found earlier."

Nilane and Misuma! These bastards had killed them!

"All I need to know," the black-clad figure continued, "is the whereabouts of your son."

What has that boy gotten himself into? Arvan thought. *Who are these men?*

The Phucak walked up to him. "Where is Adir?" he whispered. Arvan still did not respond. Abruptly, the man clutched his face in a firm grip. "Where is your son?" Arvan could hear the frustration in his voice.

The door to the house slammed open and another figure, also dressed all in black, strode out, dragging Athvan by his hair. "I ran into some Kheryne Khuun," the person said in a female voice. "They have been dealt with." She shook Athvan. "Found this one upstairs," she continued. "I was going to kill him too, but I wanted to make sure you agreed. I think he's the creature's brother. I see a resemblance."

The woman's accent marked her as a Herran. It was unheard of for a Herran and a Phucak to be in each other's presence, let alone work together. Phucao and Herraland had been mortal enemies ever since the War of Remaking.

"Akka!" Athvan cried.

"Athvan! Are you hurt?" Arvan asked, somehow managing to keep himself from screaming.

"My head!" Athvan wailed.

"Ah. So this *is* your son!" the Phucak said, then turned to the Herran woman. "Seems like it was a good thing you did not kill him."

"Don't hurt him," Arvan said. He suppressed the trembling that threatened to show his terror.

"A little trust would do us all some good," the Phucak replied without turning. As he approached Athvan, the Herran woman stood the boy up, still clutching his hair in her black-gloved fist.

"Do you know where your brother is?" the Phucak asked. Athvan did not reply. The man looked back at Arvan, shook his head, then slapped Athvan across the face.

"Athvan!" Arvan yelled, trying desperately to shake off his captor, but his captor simply strengthened his grip and pushed the blade into his throat slightly. Arvan immediately stopped moving—he couldn't help his son if he was dead.

"Do not make me hurt you again," the Phucak said to Athvan. "Do you know where your brother is?"

"I don't know!" Athvan cried.

The black-clad man didn't speak for a long moment but simply studied Athvan. "I know you are lying," he said. "Maybe we can try something else." Pulling out his long dagger, the man turned and walked back to Arvan. He swiped at him with one fluid motion. Blood seeped through Arvan's shirt before a sharp burn engulfed his chest. Arvan gritted his teeth.

"Akka! NO! NO!" Athvan cried.

"Tell me where your brother is or I will kill your father!" the Phucak yelled.

"He's in Meneres! Meneres!"

"Do you know where he went after Meneres?" the Phucak shouted.

"NOOOO!" Athvan was weeping. "He told me he was going to Meneres!"

"I think he's telling the truth," the Herran woman chimed in.

"I'll decide if he's telling the truth," the Phucak snapped. He glared at his companion for a long moment. "Fine. He's telling the truth," the man said then began walking away from Athvan. "Kill them both."

The words had barely left the Phucak's mouth when Arvan pushed off the table he was seated behind, sending himself and his captor crashing against the veranda's railing. His captor dropped his dagger. The table slid into the bench on the other side, which knocked against the Phucak's knee, tripping him. Taking advantage of the confusion, Arvan grabbed the dagger on the floor, turned, and stabbed his captor in the heart. The large masked figure dropped to the floor with a thump.

Arvan swung around in time to see the Phucak get to his feet. Stepping onto the bench, Arvan lunged downward toward the Phucak, but the Phucak simply spun away. The next moment, Arvan felt three quick slices across his back. And the moment after that, he was lying flat on the floor.

The Phucak stomped on Arvan's back. He felt a few ribs snap. Then he was grabbed by the hair and pulled up, his back bending the wrong way. Arvan felt the Phucak's mask brush against his ear.

"You were both going to die together," the Phucak whispered angrily in his ear. "But since you have been so … uncooperative, I think I will let you watch your son die." With that, the man slammed Arvan's face into the floor.

Arvan's head spun as a trickle of blood made its way down his nostril. Despite the pain he felt, Arvan managed to prop himself onto his knees. Immediately, the Phucak turned and sliced both his hamstrings. Arvan cried out in pain as he dropped to the floor once again. But the pain didn't matter. He had to get to Athvan. He could not fail him—like he had failed Malia and Adir. With useless legs dragging behind him, Arvan used his arms to pull himself toward his son.

"You are persistent," the Phucak said as he sliced under each of Arvan's armpits.

Once again Arvan cried out, though this time it was not because of the pain. He could no longer get to his son.

The Phucak calmly approached a sobbing Athvan. "Look at your akka." Athvan's tear-filled eyes met Arvan's. "Good." Then he slowly sliced Athvan's throat, his blade disappearing into the boy's neck. Athvan's cries were replaced by gurgling grunts. The Herran woman let go of him and he dropped to the floor, convulsing.

"NO!" Arvan yelled. He tried to will his limbs to move, but they did not. He tried to go to his son, but he could not.

The Phucak returned and plunged his blade into Arvan's back. Arvan felt the warm ooze of blood drenching his shirt.

"We'll need to carry Afzar's corpse all the way to the runeport," the Herran woman complained.

"We'll take their horses," the Phucak said, whipping the blood off of his blade in one smooth motion. "They will not need them anymore."

Arvan heard the Herran and the Phucak shuffling about as they gathered their dead companion. But Arvan could not take his eyes from his son who lay dying only a few paces from him. If Malia were still alive, would she forgive him for what he had done to their family?

Adir was right. He should never have married. He'd been a failure, as a husband and as a father.

Chapter Thirty-Three

Ekren sat at a small table at the front of the Ostark section, in a black leather chair. Other heads of state, except Herraland, sat at their respective lead tables as well. The sections of the eight civilized nations of Leakarha were arranged in a circle denoting the equality of nations in the Grand Council. Dina, Ferrith, and a few influential Ostarks, along with their aides, sat behind her. This year, she, as the Alamand of the Grand Council, had decided to hold the annual gathering at the Cayani Palace, and Muslar Hishayi had provided the use of his Gallery of Divinity. This location made the most sense, as all the rulers of nations would be present in Omanna for Daroongaamen.

"King Dooghlas apologizes that he was unable to make his presence at this gathering." The voice of one of the Herran representatives echoed in the expansive Gallery with its domed ceiling, painted with images of the seven Gods looking down on those gathered. "He is needed in our lands to squash the rebellion in the north."

Squash the rebellion? Ekren thought, adjusting her yellow salwar. The latest reports from her forces at Ghatirodh had reported that Kierand was pulling his forces closer to Pacca Nirum to defend the capital city. It seemed the Herran monarch had underestimated the rebel Sorcha Camran.

"Furthermore," the Herran representative continued, "his majesty would like to bring to attention the ineptitude of the Grand Council at providing any meaningful support to help secure the Lands of Herra!"

Muslar Mahmal Hishayi huffed. Even Cayani emotions seemed to have a lilt to them. "We are merely calling roll, my lord," the ruler of Cayan said. "You may bring up your grievances during your allotted time." The Herran representative grudgingly took his seat. The Muslar turned to Ekren. "Alamand Arinol," he said, his face disdainful, "we have quorum." Flaring the bottom of his seherwani, the Cayani king seated himself at the head of his section, pointedly looking away from her.

Ekren decided to ignore him. Cayani men were used to women serving their every whim. Strong women, like her, seemed to make them nervous. She swept her gaze across the Gallery. "On day thirteen of the eleventh month of Hrensa in the year of six thousand nine hundred ninety-six, I, Ekren Arinol, Alamand of the Grand Council and Regent of Ostarium, call this seventy-second annual gathering of the Grand Council to order," she said.

Presiding over Council gatherings was part of the Alamand's duties. That, and leading an inept organization. Kierand was absolutely right. The Grand Council no longer held the same sway in world politics as it once had. Ekren put the blame for the organization's fall on the bylaw that required a constant rotation of the position of Alamand. Every nation except Guerradrith, Aemonne, and Phucao—the perpetrators of the War of Remaking—held the position for five years. During its time as the Alamand of the Grand Council, each nation tried to use the position to advance its standing in the world, usually to the detriment of the other nations. Eventually this arrangement had led to mistrust and the inevitable impotence of the Grand Council.

"Before the floor is opened to the members of this esteemed Grand Council," Ekren continued, "the Council would like to make a statement." She paused and looked squarely at Tyndar Syanuenan, the

Guerran King. "The Council would advise Guerradrith to cease all acts of violence against their Herran and Aemonnil neighbors."

A few of the Guerran nobility snickered. Here was the significance of the Grand Council in full display. The Guerran men all wore their traditional garb of brocaded shirts, decorative longis—a thin fabric wrapped around their waists that fell all the way to their ankles—and embroidered headbands with the seal of Guerradrith that held their thick, curly hair in place. The two Guerran women wore long flowing dresses cinched at the waist by a thick leather belt.

"We'll cease our *acts of violence* when the Grand Council recognizes Guerradrith as a full member afforded all the privileges of the Council, which includes the position of Alamand," King Syanuenan said. The haughty Guerran accent was quite prevalent in his speech.

Ekren clenched her fists as a jolt of anger passed through her. Keeping her voice calm, she said, "You may bring up your petition for full membership during your allotted time."

"You know very well that my allotted time is naught but a farce!" the Guerran king spat, standing up. "You'll never consider our *petition* for membership." He made a disgusted expression.

"If you behave this way, your petition will never be considered," Muslar Hishayi said off-handedly. "You Guerrans are so barbaric!"

"Your day will come, Mahmal," King Syanuenan said. He was about to take a step toward the Cayani ruler seated to his left, when his queen reached forward and grabbed his hand, guiding the self-proclaimed Warrior King back to his seat.

Ekren stifled a sigh. Men were nothing but overgrown children; the world would be much better off if it were ruled by women. Facing King Jonnan Taschari, Ekren said, "King Taschari, you have the floor."

"Thank you, Alamand Arinol," King Taschari said, standing up. The rotund king of Naven garbed in the traditional Navenite two-tailed coat and turban began. "Esteemed Grand Council. Naven is in a time of need. A large number of Kheryne have left their lands and have crossed the Bahzenelyn Range."

Gasps and whispers escaped from those gathered. Ekren managed to keep her own surprise in check. What did the savages crossing the Bahzenelyn mean?

"However," King Taschari continued. "Reports from the towns and villages that have seen this influx of Kheryne do not report any savage behavior. In fact, the Kheryne are blending into our society well. But more and more of them trickle in every day and no end seems to be in sight. They are stretching small towns and villages thin and many have found their way to the capital. We are worried that we will be unable to feed and shelter all those who come. We'd like to ask the members of this esteemed Council for aid. Right now, we need food and clothes, but soon we will need to find them homes."

"We will be glad to help," Ekren said without hesitation. As one of the more powerful nations, Ostarium was obliged to help the lesser nations in their time of need. She would send them food and clothes, but even the Gods themselves could not force her to let any of the savages onto Ostark soil.

"We will be glad to help as well," said one of the Council of the Nine, the governing body of Peleria, with the characteristic metallic ring of the Pelerian accent. As usual, the Pelerian representatives flaunted their wealth with expensive velvet clothing, gold rings on every finger, and diamond-studded earrings in each ear. "We can negotiate the terms of the aid after this gathering." The Pelerians never missed an opportunity to trade and make a profit.

"That is very kind of you both," King Taschari said with a nod. "In addition, we'd like to ask for military aid."

"I thought you said the savages were not causing trouble," Ekren said. From all that she had heard about the savages, she was surprised to hear that they were peaceful. They were said to murder each other in cold blood for no apparent reason.

"They're not, Alamand Arinol," the Navenite king said. His face took on a serious expression. "But we fear we may be on the brink of a large-scale rakhor attack." His expression grew dark. "The Kheryne refugees say that bands of rakhor attacked their homes, killing all those who weren't lucky enough to escape. That's why they fled west across the Bahzenelyn Range."

Muslar Hishayi let out an uncomfortable laugh. "Large-scale rakhor attack? We all know that the God Daroon sealed those demonspawn in the Precipice at the dawn of humanity!"

"Rakhor? *God* Daroon?" King Syanuenan mocked. "You Annadis believe in such fantasies! When will you people see the truth? There are no Gods and there are no rakhor! It's shameful that grown men believe in childish fables!"

"The rakhor are real!" exclaimed a voice.

Ekren turned and spotted a lanky young man with black hair down to his shoulders, standing in the Cayani section. The boy spoke with a Navenite accent, however—his words had the characteristic jagged edges.

"What makes you so sure?" King Syanuenan asked the young man through veiled anger. "Have you seen a rakhor?"

"No, my lord," the young man said, "but I've seen what they can do."

King Taschari frowned. "What did you see?"

After a moment of silence, the young man began. "I saw a man decapitated by a rakhor. His chest and stomach were ripped open by three large claws." He paused, seemingly gathering himself.

Ekren glanced at Muslar Hishayi and found the ruler staring at the young man with smoldering eyes. The Cayani were far from flexible when it came to the breach of proprieties, especially the muslar. Before the young man could continue speaking, the muslar interjected. "If you have not seen a rakhor, how can you say with certainty that the dead man you found was killed by one?" The young man dropped his gaze and did not respond—a very wise decision, Ekren thought. "Sit down before I have you thrown out!" the muslar scolded and the young man immediately took his seat.

"The boy's description of the three claw marks matches what the Kheryne and our very own Mountain Watch report," King Taschari said, addressing the whole gathering. He then turned to face King Syanuenan. "You don't believe in the rakhor, King Syanuenan. And why would you? The rakhor never make it that far south because the men and women of the Navengaard Mountain Watch track them down and slay them." The Navenite king's pride in the Watchmen was evident in his posture and voice.

King Taschari then turned to Muslar Hishayi. "The Word does say that Daroon sealed the rakhor at the Precipice, and as any true Faithful, I believe in the teachings of the Word. I believe that the God of Courage did indeed do so. But that was almost seven thousand years ago. Don't you think that the demonspawn could have found a way out?" He paused as if waiting for a response from the muslar. When none came, he continued. "We cannot turn our backs on this matter. I don't know what will happen if the rakhor attack."

"The savages could be making it up," chimed in Emperor Ilyucu Ken, the ruler of Phucao. He was garbed in a loose-fitting robe that fell in ripples over his frail body, and a headdress of eagle plumes that weighed his head down. Though Phucao was now a small, impoverished nation, it had once been the seat of the Gronelle Empire and its rulers still used the title of Emperor. A title without meaning. *Like Alamand of the Grand Council*, Ekren thought. The Emperor's accent, however, reminded Ekren of her Phucak operative—the one who was out searching for the venna. She briefly wondered how his mission was faring.

"I can entertain the possibility that a small number of Kheryne could make up such a story," King Taschari responded, "but scores of disparate groups of Kheryne, entering Naven hundreds of miles from each other, all share the same story. I don't think they are making it up." The two rulers held each other's gaze as an uncomfortable silence fell upon the Gallery.

"The Cayani are not keen on wasting our men on such a ridiculous mission," Muslar Hishayi said, breaking the silence.

King Taschari looked visibly upset. "Very well. That's for you to decide. But might I remind you that when Cayan was at the brink of destruction during the War of Remaking, it was the Navengaard who came to your rescue."

"You Navenites will never let the past be the past, will you?" Muslar Hishayi asked, sounding disgusted. "The Ostarks came to our aid too, but you do not see them rubbing our noses in it."

"Is there anything else you would like to add, King Taschari?" Ekren interjected, attempting to avoid any further arguments of who did what for whom.

"No," the Navenite king said angrily. "I yield the floor." With that, he seated himself.

"Thank you, King Taschari," Ekren said. "Well then, let us continue."

This gathering was already off to a bad start. Blame was being thrown all around. And what was worse, there was nothing Ekren could do to stop it other than ensuring a swift end to the day's proceedings. If only her grandfather had formed the Grand Council under Ostark leadership. The world would have been a much better place.

THE CAYANI WERE NOT adept at getting many things right, but these ocean-facing balconies were a marvelous addition to the rooms at the muslar's palace. The ocean breeze, though a bit on the colder side now during the fall months, seemed to lift Ekren's perspiration away, pleasantly cooling her on an otherwise humid afternoon. Such was the boon and the bane of living on the coast. Breathtaking views and refreshing ocean winds, but when the winds went silent, bodies wept.

Since the Cayani did not use cutlery, Ekren was forced to use her hands to pick up a piece of cauliflower, grilled with a medley of spices. When she stuck it into her mouth, an explosion of flavor threatened to overwhelm her oral and olfactory senses—it was splendid! The spices, she knew, came from Naven, but it was the Cayani who knew how to use them properly.

All that the Cayani got right, however, paled in comparison to all they got wrong. It seemed as if the world had marched into the future but Cayan was stuck in the past. Ekren wondered whether the Cayani ways, which mimicked something from a time long forgotten, would be as relevant today if they did not have the support of the Sanctum of the Seven. An insincere freedom of religion. Overly compliant women. Mopra! Yet the Cayani considered themselves to be the true Faithful, though they were far from it. She had to spend three more days in this godsforsaken land. At least the Grand Council gathering had come to an end; that was something she could be glad for.

"You have been very quiet, mara," Dina said from across the table.

"Just thinking."

"About what?"

"Nothing important," Ekren replied, then realized that she was not being much of a conversationalist. "What did you think of the gathering?"

"It was … enlightening," Dina said, then smiled. "Is it always this way?"

"You mean a bunch of old men bickering about small slights and reveling in the glory of past years? Then yes. That is exactly how it is." Dina laughed. "Although," Ekren continued, "that young man's outburst when King Taschari had the floor was new. I have to admit, I admire his bravery. No one ever speaks up against monarchs."

"He is either brave or profoundly stupid," Dina said. "He thinks the rakhor are real!" She laughed.

Ekren laughed with her daughter, but she knew the truth of things. The rakhor were as real as she. "You do not believe that the rakhor are real?"

Dina shook her head. "Not everything in the Word is based on reality. The rakhor are described as such fantastical creatures—spikes on the back, fading away when killed. Such things do not exist."

"There could be fantastical things in this world that we do not know of," Ekren said.

"Like venna," Dina said, and Ekren's breath caught. "You seem to be picking up a real liking for such things," Dina added.

"Venna?" Ekren decided to play the fool. *What does Dina know?*

"Yes," her daughter said, her voice as flat as a tabletop. "I read about it in a book in your study."

"Why were you going through my books?" Ekren asked, perhaps more harshly than she had intended.

"I was not going through your books," Dina said. "The book was open and I happened to read it. I did not read very much."

"O," Ekren said, then pretended to ponder. "I cannot quite remember what book you are referring to."

Dina looked puzzled. "You do not remember reading something about a creature that glows with a rainbow aura? It is such a striking image that I could not get it out of my mind. I even went to the Lanmeria Library trying to learn more, but they only had a few books of little worth." Dina paused. "I found a Kheryne poem ... I did not realize that the Kheryne could write. I also read the accounts of an adventurer who spent a while living with the Kheryne. But all he mentioned about this creature was that it was part of some Kheryne prophecy regarding their salvation. And then there was a book by a discredited author who believed that there was a secret society called the Khasmia Shadow that hunted venna."

How did the Shadow not retrieve these books? Ekren thought with an angry apprehension. Especially the one about the Shadow. She wasn't aware that such a book existed. *No matter!* At least no harm had come from the books being out in the world, all thanks to the Shadow's painstaking efforts to wipe the world's memory of the vile creature. However, she would have to alert her operatives to go to the Lanmeria Library and have those books retrieved. But what was she to do with Dina? Her only daughter? *Dina would not repeat such things,* Ekren rationalized. *She thinks it is all fantasy.*

"I have been so busy with the Herrans and the Grand Council that I had completely forgotten about it," Ekren said. "But now that you mention it, I do remember reading something about such a creature." She smiled, hoping it looked convincing. "You are right. In my older years, I seem to want to believe in something grander than the reality our senses weave for us."

"Do not go crazy on me, mara," Dina said, smiling slyly.

"Not anytime soon, daughter," Ekren said. "My mind is sharper than ever. Anyway, are you excited for Daroongaamen tomorrow?" she asked, turning the conversation away from topics that needed to be discussed in a different place, but more importantly, at the proper time.

"I am," Dina said, " but not as excited as I was three years ago, when we hosted the games in Lanmeria."

"It does not matter where the games are hosted. The spirit of competition is the real essence of these games," Ekren said as she gazed over Omanna's harbor dotted with scores of sea vessels.

"That and keeping the world's aggression in check by channeling it into *friendly* competition."

"You are too wise for your age," Ekren said, smiling. Dina would be a great Regent, a great world leader, as long as she took control of her destiny. And did not reveal more than she should.

Chapter Thirty-Four

Massive didn't begin to describe the size of the tournament arena in Omanna. The bowl-shaped structure rose about fifty paces above its circular dirt floor. People crowded every tier, with finely garbed nobility seated in roofed pavilions closer to the bottom, while common folk filled the higher levels. Several in the crowd carried banners of their respective nations, while many others chose to display their patriotism by slathering their nation's colors all over their bodies. Puffs of confetti and arcs of colorful streamers appeared and disappeared amidst the sea of people gathered to watch the games. Horns blared, drums beat, and voices from all eight nations of the civilized world echoed through the arena. Daroongaamen was quite a sight!

How many people are here watching the games? Rein wondered as he strung his horned bow. *Twenty thousand? Thirty thousand?* He found that his knack at gauging distances didn't work too well in estimating the size of a crowd—a crowd that was quite frankly making him a little nervous.

The tent that the Navenite competitors were in was dyed in the crimson and white of the nation. And like the tent, the competitors were all dressed in crimson and white as well. Rein was joined by other archery competitors, as well as those competing in the sword and staff tournaments—winners of the various Regional Games held across Naven. All in all, Naven had three competitors in archery and sword, while only two in staff. Since Boar Sayarna had died, the Navenite team had decided to leave his spot empty, in honor of his memory.

After gathering in Meneres, where King Taschari had wished them luck, the Navenite Daroongaamen team and their families had boarded a riverboat that took them down the Penner to Shi'jazha in three days time. That was the first time Rein had stepped foot in Cayan, a land whose very air and water felt strange. Though the Cayani were considered the most pious of the Faithful, their customs seemed so very alien that Rein wondered if they worshipped the same Gods.

From Shi'jazha, they were escorted to Omanna by a Navengaard honor guard. The journey had taken five days through Cayani plains and rolling hills. Once in Omanna, they had been paraded through the city with pomp and fanfare.

"How are you feeling?" Keya asked. She was an archer from a small village called Badallur, somewhere northwest of Meneres.

"Nervous," Rein replied, more so now that a woman was talking to him.

"Don't be," Keya said. "The worst that could happen is you lose."

"That doesn't make me feel much better."

"Trust me,"—the woman tucked her black hair behind her ears—"I know what I'm talking about."

Rein nodded at that. Keya did know what she was talking about. After all, this was her second time competing in the games. "How much longer before they begin?" he asked.

"Not much longer." Keya looked out at the arena, brightened by the soft rays of the fall sun typical for the month of Hrensa. "I'm excited that we're going to be the first ones out there!" Keya added, pointing at several targets lining the circumference of the arena floor.

"Me too."

"You say that as if you don't mean it."

"No, I do! I've been waiting for this moment long before I came of age."

Keya laughed. "Well, I'm glad you get to fulfill a childhood dream."

Rein felt a little embarrassed but realized that he was no longer nervous about talking to Keya. "I'm pretty good with a bow," he said.

"Should I consider that a challenge?" Keya gave him a devious smile.

"No, just an objective fact."

"What makes it an objective fact?"

"I know I am good," Rein said, amused.

"That sounds quite subjective to me."

"Others say I'm good too."

"So, others share your subjectivity. That doesn't make it objective. Unless you think that objectivity is merely widely accepted subjectivity."

Rein's head hurt. This wasn't where he thought this conversation was headed. Women were certainly strange. "Right," he said. "I guess we'll let the games prove my subjective fact?"

Keya laughed. "I hope you're not disappointed," she teased.

At that moment, a wave of silence passed through the crowds, engulfing even the highest tiers. Rein wondered if those up there could see what was happening on the arena floor.

An entry gate to the arena opened and seven figures walked out side by side; each garbed in a robe solidly colored in one shade of the Union, with a golden cord at their waists and raised hoods that obscured the faces beneath.

"They are the Miakos," Keya said. "The high priests of the Sanctum of the Seven. They are here to bless the games."

Rein had only heard of them during Akka Hallen's sermons. It was believed that each Miakos could channel the voice of the God they were attuned to; the color of their robe denoted their attunement.

Once the Miakos approached the center, they formed a circle, facing inward and waiting in silence. The whole arena shuffled as the crowd took to its feet. Rein did likewise. Then the Miakos began chanting.

Guide us, our Gods
On the path to a Worthy Life.

So we may serve you in your glory
In Amarna.
Guide us, our Gods
To the end long promised.
We will strive not to falter or fail
Though weak and craven we might be.
If in the end we are judged Unworthy
To enter Amarna
Gladly shall we live once more
That we may prove our worth again.

Once their chant ended, the Miakos in red stepped forward. He raised his arms up, hands waving, and said, "Daroon blesses us!" then stepped back.

Next, the Miakos in the orange robe stepped into the circle and bestowed Menera's blessing. She was followed by the Miakos in yellow who bestowed Pharrahmin's blessing. Then came Herra's blessing from the Miakos in green, after which Hrenwaldt's blessing was bestowed by the Miakos in blue. Finally, Berron and Corranine's blessings were bestowed by the Miakos in violet and indigo. Each of their voices—male and female—held a distinct, otherworldly quality.

After the blessings, the Miakos formed up side by side again and exited the arena. The crowd remained hushed.

"Welcome to the twenty-third Daroongaamen in OMANNA!" a voice echoed, and the crowd immediately erupted in applause and cheers.

"Who is that?" Rein asked, locating a green-and-red pavilion in the Cayani section as the source of the voice.

"I think that's the Cayani king," Keya replied as she cheered and applauded with the rest. "The ruler of the land that holds the games typically makes a speech at its commencement."

The Cayani king, dressed in a long shirt that fell all the way to his feet, held up his palms and the crowd fell silent. "Today, we celebrate each and every nation that form the Grand Council by raising their very best onto the pedestal of competition. For decades, these games have been cherished by one and all and I sincerely hope that we continue this tradition for generations to come." He paused and the crowd cheered again, this time reining themselves in without needing a signal from the Cayani king. "Though in each tournament of bow, staff, and sword, only three will claim victory," the king continued, "let it be known that each of you is exceptional to have simply made it here. Let the games commence!" Once again, the crowd boomed.

"Come on," Keya said, beckoning him. "Let's go grab targets that will have the sun to our backs. Those are the prime targets everyone will go for!"

Rein grabbed his bow and quiver and ran after Keya, as several other archers did the same. Dodging a few slow-footed ones, Rein stopped at the target next to the one Keya had claimed for herself.

"These should do nicely," Keya said, strapping her quiver to her waist.

"If you say so," Rein said. "The sun doesn't bother me."

"My, my, aren't you a cocky one?" Keya retorted absentmindedly as she examined her shafts.

Rein felt a little unsatisfied that his quip had gone unappreciated, but he chalked it up to the strangeness of women. He looked around the arena, eyes moving through the dozens of archers staking their claims on targets. As he strapped his quiver to his back, an official walked up to him.

"You get two arrows at each distance to hit the red dot on the target," the official said in the lilting Cayani accent. He pointed to the target in front of him.

Rein looked in that direction and noticed the red dot, painted at the exact center of the round target. It was quite a bit smaller than the ones on the targets at the Regional Games; in fact those targets were a series of concentric rings. "If you miss both you will be disqualified, unless you are one of the final three. I will verify if each shot has hit true."

Rein nodded. "Once it's verified, I move back to the next line and shoot again?" he asked. This was different than in the Regional Games where the distance was fixed and the competitors had to shoot ten arrows at a target, scoring points based on how far from the center the arrows hit.

The official looked annoyed. "I am getting there," he said. "You start here at the line for ten paces. If you pass, you move back to the twenty-pace line, then thirty and so on."

Cheers erupted from one section of the crowd and Rein looked over. One of the competitors had moved to the twenty-yard line. Then more cheers began to erupt in various sections of the crowd as competitor after competitor began moving to the twenty-yard line.

"Looks like they have already started," the official said. "Do you have any questions?"

Rein shook his head.

"Good." The official moved aside. "Remember to wait for me to verify the shot before you move to the next line."

"Wow!" Keya's voice called out. "Your objective greatness is quite slow," she said as she walked to the second line with her official by her side.

Quickly, Rein grabbed an arrow from his quiver and shot it at the target. "I've already caught up," he called out to Keya, then began walking to the next line.

"I have not verified your shot yet," Rein's official said.

"It's good," Rein replied and continued walking. Momentarily, his official caught up to him, with Rein's arrow in hand.

Together, Keya and he shot arrow after arrow, moving back line after line, disappointingly slowed by their officials who had to run back and forth to verify their shots and retrieve arrows. At forty paces, Keya challenged him to shoot with his eyes closed and he did. And to his surprise, so had Keya. At seventy paces, she had sneezed—*quite intentionally*—at the exact moment he was about to let loose, causing his arrow to miss the mark; his second arrow had hit true. Keya, however, had only used one arrow. She gloated about it all the way to the ninety-pace line, where Rein hit his target with only one arrow, while Keya needed two. The farther they got, the smaller that red dot was.

Rein had almost forgotten that he was competing in Daroongaamen; he was completely wrapped up in his personal competition with Keya—that woman could shoot an arrow! But the explosion of sound that followed his true shot at the hundred-and-twenty pace line brought him back to the here and now. He looked around and found that only three archers remained. Someone in Guerran colors of blue and gold, Keya, and him.

"I'm impressed!" Keya said. "You've managed to place in the top three in your first Daroongaamen." She clapped softly. "Beating you will be a lot more satisfying now!" She smiled.

"We'll see," Rein replied.

REIN, Keya, and the Guerran archer stood in front of three adjacent targets on the other side of the arena. An official joined them.

"You may begin when you are ready," he said.

The Guerran pulled an arrow, nocked it to his bow, then aimed and let loose. The arrow pierced its target, but Rein saw that the Guerran had missed the red dot at its center, although only slightly. An official who stood near the target examined the shot, pulled the arrow out, and held his arms ups, crossed at the forearms.

"That's a miss," the official said.

The Guerran archer let out an annoyed huff, nocked another arrow, took aim, and let loose. Once his second shot was examined, the official at the other end held up his arms, parallel to each other.

"It's good," the official said.

Next, Keya took her shot, missing with her first arrow but hitting true with her second. "The sun was in my eyes," she said.

"Stop complaining." Rein aimed his arrow at the target and let loose, hitting the edge of the red dot. He had almost missed that shot. *I need to stop talking and focus,* he thought.

The three competitors and the official moved back to the hundred-and-forty pace line. Rein shot first and only managed to move on to the next line with his second arrow. He was shooting at a very small target from distances he wasn't quite comfortable with.

Next, Keya managed to hit the target with only one arrow, making her shot look effortless. Rein suddenly got the feeling that Keya might have been toying with him this entire time.

The Guerran archer missed both his shots. The crowd cheered him for securing the third-place victory, as he walked out of the arena, shoulders slumped.

"It's just you and me now," Keya said as they walked to the hundred-and-fiftieth line. "I'm glad you'll get second place."

"You mean you're glad that you'll get second place."

"Well crafted," Keya said mockingly.

Since Rein had shot first at the last line, it was Keya's turn to go first. She pulled out her arrow and stepped back with her left leg. With the bow in her right hand, she nocked her arrow, pulled, and aimed. Rein wondered how such a slender woman had the strength to bend a Navenite horned bow. Her form was so elegant, her stance so precise. She reminded him of Herra, the Goddess of the Wild. He watched as Keya's eyes locked on to the target, now barely more than a thumb-sized dot. She loosed!

Rein traced the arrow's path as it tore through the air and stuck itself in the circular target. But, unfortunately, she had missed the red dot. Keya already knew that for Rein saw her hold back a surge of emotion through gritted teeth, then pull out another arrow even before the official by the target had raised crossed arms.

Once again, Keya nocked her arrow and took aim. The arrow sprang forward, propelled by the energy held in her bow, soaring to its target. But she dropped her bow in despair. The arrow hit the target, but once again, it had missed its mark. The crowd moaned at first, then cheered.

"That's a tough shot," Rein said consolingly. Despite their heated competition, he truly meant it.

"Thanks," Keya said, "but you could still miss!"

Rein laughed. "I could," he said and pulled out an arrow. Nocking it, he held his bow up and took aim. And at that moment, the silence of the crowd made him acutely aware of the tens of thousands of scrutinizing eyes on him. The thumb that gripped the arrow began to spasm. His heart raced. Inhaling deeply, Rein attempted to calm himself and shut out the crowd. He loosed … and missed. The crowd echoed his disappointment.

"Looks like you missed," Keya said cheerfully.

"I know," Rein said shortly, angry at himself.

"One more miss and I have another shot at this."

Rein nocked another arrow to his bowstring, still inhaling deeply. Once again, he raised his bow and took aim, thumb still in spasms. *What do I see?* he asked himself. He saw the target, the arena wall behind it, the officials next to the targets, and a few tiers of the crowd. *Too much,* he thought. *Only the target!*

Rein unfocused his vision then refocused it. This time, he saw nothing but the tiny red dot at the center of the target. He focused harder and the red dot seemed to grow in size. At the same time, his ears shut off the crowd. There was only the target.

Rein held his breath and loosed. His arrow flew, but his eyes didn't follow his missile. All he saw was a red dot with an arrow at its center.

"SECOND PLACE ISN'T BAD, I suppose," Keya said, seated across the table from Rein. She bit off a chunk of chicken leg. "I moved up from last time."

Rein smiled, then slurped up a spoonful of fish stew. It was incredibly flavorful, just like every other food served in the competitor's lunch hall. Several others were seated at tables around him, enjoying Cayani delicacies. "Now do you accept that I am objectively good with a bow?" he asked.

"No."

"What? I just beat you! I just beat the whole world! I won at archery in Daroongaamen!"

"That you did. But I can still beat you," Keya said with an amused look.

Rein shook his head in exasperation. How could he argue with someone who completely ignored the facts? "Never mind," he said, deciding to change the subject. "Have you tried some of this fish stew?"

Keya made a disgusted sound. "I hate fish," she said, pretending to gag. "They are smelly and foul. Did you know that a lot of them live off the leavings of other fish?"

Rein dropped his spoon into the bowl and pushed his stew away. Why was she bent on ruining small talk … and his appetite?

"Don't push it toward me!" Keya exclaimed, leaning back.

"Congratulations on your victory, Master Maranda," a voice said from behind him.

Rein turned. "Adir!" he exclaimed. Jumping out of his seat, he embraced his childhood friend, only pulling away after a long moment. It was good to see Adir, who seemed to be trying to grow a beard, though it wasn't much more than fine stubble. "How did you get here?"

"I know one of the guards on duty," Adir said nonchalantly. "He let me in."

Adir knows Cayani guards? "All right. But what I meant was how did you get to Cayan?" He'd have to ask Adir about the guards later.

"That's a long story," Adir said with a sigh.

"I have time," Rein said, feeling a burst of laughter build up in his chest out of sheer joy of reuniting with Adir. "O, and you owe me some money for my journey to Cayan!"

Adir laughed, "I didn't promise to pay your fare."

"Yea, you did!"

"Why would I do that?"

"I don't know. But you did!"

From the other side of the table, Keya coughed. "O. This is Keya," Rein said.

"May the Gods favor you, Keya," Adir said, "though their favor did shine upon you today. Congratulations on placing second. Two Navenites victorious at Daroongaamen for the first time in history!"

"Thank you," Keya said smiling graciously, then she looked at Rein. Somehow her smile had managed to turn into a grimace within the fleeting moment it took to switch her attention. "And thank you for finally acknowledging that I was here."

Rein threw his hands up. "I'm sorry. I'm sorry," he said. "I didn't forget. It's just that I haven't seen Adir since"—he looked at his friend —"the month of Marayi."

"I can take a hint," Keya said, standing and grabbing her tray. "I'll leave you two to it then. I'm sure you have a lot of catching up to do. It was nice to meet you, Adir."

"It was nice to meet you too, Keya. May the Gods favor you."

They watched Keya leave, then turned to each other with broad smiles. Rein gestured for Adir to sit, who awkwardly straddled his seat instead of unstrapping the odd, staff-like weapon he carried and sitting like a normal person.

"So, has shy Rein finally figured out how to talk to women?" Adir asked.

"No. I haven't. She does most of the talking."

"That's what it's like when you're with a woman."

"I'm not *with* her," Rein said, feeling a little hot under his clothes.

Adir looked disappointed. "Well, maybe some day."

"Speaking of women, how's Tia? Are you two married yet?"

Adir's expression darkened. "She's not in Marafel?"

"No. Wait. Didn't you two elope?" Rein asked, confused.

"Not exactly," Adir said. "We did leave together, but ..."

"But what?"

Adir remained silent for a long moment. "She left me, Rein. In Meneres."

Meneres, now Omanna; it seemed that Adir had seen quite a bit of the world. "When were you in Meneres?"

Adir seemed distant. "Hmm ... ? I got there almost four months ago now," he said, then added slowly, "Tia left for Marafel more than two months ago. Are you sure she's not back yet?"

Rein heard the worry in Adir's voice. "Yea, I'm sure," he said. "We all thought she was with you. Maybe she got home while I was on my way here. Or maybe she decided to go elsewhere."

Adir nodded. "Maybe." He paused and met Rein's eyes. "I wasn't very good to her, Rein. Wherever she is, I hope she's happy." He let out a sigh. "How are Morena and Athvan doing?"

Now it was Rein whose mood darkened. *Adir doesn't know. How could he? No one had known where to find him.* "Adir," he began. "I ... I ..."

"Rein?" Adir sensed his discomfort, as always. "How are Morena and Athvan?" he repeated slowly.

"Your akka and Athvan are dead," Rein blurted out, then cursed himself for his bluntness. He never had been any good at delivering bad news.

To Rein's astonishment, Adir didn't react the way Rein thought he would. He expected Adir to have one of his usual outbursts, but he remained still. Motionless. Calm. It was more than a little unsettling.

"And Morena?" Adir asked finally.

"She's fine," Rein said, hoping that the news of his sister's well-being might bring his friend some relief. But was that enough? Rein had no idea what it felt like to lose someone.

"How did they die?"

"They were killed," Rein said, unsure of how to soften the blow of his words. "Kirsch, the maids, and the Kheryne your father housed were also found dead." There had been a lot of death at that house. A lot of death.

"Do you know who did it?" Adir was still unnaturally calm.

Suddenly, Rein realized that the Adir sitting in front of him was not the one he had last seen at the courthouse in Marafel. This man seemed very different, though he looked and sounded like his childhood friend. What had happened in the last four months to bring about this drastic a change?

"No," Rein said, truthfully. "The Village Watch looked into it but found nothing substantial. But some Marafellens were panicked that the rakhor that had killed Tamaar had … but akka said that the Village Watch didn't report any claw marks."

"I know it wasn't a rakhor," Adir said, his jaw clenching. "It was Syfis."

Syfis? Where had Rein heard that name before? He couldn't remember. "Who's Syfis?"

"Syfis Sayarna," Adir said, anger finally bleeding into his voice.

"Boar's brother?" Rein asked, surprised.

Adir nodded. "Syfis swore to avenge Boar's death. You were there. At the courthouse. He tried to kill me in Marafel but I escaped. Then he found me in Meneres, but still I escaped. When he lost my trail, he must have turned on my family!" Adir was breathing heavily, his nostrils flared.

Several questions floated around in Rein's mind. "Why would he do such a thing? Why would he kill everyone?" Rein found it hard to believe that Syfis would go to such lengths to avenge Boar. But then again, he didn't truly know.

"Because I killed Boar."

"But you didn't kill Boar," Rein said. "The Arbiter himself said that there wasn't any evidence. And the Village Watch didn't find anything new since the hearing, or I would have heard about it."

Adir didn't respond.

"You didn't kill Boar, right? Syfis just thinks you did." *Adir wouldn't do such a thing. Would he?*

"Not intentionally, but I did kill him." Adir spoke with a cold intensity.

Rein didn't want to believe him. "How do you unintentionally kill someone?"

Adir looked around. "I don't have enough time to get into it," he said, standing, "I need to get back to work."

"Adir, what happened with Boar?" Rein had to know why his friend had done what he'd just admitted.

"The Cayani are sticklers for the proprieties," Adir said, "and being late for work is considered a breach. But I'll take you out for dinner tonight and we'll talk."

Rein nodded. At least it wouldn't be months before he saw his friend again. "All right," he said.

"May the Gods favor you, Rein," Adir said, then he turned and walked away.

"May the Gods watch over you," Rein called out, watching Adir as he made his way out of the dining chamber. *May the Gods watch over you, my friend.*

Chapter Thirty-Five

As Adir walked down the street back to Lord Si'Pyaara's villa, he felt as if reality was spinning out of control, with him at its very edge, desperately trying to hold on with his nails. But the harder he tried to hold on, the more he blamed himself for everything.

It's my fault that my little brother is dead! Memories of a four-year-old Athvan mimicking his every action and mannerism flooded into his mind. A wave of sorrow swelled in his chest as the loss of that sweet and curious and annoyingly energetic boy settled in. He wanted to drop down onto the street and weep! Athvan hadn't deserved such a terrible end.

It's my fault that akka is dead! Though Adir searched for fond memories of his father, he was unable to find any. All he could recall were endless arguments and resentment, especially the last argument he'd had with his father, right before he left Marafel. The last thing he'd told Arvan was that he'd been an uncommitted husband and father. *Is that how I will remember him?* His father deserved a better memory, but there were none. There was only a cold finality.

SYFIS! The name sprang up in his mind, draining his sorrow into a boiling pool of anger, hissing and spitting. *Syfis!* The man truly responsible for the death of his father, brother, and the entire Nathar household. He'd killed Kirsch and Nilane and Misuma. And Kheryne? *That swinespawn deserves to die!* Clarity of purpose suddenly enveloped him. He looked up and spotted the Chariot of the Gods racing across the dark backdrop of the night sky. He was going to leave for Akkasha and kill Syfis Sayarna.

Walking through the villa gates, Adir made his way down the stone path to the gardens at the west end. He couldn't leave before making things right with Habya, though telling her his true reason for departure seemed foolish. She would only try and stop him and her words could easily sway his decision. No, it was best if she didn't know, but he couldn't leave without making his commitment to her known. He wouldn't make the same mistakes he'd made with Tia.

Approaching the morningdew bushes, Adir stopped and plucked three flowers.

⚜

"WHAT ARE the five principles true Annadi women should live by?" Habya asked, quizzing Sumaiyah on the proprieties of Annadi womanhood. However, through her travels to Naven and Ostarium, she had found that only the Cayani truly adhered to the proprieties. The rest of the Faithful seemed to pick and choose which proprieties to follow. *Their poor souls are sure to be deemed unworthy by Corranine, and reincarnated.*

"Uh …" Habya's second sister began, seated across from her at the small table in one corner of her room. "Wake before the sun … worship the Gods … take care of the home … respect and support your husband and …" Sumaiyah trailed off and shrugged.

Habya considered the twelve-year-old girl for a moment. She looked so much like her mother—Habya's second mother, Phawzia—with her blonde hair, blue eyes, and thin lips. "You need to know this, Sumaiyah," Habya said. "You are a proper woman now."

Sumaiyah's face dropped. "Everyone keeps telling me that," she complained, pouting, "but I don't feel any different."

"You will and you need to be ready when you do. So what's the last principle?"

Sumaiyah scrunched her face into a pensive expression. Suddenly, she looked annoyed. "I cannot think with that tapping."

"I do not hear any tapping." Sumaiyah was always trying to find ways to squirm out of her studies, though Habya could not blame the girl for that. She herself had detested them when she was younger.

"There it is again!" Sumaiyah exclaimed, jumping out of her seat and running to the window.

Habya turned to look and spotted the sun setting into golden waters, then she saw something suddenly appear from below and hit a glass pane on the window. Curious, she stood.

Sumaiyah swung the window open and peered out. "It's Adir," she said, turning to face Habya. "Why is he throwing pebbles at this window?"

Confused, Habya approached the window and took a look herself. *What is that foolish man doing? He is not allowed in the women's wing of the house!* As soon as he saw her, he gestured for her to go to him.

"I am going to tell akka," Sumaiyah said. "He is not supposed to be here."

That would be disastrous, Habya thought as a fear-induced chill passed through her. Adir could be such a mule sometimes. "No, that will not be necessary," she said quickly. "I will go take care of this. You stay here and read the Word. When I get back, you had better have found out what the last principle is." She could have easily told her second sister that the last principle was to beget and care for children, but this way, Sumaiyah would stay in one place and not cause any trouble.

"Fine," Sumaiyah said grumpily, thumping into the chair and opening the thick, leather-bound Word of the Gods, the Union on its front cover.

Hurriedly, Habya made her way downstairs, passing a few mopra tending to their chores. She wondered if they had seen Adir, but she knew that even if they had, they would keep their mouths shut. But if he was seen by any of her mothers or sister—except Nabila, of course—then he would be in a lot of trouble.

Pushing open the door to the lawn, she walked through to where Adir had been. Sure enough, he was still there, standing with his arms behind his back.

As she approached him, Habya glanced up at the windows that faced the lawn and found them all to be clear. *Good,* she thought. Sumaiyah was not trying to peek out. She turned her attention on Adir, furious and ready to unleash a flurry of reprimands, but then she saw his eyes. They seemed … conflicted. Whatever anger she had toward him melted away.

"Adir. Is everything fine?"

"Yea." Adir smiled unconvincingly. "Everything is fine."

"Then why were you throwing pebbles at my window? Sumaiyah was in there with me. She almost went to akka!" She glanced up at the windows again; they were still clear.

"I'm sorry about that. I needed to see you before I leave for home tonight."

"You are going back to Marafel?" *Is he leaving me?* "Why?"

Adir dropped his gaze to the ground. "I got word today that my akka has taken ill."

"How did you get this news?" Habya asked, overwhelmed by the thought of Adir leaving her. "No one knows you are in Cayan."

"No one did till today," Adir said, meeting her eyes. "You know the man who won at archery today? At Daroongaamen."

"Reinard something?" *What does that have to do with anything?* And then Habya remembered. Adir had regaled her with countless stories of the archer from his younger days. "That's your friend Rein, isn't he?"

Adir nodded. "I met him this afternoon to congratulate him on his victory and he told me about my akka. He said—" Adir choked up and Habya could see him straining to fight tears. "He said that akka may be on his last breaths. I need to make things right, Habya."

"Of course you do!" Habya knew of the strained relationship between Adir and his father and she was glad that he was taking this step. Nabila had once told her that losing someone without reconciling past differences could eat away at one's soul.

"I'll be back," Adir said, flashing her a tight smile. "I give you my word."

"I know you will."

"But before I go, there is something I must do."

"What is it?"

"Habya," Adir began, "most of the time I don't know what I'm doing. I feel like I'm floating in a sea of errant thoughts that pull me this way and that, threatening to rip me apart into countless little pieces. I'm afraid that if I ever let go, I'll lose myself. But in those moments, those moments of, quite frankly, terror, I think of you and suddenly everything is fine. My thoughts become coherent and my actions have purpose. You are the anchor of my existence."

Bringing his arms from behind his back, Adir opened a loose fist, revealing three flowers with blood-red petals, lined with yellow streaks.

Morningdews. *Three* morningdews. Habya knew what Adir was about to do. Her palms began to sweat. Her pulse quickened and her breaths were shallow.

Adir dropped to his knees and placed the flowers at her feet, then his eyes the brown of burnt wood met hers. "Habya, will you be my wife?"

Habya's ears heard the question, her mind saw the answer, but her mouth did not speak it. She stood staring at the lanky Navenite on his knees, expectantly looking up. There was absolutely no way that Adir had gained permission from her father to ask her that question. No matter how much she wanted it, her father would never allow such a thing to happen.

"So?" Adir asked.

"Ya," Habya answered, "I will be your wife." She would worry about what her father thinks at a later day. Or maybe she would not worry about it at all!

Adir's face lit up in a broad smile. He got to his feet and moved in to kiss her, but she stopped him.

"Not till we are married," Habya said.

Adir's face fell, but he respected her wishes. "Very well," he said, then clasped her hands. "I'll be back in a few weeks. May the Gods watch over you, Habya."

"May the Gods keep you safe, Adir."

Habya watched him walk away until he eventually disappeared into the dimming fall evening. She had breached many of the proprieties she had been teaching Sumaiyah. *For a man.* And now she had agreed to marry him without her father's consent. Her sins were adding up and she wondered if the Gods would forgive her. But she loved Adir and would do anything to be his wife—even it meant getting reincarnated a thousand times.

GHAREEB WALKED, amidst the echoes of his own footsteps, down the hallway in the service quarters of Lord Si'Pyaara's villa, hoping to find Adir in their room. Sinain had approached him earlier in the evening, looking for the lanky man. Apparently, Adir had not returned to work after lunch and Sinain had wanted to ensure that everything was all right with Ghareeb's *master*.

Once at the door to their room, Ghareeb turned the knob and pushed the door open. It was a fair-size room with two beds that overlooked a street, comfortable enough for the two of them. Adir stood by his bed, strapping his pack closed.

"Going somewhere?"

"Yea," Adir responded, not looking up.

"Where?"

"Marafel." Adir let out a breath of impatience.

Ghareeb felt a surge of irritation. The only reason he was in Cayan was because of Adir and now he was leaving? "Why are you going back there? Will you not put yourself in danger?"

Adir shrugged. "My akka has taken ill and I need to go see him."

Something about the way Adir spoke did not sit well with Ghareeb. "O. I'll go with you."

"No," Adir responded, almost too quickly, further raising Ghareeb's suspicions. "This is a personal matter. I'd rather go alone. You'll be fine here without me."

Ghareeb nodded, but he was not convinced. Sure, Adir's father could be ill, but the way he was acting right now—all shifty and restless, refusing to meet his eyes—seemed to indicate that something else was afoot. This did not seem like a visit to a sick relative. He had lived long enough to pick up on the subtle messages of the body.

"All right," Ghareeb said. "I hope your father has a speedy recovery."

"Thank you," Adir said, slinging his pack over his shoulder and grabbing his palma—Ghareeb had heard that Adir was getting quite adept at wielding that weapon. "Could you tell Sinain of my departure?"

"Sure. When will you be back?"

"In a few weeks," Adir said. "May the Gods watch over you, Ghareeb." With that, Adir walked out the door, shutting it behind him.

Ghareeb sat on Adir's bed, trying to determine the reason for Adir's sudden departure. *Had he been found again?* Maybe. But if he had indeed been found, why would Adir keep it from him? It did not make any sense. However, he was oddly glad that Adir had not coerced him into going with him, like he had in Meneres.

After he'd found his freedom in Nagra, the thought of returning to Cayan had been dreadfully unpleasant. But now that Aiysta was back in Omanna, he found that he did not want to leave this godsforsaken city. If it hadn't been for Adir, he would never have come here and been reunited with his lost love, even though she may not see a future for them.

Ghareeb let out an exasperated sigh, realizing that yet again, he owed Adir everything. If Adir were truly returning to Marafel, his life would be in danger. And what if he turned into a venna on his journey? What would happen then? The more Ghareeb thought about it, the more he became convinced that he could not let Adir travel alone.

PART IV
ALLEGRO

Chapter Thirty-Six

This was not the first time Ekren had entered the Chamber of the Staff at Shadow Keep on Mount Schinay. No, she had been to this long, columned chamber, lit by floating lumenotes, many times before, running drills with her operatives and keeping their skills sharp. Many had grumbled about the drills, questioning the need for them, as most believed that the last venna had been killed off more than two centuries before. Some had even questioned the need for the Shadow itself. But the Khasmia Shadow would always live on. Only Daroon, the God of Courage, could disband it.

However, in light of recent events, those drills might prove useful. Sure, the venna had slipped away from her operatives, but Ekren did not worry. Her operatives were resourceful and well trained. They would find a way to capture the creature. If not, the allure of the Staff of Beckoning would pull at the venna, like a bee being pulled to a nectar-filled flower, allowing her operatives to capture it. Daroon had stated so in his Warning to the Khasmia Shadow, which served as the very essence of the Shadow's existence.

Ekren regarded the sleek black staff floating erect a few hands above a circular floor that was painted with the seal of the Shadow—seven silvery wisps of shadow, symmetrically arrayed over a circular ring. Below the seal, the language of the Gods spelled out the Shadow's creed in square silver tiles: *For Humanity's Survival.* The staff itself did not seem like anything special, but the Warning described it as being made of titansteel, the only material that could amplify and withstand the awesome, destructive power of a venna.

Why did the Gods create such creatures? Ekren wondered. *And why did the Gods make a weapon that when wielded by the venna made it stronger?* These were questions that had plagued her for decades. Sure, a case could be made that the Staff was created to destroy the venna and that an amplification of its powers was the means to do it. But the creatures themselves seemed to serve no purpose other than their single-minded destruction of anything in their vicinity. Next to the venna, the rakhor were mere kittens. That was why the Warning was to be heeded and all venna had to be destroyed. The only way to accomplish that was to use the creature's own power against it.

According to the Warning, if the venna's power could be controlled at a certain level, then the Staff of Beckoning could be used to trap that power, effectively killing the venna. In addition, the Staff, imbued with that awesome power, could be used to destroy other venna.

Getting a venna to unleash its power was simple enough. A high degree of physical or emotional stress did the trick. But controlling a venna's fully unleashed powers had proven difficult throughout the entire history of the Khasmia Shadow. Every Khasir before her who had successfully captured a venna had been unable to do so, as the venna's powers had turned wild so quickly that it ended up consuming the creature itself before its power could be trapped in the Staff. That was not a complete failure though, as the world was rid of a creature of doom. Would she be one of those Khasir? No, she would be different! And she had already proven as much.

Under Ekren's leadership, the Shadow had become a force to be reckoned with, though no person to the west of the Bahzenelyn knew about them. With almost three hundred deadly operatives, the Shadow could wield substantial political influence, but they preferred to remain in the shadows. Furthermore, her insistence on comparing ages-old godly relics that the Shadow had so meticulously gathered over centuries against those detailed in the Warning had led to the discovery of many wonders that only the minds of Gods could conjure up. One such wonder was the nostateho.

In the past, the Shadow had to rely on the venna to unleash and raise its power. Today, the venna still had to be the one to first unleash its power, but the nostateho would enable the Shadow to control it. The Warning claimed that this relic could modulate the venna's power, allowing the Shadow to hold it at just the right point for extraction into the Staff. The rub of it though was that the nostateho had never been used before given that the last known venna had been killed long before Ekren's operatives had discovered the relic's purpose. But who was she to question the Warning that was handed to the first Khasir of the Shadow by Daroon himself?

"Khasir." Ferrith began to drop to one knee, struggling to maintain his balance in his old age.

"You do not need to salute me, Ferrith." Ekren dropped the hood of her brown robe.

"You are very kind, Khasir," Ferrith thanked.

"Do not say that out too loud," Ekren said, "I do not want the operatives to think I am lenient." Ferrith smiled. "Any news on the venna?"

"The creature is yet to be found. We also lost an operative at an altercation during some information gathering."

Ekren did not like the sound of that. "What happened?"

Ferrith looked uncomfortable. "Apparently, the Phucak operative, Uaqui, pushed the creature's father a little too far. The man snapped and killed one of ours before being cut down. Also, the village folk found the bodies—"

"Bodies?" Ekren was horrified. "How many were killed?"

"Eight in all," Ferrith said.

"Gods save me!" Ekren exclaimed. "Eight! I can understand a few casualties, but this is a massacre. And they did not cover their tracks! Are they amateurs?"

"I apologize, Khasir. They should have been more careful." Ferrith paused for a moment. "But they did manage to capture someone close to the venna. A young woman."

Ekren grew curious. "Has she said anything useful?" At least the Phucak had managed to keep this one alive.

"No, Khasir. Nothing more than what we already know. But if the operatives are successful in capturing the venna, we could use her to coax him to unleash his power."

Ekren felt a lump form in her throat. She knew exactly what Ferrith was hinting at. *Torture!* Ekren hated such methods—she did not understand how some found pleasure in performing such a sadistic act. But she could not deny its effectiveness, and when it came to killing venna, nothing was off limits. "Where are the operatives now?" she asked, directing the conversation away from uncomfortable topics. "I need to have a talk with Uaqui. He needs to control himself!"

"I am afraid they have already left," Ferrith said. "They are out retracing their steps, still searching for the creature."

Ekren nodded. The venna had to be found, with urgent haste. For if what the Navenite king said at the Grand Council gathering ten days before was true, and the rakhor were to attack, the world could not afford to deal with two catastrophes at once.

Chapter Thirty-Seven

The night was still, though Adir's mind was anything but. With sweaty palms and a racing heart, he made his way around the back of the Sayarnas' house. It hadn't been very difficult to find the place, as everyone in Akkasha knew where Boar Sayarna's house was.

A couple of windows were lit with lamplight, while the rest were dark. It was an hour of the night when most people were asleep. Slowly, he crept up a short flight of stairs that led to the front door and pushed at it. Locked. As expected.

Along the side of the house, Adir spotted an open window that led into a dark room. He pulled himself into the house, entering a soundless room furnished with a desk and a few chairs. Now he had to find Syfis!

On his journey to Akkasha by boat and horseback, Adir had second-guessed his conviction to avenge his father and brother. No matter how brave or courageous he thought he was, he had never killed a man. At least not intentionally. Would he actually be able to do it? He did not know. But every time he thought of young Athvan, a primal rage stirred in him, pushing him on.

Adir slowly opened the door to the room and entered a dark hallway, then walked down it passing the kitchen and sitting room till he came to a closed door to his right. Putting his ear against the door, he listened for sounds on the other side. When none came, he slowly opened it and peered in. The room held a bed, but no one was in it. Adir continued down the hallway and ascended the stairs at its end. Once on the second floor, he was met with another hallway with a few doors. He approached one and placed his ear against it.

Movement—it sounded like someone was walking toward the door. Adir took a step back, unstrapping his palma and holding it at the ready, completely unsure of what he was going to do.

The door opened, revealing a balding old man holding an oil lamp. Thankfully, the man did not shout upon seeing Adir, though the palma pointed at him might have had something to do with it. Adir thought he recognized the man but couldn't place him.

"What do you want?" the man asked in a gruff voice, seemingly unperturbed by his current situation.

Using his palma to coax the man back into the room, Adir shut the door behind him, keeping his eyes and palma on the old man the whole time. The room held a bed and a few other pieces of furniture.

"Where's Syfis?" Adir asked.

The old man gave Adir a long, hard look. "He's not here."

Adir felt his heart sink. He had come all this way and Syfis wasn't there! "Where is he?"

"He's away on some business."

"Where?"

"I don't know," the old man said. "And even if I did, I would never tell you! You've already taken away one of my sons."

The old man was Syfis's father! The same old man who was at the Judgment Hall on the day of Adir's trial. "Fine! You'll have to do then."

At that moment, there was a knock at the door. "Akka," came a voice, "is someone in there with you?"

With a lot of effort and deep breathing, Adir managed to control his anger as he realized that the old man had been lying. The voice from the other side of the door belonged to Syfis. Adir would recognize that voice anywhere. It had been etched into his memory ever since the night Syfis had tried to kill him.

Raising a finger to his lips, Adir got behind the door and gestured to the old man to open it.

The old man didn't move.

"Akka?" Syfis called again.

Adir gestured to the old man again, but again he did not move.

"Akka?" came Syfis's voice, then the distinct click of a door knob, followed by footsteps. "Akka. Who were you speaking with?"

Adir shoved the door shut and placed the tip of his palma on Syfis's back. Syfis stiffened. "It's unnerving when you're ambushed, isn't it?" Adir asked. "Now you know what I felt when you snuck up on me ... your *brother* snuck up on me."

Syfis remained silent for a long moment. Finally, he asked, "Who are you?"

"Turn around," Adir said. "I'll give you the courtesy of looking your death in the eyes. It's more than you gave my family, I'm sure."

Syfis turned slowly and Adir relished the look in his eyes: recognition, surprise, *fear*.

"You! What are you doing here?" Syfis asked.

"Did you think I would let you get away with killing my family?" Adir asked, looking deep into the eyes of this monster. He had killed eight people!

"I didn't! I didn't kill your family." Syfis looked confused.

At the same time, his father said, "Syfis would never do such a thing."

Lies! Adir felt his anger rise and swallow him up. Memories of his father and brother came flooding in. *Athvan had been so young.*

"Enough!" Adir glared at Syfis. "You don't deserve to live." He lowered his palma to Syfis's chest. One thrust would end it all.

Suddenly, Syfis shifted left and Adir instantly reacted with a thrust and a twist. Syfis slumped, mere deadweight, at the end of his palma.

"No!" the old man cried out and rushed at Adir.

Adir pulled his palma back, dropping Syfis to the ground. A surge of energy filled him with a sense of invincibility as he thrust the polearm into the old man's chest.

The old man grunted, his eyes fading. "What are you?" he asked through labored breaths.

Adir looked down and found all of him to be covered in the rainbow-hued haze. He had transformed into a venna. Wordlessly, he looked into the old man's eyes and twisted the palma, then looked back at himself. The haze was gone.

How did I transform? Why did I transform?

Footsteps in the hallway. Deducing he couldn't escape through the door, Adir looked around and found a window. He climbed through it and hurriedly made his way across a flat roof, swung off its edge, and landed on the ground. A scream echoed from above. Adir ran as fast as he could away from the house and back to the grove where he had tied Veyka. Louder shouts and sorrowful screams joined the first one.

Adir swung himself up onto Veyka and made his way out of the grove and onto a moonlit trail that led through some fields, crisp dead leaves crunching under the mare's hooves. He looked up and found the Chariot of the Gods zipping along in its usual unspoken hurry.

Syfis was dead and so was his father. Adir had accomplished what he'd set out to do and then some. The old man's death had been unfortunate, but then again Syfis had killed both his father and his brother. Two for two seemed appropriate. *Didn't it?* But why wasn't he elated? Or even satisfied? Why did he feel as though he'd done something horribly wrong? It didn't make sense. Honor justified his actions, but *… does honor really justify killing someone?*

Adir found himself at a loss, once again questioning all that he held true. Why did doing the things that were supposedly right make him feel so rotten inside? Did everyone feel that way or only him? Though everyone else seemed to know the what and why of things, he feared that he may never. Did he feel differently because he was this monstrous venna?

Once again, Adir felt as though reality was spinning out of control, with him at its very edge, desperately trying to hold on with his nails. The very feeling he had while walking through the streets of Omanna after learning about his family's death.

Tears welled up in Adir's eyes and he wept. Uncontrollably. He hadn't cried like this since realizing that his mother was never coming back. *Athvan, akka, I'm sorry. If it weren't for me you two would still be alive.*

But that was not all. He had been the cause of Kirsch's death—the steward who had carried Adir on his shoulders when he was little. He had been the cause of Nilane and Misuma's deaths—the housekeepers who had cared for him as if they were his mothers.

I am a monster!

With effort, Adir managed to get a grip on himself. A cold fall wind blew, freezing streaks of tears onto his face.

Soon, Adir would return to Cayan, back to the loving arms of his Habya. He wondered whether he should tell her of what he had done, or continue the lie he'd told her when he left. He felt terrible about lying to her. But what if truth made her see him for who he really was? Should he even go back to Cayan? *She deserves someone better!*

Depressed and confused, Adir tried to determine what to do next. A comforting notion came to him. *I'll go see Morena,* he thought. His keki had always given him sound advice. And she was the only family he had left.

◉

WHAT DID ADIR DO? Ghareeb wondered as he followed his longhaired friend at a safe distance. The screams he heard emanating from the house had raised coldbumps on him.

After notifying a sympathetic Sinain that Adir and he were headed to Naven to visit Adir's ailing father, Ghareeb had carefully followed Adir at a distance as he made his way to Shi'jazha. There, Adir had boarded a riverboat to Meneres forcing Ghareeb to take a different one to the Navenite capital as he had not wanted to get spotted. He lost Adir somewhere in Meneres but found him next on the road heading east to Marafel. Ghareeb had been surprised when Adir went north instead of east from Nagra, eventually ending up in the village of Akkasha.

A slice of moon in a cloudless sky was enough for Ghareeb to clearly distinguish Adir riding his horse. He had never needed much light to see, a skill he picked up while growing up in the streets of Peleria. Orphaned so early that he did not even remember his parents, he was forced to steal, sell, and eat whatever he could, and the best time to steal was night. He had been quite wily in his younger days, slipping away with his loot, flying free as a bird.

Of course, all that had ended when he was caught. That had been utterly foolish. But that was what came of taking unnecessary risks fueled by hubris. On that day, his life had changed; his wings had been clipped. He had been branded mopra. However, if it hadn't been for that unfortunate incident, he would never have met Aiysta.

How he loved that woman! Her ice-blue eyes, her short hair hued in shades of golden wheat, her perfectly melodious voice. He loved her utterly and completely. And she loved him too, but she refused to give that feeling a voice. How could she? She was a mopra and they did not know they had a voice. But he would help her find it. All she needed was to be free of her bondage.

Ahead, a figure moved to Adir's right, then another one to his left. "Adir! Adir!" Ghareeb shouted as fear and panic propelled his actions. Kneeing his horse to a gallop, Ghareeb closed the distance between him and his friend. "Adir! Look out!" he shouted loud enough to wake the sun.

Adir seemed to notice the two figures, but in the next instant he was pulled off his horse. One of the figures pulled out a long dagger, then slammed its hilt onto Adir's head, knocking him out.

O no! I have to do something! Ghareeb thought desperately, suddenly realizing the futility of charging at assailants with only a dull knife. Yet he pressed on. He was only a few yards away.

"Ad—"

Something small but hard smashed into the side of Ghareeb's head, toppling him off his horse. He smashed his face on the frozen ground and felt his front tooth get knocked out. A sharp knee dug into his spine generating a shot of dizzying pain, which made him yelp. As his arms were yanked behind him in a strong grip, he heard the distinct click of manacles locking in place.

"This certainly is a very blessed night for me," Ghareeb heard a voice say in an accent he had never heard before. Roughly, he was forced onto his back.

A man in black stood over him, looking down. All Ghareeb could see were his eyes and four blades protruding out from hips and over shoulders.

"I thought I had lost you," the man said. He sounded as though his tongue filled his entire mouth. "But I should have known that if I found him"—he jutted his chin at Adir—"I would find you. Daroon's blessings are boundless!"

"What do you want with us?" Ghareeb asked. He had no idea who this person was or how this person knew of his association with Adir.

"You? Nothing much," the man said, "but him, quite a lot." He sounded amused.

"The netralodas are on him," came a male voice from near Adir, speaking with rolling *R*s and popping *T*s. Ghareeb looked over at the two figures standing over his friend, both dressed just like the man looming over him. The one who had spoken held Adir's arms up by manacles.

"Do you think the manacles will work?" questioned the other figure in a female voice with a Herran accent Ghareeb had heard a few times before. "Do you think the netralodas will stop the creature from transforming?"

"Who knows?" the man by Ghareeb shrugged. "The Shadow hasn't had to use them for a long time." He paused for a moment, looking over at Adir, who lay motionless. "The Khasir will be pleased with us," he said gesturing to his companions, then looked down at Ghareeb. He pulled out his long dagger and raised it up high. "I am so glad I found both of you."

"Wait—"

The last thing Ghareeb heard was a loud crack in his skull.

Chapter Thirty-Eight

News of Rein's victory at Daroongaamen had reached Marafel even before he had made it back home. The Village Council, which was usually miserly when it came to shelling out money for celebrations, had decided to hold a feast in his honor. And today, the first day of Besava, was that day. Rein sat at the center of a long table on a raised dais with Mayor Alameah and the Village Council. A light breeze from the west carried the savory smells of roasting meats, steaming vegetables, and freshly made confectionaries.

All of Marafel, as well as well-wishers from neighboring towns and villages, were gathered in a large field at the edge of Daaman Woods. At the other end of the crowd, almost a hundred paces away, stood a circular target atop a ten-foot-tall wooden post. Laraan had instructed him that, on his cue, Rein was to hit the target to display his marksmanship.

Unbidden, the crowd began a chant of "Rein, Rein, Rein Maranda!"

Rein felt his face stretch out in a smile. *Recognition*, he thought. That was all he had ever wanted. Ever since his childhood, he'd wanted to be well-known. It wasn't something he was proud to admit—after all, the Word had several cautionary lessons regarding the repercussions of hubris and fame. Yet this adoration was intoxicating!

"Looks like they are ready to start," Laraan said, leaning over to him before standing up. He held up his hands to quiet the crowd. "Marafellens! Navenites! Tonight is a very auspicious night. For tonight, we honor one of our own. Three weeks ago at Daroongaamen, Naven returned with three victors! And the one to clinch the first place victory in archery was our very own Reinard Maranda!"

The crowd erupted into cheers and applause. Once again, they took up the chant of "Rein, Rein, REIN MARANDA!" only this time, the chant echoed off the tall mountains to the east, making it seem as if the lands themselves were cheering him on. Caught up in the moment, Rein stood, grabbing his bow, then nocked an arrow.

"Not right now," Laraan whispered, but Rein didn't pay the mayor any heed.

Raising his bow and taking aim, Rein shut out everything but the target atop the post. Rein loosed his arrow, immediately pulling, nocking, and shooting another, then another. Each arrow arced through the air, soaring above the crowd, and piercing the center of the target, right next to each other. Awestruck shouts traveled like an ever-growing wave from the back of the crowd, till once again the mountains echoed his name.

When the cheers eventually died down, Laraan continued. "Well that was a much better introduction than I could have ever given," he said. The crowd laughed. "But I do have here a letter that arrived a few days ago. It's from King Jonnan Taschari." The crowd went silent. "It reads, 'Day twenty-seven in the eleventh month of Hrensa, year six thousand six hundred ninety-six. Reinard Maranda, Son of Naven.

'Congratulations on your victory at Daroongaamen. Your prowess in archery is the envy of the rest of the world. You have made me proud. You have made your nation proud. I hope that this gift is to your liking. Use it well and, hopefully, you may choose to use it in my service. Naven can always use exceptional men like you! May the Gods favor you. King Jonnan Taschari, Sovereign Ruler of Naven.'"

The crowd cheered once again as Laraan brought out a long case made of oiled wood and placed it on the table in front of Rein. The three-headed taygar of Naven was carved on top of it in painstaking detail.

Rein undid the metal clasps and opened the lid. Inside the case lay an expertly crafted horned bow. Rein picked it up and ran his finger down its length—from the tip of the recurve with a taygar head, along the limbs of sturdy yet flexible maple wood, and the riser made of elk horn. It was lighter than any bow he had used before.

"So what do you think, Rein?" Laraan asked loud enough for all to hear.

Rein looked up. "Thank you, your majesty," he said, holding the bow up for everyone to see. "I shall cherish this gift for the rest of my days!" Everyone cheered.

"I believe the food is all prepared," Laraan announced. "Enjoy yourselves tonight, Marafel!"

The crowd began to disperse among intermittent cheers and shouts. Quite a few folks remained standing by the dais, while the majority began making their way to the feast. Bonfires went aflame, emanating light and warmth as the sinking sun slowly drained the world of its heat, letting the mid-fall chill set in. Rein decided to wait on the dais rather than brave the crowd below. He didn't have to rush to get his food. The Daroongaamen victor would surely be fed.

"Congratulations, Rein," Ellyn said, walking up behind him. "We're all very proud."

"Thank you, Mistress Kalathar," Rein replied, meeting her eyes. They didn't seem to hold the same excitement as the rest of those gathered tonight.

Rein watched her walk away and wondered whether the pressures of the Village Council were finally getting to her. The village had been overrun by Kheryne, and until tonight, Marafel had lost its luster. Such a large gathering of people hadn't occurred for months now, ever since the string of deaths that had plagued the small village nestled in the foothills of the Pharrahmin Mountains.

Considering the woes of Marafel reminded Rein of the day he and Adir had found Tamaar's body. It seemed such a long time ago now. But that had been the start of Marafel's troubles. The village might have moved on, had it not been for Boar's death. And the Nathar household.

The worst of it all was that Adir had admitted to *unintentionally* killing Boar. Rein had wrestled with whether or not to tell someone about Adir's admission but had decided against it, giving his friend the benefit of the doubt. Rein had hoped to hear the whole tale from Adir in Omanna, but Adir hadn't shown up for dinner as promised, leaving Rein to wonder if he had taken off again. It seemed that his childhood friend had developed a knack for running away from his problems and responsibilities—something Rein found to be cowardly. Rein had expected better from Adir, for if he were in Adir's shoes he would face his trials head on.

"Master Maranda! Master Maranda!"

Rein looked down and found a little girl, not much older than his sister, Martha. She stood next to her mother, who was wearing a high-necked dress with embroidered sleeves. People had dressed up for tonight's feast. "Yea, little miss," Rein said.

The little girl suddenly looked shy and stepped behind her mother. "Ask him your question," her mother prompted. The little girl shook her head. "Go on," her mother nudged.

"What's your question?" Rein asked, putting on his best smile.

Slowly, the little girl came out from behind her mother. "Ummm … I was wondering," she began hesitantly. "I was wondering if my akka was making my arrows wrong. They wobble when they leave my bow. I keep telling him that shouldn't happen." She seemed to have overcome her initial timidity.

Rein laughed. "All arrows do that, little miss. You just have to shoot enough arrows and learn to anticipate it." The little girl looked confused. "But, you know what, I'm impressed that you know about the wobble. Most people don't. Keep practicing and I'm sure that one day I will be at a feast celebrating your victory at Daroongaamen."

The girl's face lit up in a pretty smile. "I will practice every day, Master Maranda!" she said enthusiastically.

Abruptly, a chilling scream echoed through the crowd, then came another, and another.

"What is it, mara?" The little girl stared up at her mother, wide-eyed, as more screams rose.

"I don't know," her mother said, plainly worried and turning her head one way and another.

From atop the dais, Rein had a clear view of the entire area. Screaming and pushing, those gathered by the edge of the woods were now running west, away from the bare-limbed trees and toward the village. Then, as clear as the Temple bells, Rein heard "Rakhor!" And then he saw them.

Several looming creatures, almost twice the height of men, strode in from the woods. Six spikes, each about the length of a spear, jutted out in three pairs down the lengths of their backs. Some rakhor vanished then seemed to appear a few paces ahead of where they had been only an instant before.

The whole crowd took to its feet, running. It was complete pandemonium. Then the rakhor began killing.

Those closest to the edge of the woods were the first to fall. Men, women, children, all fell prey to the unbiased tide of death that rolled in. Some rakhor used their long claws to hack and slash at anyone within reach, while others snatched people up and whipped them around, tearing apart their bodies.

Rein stood frozen in shock. He looked around and saw the Village Council shouting out instructions in vain. No one was listening.

Without a second thought and energized by fear, Rein jumped off the dais and took off running west with King Taschari's bow in hand. Shortly, he found himself being pushed in every direction by the throng of people trying to escape their imminent death. Screams and shouts filled the ever-darkening evening.

My parents! My siblings! Rein suddenly thought. They were in the crowd with the rest. *Gods, watch over them!*

As Rein got farther away from the field, the crowd began to loosen and spread out in various directions. Rein continued west, running toward his house, hoping to find his family alive.

Some distance ahead, he came across two groups of uniformed soldiers running toward Daaman Woods, ordered in rank and file. *The Mountain Watch!*

Over the last few months, the Watchmen had conducted regular patrols of the foothills, looking for the rakhor that had killed Tamaar. When they were off duty, they'd visit the Rainbow Inn for drinks, where Rein had come to know a few, some of whom were barely older than he was.

"Rein," Bhavain called out as he passed by. "Are there really rakhor by the woods?" The Watchman's voice carried the trepidation Rein felt.

"Yea," Rein managed to say. That familiar lump in his throat was back.

"Gods save us!" Bhavain exclaimed. "Pray for us, Rein," he said, then continued on with his brethren.

Rein stood for a moment watching the men and women of the Mountain Watch march toward the demonspawn. With sword and quiver on hip, bow across back, and spear in hand, the brave Watchmen waded against a strong current of lesser folks running away. Rein felt ashamed as he realized that he was one of those lesser folks. Suddenly his victory at Daroongaamen began to feel empty. The recognition he got from the world seemed worthless.

Is this how he stood and faced his obstacles? Sure, his obstacles were rakhor. Even Daroon himself hadn't been able to kill the demonspawn, instead being forced to seal them in at the Precipice. How was he, a mere mortal, to face that? But then again, Bhavain had never faced a rakhor either, yet there he was willingly marching toward them. Could Rein live with himself knowing that he had chosen to run away?

Suddenly, Rein remembered what his father had told him when he had come of age. *In life,* Eli had said, *opportunities to prove who you are to yourself don't come by too often. It's up to you to recognize and seize them. Or risk regret.*

Something in Rein hardened as a new resolve took hold of him. "Bhavain!" Rein called out. "I want to help!"

"ALL RIGHT, THIS IS FAR ENOUGH," Bhavain said, holding up his fist and signaling the halt.

Rein's heart thumped so loudly that he was afraid the three rakhor in front of him would hear it. The demonspawn were merely thirty paces away, but the darkness made them seem closer. At this distance, Rein was able to see the rakhor a lot more clearly; though there was no moon, the bonfires lit during the feast provided enough light.

Based on the stories he'd heard, Rein had always pictured the rakhor's spikes as being rigid, but they were far from it. As the creatures moved, the spikes bent, swayed, and bounced with a smooth fluidity. Their whole body, including claws and face, was covered in an armor-like skin, blacker than the darkest hour of night, reflecting the light of the bonfires. Their faces held no features. None. No eyes, no nose, nothing! Just the same armor skin.

"Looks like only three," Sarish said, voice barely a whisper, as the large man scanned the surroundings from where he crouched behind some tall brush.

Abruptly, one of the rakhor vanished then appeared again, a few paces from its original spot, still about thirty paces from Rein and the Watchmen. The creature lifted its arm and speared its sharp claws downward. A man, who lay among several dead or wounded, cried out, his last breath leaving his body.

Rein felt his stomach twist. A nauseating feeling caused his forehead to bead up with sweat. He brought his fist up to his mouth as his earlier meal threatened to exit.

"Breathe," Bhavain whispered.

Rein obliged and his nausea dissipated slowly. "Where did the rest go?" Rein managed to ask.

"I don't know," Sarish said. "Gods' favor, they didn't chase everyone into the village. But looks like these here are killing anyone left alive."

"All right," said Bhavain, "on my signal, Sarish and I will charge and surprise those demons. Rein, I need you to take down as many as you can."

Rein nodded assent, but he wasn't sure he was up to the task. Earlier, when Bhavain requested of his lieutenant that Rein help them, the lieutenant had not been thrilled about having an untrained civilian join his ranks. However, being severely outnumbered by the rakhor forced his hand. At the time, Rein had been only too eager to help, but now that he was facing three rakhor, he seriously worried that he hadn't thought this whole thing through. Even if he somehow stopped shaking, it was nighttime and he could hardly see. And what's more, the lieutenant had mentioned that a rakhor could only be killed by a fatal attack to the throat. Rein fearfully looked at the rakhor. Cries of pain emanated from the darkness.

Bhavain held up three fingers, then two, then one, then pointed ahead. As one, the two Watchmen launched themselves out into the open. "For Gods, family, and nation!" they shouted.

All three rakhor turned to face the Watchmen as the men closed the gap. Rein stood watching, frozen by fear and awed by the Watchmen's bravery.

"Rein! SHOOT!" Bhavain's voice cried out.

Snapping back to the moment, Rein pulled out an arrow and nocked it to the new bow. Though the bow was light and easy to draw, his arms swayed, destabilizing his aim. To make matters worse, Sarish had run into his line of fire.

"REIN! SHOOT!" Sarish yelled. The two Watchmen were barely ten paces from the rakhor.

One of the rakhor spread its arms out while another appeared to ready itself.

Despite his uncertain aim, Rein loosed when his instinct compelled him to. Arcing over Sarish's head, the arrow found the neck of the rakhor the two Watchmen were charging toward. The rakhor *flickered* a few times, then sublimated into a mist of colors that looked a lot like the Aurora, then the mist faded away into nothingness. *The stories are true!*

Bhavain leapt at another rakhor, spear extended, but the rakhor dodged away. The third rakhor joined his companion separating the two Watchmen.

Sarish struck at one of the rakhor as Rein nocked another arrow and loosed. Just as the rakhor turned to face Sarish, the arrow stuck into its throat. And like its companion, this rakhor flickered, misted into colors of the Aurora, and faded away.

The third rakhor whirled around and raced toward the woods, vanishing intermittently and appearing farther away.

"We have to kill it!" Bhavain yelled, taking off after it, closely followed by Sarish.

Rein pulled out another arrow and tried to aim but found it impossible to track the rakhor. *Such speed!* Rein put the arrow back in his quiver and chased after the Watchmen.

Rein followed the Watchmen in the woods, running as fast his legs allowed. Before long, the tree-topped flat ground turned into a steep uphill slope, slowing the Watchmen down and enabling Rein to catch up to them. The run turned into a walk, which deteriorated into unsteady, intermittent steps. Breathing heavily, Rein stopped, leaning on a tree.

"We have to keep going, Rein," Bhavain said. He pointed northeast. "I saw it go that way."

Rein nodded, then looked up with a sigh spotting the Chariot of the Gods hurriedly tracking its usual path. His legs hurt, his chest burned, and he was covered in a cold sweat. Unlike Bhavain and Sarish, he wasn't used to this much strain, but he wasn't about to let them down. He pushed off from the tree and followed.

Farther up the incline, Rein and the Watchmen came upon a small cave. Several boulders of varying sizes were strewn about, as if carelessly discarded by the Goddess Pharrahmin.

"Are you sure it went in there?" Sarish asked.

"Yea." Bhavain nodded. Cautiously, he approached the cave that seemed too small to hide a rakhor. Abruptly, he stopped. "There's a hole in the ground here," he said. "Light a torch."

As the three men got closer, the torchlight illuminated the shallow cave of brown stone, that was concealing a hole large enough for a rakhor to drop down width-wise.

"Where do you suppose it goes?" Rein asked.

"I don't know," Bhavain said, "but that's the only way it could've escaped."

"It would be foolish to go in there after it," Sarish said.

Bhavain nodded. "Yea. We don't know what's on the other side."

"So we just go back?" Rein asked. "We can't just leave, can we?

What if it comes out later and heads into the village?" Rein felt horror at the thought of a rakhor wandering through Marafel killing more people. There had been enough death!

"You're right," Bhavain said, looking around. Pointing at some boulders, he continued, "Sarish, help me drop some of these in there. Hopefully, it'll block their path buying us some time to get help from our comrades."

Sarish nodded, handing Rein the torch. "This one here looks light enough to move," he said, pointing at one. "You keep watch, Rein."

Bhavain joined Sarish and the two managed to roll the boulder into the hole. That boulder was followed by six more of similar size, till the last boulder stuck halfway out of the hole. Rein watched in awe as the two men, barely older than he, accomplished a feat most men would be too lazy to even attempt. And all that after running almost eight hundred feet up the side of steep slopes. These Watchmen truly lived up to their reputation.

"That should hopefully do it," Bhavain said.

Sarish laughed a rumbly laugh. "Are you sure? One rakhor is as strong as ten men."

"It has to be, at least till we get some reinforcements." Bhavain turned to Rein. "I need you to go to Lieutenant Meehra and tell him of what you saw. We'll stay here and keep watch."

"I will." Rein handed the torch back to Sarish. "Help will be here shortly," he said as he turned to run downhill.

"One more thing, Rein," Bhavain said, pulling off the pin holding his cloak together. He held it out to Rein. "I also need you to give this to the lieutenant."

Rein looked at the metallic pin in the yellow torchlight. It was a solid black triangle, about as wide as three fingers, with an eye in its middle. "Why?"

"It's the seal of the Navengaard Mountain Watch," Bhavain said, "and by giving this to you, I'm nominating you for entry into our ranks."

Rein felt pride fill him. Yet at the same time, he also felt doubt creep in. "Why me?" he asked.

"Are you serious?" Sarish asked. "Without you, Bhavain and I would be dead."

"I almost didn't shoot," Rein admitted, remembering how he'd forgotten to follow simple instructions in the heat of the moment.

"You also don't have any training"—Bhavain gestured dismissively —"but despite that, you killed two rakhor and stuck with us afterward. If you ask me, I want you watching my back always."

"I agree." Sarish smiled.

"So what do you say?" Bhavain tilted his head. "Will you hand it to the lieutenant and join our order?"

Rein pondered for only a moment. What he wanted most out of life was recognition, and he felt he'd achieved that at Daroongaamen. But next to this, that recognition paled. He realized that what he truly wanted out of life was not just mere recognition, but recognition from those he felt he belonged with. And it seemed that the Watchmen might be the very thing he was looking for. "Of course I will," he said.

"Gods' favor!" Sarish clapped Rein on his back. "That's the right call. Now all you have to do is finish training and run the Gauntlet to be officially sworn in."

Chapter Thirty-Nine

He awoke with a long breath, inhaling deeply through his nose and exhaling out from his mouth. A few breaths later, sensation returned to his body that was anything but pleasant; it felt as if he had been trampled in a cattle stampede. He stood, abruptly realizing that his wrists and ankles were cuffed. Loose chains ran from the cuffs to the wall. To his left, he spotted two dimly lit shapes bound as he was; both were slumped and motionless.

Looking around, he saw that he was at the end of a long stone chamber with two rows of tall stone columns running down its length; he couldn't see its end. The chamber appeared to be lit by white and yellow motes of light that floated along the walls. Awe pit itself against fear for control of his emotions.

He looked down. The floor on which he stood was circular with a circular symbol at its center. Words in a strange language were inscribed below the symbol. Strangest of all, above the symbol was a black staff, floating a few hands off the floor.

What is happening? he thought as the sound of distant waves washed into his hearing. He looked up. The ceiling ended where the circular floor began. The black night sky stretched above, dotted with stars on a moonless night as the Chariot of the Gods zipped across it.

A door opened somewhere, sending echoes of footsteps bouncing off the long walls. Shortly, several shadowy figures appeared, walking toward him. His heart began to race. As they passed by the floating motes of light, he could see that they were clad all in black, with swords protruding from their shoulders and shorter blades attached to each hip.

The rush of memories overwhelmed him into remembering. He had been taken by these black-clad people in Akkasha. But why? What did they want from him?

Three of the figures waited behind, while the rest approached the circular floor and fanned themselves around him. Suddenly, Adir felt a rumble under his feet as the stone floor in front of the three figures slid away. Three black stone blocks with gold trims and flickering lights rose out of the ground, accompanied by the sound of stone grinding against stone. Once the lighted blocks ceased their rumbling emergence, the black-clad figures around him unsheathed the swords from their backs with a unanimous rasp, holding them out with extended arms. Then there was only silence, save for the dim crash of waves. *Gods save me!*

Another door opened, this time to his right. A backlit, hooded figure emerged through the doorway. As the figure approached, the motes of light arrayed down the length of the chamber's walls suddenly flared. Adir shielded his eyes against the unexpected brightness. When next he looked, the hooded figure stood only a few paces in front of him. Adir couldn't see a face under the shadowy cowl of the brown robe.

"I apologize for the rough treatment you received when my operatives found you." The person under the robe was a woman, speaking in a polished and proper accent, typical of the Ostarks who had visited Cayan for Daroongaamen. "But apparently you were quite uncooperative."

Adir decided to remain silent, though his fear tried to persuade him to scream.

"If I had known that it was you when I saw you in Cayan," the brown-robed woman continued, "I would have brought you in myself."

Adir tried placing the voice but couldn't. "Where did you see me in Cayan?" he asked with a fearful curiosity, his voice sounding pathetic to his own ears.

"That is not important," the woman said, turning away. "How does he look?" she called out.

"Well enough, Khasir," said one of the black-clad operatives in a Navenite accent. He was behind the central lighted block and appeared to be looking at something on the other side of it. "He is healthy."

"Good." Khasir turned back toward Adir. "Are you ready, Adir?" she asked.

"Ready for what?" Adir asked, panicked. "What are you going to do to me?" *How does she know my name?*

"You? Nothing yet." She pointed at the two prisoners bound to his left. "They are first."

Two motes of light blossomed above each of the other captives, illuminating them.

Tia and Ghareeb! Adir's stomach dropped. How had they been captured? "What are you going to do to them?"

"Let me show you." Khasir pulled out what appeared to be a pane of glass that lit up with strange symbols. "The wonders of the Gods know no bounds."

The cuffs on Adir's wrists went frost cold when Khasir tapped on a few symbols. The next instant was pure agony. It was as if his whole body was aflame while thousands of knives stabbed him simultaneously. Adir screamed as he shook and convulsed in an effort to rid himself of the torture, but that only made it worse. Then, suddenly, the pain stopped.

"How did the creature do?" Adir heard.

"No rise, Khasir," the Navenite operative replied.

Khasir let out a heavy sigh, then walked up to him. "You have a strong constitution," she said. *Why does she sound disappointed?*

"Why are you doing this?" Adir asked, gagging from the echoes of pain. "What have I done to you?"

"You have not done anything yet, at least that we know of. But you could."

"What does that mean? Who … who are you?"

"You would have never heard of us," Khasir said, "but that is how we like to operate." She paused. "But since your time on Leakarha is short, I suppose it would not hurt for you to know." She paused again, for longer this time. "We are the Khasmia Shadow," she announced, "and I am its Khasir. We have been charged by the God of Courage himself to rid the world of venna. Like *you.*"

How does she know about venna? Based on what Ghareeb had told him, no one knew about venna. It was nothing but a fabled creature from Kheryne lore. "What is a venna?" Adir asked, though he knew he sounded far from convincing.

"What is a venna?" The Khasir scoffed. "A venna is the most dangerous creation of the Gods. Tainted creatures that channel their corruption with the sole purpose of destruction. A creature of doom. A monster. You are a curse upon this world!"

"I'm not a venna," Adir said forcefully, maybe too forcefully.

"Of course you are!" The Khasir pointed at the chains that bound Adir. "When you are bound by those cuffs, we can see your vitality, your essence, on these marvelous relics," she pointed at the lighted blocks behind her, "called the nostateho. Your essence does not lie."

"No," Adir said, shaking his head. "This sounds insane!"

The Khasir laughed in an unsettlingly melodious manner. "I can see how it does, but let me assure you that it is not. Every incredible, fantastical thing you see here was made by our Gods when we lived with them on Aedenin. The Word calls them Gifts of the Gods, but these relics are much more than mere gifts."

Adir recalled the many sermons of Akka Hallen where the sage had narrated the story of Genesis. The Goddess of Justice, Corranine, had left humans with many Gifts that had been lost over the ages. But Adir had always assumed that the Gifts were some religious metaphor, not to be taken literally. "The Word is true?" Adir blurted out, though he'd meant for it to be an internal thought.

"Not all of it." The Khasir laced her fingers together. "A lot of it was bastardized to fit the whims of the Sanctum of the Seven, but some of it …" she trailed off. "The Khasmia Shadow does not live by the Word, however. We live by a higher philosophy, the true calling."

She paused. "But I digress. Rest assured, we know you are venna. One of my operatives saw you covered in a rainbow-hued haze with his own eyes."

No matter what, I will not admit to it, Adir thought. "I don't believe you," he said, "I'm not this venna. I'm just a nobody from Marafel."

The Khasir's brown hood bobbed up and down as the woman nodded. "Such stubbornness," she said, sounding disappointed again. "But I suppose it is possible that you do not know. Very well. I will just have to show you then." She pointed at Ghareeb. "Wake him up!"

"Ya, Khasir," an operative from another lighted contraption said, speaking with a lilting Cayani accent.

Ghareeb lay limply on the floor bound by his shackles. Then one of his fingers twitched, then another. Then he grunted. He moved his head around, eyes barely open. "Where am I?" he asked with a voice of recent awakening.

"Ghareeb!" Adir said, incredulous that his friend had been woken up on command. *How is this possible? Are those truly relics built by the Gods?* No, that was preposterous!

"Go ahead," the Khasir said.

Ghareeb looked at Adir with a worried puzzlement. Then his eyes shot open, his whole body stiffening as straight as an arrow. Blood-churning wails emerged from the man as he twisted and contorted. The torment was plain for anyone to see.

"Stop it! Stop it!" Adir yelled at the Khasir, but Ghareeb's screams of agony continued. He knew the pain that his friend was in, intense and unceasing. Yet he couldn't get himself to admit to what he was.

"Any change in the venna?" the Khasir asked calmly through Ghareeb's screams.

"Only a slight rise in its power. But nothing significant," the Navenite operative said.

Abruptly, Ghareeb went limp, dropping to the floor like a heavy sack.

"He's unconscious," the Cayani operative said.

"Wake her up!" The shadow-faced, brown-robed woman pointed at Tia, her voice and posture betraying her frustration.

"No! Not her!" Adir pleaded. "Please! Please! Not her! Do what you want to me, but leave Tia alone!" But still his fear didn't let him admit to what he was.

"Unfortunately, the best way to get what we want from you is through her." The Khasir sounded truly apologetic. "I wish there were a simpler way."

Adir heard Tia waking up. "No, no. Please don't do this," he begged, but the Khasir simply turned away from him.

"Adir?" Tia's sweet voice called out. She sounded very weak. "Adir?"

"I'm here, Tia," Adir said, facing her. He felt the wet trail of helpless tears creep down his cheeks. "I'm sorry."

"Sorry for what?" Tia asked, her eyes blinking slowly as if still dazed. The green dress she had on was tattered and covered in stains; it had been Adir's favorite dress.

Before Adir could get another word out, the beautiful woman stiffened with bulging eyes. And then she screamed. O how she screamed.

"Please stop!" Adir cried out as he watched Tia drop to her knees, clutching her stomach. "Leave her out of this! It is me you want!"

"Any changes?" the Khasir asked, ignoring Adir's pleas, annoyance plain in her voice.

"No, Khasir," the Navenite operative said.

Watching his once-beloved Tia writhing and screaming, something in Adir broke. "I am a venna!" he admitted. "Please stop!"

"I already know that," the Khasir said as Tia bent forward and vomited. "I want you to unleash it!"

"I don't know how!" Adir cried.

"Most of you do not," the Khasir said as Tia's screams rose in intensity. "But this will help," she added, pointing at Tia.

Tia had been through enough suffering for him. He had to end this. Adir dropped to his knees. "Please, my lady," he pleaded. "Please show some mercy!"

The Khasir's shadowed face regarded Adir for a long moment. "A few of my operatives," she began, "the ones who captured you, tell me that your father begged just like you."

At the mention of his father, Adir fell silent.

"Yes," the Khasir continued, "your brother too. They had no self-respect, no dignity to face what was coming."

Tia's screams appeared to fade into the background.

"Pleaded like dogs to the very end," the Khasir spat.

Syfis didn't kill akka and Athvan? Adir thought, remembering the death of the Sayarna men at his hands. An ugly truth was revealing itself, but Adir didn't want to acknowledge it, couldn't acknowledge it. He had to believe that Syfis had killed Arvan and Athvan. If not, he was every bit the monster his actions made him.

Abruptly, Tia's screams stopped.

"She's dead, Khasir," an operative called out in an accent Adir had never heard before.

Adir looked to his left where Tia lay doubled over. *Tia's dead?*

"What about the creature?" the Khasir asked.

"Its power is much higher than before. But—"

"Enough of this!" the Khasir bellowed and tapped on her pane of glass.

Adir's cuffs instantly went cold and intense pain engulfed every point throughout him. His body writhed in agony, screaming. But his mind was lost in the sobering realization that he was the cause of all the turmoil in his life. Not his father, not Tia, not the Sayarnas, or anyone else. His loved ones had all been there for him while all he did was push them away. And in return for their love and kindness, he brought them suffering and death.

"It's rising, Khasir. Quickly!" the Navenite operative called out.

"Good," the Khasir said. "Bring the Staff."

Through unfocused vision, Adir watched as an operative grabbed the floating black staff with undue reverence, then walked up to him and stood a few paces away. The Khasir tapped on a few symbols and Adir's arms began to move to his front on their own accord, till his palms stopped a short distance from each other, cupping air in between.

"What is taking so long?" The Khasir sounded furious.

"I don't know," the operative said.

The Khasir let out an angry shout and tapped again on the lighted pane of glass.

Adir could no longer breathe. It was as if his own neck was squeezing down on itself. The sudden prospect of death jolted Adir back to the moment. He struggled for a breath, but none came.

Without warning, a surge of energy rushed through him. That intoxicating well of unimaginable strength had somehow been tapped. Adir found himself engulfed in the resplendent rainbow haze. He had transformed!

"Good," the Khasir said, tapping on some more symbols.

Immediately, Adir's pain vanished and his lungs filled with air, but all he could move was his head. The rest of him was immobile, seemingly under the Khasir's control.

"Raise its power," the Khasir commanded. She sounded apprehensive.

Suddenly, Adir found himself tapping deeper into the well of strength. His power grew. Every muscle, every hair on his body felt as if they could shatter mountains. He'd never experienced this kind of power before. Yet it was useless. The godly relics of the Khasmia Shadow had him immobilized.

"Hand him the staff," the Khasir commanded.

Though Adir couldn't see the face hidden behind the black mask, the operative's eyes betrayed fear. The black-clad operative stepped toward Adir slowly.

"What are you worried about?" the Khasir asked. "The netralodas have him securely bound!"

Cautiously, the operative placed the staff in the space between Adir's hands then hurried away. The Khasir tapped on her lighted glass pane and Adir's fingers began wrapping themselves around the smooth surface of the staff. And Adir experienced something new.

Adir *shifted*. Not a physical movement, but rather a displacement within himself. Abruptly, he found himself in the middle of a vast ocean of countless loops of indeterminate color, all undulating in different patterns. A soothing, ethereal sound pulsated all around him. It was as if the undulating loops were singing to him!

Where am I?

With great apprehension, Adir touched one of the undulating loops, though he didn't truly have hands. Or a body. The undulating loop wobbled and deformed, then settled into a new pattern, its sound standing in stark dissonance with those around it. Adir watched with growing unease as the loop, no larger than a copper crown, wildly varied its pitch, sweeping through myriad erratic undulations. Then with a snap, it settled back to its original form in harmony with the other loops around it.

Adir *blinked* in astonishment. Immediately, he shot away at an incredible speed, the undulating musical loops getting smaller, their individual notes fading yet merging into something new. The farther he got, the once-countless loops retreated and coalesced into shapes, shapes his eyes were seeing. It was as if he were seeing through a new lens. The chamber, the relics, the people, the air itself. *Everything* contained undulating loops. *Everything* had a unique song. And he could hear them all, see them all, *feel them all.*

"Khasir," the Navenite operative called out, his voice tremulous, "the creature seems to be modulating its power."

With a rush, Adir came back into himself, confused and disturbed. Something was different, though he couldn't say exactly what. It felt as if a veil had been pulled from his eyes, revealing things he didn't understand. He was still transformed as a venna, engulfed in the rainbow-hued haze. But what was this new sensation, this new connection?

"Impossible!" The Khasir walked over to the lighted block in the middle and stared at it intently. "The staff is supposed to extract the creature's power and destroy it!"

"Yea, Khasir," the Navenite operative said uncertainly. "It should, but …"

Something around Adir changed. He felt it through his new sensation, prompting him to look to his right. One of the black-clad operatives was charging toward him, his swords lowered to his sides, parallel with his legs. Instinctively, Adir moved into a defensive stance and was surprised to find that he was free of his bindings.

"How did he slip of out of the netralodas!?" The Khasir's tone was an amalgamation of shock and awe.

"I don't know, Khasir," came the reply from the Navenite operative, his voice dripping with fear.

The charging operative stopped in front of Adir and turned as if standing in his defense. "We need to get out of here! NOW!" the operative urged in yet another foreign accent. His *R*s rolled and *T*s popped.

A cautious curiosity stayed Adir's attack as four other operatives charged forward. The rest stood with gaping mouths. One operative charging from his left leapt, though Adir didn't actually see it with his eyes—it was as if the air to his left had changed its song.

An instinctual knowledge made Adir shift once again, returning him to the vast ocean of undulating loops, singing, resonating. He *reached out*, fearfully realizing that they responded to him. Moving several around, he changed their sound then shifted back, once again seeing the world through the lens of undulating loops. He didn't know what he'd done, but it felt right.

The air in the chamber stirred up into a forceful wind that grabbed the leaping operative and slammed him into the floor by Adir's feet. Adir raised the black staff with both hands, in the manner Sinain had taught him to kill a downed opponent using a palma. As he thrust the staff downward, its tip morphed into the blade of a palma, piercing the operative's heart.

From the other end of the staff, a blindingly bright beam of white light shot into the night sky.

Daroon save us! Ekren thought, looking through shielded eyes at the incredible bar of light shooting out of the Staff of Beckoning. The Warning had said nothing of this. The Staff was to unravel the venna, killing it. Her eyes traced the beam piercing the sky till it was intercepted by the Chariot of the Gods, seemingly getting absorbed by the star.

When darkness returned, Ekren looked at the creature. It was no longer covered in a rainbow haze. Ekren grabbed the operative next to her. "Seize it!" she commanded, furious and afraid at the prospect of a venna loose in the world with the Staff of Beckoning. "NOW!"

The operative pulled out his swords and charged, yet his charge seemed halfhearted. Looking around, Ekren found other operatives cautiously surrounding the venna. This was no time for caution!

The Shadow had performed multiple drills for such situations, yet the fact that they had not dealt with a real venna was apparent in their hesitation. *The drills had not accounted for Shadow turning on Shadow,* Ekren realized with a heartsinking sense of betrayal. Four of her operatives were now protecting the vile creature. How had this come to pass?

A door down the wall opened and several footsteps rang through the long chamber. Could she trust them? It did not matter. For now, she needed to capture the monster. "Seize it!" she commanded. "And kill anyone who gets in your way!"

"We need to go now!" one of the traitorous operatives said in a clear Kheryne accent.

"Not without them!" the venna said, pointing at the Pelerian man and the Navenite woman.

"We do not have any time," the Kheryne operative said, lifting his chin at the approaching mass of operatives cautiously moving toward them in three files. Their swords were drawn and held at the ready.

"I'll deal with them," the venna roared, stepping out from behind its defenders.

"Cut them down!" Ekren commanded, disgusted at those willing to protect the greatest threat to humanity.

Abruptly, the venna unleashed its power, its rainbow haze engulfing its whole body in colorful wisps, revealing only a silhouette of the creature.

It cannot be! Ekren had captured a venna that could control its power. The realization formed a pit of fear in her stomach that slowly drained her resolve.

The venna rushed at the approaching operatives with incredible speed. It was as if the creature had vanished from where it was and appeared in front of the operatives, like rakhor!

With the Staff—*that now looked like a Cayani palma*—the venna tore through the front line of operatives, slicing their bodies in half, blood, flesh, and guts spraying and spilling. Stepping forward and cutting an arc in the other direction, the venna sliced the second line of operatives in twain with no apparent effort. Then it swung once more and all but three operatives in the third line fell, their blood staining the seal of the Shadow.

"Let us leave!" the traitorous Kheryne operative said. He carried the Navenite woman on his back. "Through there!" he pointed, then ran toward the door Ekren had used to enter the chamber. The other traitors—one of them carrying the Pelerian—took off after him. The venna feinted a lunge at the three surviving operatives, then followed the traitors. The three operatives did not pursue.

Ekren regarded her dead operatives in horror. Within the blink of an eye, the monstrous creature had decimated several seasoned men and women. How could the Shadow be expected to contain that?

But that was not a thought Ekren could even entertain. She would not be known as the Khasir that brought about the end of the world. If the Khasmia Shadow did not destroy this creature, it would destroy the world. And it had the Staff of Beckoning, an ancient relic that amplified its corrupt powers. Ekren could not let it escape!

"You!" Ekren said, pointing at one of the three operatives still alive. "Have all the exits sealed!"

The door the venna had escaped through could lead them to any number of places within Shadow Keep, but to get off Aedenin, they would need to get to a runeport. And there were only two of those on the island—one at the front of the Keep and the other in her den.

"Alert the other operatives and inform them we have traitors in our midst," she added. "Make sure to seal off the front runeport. NOW GO!"

The operative took off down the long chamber.

Pointing to the other two, Ekren said, "Come with me. We are going after the vile creature."

Chapter Forty

"Get on here," the operative the others called Rusane said. "We have to leave!" He spoke with an accent that emphasized his Ts and rolled Rs.

The urgency in Rusane's voice sounded real. Yet Adir couldn't help but feel that this was some kind of trap. "Why do you want me to get into a corner? Was rescuing me some kind of joke?"

Through the slit in his mask, Rusane's eyes flashed with annoyance. "I will explain later. For now, trust me!"

Adir didn't trust this man. He was with those who had captured him. They had killed his family, killed Tia. A pang of sorrow shot through him. At least Ghareeb was still breathing. However, with no other choice, Adir stepped into the circular corner of the windowless room, confused as to how they were to escape. They'd just locked themselves in the Khasir's den and were now crowding into a corner?

Rusane stepped on two tiles along the circumference of the circular corner. Immediately, the floor began to shimmer with the rainbow haze. It looked like the same haze that surrounded Adir when transforming into a venna. He checked his arms. Nothing.

"What's happening?" Adir asked, panicked, as the rainbow haze ascended, covering him from the bottom up.

"We are going to Lanmeria," Rusane said, adjusting Tia's body across his shoulders.

"Going to Lanmeria? Isn't that in—"

All sound and sight ceased for a brief moment. Then, with a pop, his hearing returned, immediately followed by sight as the rainbow haze descended.

Adir found himself in one corner of a lavishly decorated room with large open windows looking out at a dawn sky. *How is this possible? What happened to the Khasir's den?* He almost jumped out of his skin when a hand fell on his shoulder.

"It is called a runeport," Rusane said, nudging him into the room. "I had the same look you have now when I first went through one."

The other operatives followed. The one that carried Ghareeb placed the bearded man on a black leather chair and stretched his back.

"A runeport?" Adir asked. "What is that?"

"It takes you from one place to another in an instant," Rusane said matter-of-factly.

"So, we are actually in Ostarium?"

"Yes, we are." Rusane placed Tia's lifeless body in another chair and cracked his back, then pointed out the window. "Look, it is almost morning."

"How?" Adir was utterly confused. None of this made any sense. He felt as if he was in a surreal dream.

"I do not know for I do not know the mind of the Gods."

This preposterous notion again! But after what he had just seen and experienced, preposterous might be the new normal.

"Rusane!" another operative called out, in the same accent as Rusane. He pointed at the runeport—its floor had begun to shimmer.

Rusane's eyes widened. "We must make haste," he urged, heaving Tia back onto his shoulders and moving rapidly to the door. "The other Shadow operatives are following us. We do not have much time. And the palace will be waking up soon." The other operative picked Ghareeb up and followed Rusane.

"You go ahead," Adir found himself saying. He had just discovered a deep thirst for vengeance. "I'll stay behind and buy us some time." But really, he just wanted to hurt those who had hurt the ones he loved and made him wrongfully kill Syfis and his father. He had so much blood on his hands.

"No! You are the whole reason why we need to leave now!" Rusane said stubbornly. The shimmer had risen about a foot off the ground.

"I can take care of myself," Adir said. "Besides, carrying them will slow you down." He pointed at Tia and Ghareeb. He had to get Ghareeb to safety and he had to give Tia a proper burial. They had sacrificed so much for him.

Rusane squinted. "So you can control it now?"

"Yea," Adir said. The unveiling of a new understanding just out of his reach had somehow given him the ability to transform at will. The sense of invincibility that accompanied the control over his transformation had allowed him to slay all those operatives, scything through them as if they were rice stalks during harvest.

"All right," Rusane said. "If they come at you with cuffs, run away! They are called netralodas and they are meant to instantly incapacitate a venna."

"I have no intention of being captured again," Adir said. Whoever appeared in that corner alcove wouldn't be alive long enough to even try.

"When you leave, run down the hallway then turn left. At the end of that hallway, you will see an atrium below. We will meet you there."

Adir nodded. Rusane gave him one final look, then he and the other three operatives exited the room, shutting the door behind them.

Adir gripped the palma, that was once a staff, in both hands as the rainbow shimmer neared the ceiling. How had the staff turned into a palma? All he had done was picture thrusting with a palma in his mind as his eyes looked at it through the lens of undulating loops.

The rainbow shimmer hit the ceiling then began descending, revealing the brown-robed Khasir.

"You've come alone," Adir stated. "It doesn't seem safe to pursue a venna alone."

"I did not want my operatives harassing this place," the Khasir said, walking into the room and stopping a few paces in front of Adir.

"O. So you are concerned for the people who live here?" Adir spat as his closest companion, anger, returned. "Where was this concern when you had my father killed?" He thrust the palma toward the Khasir's heart but stopped short of piercing through. The Khasir didn't even flinch. "Where was this concern when you had my brother slain?" He raised the sword blade to the Khasir's neck. "Where was this concern when you tortured Ghareeb and killed Tia?"

"That is not how I wanted things to go," the Khasir said, "but circumstances forced my hand."

"Circumstances are forcing my hand too," Adir said, his heart desiring nothing but this woman's death. "Drop your hood." He wanted to see the face of this unknown woman who had caused him so much pain. He wanted to savor the look on her face as her last breath left her body.

Slowly, the Khasir lowered her hood.

"You!" Adir exclaimed. The Khasir of the Khasmia Shadow was none other than the Regent of Ostarium, the Alamand of the Grand Council, Ekren Arinol! What was going on?

Suddenly, a sword appeared in Ekren's hand. She shoved aside the palma, stepped inside Adir's reach, and swung.

Adir ducked, the sword whizzing over his head, then immediately lunged forward. To his surprise, the Regent simply stepped aside, just as Sinain would have, as if she were a practitioner of the art of Continuity.

Adir tumbled and crashed into a chair by the large desk at the center of the room. If Ekren knew the Cayani fighting philosophy of Continuity, not many would be able to best her. But he was no mere man.

Adir transformed, the rainbow haze fully engulfing him. He could see every detail of every little thing in the room. He could hear the operatives' footsteps making their way down a flight of stairs. He could smell the ocean breeze being warmed by the rising sun. Above all, the well of unimaginable strength had been tapped. But that lens of undulating loops, for some reason, eluded him.

"So, you have to resort to using your corrupt powers to defeat a true human?" Ekren asked mockingly. "Your father never taught you honor, did he?"

"He did," Adir said with a cold determination, "but I choose to use every advantage I have." Adir took three steps forward, then thrust the palma into Ekren's chest, intentionally missing the Khasir's heart. This woman didn't deserve a quick death! He pulled the blade out then thrust it once more into the Regent's belly.

Ekren fell to the ground, her brown robe darkening from her oozing blood. "Daroon save us all," she muttered through labored breaths. "I have failed." Her fading green eyes looked directly into his. "I have loosed destruction upon the world." She inhaled in a long breath, but didn't exhale.

Adir felt a chill pass through him at the dying woman's words. Everyone who knew about venna had nothing good to say about it. But he wasn't a monster. He wouldn't destroy the world. Or would this venna one day take over his self and … ? *No, that's preposterous! Right?*

"Where is he?" Adir heard Rusane's voice through his heightened hearing. It sounded like it came from below.

They're waiting for me. He also heard casual footsteps shuffling through various parts of the palace.

Adir ended his transformation and opened the door, looking out into a long, empty corridor with several arched windows. Quickly, he ran down the corridor and just as he was about to turn left at its end, as per Rusane's instructions, he bumped into someone.

A beautiful woman with green eyes and auburn hair looked up at him. Adir immediately recognized her from the Grand Council gathering—it was the Regent's daughter.

"Look where you are going," the woman said, meeting his eyes.

Shoving her aside, Adir ran toward where Rusane had said the atrium would be.

"You!" the woman called out. "Stop!"

Approaching a railing, Adir looked down at the atrium. He contemplated transforming and jumping, but decided against it as he didn't want to attract any more attention. Thankfully, there were stairs nearby.

Running down the stairs as fast as he could, Adir made his way in the direction from which he'd heard Rusane. Shortly, he found the whole group huddled behind a row of potted plants.

"It is daylight outside," Rusane said with concern in his voice. "We will need to stay low and quiet."

Suddenly, a scream echoed through the palace.

"What was that?" Rusane asked.

"I think the Regent's daughter found her mother's body," Adir said.

"How do you know that?"

"I ran into her on my way to you."

Rusane did not look pleased. "So, now you know that Ekren Arinol was the Khasir." Adir nodded. "There's a lot more you need to know," Rusane continued, "but now is not the time. Now, we need to run." He took off toward a small metal gate at the other end of the atrium.

Once outside, Adir found himself in a garden with servants dressed in yellow and white livery tending to various chores.

"The other runeport is right there," Rusane said, completely ignoring the confused stares of the palace servants.

How many of these things are there? Adir wondered.

Behind a large banyan tree with thick, gnarled roots hanging from its limbs, Rusane halted the group on a stone circle. It was well hidden from plain sight. "Everyone get on! I am sure guards are looking for us after you revealed yourself to the Heiress Regent."

Adir felt his anger surge at the accusation, but he managed to rein it in. Rusane pushed on three stones on the edge of the circle. And as before, the ground began to shimmer with a rainbow haze. The haze ascended.

"Where are we going now?" Adir asked apprehensively.

"To the other end of the world!"

Chapter Forty-One

Dina had always known that one day her mother would stand judgment at the gates of Amarna—a day that was far in the future. But she had been proven wrong when she walked into the Regent's study two days before to find Ekren lying on the floor, unbreathing.

This morning, on the sixth day in the month of Besava, in a funeral with all the honor and ceremony worthy of an exceptional woman, Ostarium bade goodbye to its beloved Regent. But while Ostarium would mourn for a short yet appropriate amount of time, Dina feared she would weep forever. Ekren Arinol might have been the greatest Regent of Ostarium, but to her, Ekren had been both of her parents.

"The Elevation will take place three days hence, Heiress Regent," Ferrith said. "The necessary preparations are under way."

"Does it have to be this soon?" Dina asked from across the table from him in her chamber. She should have used the Regent's study for this meeting with Ferrith, but she could not get herself to go back there. The image of her mother lying dead in a pool of her own blood was still too fresh. "Mara's ashes are barely cold."

Ferrith's expression turned sympathetic. "Child," he said gently, "I grieve for your mother's loss as well, but the Ostarks need a new Regent. They are looking to you to lead our nation into the future."

"It does not seem right, Ferrith," Dina protested. "It feels rushed!"

"I know," Ferrith replied, "but such is the burden of your Regency. You have to dig deep and find the strength to push aside your woes for the sake of your people. Your mother would have wished it so herself."

Dina held back a sudden flood of tears with effort. Breathing in deeply, she collected herself. "Very well," she said. She would be strong. For her mother!

And Dina would do more than just be strong. She would find and kill the man who took her mother away from her. "Any news on mara's murderer?" she asked.

"No, Heiress Regent," Ferrith said. "Rest assured we are looking for him."

"What is taking so long?" Dina said with an impatient anger. "This is not just any murder we are dealing with. The Regent of Ostarium was assassinated!"

"Yes, Heiress Regent. But that is exactly why we cannot move quickly. Political assassinations are a tricky business." He paused. "We have told the world that your mother died of natural causes, for if the world found out that the Regent was assassinated, it could easily undo the international stability we have worked on for generations."

"The way I see it," Dina said with a bitter taste in her mouth, "that stability was undone the moment mara was killed." She had not liked the idea of lying about her mother's death, wanting to scream about it from the highest peaks and in the lowest valleys, till every person in every nation was looking for her mother's murderer. She wanted to burn the world to ashes to find the man who had killed Ekren. But she had grudgingly agreed to Ferrith's plan.

"I understand, Heiress Regent," Ferrith said. "But if we move too quickly trying to find this man, we will attract too much attention." He smiled ingratiatingly, but Dina kept her face impassive. Ferrith shifted uncomfortably. "Heiress Regent," he said, "since you say that the man who killed your mother was the one who spoke up at the Grand Council gathering, then we cannot say for certain who wanted your mother … eliminated."

Dina shot the old man an angry glance.

Ferrith tightened his lips into a thin line. "That man was in the employ of the Cayani but spoke with a Navenite accent. Either nation could be behind this heinous deed." Ferrith paused and regarded her with his aged green eyes. "We need time to find out who the true culprit is, and only then can we act. If not, I fear we may find ourselves in another War of Remaking!"

Dina did not like what Ferrith was saying, yet her mother trusted this grey old man with his bony fingers. And so she would trust him too. "Very well, Ferrith," she said with a sinking disappointment, "but I would like regular progress reports. At the very least, I want this man found! If not killed!" Her disappointment ignited a molten anger in her heart as she remembered her mother laying dead in a blood-soaked brown robe. "Ferrith, the robe that mara was in … I had never seen her in it before. Had you?"

Ferrith did not answer for a moment, seemingly searching his memory. "No, Heiress Regent."

It was utterly odd that the robe that her mara had died in seemed to fit the description of the robe worn by the Khasir of the Khasmia Shadow. At least according to the accounts of the discredited author whose work on the Khasmia Shadow had been an intriguing read.

"Is there anything else you require of me, Heiress Regent?"

"No. You may leave, Ferrith. Thank you for your council."

"Anytime, Heiress Regent," Ferrith replied, rising. "May the Gods give you strength." With that he walked to the door, but before he left the room, he turned. "And Heiress Regent," he called, "if you need someone to talk to, I am always here. I know a thing or two about losing the only living parent at your age." He smiled warmly then closed the door.

Dina found that deciding to trust Ferrith did not allay her anger any. In fact it only made it worse. She would not get the instant retribution she so desired.

The molten anger in her heart erupted, sending burning rivers of rage throughout her body. Looking for a release, Dina tapped into that familiar well of unimaginable strength—a trick she had learned in her teenage years. Immediately, she was engulfed in a rainbow-hued haze, wisps of which rose up into the air. An intoxicating sense of invincibility washed through her.

Venna! She had not known what she was till she had found the book in Ekren's study. Since the first day she had learned how to transform, she had lived in constant fear of being found out. Normal people did not engulf themselves in a rainbow-hued haze.

But upon finding the book in Ekren's study, she had flirted with the notion of telling her mother, overjoyed at the prospect of unburdening herself. Alas, her research with Bilgan and the Master Archivist had revealed the venna to be a vile creature of destruction. Not to mention that venna were hunted by a secret society called the Khasmia Shadow. She was not sure if she was being hunted, since the existence of the society had not been proven, but any thought of revealing her true self to Ekren had been snuffed out. Yet she had hoped that one day she would have had the courage to tell Ekren. But her mara was now gone, murdered by the hands of a long-haired, lanky man.

I will find you! Dina thought with furious conviction, tapping deeper into her well of unimaginable strength. The rainbow-hued wisps flared. *And when I do …*

Chapter Forty-Two

Agusty fall wind swept across the Kheryne Steppes, bending the brown grass nearly flat under a wide grey sky. Adir pulled his coat a little tighter around him and adjusted his hat as he tried to gain control over his thoughts. Tia was being put to rest.

Draped in a green dress, one the idgiich picked out at Adir's behest, Tia lay on a bed of grass bordered by wildflowers. Adir had spent two whole days scouring the steppes for these flowers, while the idgiich prepared Tia's body and cared for a recovering Ghareeb. With fall in full swing, it had been difficult finding enough flowers to border the entirety of the bed of grass. But seeing how he'd never done enough for a woman who'd given up her life for him, the meager collection of flowers seemed appropriate.

The idgiich, garbed in a woolen garment that the Kheryne Khuun called dealhe, stood next to Tia's body holding a small metal bowl. The wind picked up in strength, flinging the strands of grass on her headdress in every which direction, threatening to snatch it off her head. Yet the idgiich didn't move a muscle to adjust her wild headdress. She simply stood with eyes closed, face solemn.

"Every time we lay someone to rest, the wind comes to whisk their souls away to the gates of Amarna," Rusane whispered to him. "Every time."

Adir simply nodded. If Tia had heard those words she would have pointed out that the lands of Kheryne were inherently windy, which would make the presence of wind tonight nothing special. And she would have also pointed out that humans didn't have souls.

None of that mattered though; Tia was gone forever. Like his father and brother.

To Adir's other side, Ghareeb shifted from foot to foot. Though he had recovered well enough, Ghareeb, who now had a missing front tooth, still suffered from lingering effects of his torment at the hands of the vile Khasmia Shadow. He seemed to have difficulty standing for very long. Guildnar, Rusane's brother, had offered to get him a stool for the funeral, but Ghareeb had declined, arguing that he preferred to stand to show respect for Tia. The red-bearded man smiled at Adir with sad and tired eyes. "She was a good woman," he said, awkwardly nodding his head.

"Yea, she was," Adir agreed. Painful guilt pushed at his chest. *But I'm not a good man.*

"I am going to miss her," Ghareeb added.

The idgiich opened her eyes as the evening sun began sinking behind the tall peaks of the Bahzenelyn to the west. "Brothers and sisters of Blood Akh'Khamgaal!" she exclaimed over the wind, loud enough for those gathered to hear. The entire yiria was present. "Let us rejoice that a soul stands at the gates of Amarna deciding whether or not to enter!"

Everyone cheered, although it wasn't a boisterous cheer for it lasted no longer than the space of a single breath.

What? Adir thought, confused at the idgiich's words. *Rejoice?*

"The soul that called itself Tia in this life," the idgiich continued, "began its journey in a village called Marafel on the other side of the Bahzenelyn. Though I do not know much about this being, I do know that this enchanting soul was loved." She looked directly into Adir's eyes. "Love, the most sought of all experiences, yet one so elusive. For if grasped too tightly, it slips away."

Adir felt as if he stood naked under the scrutinizing gaze of the idgiich's grey eyes. He'd heard some of the Kheryne Khuun mention that the idgiich, who dealt in matters of life, death, and beyond, could commune with the dead. Surely that was a preposterous notion, yet her words seemed so pointed.

"Adir, my child," the idgiich called. "You knew Tia's life best. Would you share some memories?"

Memories? Adir certainly had fond memories of Tia. Like the day when she taught him how to skip rocks across water. Or the time they stole Niman Mummfar's mule and left it by the Penner because they were too afraid to return it. Or the first time Tia responded to his advances. He opened his mouth to speak, but an overwhelming guilt silenced his voice.

Suddenly, all Adir could think of was how he had led Tia on, tricking her into going to Meneres with him. And how he had left her in Nagra. And how he had shoved her aside when Habya came into his life. Her screams at the hands of the Khasmia Shadow! If it weren't for him, Tia would still be alive.

"Adir is too grieved to speak," Ghareeb said. "He loved her very much."

The idgiich nodded once. "I understand," she said, sounding sympathetic. "It is always difficult to lose a loved one, but remember that a person is much more than their body. The body is but a vehicle for the soul, which lives as many lives as it desires. Rejoice! For you were fortunate enough to have been a part of its journey. Rejoice! For this soul is free once again to decide to enter Amarna or chase after its desire for experience."

Kneeling next to Tia's body, the idgiich scooped out three spoonfuls of water from the metal bowl, pouring one onto Tia's forehead and one onto each of her eyes. Setting the bowl aside, she touched Tia's forehead and her own with her fingertips. "Gods in Amarna! Welcome this soul if it chooses to enter."

"Peace in eternity!" the whole yiria chanted.

"Peace ... in eternity!" the idgiich echoed.

In the silence that followed, four Kheryne Khuun, dressed in ceremonious black dealhes with black sashes around the waist, approached Tia's body. They circled her seven times, then stood at each corner of the grass bed.

"You should go say your final goodbyes now," Rusane advised in a whisper. "The urshool are about to take her for burial."

Adir moved close to Tia. Her long black hair was slightly fanned under her back, making it seem as if she had wings. If only she really had wings, she could have flown away. Free from him. He studied her face, trying to etch it into his memory. However, he knew full well that one day he wouldn't remember her face—a harsh truth he had learned after his mother had been missing for years. All that would remain would be a feeling of Tia. But for him that feeling would be tainted by his guilt.

"I'm sorry, Tia," Adir said. "I'm sorry you wasted your life on me … I'm sorry you didn't find what you deserved." His eyes welled up with tears, but he held them back. "I'll miss you."

With a heart laden with sorrow and guilt, Adir looked up and nodded to one of the urshool. The four undertakers wrapped the grass bed around Tia like a blanket and carried her away to her final resting place.

As the urshool faded from sight, the yiria began to disperse. Ghareeb walked over and stood next to Adir in silence. After a while, he said, "Rusane wants to talk in Guildnar's gehr. But he said to take as much time as you need."

"We can go," Adir said, looking up at the sky. He spotted the Chariot of the Gods, but it seemed to move slower—much slower—as if mourning Tia's loss. Despite Tia being Faithless, he hoped that the Messenger in the Chariot would vouch for Tia's entry into Amarna.

"Are you sure?" Ghareeb asked, quickly masking a look of incredulity.

"When I had time with Tia, I didn't use it well," Adir said. "Taking as much time as I need now seems … meaningless."

THE CIRCULAR TENT made from animal hide, that the Kheryne called a gehr, was warmed just right by a low yellow fire burning at its center. The Kheryne Khuun didn't bother with hearths or floors. From what Adir had gathered, their clan or *yiria* or *blood*—it got quite confusing sometimes—wandered the steppes with the seasons, chasing herds or just *following our hearts*, as Rusane had put it. Floors were not much of a priority when you picked up and left every so often.

Across the fire sat Rusane and his brother Guildnar Romakhai. Guildnar was the *yearon*, which Adir supposed meant leader or mayor, of Blood Akh'Khamgaal. From looks alone, it was hard to tell the two Kheryne Khuun apart. Both had long, wispy black hair, and thin mustaches hanging down to their chins. Both displayed the same calm, arrogant look that Adir had seen in battle-hardened veterans like Captain Marwar, Sinain, and his own father. If it weren't for Rusane's Khasmia Shadow garb and the hints of white in Guildnar's hair attesting to his seniority over his younger brother, the two would have been indistinguishable.

"What did you think of the funeral?" Guildnar asked in a commanding voice.

"It was strange, Yearon Romakhai," Adir said honestly, taking a sip of eirag, an alcoholic beverage made from fermented goat's milk. It was quite strong and quite sweet.

Guildnar looked offended. "What do you mean ... strange?"

Adir didn't care if Guildnar took offense to his honesty. "Souls don't *choose* to enter Amarna. Corranine, the Goddess of Justice, lets you in if you've lived a worthy life."

Guildnar bellowed a hearty laugh. "Is that what you believe?" He paused as if waiting for a response. "Why would Corranine care if you entered Amarna or not? Do you not think that a God has better things to do than be a doorkeeper?"

"So ... the soul simply chooses to enter Amarna?" Adir asked.

"Yes," Guildnar replied. "When a soul has had its fill of experiences, it chooses to enter Amarna."

Adir was confused. He turned to Ghareeb, hoping for some explanation, but the man simply shrugged.

"Do you know what a soul is, Adir?" Guildnar asked.

The yearon's question took Adir by surprise. "It's ... uhh ... a life force," he said, remembering the teachings of the Word. But, truly, he didn't know.

Guildnar smiled. "It certainly is a life force in the sense that a soul makes a body seem alive. But it is much more than that. It also makes the body a person." He paused, taking a sip from his cup. "The Kheryne Khuun," he continued, "believe that the soul is an eternal being, living many lives to fulfill its desire for experiences. Once it has satiated its desire, it decides to enter Amarna and become one with existence. As such, we Kheryne Khuun live our lives to fulfill our desires. To aid our souls on their quest."

"It is Adis Vilgaan," Rusane said, seated with legs crossed.

Adir looked at the man clad all in black, swords and daggers protruding from behind the corners of his body. Rusane and the other Kheryne operatives of the Khasmia Shadow had not once masked their faces since their arrival. "Adis Vilgaan?"

"Yes," Rusane said with a nod. "Adis Vilgaan. It is the foundation by which the Kheryne Khuun live our lives. Unlike Annadism, which views reincarnation as a punishment, a penance for an unworthy life, Adis Vilgaan teaches that reincarnation is a blessing bestowed upon souls by our Gods. For only through reincarnation can a soul fulfill its desire for experience."

"That is fascinating," Ghareeb interjected.

"Because of our belief in Adis Vilgaan," Rusane continued, unperturbed by the interruption, "we band together in yirias to help each other fulfill our soul's desires. And, Adir"—Rusane looked into his eyes—"that is why we risked life and limb to save you from the clutches of the Khasmia Shadow."

"What do I have to do with Adis Vilgaan?"

"Nothing beyond the fact that you are another soul fulfilling your desire for experiences. And you are a venna."

"Why would you want to save a monstrous creature that will destroy the world?" Adir asked. None of this made any sense.

Rusane remained silent for a long moment. "As far back as our histories can remember," he began, "the venna were indeed monstrous. They wandered these steppes covered in a rainbow haze, and wherever they went, destruction followed. The Kheryne Khuun had fables and stories that warned of venna. My people lived in fear for thousands of years.

"One day, a stranger crossed over from the Bahzenelyn, claiming that Daroon had charged him with ridding the world of venna. Desperate and afraid, a few joined the man and became the first Kheryne Khuun to become Shadow operatives. These operatives, and those that followed them in generations to come, hunted venna with a fervent resolve to save humanity. But in doing so, their resolve turned into blind zeal. They committed many atrocities in the name of the Shadow, killing men, women, and children with no thought or remorse. Such is the power of desperation—it rids us of our humanity. Eventually, the Shadow erased all knowledge of the venna from the world."

"Why did you do that?" Ghareeb asked.

"The Warning says that the world would be better off not knowing about the venna. So the Shadow killed those who knew of the venna and confiscated or destroyed books, scrolls, and relics that spoke of the creature. Over time, the world forgot and the operatives continued their work in secret." Rusane paused and sipped from his cup.

"But," Adir said, realizing that something didn't make sense, "the Kheryne Khuun know about venna and the Shadow. Why didn't the Shadow go after your people?"

"They tried, but they soon found out that the Kheryne Khuun are hard to track," Rusane said.

"They also realized," Guildnar added, "that no Kheryne Khuun operative would give up the typical whereabouts of their yiria."

Rusane nodded in agreement. "Eventually, the Shadow decided that the Kheryne Khuun were too spread apart and cut off from the rest of the world to warrant any real effort. Besides, at that time, the Kheryne Khuun would voluntarily send our venna to the Shadow. Wives surrendered their husbands, siblings turned in each other. Even parents gave up their children."

"That is awful!" Ghareeb exclaimed. "Is that why the rest of the world considers you to be savages?"

Rusane shrugged. "When people do not understand something, they assume the worst. Nonetheless, it was a dark time of our past. But all that changed more than five hundred years ago because of a Kheryne Khuun operative called Tallena.

"Tallena was the first Kheryne Khuun operative to rise through the ranks of the Shadow. She was groomed to take over as Khasir. As part of her grooming, she was present for the torture and death of a venna called Altansar." Rusane paused for a long moment. "She watched as Altansar was tortured and eventually killed. His death affected her deeply.

"Then one day, while fulfilling her duties to the Shadow, Tallena recovered a relic in some ruins in the south of Kheryne. It was part of a parchment that seemed nothing special; it just contained some writings in the language of the Gods. But loosely translated, it said *rainbow-hued haze will be our salvation.*

"This revelation astonished Tallena. She came to the realization that Altansar, and indeed all venna, were not monstrous creatures but special souls chosen by the Gods. They needed to be protected from the Shadow!

"When Tallena shared her revelation with the other Kheryne Khuun operatives and invoked the teachings of Adis Vilgaan, she managed to recruit them to her cause and formed the Tallenata Venna. Since Tallena's time, every Kheryne Khuun that became an operative was also a Tallenata Venna, working to save venna so their souls may fulfill their desire for experience."

"The Tallenata Venna," Guildnar spoke, "spread Tallena's revelation to all Kheryne Khuun."

"So where are these other venna you've saved?" Adir asked.

"Sadly, Adir," Rusane said, "you are the first. But that is because the Shadow has not found a venna in over two hundred years. Some had begun to believe that the venna had been eradicated. And before that, according to the Shadow's records, every other venna had simply faded to nothingness when they unleashed their power and could not control it."

"I'm the first venna who can control his powers?" Adir asked in surprise.

"Yes," Rusane nodded. "It is quite remarkable actually. The

Warning says that you are not supposed to be able to do that. That your power should kill you."

"What is the Warning?" Ghareeb asked. "You have mentioned it a few times."

"It is said that the Warning was written by Daroon himself and handed to the first Khasir of the Khasmia Shadow," Rusane explained. "It is the essence of the society's operations. We are taught to live and breathe by it."

"All right, but what is it?"

"I suppose you could call it the holy book of the Khasmia Shadow, akin to the Word of the Gods. It teaches about the venna and how to destroy them. It is the Shadow's code of conduct. It even lists several relics with detailed descriptions of design and use."

Ghareeb nodded then looked at Adir. "So you believe that the venna are your salvation?"

Rusane and Guildnar both looked pointedly at Adir, but only Rusane spoke. "Yes."

A strange sensation of pride and fear mingled in Adir's chest. *I can't even save myself. How am I to be their salvation?*

"Salvation from what?" Ghareeb asked. Adir wasn't sure if that was a veiled insult.

"I do not know," Rusane admitted. The gehr fell silent.

"So now what?" Adir asked.

"The Shadow will not rest till they find you," Rusane said with a sigh. "They will come after you. You will have to be on your guard."

"So I can't go back home to see my sister?" Adir asked. *Or back to Omanna and Habya?*

"I would advise against it. Operatives will be sweeping every nation west of the Bahzenelyn looking for you. For now, you should be safe here. With their Khasir dead, it will take the Shadow some time to organize and discover that all of their Kheryne Khuun operatives are missing. But they will eventually come here too."

"So I can't go back home and I can't stay here," Adir said as hopelessness crept in.

"The only way out"—Rusane ran his fingers down the length of his long mustache—"is to destroy the Khasmia Shadow."

"Destroy the Khasmia Shadow!" Ghareeb slapped his hands on his thighs. "As much as I would like to see each and every one of them burn, I do not think that is a practical option."

"It was not before, but it is now," Rusane said. "We have never had a venna on our side." He pointed at the palma that was once a staff, strapped to Adir's back, "and you have the Staff of Beckoning. When wielded by a venna, it is said to amplify your powers." Rusane leaned forward, his expression intense. "Did it? Did you feel stronger?"

It was when his hands touched the Staff that Adir was transported to that ocean of undulating, musical loops, somewhere within himself, yet without. But did he feel stronger? No. He had, however, felt a strange new connection. A connection that somehow allowed him to control the air around him. *Did I really do that?*

"Adir?" Rusane called. "Did you feel stronger?"

"I don't know," Adir replied, snapping back to the moment. "Maybe?"

Rusane looked disappointed. "Are you sure? We all saw that white bar of light shoot out of the Staff. And the Staff of Beckoning somehow turned itself into a palma!" He shook his head. "My mind cannot fathom such things. But all that aside, would you help us destroy the Khasmia Shadow, Adir?"

"Your help will be greatly appreciated," Guildnar chimed in. "By destroying them, you will not only help yourself but those who saved you as well. And other venna like you."

Every instinct in Adir screamed *NO!* But he knew that what Rusane was saying was true. The Shadow wouldn't rest till he was dead. That much was evident when Ekren Arinol herself pursued him, though Ekren had known what Adir was capable of.

As long as the Khasmia Shadow was after him, Habya and he could never have a life together. And that would mean he would once again break his word and pull an innocent woman into danger. Determined not to repeat the mistakes he'd made with Tia, he was left only one choice. "Yea," he said. "I'll help you."

"Excellent!" Guildnar raised his cup. "You are welcome in my yiria for as long as you wish, Adir."

"Thank you, Yearon Romakhai," Adir said. Guildnar responded with a gracious nod.

"Well, I would like to return to Cayan as soon as possible," said Ghareeb.

Adir looked at his friend. "The Shadow will be looking for you too, Ghareeb."

"Ya, but I have something I need to tend to," Ghareeb said vaguely. "It has already been too long."

"If you so wish, Ghareeb," Rusane said. "You can take a runeport to right outside Omanna."

"Runeport?"

"Ah, yes! You were unconscious when we traveled here," Rusane said with an amused smile. "Runeports are relics left behind by the Gods that lets one travel from one place to another in an instant."

"All right," Ghareeb said slowly, with a look that seemed to judge Rusane's sanity.

"And Ghareeb," Rusane said, "I am sorry for my part in your suffering." He sounded sincere.

"It is all right," Ghareeb said with a smile. "I have suffered worse. And besides, you ended up saving me."

"Thank you. You are a forgiving soul."

"Well," Guildnar said, getting to his feet, "it is getting late. I am ready for sleep. I need to be awake early to milk my goats." Everyone stood.

Adir smiled on the outside and cried on the inside, Guildnar's mention of milking bringing back strong memories of home. Would he ever go back to Marafel?

"May the Gods aid your soul," Guildnar said, then he escorted Adir and Ghareeb out of his gehr.

ADIR AND GHAREEB walked side by side toward the gehr Guildnar had given them, navigating around stakes and ropes. The wind had died down, yet the cold was still biting.

"It seems you are their salvation," Ghareeb said mockingly. "How does it feel to go from monster to salvation?"

"Confusing," Adir answered truthfully. "Long ago, the Kheryne thought I was a monster, then they changed their minds? All this sounds like a bunch of cow dung."

Ghareeb laughed. "Like runeports."

"Runeports are real. How else can you explain how you made it all the way across the Bahzenelyn so quickly?"

Ghareeb looked visibly shaken. "I thought that my sense of time had been warped after what those Khasmia swinespawn did to me." He paused for a moment. "Then that must mean you really are chosen by the Gods."

"That's quite the leap," Adir said, shaking his head. But was it? "I don't know, Ghareeb. I don't know what to believe. Everyone is telling me something different." It was maddening. "You're the learned one. What do you think?"

Ghareeb smiled. "I would not say I am learned, but from the little that I have read, and having traveled a bit, the only thing I can say is that no matter where you go, everyone has crazy, unbelievable stories. The funny thing is, everyone believes their own crazy stories are true and all others are heresy. So ... believe what you want, because no one truly knows anything."

"What if my beliefs are wrong?"

"Does it matter?"

Does it? Shouldn't it? He needed more time to mull this over. "You should stay here, Ghareeb," he said. "Cayan is not safe for you."

"Ya, I know," Ghareeb replied. "But it was not safe for me before either. And besides, I need to go there."

"Why?"

"For a woman," Ghareeb said as a small smile briefly touched his lips. "She needs me and I need her."

"I understand that," Adir said, wishing he could go back to his Habya.

When they approached their tent, Ghareeb pulled the doorflap open and entered, but Adir didn't follow.

Shortly, Ghareeb poked his head out. "Are you planning on sleeping tonight?"

"Not right now," Adir said, shaking his head. "I feel awake."

"Well, I am tired." Ghareeb rubbed his eyes. "It has been a long day." He looked at Adir, sticking his tongue through the gap where a tooth once was. "May the Gods watch over you, my friend."

"You as well," Adir said reflexively.

Adir walked down the goat-mowed path, as Rusane had called it, with an almost half-moon lighting his way. Far to the northwest, the Aurora danced low across the sky, displaying its rainbow-colored wisps in splendor, subtly reminding him of who he was.

Venna. What that meant he hadn't the slightest notion. Others seemed more knowledgeable about him than he himself.

The more Adir thought about it, the more his mind spiraled into confusion. What had happened when he touched the Staff of Beckoning? What were those undulating loops that serenaded him with dulcet, singular tones? What had been that bright light shooting from the Staff of Beckoning?

Nothing made any sense. And when combined with fantastical talk about Gods and revelation and salvation, it was all ... *incoherent and inconsistent*. There had to be another explanation, though there were enough explanations already and none seemed to clarify anything.

If the Kheryne were to be believed, he was their salvation, but if the Shadow were to be believed, he was a monster, and both were claiming a divine hand in shaping their beliefs. However, if the Faithless were to be believed then the Gods didn't exist and that would make him ... *what?*

Am I even an I?

A feeling of surreality washed over Adir. Everything seemed out of place and he had no idea how anything was actually supposed to be. He was stuck in an unraveling dream—a dream he wanted to wake from, but with no clue how.

Epilogue

A soft yet clearly audible beep yanked him out of his concentration.

What was that? He waited for a short time, listening. When no more beeps sounded, he returned to his work.

The analysis seems to work. A theoretical possibility exists for a barrier, but the energy for modulation is so high that the possibility might as well be an impossibility. To be able to get that kind of output, we would need—

The beep sounded again.

Irritated, he looked up from his work and across the brightly lit room. His eyes fell upon the thin, light-complexioned woman wearing a tightly fitted yellow shirt. She was blissfully reading, seemingly unbothered by the beeps. He wanted to ask her to close her book and investigate the beeps—after all, that was her job—but that was not his way. He despised confrontation. He'd rather just let things slide or do it himself if it meant he could avoid unpleasantness. Though in this case, he did not know how to stop the beeps. Ignoring them wasn't working either. He needed her help.

He coughed, hoping to get her attention. It worked. She looked up from her book and smiled at him. He met her eyes for a long moment then smiled weakly and looked away. He should have asked her to investigate the beeps, but he couldn't find the appropriate words. Besides, it hadn't sounded for some time; maybe it had stopped.

Just as he returned his attention to his work, the beep went off again. It was as if the beep was actively trying to hinder his contemplation.

"Did you hear that?" he asked, irritation overcoming his non-confrontational nature.

"Hear what?" she asked, still reading.

"That beep," he said. "It's been going off for a little while now."

"All right. I'll take a look at it."

"Thank you," he said half-heartedly and returned to his work.

A few moments later, the beep sounded again. He looked up and found that she was still reading!

"Pharrahmin," he said gently, "can you please find out what that beeping is?" He had known her for … a very long time, yet he felt uncomfortable *ordering* her.

"All right." Pharrahmin shut her book with hyperbolic frustration, then rose and walked into the other room.

He sat watching the door to the other room as the moments passed, his impatience growing. He still had a lot of work to do and not enough time. "Did you find it?" he called, unable to hold out any longer.

The beep sounded, as if in response.

Some more time passed, yet no word came from Pharrahmin. *What was taking so long?*

"Pharrahmin," he called again. "Any luck?"

"You better come take a look at this, Berron."

Berron stood and walked slowly toward the other room, reluctant to pause his work. Pharrahmin had never asked him to take a look at anything before. In fact, she had always been of the mind that his theoretical smarts did not translate well to practical applications. *She* was the expert in engineering.

The beep sounded again as he entered the large room that hummed with a low, ambient buzz from the workings of Pharrahmin's various contraptions. "Doubt I'm going to be of much help," Berron said, approaching her. "What did you want me to look at?"

Pharrahmin met his eyes, a single lock of her blonde hair sliding onto her face. She tucked it behind her ear, adjusted her diadem that carried a thumb-sized, bright yellow citrine at its center, then nodded toward the screen.

Berron faced the screen … and his breath caught. The screen displayed 'SIGNAL DETECTED' in large green letters. It disappeared and returned with the next beep. "This must be a mistake," he said in disbelief.

"Maybe," Pharrahmin said, "but I ran a quick diagnostics on the system and it's working fine. The signal integrity is also good. No corruption."

Abruptly, three beeps sounded and the screen displayed 'SIGNAL LOST' in large red letters.

Berron turned to Pharrahmin. "We should have used something louder and more dominant than a beep."

"We did not expect to get a signal at all," Pharrahmin replied, sounding a lot more excited than defensive. "We should analyze it."

The screen flickered, replacing the letters with a signal-processing tool. Berron realized that Pharrahmin had taken cerebral control of the console. *She really outdid herself by inventing the external cerebral augments.* Of course, if it weren't for him, she would never have been able to build it in the first place; she did use the results from his research on Venebra Modulation after all.

"It's a short burst, but very powerful!"

Berron leaned in to look at the results displayed on the screen and caught a whiff of Pharrahmin's perfume—it was fetching. *What?* He dragged himself back to the moment and examined the results. The peak amplitude of the signal was indeed very high, affirming Pharrahmin's conclusion. "I'm surprised the probe's transmitter withstood that much energy passing through it."

"I built it to withstand quite a bit," Pharrahmin said with a smug smile.

How very typical, Berron thought. She always over-engineered her inventions—case in point, the augments. They were initially supposed to merely be a field-analysis tool, but by the time she was done with them, they were capable of console controls and intra-augment communications. He felt an inexplicable sense of pride in her.

"We have to tell the others," Pharrahmin said.

"I agree. I'll contact them." Berron accessed his cerebral augment. *I need you all to come see something,* he thought and sent it through his augment to the others.

A few moments later, he got a reply from Hrenwaldt: *Does it have to be now?*

Berron's nature fought him. He hated forcing people to do anything. But this was not the time to be timid. *Yes,* Berron replied, trying to sound commanding. But Hrenwaldt was always better at that.

What's this about? Hrenwaldt sent.

I'll come over. I have nothing better to do, Corranine sent.

I shall be a while, Menera sent. *I'm in the middle of a bath and I'm rather enjoying it.*

Berron shook his head. He did not think it would take this much discussion to get them there. *We've received a signal from Leakarha,* Berron sent. He was getting impatient.

What signal? Corranine sent.

The signal? Hrenwaldt sent.

Yes! The signal! Now get over here! Pharrahmin sent.

After a long pause, Hrenwaldt sent, *I'll be right over. Just need to get to a ring.*

Menera? Pharrahmin sent.

After a long pause, Menera sent, *Fine. I shall be there.*

In a few moments, the door to the room shimmered with a rainbow-colored hue, transforming into a ringway, and Corranine walked through it. The fair-skinned woman was dressed in a light violet blouse and skirt, with a diadem with a deep violet iolite encircling her head.

"Looks like you owe me a decade of service, Berron." Corranine smiled broadly.

"Let's discuss that after we've had confirmation," Berron said. Why had he ever made that idiotic bet with her?

"It's pretty much confirmed," Pharrahmin added, grinning. "We're just waiting on consensus." She winked at Corranine.

Women! Always banding together.

Menera walked in wearing an orange dress and looking uncharacteristically messy with her hair still dripping wet. She had obviously rushed out of her bath to get there. She even held her diadem with its bright orange moonstone in her hand instead of wearing it. She placed it around her head as she approached and the combination of orange moonstone, tan skin, and green eyes gave her a beauty that surpassed her current dishevelment.

Hrenwaldt entered through the ringway immediately after Menera. Berron was not sure how he always managed to look regal. Perhaps because he always wore a cloak over his clothes, all in hues of blue, along with his sapphire diadem and sharp-angled beard.

"So let's take a look," Hrenwaldt said, command cutting through his voice.

"Where's Herra?" Pharrahmin asked. "We should wait for her."

"She's not coming," Hrenwaldt said, suddenly sounding a little sheepish.

Ask him why, came Herra's thought through the augment.

Herra, let's not do this now, Hrenwaldt sent, pleading. *We have much more important matters to deal with right now.*

A few moments later, Herra sent, *Fine! I'll be there.* And another few moments later, she walked through the ringway, wearing a loose-fitting, sleeveless dress of green and a diadem holding an emerald around her head.

"Good," Hrenwaldt said. Berron noticed how Hrenwaldt met everyone's eyes except Herra's. "Let's get started, then. So, we have a signal?"

"Yes," Pharrahmin said matter-of-factly. "It was detected a few minutes ago. It was short but very strong."

"Did you analyze it?" Herra asked, moving to stand next to Hrenwaldt.

As Pharrahmin regaled the others with the results of her analysis, a thought suddenly occurred to Berron. He accessed another nearby console with his augment and sifted through data they had been collecting and archiving for all this time. The data had been gathered through a probe that zipped across the skies of the world of Leakarha, and had been left behind when they departed. First, he filtered out everything but images. Then he stitched them together chronologically, creating a time-lapse recording of Leakarha as it changed over the years.

" … so as you can see, the signal is quite anomalous compared with those we've encountered elsewhere," he heard Pharrahmin explaining. "Given that we see peaks at harmonic frequencies, we can be fairly certain that the various bursts are from a single source. Something down there *modulated*!"

"This is interesting," Berron said, completing his task. Immediately, he realized that he had interrupted Pharrahmin. "I'm sorry. I didn't mean to interrupt you."

"What's so interesting?" Hrenwaldt asked before Pharrahmin could respond.

"This." Berron pointed at the screen of his console.

The others gathered around and Berron started the sequence of images, then watched as they played through.

Leakarha was changing. Some lands withered away while others grew lush. Lakes and rivers dried up as new ones sprang up elsewhere. Volcanos erupted in some places while earthquakes wracked others. He looked at the others and saw a uniform look of shock and surprise on each of their faces as they watched the images unfold in front of their eyes. At one point, a small, organized civilization appeared on Leakarha before fading away.

"They multiplied and migrated! They weren't designed to multiply." Corranine said in an astonished whisper.

More civilizations appeared and disappeared as the images marched on. But through all of that, the humans seemed to have endured and shaped the land around them. As the images wound down, the last few seemed to capture a bright white light hurtling toward the probe's camera, washing out the lens. The images came to a stop.

"What was that?" Hrenwaldt asked.

"I think that was the source of our signal," Pharrahmin answered.

A long silence fell on the room. Hrenwaldt, Herra, and Pharrahmin appeared thoughtful, while Corranine continued to stare at the screen, even though it simply displayed a washed-out white image. Menera looked surprised, and had somehow managed to tidy herself up at some point.

Herra finally broke the silence. "How … how long has it been?"

Berron quickly accessed the console and calculated the time since their departure from Leakarha. "It's been slightly more than nine hundred and ninety-nine years since we got back to Amarna. That's relative to our time. On Leakarha, it's been"—he paused to do a quick conversion—"almost seven thousand years!"

"Their progress has been amazing!" Pharrahmin said. "And the signal …" She trailed off. "Who knows what they know or how much they've managed to advance. We need to go back." Everyone looked at each other, but no one spoke. "That's the only way we will find out," she added.

"Pharrah, dear," Menera said sweetly. Her voice could lull one into trusting her every word—something Menera loved to take advantage of. "I don't think it's worth the trip. All our previous attempts have ended in failure, if not disaster. What makes you think that this time will be any different? We did spend an awful lot of time with that lot and did not have any success."

"We didn't think they would multiply," Pharrahmin said defensively.

"I agree," Berron said more forcefully than intended, surprising himself. But for some reason he did not like seeing Pharrahmin get cornered. "We did not expect a signal that confirmed modulation either," he added in his normal tone.

"I don't care either way," Corranine added. "I'm enjoying the time off while we wait for our end. But a trip would be just as fun."

"Where do you and Herra stand, Hren?" Pharrahmin asked.

Hrenwaldt and Herra looked at each other. Something seemed to have passed between the couple, as the hard expression that Herra had been throwing at Hrenwaldt since they got to the room had softened significantly.

"It's been a long while since we left Leakarha," Hrenwaldt said, "assuming that our efforts were fruitless. But now the signal. The images from the probe." He paused as if to let it sink in. "We need to find out what's happening there." He paused again, then added, "Let's begin necessary preparations. We'll head out as soon as we are ready. And Menera, pack lightly."

Pharrahmin let out a victorious yelp, while Menera shook her head with a sour look on her face that somehow managed to enhance her beauty.

One by one, they exited through the ringway, leaving Berron and Pharrahmin behind.

"So, are you ready?" Pharrahmin asked. "I'm pretty excited. But I do wish Daroon was still with us to witness this."

As Berron regarded Pharrahmin, he couldn't help feeling a little excited himself. Countless failures and several millennia later, they might have found what they had lost so long ago.

Hope.

APPENDIX - CAST OF CHARACTERS

Naven

<u>**Marafel**</u>

◊ *The Nathars*

- **Arvan**: Herdsman, retired Captain in the Navengaard, previous mayor of Marafel.
- **Malia**: Previous sarawaan of Marafel, Arvan's wife.

Their children:

- **Morena**: Married to Laraan, the Mayor of Marafel.
- **Adir**: Herdsman.
- **Athvan**.

The Nathar Household:

- **Kirsch Nayal**: Steward.
- **Dahn Nayal**: Kirsch's father and previous steward.
- **Nilane**: Housekeeper.
- **Misuma**: Housekeeper.
- **Amaar**: Farmhand.
- **Tamaar**: Farmhand, Amaar's brother.
- **Tegeth**: Kheryne Khuun refugee.
- **Erebi**: Kheryne Khuun refugee.
- **Nugai**: Tegeth's and Erebi's daughter.

◊ *The Marandas*

- **Eli**: Herdsman.
- **Lora**: Eli's wife.

Their children

- **Reinard (Rein)**: Herdsman.
- **Martha**.
- **Dolaran**.

◊ *The Ellars*

- **Marcy**: Crumbcake vendor.
- **Tia**: Marcy's daughter.

◊ *The Alameahs*

- **Laraan**: Mayor of Marafel.
- **Morena**: Laraan's wife and Arvan's and Malia's daughter.

◊ *The Kalathars*

- **Ellyn**: Village councillor.
- **Lakesh**: Ellyn's late husband. Navengaard soldier.

The Kalathar Household:

- **Barma**: Kheryne Khuun refugee.
- **Batby**: Barma's son.

◊ *The Knafelles*

- **Thane Knafelle**: Owner of Rainbow Inn.
- **Sarina Knafelle**: Owner of Rainbow Inn.
- **Eddher Knafelle**: Watchman of the Mountain Watch from long ago. Thane's great-grandfather.

◊ *Marafellen Village Folk*

- **Baely Marrat**: Jute farmer.

- **Bruca Danna**: Blacksmith.
- **Charika Bremman**: Sarawaan of Marafel.
- **Gray Larrion**: Village councillor.
- **Kremmon Marwar**: Captain in the Navengaard. Adir's staff instructor.
- **Logath Kaleb**: Cheesemaker.
- **Mel Naldatree**: Village councillor.
- **Nikal**: Athvan Nathar's friend.
- **Niman Mummfar**: Village councillor.
- **Arbiter Rabinar**: Arbiter of Marafel.
- **Akka Rammel Hallen**: Sage of the Temple of Seven Truths.

Akkasha

◊ *The Sayarnas*

- **Boar Sayarna**: Staff tournament competitor at the Regional Games in Marafel, Naven. Second place victor at Daroongaamen in Ostarium.
- **Syfis Sayarna**: Boar's older brother.

◊ *Akkashan Village Folk*

- **Bhavain**: Watchman of the Mountain Watch.
- **Fetwin**: Staff tournament competitor at the Regional Games in Marafel, Naven.
- **Bendell Jetmot**: Staff tournament competitor at the Regional Games in Marafel, Naven.

Nagra

◊ *Nagran Townsfolk*

- **Master Hirnar**: Owner of the Soft Pillow Inn.
- **Muhain Shaptel**: Staff tournament competitor at the Regional Games in Marafel, Naven.

- **Daicon Trestall**: Staff tournament competitor at the Regional Games in Marafel, Naven.
- **Thirith**: Groom at the Soft Pillow Inn.
- **Waari**: Serving girl at the Soft Pillow Inn.
- **Lieutenant Meehra**: Lieutenant of the Navengaard Mountain Watch.

Meneres

◊ *Meneres City Folk*

- **Jonnan Taschari**: King of Naven.
- **Lord Preschad**: Nobleman.
- **Master Steward**: Head steward at Lord Preschad's manor.
- **Preya**: Serving maid at Lord Preschad's manor.
- **Ramika**: Serving main at Lord Preschad's manor.
- **Dhara**: Laundress at Lord Preschad's manor.
- **Sarish**: Watchman of the Mountain Watch.

Badallur

◊ *Badallur Village Folk*

- **Keya**: Archery competitor at Daroongaamen in Omanna, Cayan.

Ostarium

<u>Lanmeria</u>

◊ *The Arinols*

- **Ekren**: Regent of Ostarium.
- **Garron**: Ekren's late husband.

Their child:

- **Dina**: Heiress Regent of Ostarium

The Arinol Household:

- **Ferrith Grasek**: Vice Regent of Ostarium.
- **Bilgan Koray**: Dina's Preceptor, once a sage of the Temple of the Seven Truths.
- **Nekmi Sadi**: Captain in the Regent's Guard.
- **Captain Altrana**: Captain in the forces of Ostarium.

◊ *Lanmerian City Folk*

- **Cassail Tymanol**: Master Archivist of the Lanmeria Library.
- **Mertca Malasi**: Nobleman.
- **Hernel**: Coachman for Mertca Malasi.
- **Master Jazacki**: Previous Master Archivist of the Lanmeria Library.
- **Remzi Dalmeen**: Meat merchant.
- **Daltaar Magkli**: Father of Ostarium.
- **Ilka Torkul**: Regent of Ostarium long ago.
- **Rimul Kanuk**: Emperor of the Gronelle Empire long ago.

<u>Boloppa</u>

◊ Boloppan Village Folk

- **Saami Tabka**: Farmhand employed by Remzi Dalmeen.

Peleria

<u>**Port Rathawia**</u>

◊ *Port Rathawia City Folk*

- **Ghareeb**: Orphan.

◊ *Characters of Note*

- **Erogat**: Pelerian philosopher long ago.

Cayan

Omanna

◊ *The Si'Pyaaras*

- **Abdel**: Nobleman.
- **Barika**: Abdel's first wife.
- **Phawzia**: Abdel's second wife.
- **Rahaya**: Abdel's third wife.

Abdel's and Barika's children:

- **Nabila**.
- **Habya**.

Abdel's and Phawzia's children:

- **Munaam**.
- **Sumaiyah**.

The Si'Pyaara Household:

- **Sinain Dewarent**: Captain of the Guards.
- **Fini**: Guard.
- **Zaal**: Guard.

◊ *Omanna City Folk*

- **Mahmal Hishayi**: Muslar of Cayan.
- **Afzar**: Operative of the Khasmia Shadow.
- **Aiysta**: Mopra.

Herraland

<u>Pacca Nirum</u>

◊ *Pacca Nirum City Folk*

- **Kierand Dooghlas**: King of Herraland.

◊ *Characters of Note*

- **Sorcha Camran**: Rebel leader.
- **Rhonea**: Operative of the Khasmia Shadow.

The Land of Kheryne

<u>**Blood Akh'Khamgaal**</u>

◊ The Romakhais

- **Rusane**: Operative of the Khasmia Shadow.
- **Guildnar**: Yearon of Blood Akh'Khamgaal. Rusane's brother.

◊ Characters of Note

- **Tallena**: Operative of the Khasmia Shadow from long ago.
- **Altansar**: Kheryne Khuun venna captured by the Khasmia Shadow long ago.

Phucao

<u>Chima</u>

◊ *Characters of Note*

- **Uaqui**: Operative of the Khasmia Shadow.
- **Ilyucu Ken**: Emperor of Phucao.
- **Rimul Kanuk**: Emperor of Gronelle Empire from long ago during its fall.

Aemonne

<u>Lykusira</u>

◊ *Characters of Note*

- **Dameel Himsal**: King of Aemonne during the War of Remaking.

Guerradrith

<u>**Lonidas**</u>

◊ *Characters of Note*

- **Tyndar Syanuenan**: King of Guerradrith. The Warrior King.
- **Tagarath Syanuenan**: King of Guerradrith during the War of Remaking. Tyndar's grandfather.

The Gods

- **Daroon**: *God of Courage.* Color: Red.
- **Menera**: *Goddess of Love.* Color: Orange.
- **Pharrahmin**: *Goddess of Light.* Color: Yellow.
- **Herra**: *Goddess of the Wild.* Color: Green.
- **Hrenwaldt**: *God of Water.* Color: Blue.
- **Berron**: *God of Wisdom.* Color: Indigo.
- **Corranine**: *Goddess of Justice.* Color: Violet.

About the Author

Praneet Menon has been interested in writing from an early age, influenced by his life. He spent almost sixteen years growing up in India and the rest of his life in five different U.S. states, sprinkled in with travel to other nations. Experiencing firsthand the sheer variety of culture, language, and spirituality that make up this world helped him form his subjective baseline for the human condition.

Praneet's formal education in aeronautical and mechanical engineering, along with his work as a flight instructor, brings a meticulous attention to detail to his writings. The precision needed in engineering and the situational awareness required of pilots aid his efforts of blending technical realism with unconstrained imagination. As a lifelong student of philosophy and psychology, his narratives explore the age-old themes of identity, purpose, and destiny that are still relevant in a post-modern world.

Find out more at praneetmenon.com